THE FAERIE WARS CHRONICLES

THE FAERIE WARS CHRONICLES

THE FAEMAN QUEST

BOOK FIVE

HERBIE BRENNAN

BLOOMSBURY

LONDON BERLIN NEW YORK SYDNEY

Bloomsbury Publishing, London, Berlin, New York and Sydney

First published in Great Britain in January 2011 by Bloomsbury Publishing Plc
36 Soho Square, London, W1D 3QY

First published in the USA in January 2011
by Bloomsbury Books for Young Readers
175 Fifth Avenue, New York, NY 10010

A CIP catalogue record of this book is available from the British Library

ISBN 978 1 4088 0561 9

FSC
www.fsc.org
MIX
Paper from
responsible sources
FSC® C018072

Printed in Great Britain by Clays Ltd, St Ives plc, Bungay, Suffolk

1 3 5 7 9 10 8 6 4 2

www.faeriewars.com

www.bloomsbury.com

For Cousin Wally and his lovely Barb
with huge affection and best wishes for Luc

PART ONE

One

'We have a *what?*' Henry exploded.

'We have a daughter,' Blue repeated. 'She's fifteen years old, nearly sixteen. Her name is Mella.'

They were together in the Throne Room of the Purple Palace. Blue, annoyingly, had perched herself on the edge of the Consort's Chair, and since Henry wasn't allowed to sit on the Imperial Throne, he was squatting near her feet on the third step of the dais. The little physician seated beside him was scratching at his arm with an instrument that looked much like a wire-headed toothbrush. Henry pushed his hand away impatiently and frowned at him.

'What are you *doing?*'

'Preparing your veins for an infusion of elementals, Consort Majesty.' The physician held up a writhing leather pouch. One of the elementals almost clawed its way out before he jerked the drawstring to trap it. The creature glared at Henry malevolently.

'Don't be ridiculous,' Henry said to Blue. 'Of course we haven't got a daughter.' A sudden thought occurred to him. 'Unless . . . ?'

Blue shook her head. 'No, I'm not. One faeman child is quite enough, thank you.' She sighed. 'She used a *lethe-*cone on us.'

Henry felt his jaw muscles slacken as he stared at her. 'We have a daughter called – what was her name?'

'Mella.'

'We have a daughter called Mella who used a *lethe-cone* on us?'

The little physician was attaching a flexible transparent tube to his arm, but Henry ignored him. They couldn't have a fifteen-year-old daughter. They *didn't* have a fifteen-year-old daughter. They didn't have *any* children. Although they had been married sixteen years now, and he vaguely recalled wanting children. And even though they'd have been very young, it was a royal faerie custom to produce an heir as quickly as possible . . .

'You always do that,' Blue said crossly. 'Repeat things I say as a question. You have no idea how irritating it is.'

Henry brushed the physician's hand away again and frowned. 'I have no idea how –?'

But Blue cut him short. 'Leave the doctor alone, Henry. He has to get those elementals into your bloodstream otherwise you'll never remember.'

Her words brought him up short. *Lethe* spells made you forget things: specific, precise things like people or events. A good magician could craft one that would blank out all knowledge of your own mother. Was it possible he really *did* have a daughter? The physician rubbed some salve on his skin that caused it to tear open, then pushed the transparent tube inside.

'Ow!' Henry said. 'That hurts!'

'Won't be long now, Consort Majesty,' the physician told him cheerfully. He clipped a funnel on to the open end of the tube and tipped his pouch of elementals into it. The creatures slid down the sides, changing texture as they moved, then slipped like smoke into the transparent tube.

Henry opened his mouth to protest again and discovered he could not speak. There was a weird slithery sensation as the elementals entered his bloodstream, then a moment of utter confusion when they reached his brain and began to dismantle the crystalline structures left by the *lethe*. After that came the nausea, a gut-wrenching, toss-your-cookies-*now* sort of nausea as the debris dropped into his stomach. Then the elementals were streaming out of his ear into the physician's waiting pouch. Henry's head cleared at once.

'Oh my God,' he said.

'You remember now?' Blue asked.

Henry placed his head in his hands. 'Oh my God,' he said again. He looked back up at Blue. 'She's run off, hasn't she?'

Blue nodded. 'Yes.'

'Where?'

Blue shook her head and shrugged grimly. 'Who knows?'

'When?'

'Three days ago.'

'Three *days?*' Henry stared at her in enraged disbelief. 'Why did nobody tell us?'

'She put it about that we were sending her to Haleklind to further her education.'

The little physician had packed up his equipment and was backing out of the Throne Room, bowing as he went. Henry scarcely registered his departure. 'Didn't anyone go with her?'

Blue shook her head again. 'She took a personal flyer.'

'She doesn't have a flying licence!'

'She's a Princess of the Realm, Henry. Do you honestly think anyone was going to stop her?'

After a moment, Henry said, 'I don't suppose she actually *went* to Haleklind?'

'No. No record of her flyer moving in or out of their airspace, no record of her at a border crossing, no breaches of security involving anyone of her description – and you know how careful the Table of Seven are about that sort of thing.'

The Table of Seven was Haleklind's ruling council. Haleklind's *paranoid* ruling council. Henry stared at her bleakly. 'So she could be *anywhere*.'

Then Blue was beside him, clutching him, demanding comfort. He could feel she was trembling. 'Henry,' Blue said, 'Mella could be *dead!*'

Two

'I want the girl dead,' said the severed head of Lord Hairstreak. It stared – glared, really – at Jasper Chalkhill, a Faerie of the Night who had undergone dramatic changes in the past decade. He'd lost weight, for one thing – hadn't we all? – and a great deal of it. Did he still have a wangaramus up his bottom, Hairstreak wondered. The worms had their benefits, but they did leech nourishment. Their hosts all tended to get thinner by the month: it was almost the standard way of spotting them. Chalkhill was positively wraith-like. He was showing cheekbones for the first time in years. But that wasn't the only change. He'd abandoned his camp act, thank Darkness, and he spoke very little. He was no longer anybody's spy, not Madame Cardui's, not Hairstreak's own. He was an assassin now, perhaps the best assassin in the Realm. Which was just what Hairstreak needed.

Chalkhill glared back. There was a time when he'd been very afraid of Lord Hairstreak. But it was difficult to take the little turd seriously now he was just a severed head supported by an onyx cube. You could see the veins and sinews trailing from the stump of neck if you looked hard enough. All the same, Chalkhill had to admit His Lordship had made a miraculous – if highly secret – comeback. Working with extreme cunning through a network of proxies, he was almost as powerful as he'd ever been and a great deal richer. More than rich enough to pay Chalkhill's outrageous fees.

'Not possible,' Chalkhill said. 'The security arrangements in the Purple Palace are impregnable.'

The lips of the severed head began to writhe. It took a moment for Chalkhill to realise the contortions meant Hairstreak was trying to smile. It was a creepy sight.

'She is no longer in the Purple Palace,' Hairstreak said at length.

An interesting development, Chalkhill thought. The faeman child's condition meant she only ever left the Palace on State occasions – once, perhaps twice a year at most. And there were no State occasions scheduled for the next six months.

'Where is she?' Chalkhill asked.

The energies generated by the onyx cube were erratic and sometimes caused one of Hairstreak's eyes to roll without reference to the other. It did so now, turning momentarily white in the process, before coming to rest focused disconcertingly on a spot beyond Chalkhill's left ear. 'No one knows,' Hairstreak said.

There was a discreet *Body in a Box* sticker on the cube beneath the intertwined CMS logo of Consolidated Magical Services. The cube itself and the head resting on it were both protected by a military-grade spell field, which meant Hairstreak – what was left of him – had become indestructible and virtually immortal. The cube drew its power directly from the sun, so you couldn't even shut him down – an ironical outcome for a botched suicide attempt.

Chalkhill said, 'So I have to find her before I kill her?'

'Obviously.'

'In that case my fee is doubled.'

'I thought it might be,' Hairstreak said, but voiced no objection.

Chalkhill said, 'There's a time limit?'

'For having her killed? Of course there's a time limit. One calendar month from today. But obviously earlier if possible.'

Chalkhill did the calculation in his head. One calendar month from today was Princess Culmella's sixteenth birthday. So the job had something to do with the Imperial succession. He half wondered if he should ask Hairstreak directly, but decided against it. Probably safer not to know. He took a deep breath. 'Triple fee for fast jobs.'

'Agreed,' Hairstreak said.

Chalkhill chewed thoughtfully at his lower lip. 'Any special instructions?'

'Just one,' said Hairstreak's head. 'You must bring her here to kill her.'

Chalkhill blinked. 'Here? To your Keep?'

'Exactly.'

It made sense for Hairstreak to want the faeman girl dead, but it made no sense to have her killed in his own home. 'But if she is killed here, won't that throw suspicion on to you, Your Lordship?'

'Let me worry about that,' His Lordship said. 'The terms of our contract will be that you find her, bring her here and kill her.'

'In that case –' Chalkhill said.

'I know, I know,' said Hairstreak irritably. 'Your fee is quadrupled.' He got his eyes under control and fixed Chalkhill with a piercing gaze. 'Can I take it you're prepared to do the job?'

Chalkhill smiled benignly. 'Oh, yes, Lord Hairstreak, yes indeed.'

Chalkhill's personal stealth flyer was marked by a tiny Imperial flag stuck in a flowerpot just a few yards from the side door. Anxious though he was to get away unseen, he could not resist a backwards glance as he walked towards it. Hairstreak's Keep was a Gothic nightmare of obsidian blocks and granite towers clinging to a cliff edge above an angry sea. Rain lashed down and wind whined perpetually, the result of weather spells that, some said, were so well crafted nobody could turn them off. There were rumours of a curse on the place. It had been owned by Hamearis, Duke of Burgundy, when the demons got him. Soon after Lord Hairstreak took it over, he'd attempted suicide by flinging himself off its battlements.

Chalkhill could not decide whether that had been Hairstreak's lucky or unlucky day. He was certainly lucky not to be killed, unlucky in that death was what he wanted, lucky that Hamearis had installed safety spells designed to help guests blown off open parapets, unlucky that his suicidal leap caused him to land with his head inside the spell zone while his rain-soaked body smashed itself to a pulp on the surrounding rocks. It was nearly six months before anybody found him – he'd fallen on hard times and dismissed his servants – by which point his body had rotted. The head, however, was perfectly preserved. An admirer bought him his first *Body in a Box* – the cheap, basic version that supported brain function, but allowed no communication. Hairstreak developed an eye-blink code and set to rebuilding his fortunes. Now, just sixteen years on, he was once again among the richest, most powerful faeries in the Realm, although very few people realised it. And he still harboured ambitions for the throne, to judge by the latest developments.

Chalkhill pulled his vanishing hood over his head, climbed into the invisible flyer and grinned. Ambitions to become the *head* faerie, you might say.

Three

The rat was coming again. Brimstone could hear it. Could smell it and sense its evil little ratty thoughts. It wanted to kill him, of course. Everything wanted to kill him these days. Especially Dr Philenor.

Brimstone was squatting in the corner of his cell, spotlighted by a ray of watery sunshine streaming through the sole high window. It was his favourite spot, marked by striations and browning bloodstains on the flagstones where he'd once tried to dig his way out with his bare hands. He usually squatted naked, or covered in excrement, but today he was wearing a suit. Today was a special day.

He expanded his senses to discover what else might be threatening him. His mind flowed out into the tangled corridors of the Double Luck Mountain Lunatic Asylum and latched on to the left ear of one of the nurses, a plump attractive little Faerie of the Night, who was currently thinking of buying sardines for her cat when her shift ended. There was a special offer on sardines at a fishmonger she passed on her way home. She could buy four at a saving of thirteen per cent and cut them up for Tiddles, who liked to eat them raw. Four sardines, chopped, would be a very satisfactory supper for Tiddles, and once Tiddles was fed, the nurse could come back in the middle of the night when the asylum was quiet and use her special pass key to get in and murder Brimstone. She was just the same as the other nurses. They all wanted to kill Brimstone. As did that nurse's cat. And the fishmonger. And the sardines.

There were cockroaches in the walls. He could hear them easily with his heightened senses, clicking and feeding and singing martial songs. They were planning to get him, those cockroaches, just as soon as they'd mustered enough troops. There was an army of cockroaches stationed just inside the walls, not quite big enough to kill him yet, but they were breeding steadily in their special farms, training up young cockroaches for the cockroach army. When there were enough of them, say 3.7 billion cockroaches, they would swarm out of the walls and begin to eat him from the feet up. Cockroaches always ate you starting at the feet, leaving your eyes to the last so you could watch what they were doing right up to the bitter end.

A bluebottle squeezed through a crack in the windowpane and began to buzz lazily around the cell. Almost certainly a spy-fly for the cockroaches, Brimstone thought. Insects stuck together when it came to killing humans. Insects and germs. Dr Philenor was breeding giant germs, of course: things the size of sparrows. He kept them in old handkerchiefs and unleashed them on his enemies. They flew up your nose and made you sick.

The bluebottle buzzed within a yard of Brimstone. He caught it expertly and ate it.

The rat was definitely getting closer *and it was not alone!* With the astonishing reach of his expanded senses, Brimstone could tell the creature was bringing his wife and children, four hungry little rats, less than half the size of their parents, but with sharp, piranha teeth. It was a family outing, aimed at killing Brimstone.

They were all planning to kill Brimstone – the rats and the spy-flies and the cockroach army and Dr Philenor's giant germs and the nurses and their cats and the sardines and the fishmongers and anything else that could burrow, fly, squeeze or otherwise gain entry to his padded cell. But Brimstone was not afraid.

He had George to protect him.

There was a *scritch-scratch* at the door of his cell and for a moment Brimstone wondered if the rat family had circled round in a flanking movement, then realised, as the door swung open, it had to be Orderly Nastes.

'Are we dressed?' asked Orderly Nastes as he marched in with his tray. 'I see we are! Well done, Silas. It's an important day for us, isn't it? Do you know why it's an important day, Silas?'

'Yes,' Brimstone muttered, scowling.

'Of course you do!' exclaimed Orderly Nastes cheerfully. He was a plump bald man with an unexpected lisp and a drooping moustache, grown in imitation of Dr Philenor. 'It's the day we meet up with our Review Board. And that means our Sunday suit, doesn't it? Because we have to look our best.' He placed the tray on the floor beside Brimstone. It was set with a mug of medicinal ale, a lump of stale bread and a piece of mouldy cheese.

'Ta,' Brimstone muttered, taking care not to meet Orderly Nastes's eye. It was important not to meet the eyes of orderlies, who were equipped with special eye inserts that shot invisible rays into your head and melted your brain. He reached out for the cheese and began to break it into crumbly pieces.

'How's George?' asked Orderly Nastes conversationally.

Why don't you ask him yourself? thought Brimstone crossly. George had put in an early appearance, as he often did when there was cheese about. He was towering over them now, fangs bared, with his back against the far wall. But experience had taught Brimstone that idiots like Nastes often failed to notice things that were right under their noses, so he murmured, 'Fine.' George smiled and nodded his agreement.

Orderly Nastes gave a discreet cough. 'Word to the wise, Silas. Wouldn't want to mention George to your Review Board, I were you.' He tapped the side of his nose. 'Get my drift?'

'Yes,' Brimstone muttered. He wanted Orderly Nastes to go away now, so he could drink his ale and feed George with the cheese. If George was hungry – and George was *always* hungry – he might eat Orderly Nastes instead of the cheese. How would he explain *that* to the Review Board?

But Orderly Nastes was already on his way out. 'You have a nice breakfast now, Silas,' he said. 'Nurse will be down presently to take you for your review.' He shook his key ring and selected the three that locked the door. 'Well, best of luck now.'

As soon as Nastes was gone, Brimstone spread the crumbled cheese on the floor, laying it out in neat little lines the way George liked. But George mustn't have been hungry after all, because he didn't touch the cheese and the food stayed there until the rat Brimstone had heard crept cautiously out of a hole in the skirting.

It stared for a long time at Brimstone, who sat immobile in his corner, then crept forward and began to nibble at the nearest crumb. Brimstone caught it and ate it, starting with the head since he was not a cockroach.

It tasted even better than the bluebottle.

four

Analogue clothes were really *weird*. She'd followed the pictures and dressed herself in blue breeches (like a boy!) that clung to her bottom, and a sort of buttonless cotton shirt with writing on the front. The writing said, *Beware of Geeks Bearing Gifs*. Mella had no idea what that meant – she'd never heard of a geek or a gif – but the girl in the shop had assured her it was cool.

The Analogue World was really weird as well. She was used to the mechanical carriages now; had even ridden in one. She'd listened to the little boxes that talked to you and played music in your ears. She'd sat on a hotel bed watching a window on a scene that kept changing all the time, allowing her to watch humans doing the most remarkable – and sometimes naughty – things. But all these were just magical toys, whatever her father's journal said about no magic in this realm. What she found *seriously* weird were the huge trackways of tar and crushed stone that criss-crossed the world like spider-webs. She was on one of them now, walking along its pavement, fascinated by the houses down each side.

They were smaller than the Purple Palace, of course, but they were also smaller than most other buildings in the Faerie Realm, where town houses were seldom less than three storeys and country houses came with their own rolling parklands, gardens and estates. These were country houses (in the sense that they were houses built some distance from the nearest town) but their grounds comprised no more than a few yards of lawn, a few flowers, a few bushes and, rarest of all, the occasional lonely tree. None rose higher than two storeys. Several were just one. Not one was built from honest stone: the favoured material seemed to be rust-coloured bricks. It was incredible to think her father had once lived here.

She came to an open-fronted shelter with a sign on a pole that made her smile. The sign said *Bus Stop*. At home, 'to bus' meant to kiss. But here, of course, it was short for 'omnibus', a giant mechanical carriage capable of carrying scores of people along the trackways. She smiled for another reason as well. This was the selfsame bus stop her father had used all those years ago when he came home from school. Which meant his old home must be just a short walk away.

Mella slowed her pace so she could rehearse her story one more time inside her head. She knew from her father's journal that he was supposed to be living in New Zealand. Mella had no idea where New Zealand was, but she imagined it had to be a long way from here and nowhere near the Faerie Realm. Henry had chosen New Zealand because that was where Mr Fogarty was also supposed to be living. Mella had never met Mr Fogarty, who died before she was born, but she'd spoken to him once or twice and he'd been willing to answer questions. He'd told her the story that they'd fed to Henry's mother and reinforced with a little subtle spellwork so she would never question it. Basically she believed her son was married to a New Zealand girl and there was no question of them ever visiting England because they were looking after Mr Fogarty, now ninety-nine years old and bedridden. (The dead Mr Fogarty had found that hugely amusing.) More spellwork ensured that Henry's father believed the same thing. Neither of them were told they became grandparents fifteen years ago. Mr Fogarty had advised Henry that the knowledge of a granddaughter might encourage them to visit New Zealand where the whole elaborate charade would fall apart.

From everything she'd read in the journal, Henry's father was nice, but weak. When his wife threw him out, he took up with a girl half his age. Now he was living with her in Stoke Poges, somewhere that sounded to Mella like one of the gnomic cities, but couldn't be because it was in Buckinghamshire, a notorious gnome-free zone. Henry's mother was something else. Henry's mother fascinated Mella. She ran a girls' school somewhere close by. She was hard as iron nails, tough as leather boots. She was intelligent, opinionated, bossy and independent. She even slept with other women, for heaven's sake. Well, one other woman at least, a girlfriend named Anaïs.

(Mella had almost missed this when she was reading her father's private journal for the first time. He referred to his mother, her grandmother, as 'gay', which Mella thought meant she was happy and cheerful most of the time. Except from everything Henry wrote, Martha Atherton didn't *seem* happy and cheerful. In fact, sometimes she sounded downright sinister. It was quite clear Henry was frightened of her. Later, Mella discovered 'gay' had a totally different meaning in the Analogue World.)

But the most exciting thing of all was that Martha

Atherton was *human*. Mella's father was human, of course, but he'd spent so much of his time in the Realm he was practically a Faerie of the Light. He talked like one and acted like one and much of the time Mella suspected he even thought like one. Her grandmother was different. She'd never even heard of the Faerie Realm. She was human through and through. Mella could hardly wait to find out what sort of woman that made you. She could hardly wait to meet her grandmother.

'*Good morning, Grandmother – my name's Mella.*'

She'd spent much of the last month honing the simple sentence into a state of absolute perfection. Not, *You don't know me, but you may remember you've a son called Henry? Well . . .* Not, *This may come as something of a shock, but we're closely related.* Not, *Hello there, I've just come from New Zealand and guess what . . . ?* Not even, *Hello, Mrs Atherton, I am your granddaughter.* If everything Henry wrote about her was true, she would understand at once. It would come as a shock, of course, but she would never show it. She would say, in her stern, serious, terribly human voice, '*Come in, Culmella, and meet my girlfriend.*' It would be so *cool!*

What happened after that, what happened after she was invited into the all-girl household, what happened after she met Anaïs (who Henry said was very pretty) Mella hadn't quite worked out. But it would all revolve around *human* customs. She would probably be invited to stay. She might even be taken shopping to buy new clothes (she had gold in her purse, something she'd already discovered went a very long way in this exotic Analogue World). Mella liked to think that what would happen must remain *in the lap of the Gods.* The Old

Gods, that was, who were open to adventures. They were bound to ask her about her father, of course, but since she'd read his journal she knew exactly what to tell them. Her story was well-rehearsed: she'd even read up on New Zealand in case they wanted details about where she lived.

The houses were peculiar in that none of them had the spell-driven guardians that were standard in the Faerie Realm. There, you had only to place one hand on an entrance gate for a voice to whisper the name of the house, the name of the owner, who was currently in residence and whether you would be welcome to call. Most of them had a security setting that paralysed undesirable visitors, then tarred and feathered them if they persisted. But there was nothing like that here, not even a basic announcer. Some of the houses had nameplates, all of them had numbers, but there was no way of telling who lived in them unless you already knew. No way of finding out if you'd be welcome either.

So which house had her father lived in? Which house did her grandmother still live in with Anaïs? A dreadful thought struck her suddenly: suppose her grandmother no longer lived here? Suppose she'd sold the house and moved on somewhere else? In the Faerie Realm a guardian would give her all that information, including instructions on how to get to the former resident's new abode. But here . . .

Mella felt like kicking herself. Why on earth hadn't she thought of this sooner?

She slowed her pace, examining each house more carefully. She was absolutely certain her father had never mentioned a house number in his journal. Why should he? He knew where he lived and the journal was supposed to be private. (As if anybody expected anything to stay private without spell protection: but then her father was allergic to spells.) Had he ever mentioned a name? Mella wasn't sure. And if he *had* mentioned one, she surely could not remember. What to do?

Perhaps she should call at any of the houses at random and simply ask where Mrs Atherton lived. It seemed hideously rude to call on a total stranger demanding help, but what other option did she have? All the same, she hesitated. She simply could not imagine herself walking up to any of those doorways when she didn't know who occupied the house. What would she do if they called the police? She knew about police from her father's journal, when he'd written about the time her mother visited the Analogue World. She also knew her rank as Princess of the Realm counted for precisely nothing in this world. If the police arrested her and threw her in a dungeon, she could easily stay there for the rest of her life. She moved on slowly, reading numbers, reading nameplates.

Chatleigh. The nameplate prompted her memory at once. It was engraved on a metal plaque, decorated by a faded painting of some flowers. *Chatleigh*. Somewhere in his journal, her father had mentioned that name. She was sure of it. And why else would he mention the name if it wasn't the house where he lived?

She looked beyond the garden gate and saw the house matched the description of his home as given in the journal. (So did several other houses, but she pushed that thought aside.) Mella drew in a deep, shuddering breath. She felt a fluttering in her abdomen. This was it. Even without a guardian, her instinct told her someone was at home, told her firmly that someone had to be her grandmother. It could not possibly be any other way. Mella had come so far, risked so much. The Gods would never be so cruel as to disappoint her now.

She pushed the gate, unconsciously steeling herself for the paralysis of the unwelcome, then remembered and relaxed. It wasn't like that here. This was a whole new world.

Close-up, the house looked bigger; and a whole lot prettier. There were flowers in the garden and the lawn had just been cut. Her grandmother was clearly a tidy woman. She walked to the front door and waited, heart thumping, to be announced, then remembered again, smiled to herself at herself, reached up and pressed the little lighted button she knew to be a bell-push. She heard the chime as she released the pressure.

For a long, long moment, it seemed as if the house might be empty, despite her intuition. But then she heard the sound of someone moving inside. A woman's shape appeared briefly behind the frosted glass panel to one side of the door. Then there was the metallic rattle of the funny locks they used here and the door swung back.

'Good morning, Gra—' Mella began, then stopped. The woman on the doorstep was absolutely not her grandmother.

The woman on the doorstep was too young. She looked about Mella's father's age, or maybe a bit younger; and actually there was the look of Henry about her around the eyes. But if she wasn't her father's mother – and clearly she wasn't – who could she be? There was something about her – an arrogant tilt of the head, a flash of annoyance in the eyes – that told Mella she was certainly no servant.

It had to be asked. Mella screwed up her courage.

'Does Martha Atherton live here?' She remembered the Analogue custom and amended, 'Does Mrs Martha Atherton live here?'

'Are you one of her students?'

As a princess, Mella was not accustomed to being questioned or explaining herself. 'No,' she said coldly and stared the other woman in the eye.

The woman glared back, but eventually said (when Mella refused to look away), 'She's on holiday.' She hesitated, then added, 'I'm house-sitting.'

It was a strange term, but Mella decided to ignore it. She opened her mouth to ask another question, but what she heard come out was, 'I'm her granddaughter.'

The woman on the doorstep froze, her mouth half open. She stared at Mella, without the hostility this time but with rather more surprise, even shock. She swallowed, looked away, looked back again, then said, 'She doesn't have a granddaughter.' It was a flat statement without challenge. In fact, the hint of a rising inflection almost turned it into a question.

Mella said very seriously, 'She doesn't *know* she has a granddaughter.' She straightened her shoulders and pushed a curl of hair back from her face. 'I'm from New Zealand.'

The woman leaned forward, mouth still half open, to examine her face more closely. After a long, long moment she breathed, half to herself, 'I don't believe it. You're Henry's child.'

Mella smiled for the first time. 'My name is Culmella,' she announced proudly. 'Who are you?'

'I'm your aunt Aisling,' the woman said. 'Your father's sister.'

five

In his fourth year as Consort Majesty, Henry had taken it on himself to reform Blue's espionage service. Now he was beginning to wish he'd never bothered. The zombies seemed like a good idea at the time – they'd no fear of death and couldn't be killed since they were already dead – but as guards they frankly left a lot to be desired. Bits kept falling off them and the smell was dreadful. Madame Cardui eventually tried to sack the lot of them, but by then they had formed a trade union so that any reform proved impossible. They marched proudly beside him, singing quietly in their splendid red uniforms, through the labyrinth beneath the Purple Palace that led to the new espionage HQ. Henry sighed. At least they saved the expense of tracker coins. And food.

The mirrored complex at the heart of the labyrinth made him feel faintly ill, and one zombie laid a friendly hand on his arm to steady him. Henry closed his eyes briefly to shut out the multiple reflections and waited to be announced. 'Consort Majesty King Henry, Your Lady-ship,' whispered the zombie in a voice that crackled like dried leaves. Henry waited for a moment, then opened his eyes. The reflections were gone, as were the zom-bies, and he was standing in a roomy, antique-furnished chamber. Madame Cardui, dressed in something multi-coloured and diaphanous, floated towards him, beaming.

'Henry, deeah!' she exclaimed as she embraced him. She'd had a recent head peel that left her raven-haired with the face of a twenty-five-year-old, but the body beneath the robe was slight and delicate as the bones of a bird. He kissed her gently, then released her.

'Culmella has gone missing,' he said without preliminary.

The zombie's hand was still clinging unnoticed to his arm. Madame Cardui brushed it off and it fell to the floor in an explosion of dust. 'So I heard – it's the talk of the Palace,' she said. 'My agents are already working on it as their top priority.' She glanced behind him. 'Is Queen Blue with you?'

Henry moved over to one of the easy chairs. 'She's upset. Obviously. Actually she's very upset. The Palace physician has given her a sedative. I promised I would look after things.' He looked around him vaguely. 'Until she decides otherwise, of course, which probably means this afternoon.'

'Actually later this morning,' Madame Cardui smiled slightly. 'I received a summons from her first thing.'

It was typical of Blue, who never trusted the important matters to anybody except herself. Henry had long since stopped taking it personally. 'Well, meanwhile we can get the ball rolling,' he said easily.

Madame Cardui reclined gracefully on a floater cloud and propped herself on one elbow. 'Poor Blue. Children can be such a burden at times.' She smiled reassuringly. 'As well as a blessing.' The smile faded. 'I'm afraid Mella takes after her mother. Blue used to get up to the most terrifying escapades in her younger days. Before you

26

met her, of course: you've proven a very steadying influence.'

Henry was far from sure about that, but he wanted to focus on the most pressing matter. 'You think that's what it is? An escapade?'

'I think it's the most likely thing, given what we know about Mella. It's not the first time she's run away.'

'It's the first time she's used *lethe* on us,' Henry told her sourly. That was the one thing that worried him. *Lethe* cones were powerful magic, powerful and expensive, especially the sophisticated selective-memory types that had been used on Blue and himself. If Mella really had used them, then it had to be for something extremely important, not just some spontaneous prank. But suppose it hadn't been Mella who used them? Suppose it was somebody else? 'Can we rule out a kidnap?'

'One can rule out nothing,' Madame Cardui told him soberly. 'I *think* it's most likely that she ran away, but a skilful kidnap could be tailored to ensure that's exactly what one *would* think.'

'There's been no ransom demand,' Henry said. 'I would have expected one by now in a kidnap.'

'Assuming a financial motive.'

Henry frowned. 'What other motive would there be?'

Madame Cardui gave him a hard stare. 'Political.'

'Ahhh,' Henry said. He glanced away and chewed his lip. 'You're thinking about the birthday.'

'I am indeed. If Mella is not present here in the Palace for her formal coming of age, she forfeits her succession to the throne.'

'Well, she does and she doesn't,' Henry said. 'I've been thinking about that. She forfeits her legal right to *demand* the throne when Blue dies, of course. But faeries have always been very practical about things like that. If there's nobody else in line, she'll get the throne anyway.'

'Only if you and Blue have no more children.'

'We don't plan to have any more,' Henry said.

Madame Cardui's old eyes gazed at him out of her youthful face. 'You're a vigorous man, Henry. Blue is a warm-hearted woman. Who knows what might happen after midnight when the moon is full?'

Henry flushed. To cover his embarrassment he said, 'But there are no other children *now*. So who would have a motive to kidnap her? Who would it benefit?'

'Comma?' Madame Cardui asked.

Henry looked at her in surprise. Comma was his brother-in-law, Blue's half-brother. He'd been an obnoxious child, but somehow managed to grow into a handsome, brave and caring man. 'Does Comma have a claim to the throne?'

'Only obliquely, I must admit. If Mella forfeits and Blue abdicates and there are no other children and Blue neglects to make a *fiat* then Comma might argue sanguinageniture – the principle of blood before marriage – to argue precedence over you, for example.'

He's welcome to argue anything he likes, Henry thought: his own ambitions for the throne hung in a limbo somewhere less than zero. But Comma couldn't have kidnapped Mella unless he somehow managed it by proxy. He'd been away for the last three years clearing up an infestation of pirates in the Galiston Triangle.

'Comma's at sea,' Henry said.

'In that case, the only other real prospect is you.'

He gave her a quick, affectionate glance. Madame Cardui was almost as paranoid as Mr Fogarty: it went with the job and enabled her to do it very, very efficiently. 'I expect you've already checked out every move I've made for the past six months.'

Madame Cardui sighed. 'You must forgive me, Henry – it's not personal.'

'I know that,' Henry said. 'I assume you found nothing suspicious?' He *knew* she'd found nothing suspicious, otherwise he'd be rotting in a dungeon now, Consort Majesty or not.

'Nor did I expect to,' Madame Cardui told him.

To lighten the mood, Henry said, 'Well, at least we don't have to worry about our old friend Lord Hairstreak any more.'

Madame Cardui smiled. 'That is a blessing, deeah. That is definitely a blessing.'

Six

The Review Board was headed by Dr Philenor, who sat behind his black moustache on a raised dais at the end of a consultant's table. Five of his colleagues had grown similar moustaches with greater or lesser degrees of success. The sixth, a woman, was wearing a stick-on version made from horsehair. The crest of the Double Luck Mountain Lunatic Asylum – crossed hypodermic syringes surmounting a lobotomy scalpel – was fixed to the wall directly above Dr Philenor's head. By his right foot was a briefcase which, Brimstone realised, must be filled with giant germs. Or evil elementals. Or both.

Brimstone himself was strapped into a treatment chair bolted to the floor in front of the table. An orderly – not Orderly Nastes, but a skinny colleague who smelled of sour beer – had bolted an Endolg Skin Copper helmet to the top of his head. As a result, etheric tentacles were already crawling into his brain, making it itch. The helmet's controls were set into the arm of Dr Philenor's seat.

'Good morning, Dr Brimstone,' Dr Philenor said politely. Philenor's doctorate was in psychiatric medicine, of course. Brimstone's was in demonology, an obsolete discipline since Blue became Queen of Hael. Brimstone had never used the title even when he practised professionally, but Philenor was a stickler for formalities, especially when dealing with his patients. He'd once published a learned paper entitled *Raving Loonies: The Importance of Courtesy in their Care and Treatment*.

'Good morning, Dr Philenor.' Brimstone smiled benignly. The trick with Review Boards was to keep calm, simulate submission, pretend the treatment had worked and hide all symptoms.

'How are we feeling this morning, Dr Brimstone?' Dr Philenor asked, making a tick on a sheet pinned to his clipboard.

Brimstone knew he was safe enough since the ESC helmet had not yet been activated. The trauma suffered by the creatures as they were flayed interfered with the truthsense of the finished helmet. It often took fully five minutes to begin to function. His smile broadened into a sunny beam.

'Magnificent,' he said. 'Quite magnificent. I cannot thank you and your gracious team enough for my therapies. Such potions! Such pills! Such infusions! Such transfusions! Such surgical procedures! Due entirely to your sterling efforts, my level of health – and especially my *mental* health – is at a peak unparalleled in the past fifty years.' He wondered if he might be overdoing it, but Philenor seemed to be swallowing the rubbish without difficulty.

Dr Philenor coughed lightly. 'No . . . ah . . . threats of any sort? To your, ah, welfare?' The briefcase at his foot writhed fiercely.

He was fishing for evidence of what they called paranoia, of course – a medical term designed to keep you off your guard when everything was out to get you. Brimstone widened his eyes and batted his eyelids. 'Threats, Dr Philenor?' he echoed. 'How could anyone experience a sense of threat in such a well-run establishment as your excellent clinic? Why, I was just remarking to Orderly Nastes the other day how safe and secure I have felt here since you rescued me from my unfortunate . . . episode.'

There was a scattering of applause from the staff around the table, quickly silenced by a severe look from Dr Philenor. But his features softened as he turned back to Brimstone. 'Now, Dr Brimstone, a crucial question: on a scale of one to ten, one representing total madness and ten perfect mental health, how would you rate your current condition?'

'Tell him *eleven*,' growled George, who'd been hovering invisibly at Brimstone's shoulder throughout the whole of the proceedings.

Brimstone had opened his mouth to respond before he realised an etheric ganglia was now wrapped around his pre-frontal cortex, a sure sign that the ESC helmet was at long last activated. He closed his mouth carefully. It was Sod's Law that it had happened at this precise time. Once the helmet became functional, the endolg skin broadcast signals directly to the control console in the arm of Philenor's chair. If Brimstone continued to lie, Philenor would know at once. Worse, the doctor had only to press a button to activate the helmet's emergency surgical programme, designed to leave Brimstone in a vegetative state – hence no further trouble to anybody – for eighteen months. When Brimstone first arrived at the asylum, staff explained the surgery was a therapy, not a punishment, but it was a therapy he could ill-afford at the moment.

'Come now, Dr Philenor,' he said carefully, 'that is hardly for me to say. Only a lunatic would presume to judge his own sanity. I am content to leave my evaluation to the kindly, caring, and, above all, highly trained and eminently qualified experts gathered in this room.' He lowered his eyes modestly to murmurs of approval around the table.

'Well said.' Dr Philenor nodded and ticked another box on his evaluation sheet. He looked up again at Brimstone and actually smiled. 'What's this I hear about your invisible companion?'

Brimstone froze. Somebody must have grassed him up and now he was trapped. He knew from long experience he was the only one who could see George, so admitting his existence was asking for a diagnosis of delusional schizophrenia – a ticket to permanent incarceration if ever there was one. On the other hand, denying George while the ESC helmet was functioning would show at once he'd been lying and invite immediate surgery with eighteen months' vegetation until his brain healed up again. But there was always Plan B. After all, he'd never really expected to talk his way past the Review Board. He raised the little finger of his left hand and twirled it widdershins in the secret stand-by signal he'd agreed with George. George pulled himself erect, licked his lips and snarled in a very satisfactory manner.

But this was only stand-by. Despite everything, there remained the possibility of escaping without violence. Brimstone held Dr Philenor's eye and smiled back. 'I take it you mean my *imaginary* companion?' he said easily. 'The little friend I . . . conjured up . . . for company throughout the long days and nights of my lonely, yet therapeutically necessary and medically ethical, solitary confinement?' There was just the barest possibility the helmet might not react. His statement was not a complete lie. He *had* conjured George from the hideously dangerous nether regions beyond the deepest pits of Hael. And the techniques he used had indeed involved the use of the visual imagination. A living endolg would have spotted the deceit at once, but it might slip past the ESC.

Dr Philenor glanced at the miniature viewscreen set into the arm of his chair, but if it was glowing red (or even amber) he showed no sign as he asked, 'Did you give this companion a name?'

Brimstone fought down the urge to glance over his shoulder. 'George,' he said.

Dr Philenor glanced at him quizzically. 'Pardon?'

'George,' Brimstone said a little more loudly.

'You gave him *my* first name?'

Brimstone nodded vigorously. 'Yes, of course. What better companion could I have in my hour of need? I spent many hours in imaginary conversation attempting to envision what wisdom you might impart to me had you been really present, which, of course, I never believed for a moment you were.' Once again there was just enough truth in there to fool the helmet . . . if he was very, very lucky.

The idiot Philenor still failed to react. 'Are you telling me, Dr Brimstone, that you do not believe this companion *actually exists*?'

George leaned down to whisper, 'Which one do you want me to slaughter first?'

'None of them until I give the signal,' Brimstone hissed through gritted teeth. He was beginning to harbour a suspicion that the helmet might be broken – psychiatric equipment was delicate at the best of times. To test the idea, he said loudly and clearly to Dr Philenor, 'Of course not. Complete figment of my imagination.' There was no way such a bare-faced lie could get past the helmet unless it was malfunctioning. A risk, of course, but if he knew the ESC was faulty and Dr Philenor did not, then he could get away with murder. If, on the other hand, the alarm went off, he could always trigger Plan B and set George to kill off the Review Board, then help him fight his way out of the asylum.

A very strange thing happened. Brimstone distinctly saw the flash of red on the arm of Philenor's chair. But instead of raising the alarm, Dr Philenor only said quietly, 'Very good, Dr Brimstone' and ticked another box. He set down the clipboard and turned to his companions. 'It seems to me,' he told them, 'that our patient has been completely rehabilitated. He entered our clinic a mental and emotional wreck and is now, thanks to our patience, care and skill, a man of totally sound mind, ready to resume his place as an intelligent and productive member of society.' He paused, then added, 'Perhaps I might have your considered opinions.'

Six moustaches (one of which was false) glanced at Brimstone, glanced at Philenor, then vied to voice their agreement:

'Yes.'

'Definitely.'

'Absolutely.'

'*Certainment*, Dr Philenor.'

'You're so right, Boss.'

'Correct in every detail, Master.'

Philenor allowed them to grovel for a moment longer, then said loudly, 'But . . .'

There was a stunned silence as they looked at him. With their attention diverted, Brimstone risked a quick glance over his shoulder. George, all fangs and feathers and rippling muscles, was crouched ready to spring on his signal.

'But . . .' Dr Philenor repeated, 'it would scarcely be a kindness were we simply to release him, were we simply to *turn him out on the street,* so to speak.'

'No.'

'Oh no.'

'Perish the thought.'

'You're so right, Boss.'

'Definitely not.'

'Never!'

Brimstone stared at the doctor intently. What was the old quack playing at? The helmet had told him Brimstone was lying, yet he'd ignored it. But even before that happened, Brimstone couldn't really believe he'd bought the rehabilitation story. Not even a psychiatrist could be that stupid. There was a hidden agenda here and Brimstone didn't like hidden agendas unless he'd hidden them himself. He leaned forward in his chair and felt – to his surprise – his restraints begin to loosen.

'So what I propose . . .' announced Philenor.

'Yes?'

'What?'

'Tell us.'

'Speak, oh wise one.'

'Your proposal?'

'All ears.'

'. . . is to release Dr Brimstone *in care* . . .' Dr Philenor went on.

'Brilliant.'

'Super.'

'Great idea.'

'Why didn't we think of that?'

'You're so wise, Dr Philenor.'

'Perfect solution.'

In care? Brimstone began to scowl. In care of who? And what did *in care* mean? Was he going to be stuck with some bossy nurse? Would somebody have proxy powers over his estate? Did he have to report to a probation officer? Philenor was up to something – he was sure of it. Brimstone's scowl deepened. Maybe he should set George loose anyway.

'. . . And who better to look after him,' Dr Philenor continued, 'than that most generous of benefactors, the man who has contributed so much money to our asylum in the past few weeks, the man who has built us a new wing, doubled our pension fund and written me a personal cheque for –' he coughed, '– well, the amount is hardly relevant. I speak, of course, about the man who has waited patiently behind that curtain throughout our meeting –' he pointed dramatically, '– in order once again to welcome an old friend to his bosom. I speak of course of –' The curtain swept back.

'George!' Brimstone hissed, then stopped just short of the final attack order. He blinked, twice. The man behind the curtain was the last person he expected to see. Or wanted.

The man behind the curtain, smiling with his spell-encrusted teeth, was Jasper Chalkhill.

Seven

Chalkhill must have come up in the world. There was a stretch ouklo hovering beside the main entrance. Brimstone climbed in with a distinct feeling of trepidation. The trouble was, the last time they'd met, Brimstone had tried to sacrifice him to the Jormungand serpent. It had been a good sixteen years ago, admittedly, but surely Chalkhill couldn't have forgotten? He decided not to bring it up for the moment, just in case, and asked instead, 'How did you know where I was?'

'I didn't. But I knew you were mad and there are only a few facilities like this in the Realm. I had someone check them all.'

George was climbing into the ouklo as well, which gave Brimstone a feeling of confidence. 'How did you persuade him to let me go?'

'Philenor? I bribed him, of course.' Chalkhill was looking a lot different from the last time Brimstone saw him. He'd lost weight, for one thing, and he was a much snappier dresser for another. He rapped on the ceiling of the ouklo with his Malacca cane and his coachman triggered the starter spell. The carriage rose smoothly and surprisingly quickly for a vehicle of its size and weight.

Brimstone glanced through the window. The Double Luck Mountain Lunatic Asylum was receding into the distance. From this height it was already apparent that its buildings and grounds had been carefully landscaped so that when viewed from above they spelled out the word *Philenor.* The good doctor clearly had a healthy ego. Brimstone turned away. Now was the time for the crucial question. He gave the hand signal that put George on high alert and asked, 'What do you want from me, Jasper?'

In the old days, Chalkhill would have contrived to look hurt. He would have composed his features into a hurt expression. One of his hideous novelty spells would have flashed *HURT* across his forehead. He would have given a small, sad smile and spouted some nonsense about old friends and business colleagues. But the new, improved Chalkhill did none of these things. Instead he asked a question of his own.

'Is it true about the cloud dancer?'

It was, but why did Chalkhill want to know? Brimstone stared at him suspiciously. He weighed the pros and cons of lying, without reaching much of a conclusion. The bottom line was that the cloud dancer business was on public record – or at least on record in the asylum he'd just left. If Chalkhill could bribe Philenor to let him go, he could certainly get a copy of his records. Cautiously, Brimstone said, 'Yes.'

'I understand Lord Hairstreak sent it after you?'

Brimstone shrugged. 'Probably. It never told me.'

There was a brief flash of the Chalkhill he'd once known when the old perv licked his lips. 'What happened? Exactly?'

It was really difficult to see where this was going, unless it was just Chalkhill taking pleasure in the misfortunes of others. Which Brimstone could fully appreciate since he often did it himself. 'What happened . . .' he began.

What happened, as he remembered it, was that the creature had found him on the edge of the Buthner desert near the Mountains of Madness. Cloud dancers were blood-feeders whose natural home was on a different dimension of reality to this one. When they crossed over, it was difficult for them to maintain a physical form, but their immaterial existence on this realm was precisely what allowed them to probe faerie minds and mine their secrets. At the time, Brimstone had been harbouring a particularly poisonous secret – he'd managed to steal an angel – and had fought ferociously to keep it to himself.

Brimstone shuddered. He could remember the scene as if it were yesterday. A red sunset promised a fine day on the morrow. The angel was safely trapped and immobilised. Everything seemed to be going according to plan. Then, across the desert at the furthest edge of his vision, he noticed a movement like an approaching dust-devil or djinn. But as it drew closer, he saw it was neither and by the time he realised what he was dealing with, the thing was almost on top of him.

Some academics maintained that cloud dancers, as a species, were distantly related to vampires, but to Brimstone the creature looked far more like a ghoul. It was tall and thin and caped and fanged with the pallor and transparency of a ghost. Despite its fragility, it was capable of physical attack – dancers had been known to suck their victims dry of blood – but that was not the greatest danger. The greatest danger was that the thing could reach into your mind; which was exactly what this one did.

Most men would have crumbled at once. But Brimstone was a trained demonologist who'd spent nine years in Arcane School learning the mental techniques that allowed him to communicate with demons in the good old days before Queen Blue spoiled everything. The disciplines had toughened his mind to a degree that allowed him to withstand the initial attack.

With the creature thrown back, Brimstone created an imaginary sea-chest of thick oak with metal bandings and used it to store all thoughts and memories of the angel. Then he wrapped it in imaginary chains, fastened the chains with triple padlocks and swallowed the imaginary key. The cloud dancer recovered and threw itself against the chest. Brimstone concentrated so that the chest withstood the attack. The cloud dancer redoubled its efforts, but the chest remained sound. Brimstone allowed himself a little smile.

The little smile was probably a mistake, for it threw the cloud dancer into a paroxysm of fury. But now, instead of hurling itself futilely against the impregnable chest, it dived down Brimstone's throat in search of the key. Brimstone mentally grabbed its feet and began to drag it back up again. The cloud dancer twisted, slid back up into his head and, in a fit of pique, began methodically to dismantle his brain.

'It got a bit fuzzy after that,' Brimstone concluded.

'But it never found out about the angel?'

'No, it never found that out.'

'It just sent you barking mad?'

Brimstone snorted. 'That's what happens when you have a dismantled brain.'

Chalkhill was licking his lips again, but without the pervy light in his eye this time, which meant he was about to ask something important. 'Is it true that when you're attacked by a cloud dancer, it leaves you very sensitive?'

'It usually leaves you dead.'

'Yes, but when it doesn't leave you dead. As in your case, Silas. If it doesn't leave you dead, is it true it leaves you very sensitive?'

Brimstone leaned a casual elbow on the edge of the window. Chalkhill planned to kill him, of course, as did most of his former friends, but probably not quite yet. His questions, the way he held himself, the involuntary movements of his ears all suggested he was up to something – something for which he needed Brimstone's help. Brimstone gave the hand signal that put George back on stand-by and said, 'Oh yes, very sensitive.' He leaned forward to stare into Chalkhill's face. 'Very sensitive indeed.' He allowed himself to sink back into the buttoned leather seats of the ouklo interior. 'Once they put your brain back together, that is.'

But Chalkhill ignored the sarcasm in his enthusiasm to scrabble from his pocket something white and lacy, which he waved in front of Brimstone's face.

Brimstone drew back quickly. 'What's that?'

'It's a handkerchief, pronounced *hankerchief* or sometimes *hankie*. Humans use them.'

'What for?'

'To blow their noses.'

Brimstone stared at the handkerchief, then stared at Chalkhill. 'What do they do with the result?'

'After they've blown? They wrap it up and keep it in their pocket.'

Brimstone shuddered. 'Gross. And I'll thank you to stop waving that thing in my face.'

'It's all right,' Chalkhill said, 'it hasn't been blown into yet.' He leaned forward. 'Listen, Silas, I want you to sniff this.'

'No,' Brimstone said.

'It belongs to . . . a certain person.'

'Who?' Brimstone asked immediately.

'I'd prefer not to tell you.' Chalkhill composed his features into a look of sympathetic caring. 'It would be *better* for you not to know.'

Which might well be true, Brimstone thought, since Chalkhill was clearly trying to suck him into another of his convoluted schemes. 'What do you want, Chalkhill?' he asked crossly.

'What I want is for you to smell this, then track down where its owner is now.' He smiled. 'Like a bloodhound.' The smile vanished. 'You can do that now, can't you? Now you're sensitive?'

Brimstone hesitated. He probably could. He'd certainly developed some very peculiar powers since Dr Philenor remantled his brain. He could see George, for one thing, when nobody else could; and he could hear cockroaches talking to each other. Tracking somebody down like a bloodhound might not be beyond the bounds of possibility. And even if he couldn't, it might be worth his while pretending. Although he was free of the lunatic asylum now, his funds were limited – much of his property had been sold off to pay for treatment – and Chalkhill had always been a bit of a cash cow in the past. Brimstone looked at him steadily.

'What's in it for me?' he asked.

Eight

It was *sooo* exciting. Mella had never seen a human kitchen before and this one was absolutely nothing like the kitchens of the Purple Palace. They were huge, with great black log-burning stoves, enormous roasting pits and no less than seven rainbow-coloured flavour chambers humming with spell power. This human kitchen was extremely small by contrast, with no roasting pit at all, no open fires of any sort and no stoves that she could see, while the only thing remotely like a flavour chamber was a white metal box on a countertop that would hardly hold a chicken, let alone an ox. All of which begged the question: how did these people cook? There was nothing, absolutely nothing, here that looked like it might do the job. Yet there were pots and pans hanging from hooks on the ceiling, so cooking must be done somehow.

'What's that?' she asked Aunt Aisling, pointing to a coffin-sized cabinet standing upright by one wall. Like much of the equipment here, it had been painted white, so it was unlikely to contain a corpse. But you could never be sure. Some of the earliest faerie histories mentioned humans who *ate each other!*

Aisling glanced at her in surprise. 'It's just a refrigerator. Don't you have one at home?'

Mella almost winced. Home was supposed to be New Zealand where, she supposed, they must have refrigerators, whatever refrigerators might be. But she recovered quickly. 'Oh, yes, of course. It's just ours is a different . . . design.' She'd have to be very careful. The last thing she needed was to raise Aunt Aisling's suspicions, although Aunt Aisling was very, very unlikely to guess where she really came from. Mella allowed herself a small, secret smile.

'Would you like a cup of tea?' Aisling asked.

Mella's smile vanished abruptly. Her father had warned her there were two drinks that were dangerous to faeries when they visited the Analogue Realm. Well, not dangerous exactly, not poisonous or anything, but tricky. One was coffee, which seemed to have very little effect on humans – all it really did was keep them awake – but acted as a psychedelic on faeries, triggering visionary experiences. The other was tea, which Aunt Aisling was offering now. The trouble was, Mella couldn't remember what Henry had told her tea did to faeries. He'd only mentioned it once when she was a lot younger and hadn't really been paying attention. She hesitated, realised hesitation might seem suspicious, realised tea drinking was a common ritual among humans, tea drinking was expected, tea drinking was probably *compulsory* in New Zealand, remembered too that she was only *half*-faerie so it would probably have no effect at all, then said, 'Yes, please.'

'You put the kettle on,' Aisling said. 'I'll find the pot. Earl Grey all right for you? Mother never seems to have anything else.'

Who was Earl Grey? *What* was Earl Grey? Maybe there were different types of tea. She took a deep breath.

She was committed now, so it hardly mattered what type of tea she drank: she didn't know what any of them was likely to do to her. 'Yes, fine,' she said. She'd read somewhere that human girls her age would signify assent by saying *Cool*, but she'd also read that the English always drank tea hot, so that would hardly be appropriate. Analogue life was proving a lot more difficult than she'd anticipated.

The kettle was easy enough. The design was much the same here as in the Faerie Realm, and while the kettle on the countertop was smaller than those in the Purple Palace kitchens and there was a funny little tube sticking out the back at the bottom, it was definitely a kettle. She picked it up and once again looked around for a fire. 'Where do I put it on to boil?'

'Is there water in it?' Aisling asked.

Oh Gods, Mella thought. Where was the well in this little kitchen? Did it have a pump, or would she have to draw water in a bucket? There were no *spells*, that was the trouble. You had to do positively everything yourself. She shook the kettle experimentally and discovered to her relief it was already half full. 'Yes, there is.'

'Plug it in beside the sink.'

Plug it in? When the servants wanted to boil a kettle without using up a spell cone, they hung it over an open fire. But *plug it in?* How did you plug in a kettle? To play for time she moved slowly over to the sink – she knew what a sink was – and looked around vaguely.

'Plug's beside the microwave,' Aisling said helpfully.

What, in the name of the Old Gods, was a microwave? For the first time since she'd arrived in the Analogue Realm, Mella began to feel she was drowning. Then suddenly she noticed the wording on the chicken-sized flavour chamber: *Siemens HF26056GB 1000 Watts Microwave*. Brilliant, but what now? Plug it into the microwave? No, Aunt Aisling said *beside the microwave*. Mella felt her mind move into a higher gear, as it sometimes did when she was faced with an emergency. There were several pieces of kitchen equipment beside the microwave, but only one of them looked anything like what she was searching for: a black rubbery snake with a short, thick tube thing on the end. A plug? It *might* be a plug. It might be *the* plug. But the interesting thing, maybe the important thing, her whizzing mind told her, was that the plug (?) looked as if it might fit into the tube sticking out of the kettle. She tried pushing it in. At first it wouldn't go, then she twisted it slightly and in it slid! Mella set the kettle down triumphantly.

'You'll have to switch it on at the wall,' Aisling said.

Mella's eyes slid along the black snake. At the far end from the kettle, it entered the wall by way of a peculiar plate. On the plate was a switch. But Mella knew how to operate switches. She pressed this one down with a feeling of triumph. To her relief, Aunt Aisling was no longer watching her, but had opened a cupboard and taken out a smaller, pot-bellied kettle with its handle on the back. Unlike real kettles, this vessel wasn't used in the Faerie Realm at all, but she knew what it was from pictures: a teapot. She watched with fascination as Aunt Aisling spooned dried herbs into it from a yellow container.

'I hate tea bags, don't you?' Aisling said mysteriously.

'Positively loathe them,' Mella told her.

Minutes later, Aisling was pouring out two cups of amber liquid. 'I do hope you don't take milk with Earl Grey,' she murmured.

Mella gave an ostentatious shudder as she carried her cup to the table. 'Never touch it.' She could wing this conversation, she knew she could. She'd winged it beautifully already because clearly Aunt Aisling didn't suspect a thing. All she needed to do now was steer it. And keep her wits about her. And pick up as much about the Analogue World as possible. Things were actually working out rather well. Aunt Aisling was pretty stupid, according to her father's journal. It was just as well to get in a little practice with her before she met her grandmother, who wasn't stupid at all. She smiled benignly at Aisling and took her first sip of Earl Grey tea.

She tasted the bergamot at once and liked the way it blended into the smoky, dusty flavour of the tea itself. No wonder this drink was popular in the Analogue World: it was seriously delicious. She took another sip before remembering to go slowly. This was an infusion faeries were warned about and, while she was only half-faerie, there was still a 50/50 chance it would affect her. So careful was the keyword. 'Nice tea,' she remarked. It seemed a safe, sophisticated thing to say.

Aisling asked suddenly, 'What age are you, Mella?'

'Fifteen. Nearly sixteen. Why do you ask, Aunt Aisling?'

Aisling shrugged. 'I was just surprised Henry let you make the journey all on your own.' She looked seriously at Mella. 'Without telling us. We could have met you at the airport.'

This one she'd been expecting. Mella smiled. 'Actually, I was surprised you didn't. I've been wondering if Grandmother didn't *get* Father's letter.' She batted her eyelids innocently. This was the heart of the story she'd concocted, cunningly contrived not just to explain her unexpected appearance, but to make everyone else feel guilty about it. There was no letter, of course: how could there be?

'Henry wrote to Mother about your visit?'

Mella nodded enthusiastically. 'Oh, yes, of course. Telling her all about my visit and asking if I could stay with her. He didn't mind me taking the flight on my own – he said he wanted me to learn independence – but he thought Grandmother might meet me at the airport, or arrange for somebody else to.' She took another sip of her tea and looked at Aisling benignly. 'I didn't really mind when there was no one there. It's really not so far from Heathrow. I took a taxi.'

'What?' Aisling asked. 'All the way from Fairyland?'

Nine

Consolidated Magical Services had done quite a good job with their *Body in a Box,* but it lacked one obvious feature. There were no wheels built into the onyx cube and the delicate solid-state spell circuitry meant none could be attached once it was factory-sealed. As a result, when Lord Hairstreak wanted to go anywhere, the whole contraption had to be loaded on to a wheelbarrow and pushed to its destination with his head wobbling on top. The only servant he would trust with this task was an ancient family retainer called Battus Polydamas, who wheezed and complained incessantly, but knew how to keep secrets and would have given his life for his master.

'Careful, Batty!' Hairstreak screamed as the barrow hit a bump and the cube swayed alarmingly. If the thing ever toppled over, there was a risk that the connections would snap and his head roll off across the floor. It wouldn't kill him, of course – the head was indestructible thanks to the safety spells – but the experience was always disorienting. Furthermore, reattachment was painful and could take anything up to a week, during which he was unable to communicate except by eye-blinks.

'*Careful,* is it? We want *careful?*' Batty muttered.

'You mind your manners, young Master Hairstreak, and don't try to teach your grampa how to suck slugs.' He wheezed and tugged the barrow round in order to negotiate a corner. The cube began to sway in the other direction.

The violent weather spells that marked the approaches to Lord Hairstreak's Keep stood in stark contrast to the weather spells located in the sky above the building's central courtyard. When the Duke of Burgundy had owned the Keep, this vast area was paved with granite and used exclusively for military manoeuvers. One of Hairstreak's first actions when he began to recover his fortune was to change all that. Teams of gnomes were called in to break up the stone, topsoil was imported by the ton and the fashionable Forest Faerie designer Celadon was hired to create a garden. Not one single specified plant (with the exception of grass) would grow naturally at the northerly latitude of the Keep, but Hairstreak was taken by the scheme and approved the cost of the weather spells that would make it possible. The result was an extraordinary – and in places extraordinarily challenging – creation unlike any other garden in the entire realm. His great-niece now lived there permanently and consequently only Hairstreak ever visited it. The magical securities around the perimeter were set to spectacularly lethal levels. Batty was the only servant who could pass them safely; and even then, only when he was barrowing the cube.

Hairstreak felt the hot, humid air on his face as they entered the approach corridor and experienced a pleasant tingle of anticipation in the centre of his cube. He enjoyed these little garden jaunts for more than one reason. His great-niece was quite delightful, of course, just at that age when children ceased to be children and formed entertainingly fatuous opinions of their own. But unlike most teenaged faeries – Lighters or Nighters – she was unfailingly polite to him and affectionate; one might even say *loving*. As he'd trained her to be, of course, but an unusual experience for Hairstreak just the same. He quite looked forward to these little visits, although he purposely limited them to once a week: it would never do if the girl became too familiar. At the moment she remained in awe of him, a useful reaction that could only be maintained by distance. In his experience, familiarity all too often led to the discovery of one's weaknesses and at the moment he had all too many weaknesses waiting to be discovered, any one of which might prove fatal to his plans. The last thing he needed was to have to kill her. That would mean scrapping years of effort and starting afresh, something that scarcely bore thinking about.

As he bumped through the archway into the open air, the full, lush beauty of the gardens struck him like a physical blow. In some ways the loss of his natural body had proven a boon; and this was certainly one of them. The cube enhanced all his senses, except touch, so that when he happened upon something aesthetically pleasing, like a painting, concerto, olbonium or a natural wonder such as this garden, his appreciation was heightened several-fold. He often wondered what it would be like when he ruled the Realm and could order the wonders of the world transported to his doorstep. It was difficult to imagine the sheer delight he would experience, but it was something to which he looked forward enormously.

The spell-driven securities were, of course, invisible

and randomised, but anyone venturing beyond the low perimeter hedge could confidently expect to be vapourised within ten to fifteen seconds. With some exceptions, of course. Hairstreak could come and go as he pleased, barrowed by Batty, but the girl could not. Although the spells would not kill her, she was absolutely confined to the inner gardens in order to ensure no one, servant or visitor, caught an accidental glimpse of her. But within those inner gardens, all her needs were met. She had her own home. She had a range of magical entertainments. She had two endolg pups for company: neither would develop speech for at least another year, by which time it would be too late to damage his plans. Her servants were all an advanced type of golem, programmed to self-destruct rather than reveal her existence.

Batty pushed the barrow on relentlessly. They were on grass now, following a path that led eventually through a screen of trees concealing the silver river that marked the boundary of the inner gardens. Here the path split, one branch following the river, the other leading to a hump-backed bridge. Since he didn't trust Batty on the bridge, Hairstreak ordered him to follow the river. They reached an open gateway and the cube circuitry *pinged* audibly as it detected the spell field that stretched space, leaving the inner gardens substantially larger than the outer.

Here the real exotica began. Multicoloured fronds reached out to caress them as they passed. ('Geroff me!' Batty muttered.) Large, tubular danceflowers gyrated gently to attract their attention. Spiroform trubongs bounced sedately through the undergrowth. Tiny ground cover plants – Hairstreak couldn't remember their names – burst into song as the barrow wheels passed over them. The pathways meandered kinetically to show as much of the environment as possible without trying a traveller's patience: the very words Celadon had used when explaining his plan. And to be fair, they seldom tried Hairstreak's patience, since the moving pathways meant every visit produced its quota of surprises. This one, for instance, revealed a heroic marble statue of Hairstreak himself (still equipped with his original body) half hidden in a stand of fanferns.

Hairstreak smiled benignly as the tropical plantings gradually gave way to the forest arboretum that concealed the home of his great-niece. While Celadon had been given full rein where the tropical exotica were concerned, this area was Hairstreak's own little whimsy, worked out by him in some detail and specially commissioned as the centerpiece of the whole plan. The forest path, which followed a static meander so that the approach never varied, eventually opened out into a clearing; and in the precise centre of the clearing was the dearest, sweetest, rose-covered country cottage it was possible to imagine. A water butt stood by one corner, a pile of newly cut logs by another. There was a roofed well just yards from the front door, close by the endolg kennels. Around the back, Hairstreak knew, was a vegetable patch and herb garden. Woodsmoke curled lazily from the chimney while a delicate little spell ensured the welcome smell of home-baking wafted gently from the kitchen.

The building was an exact reconstruction, researched down to the smallest detail, of a cottage that featured in one of the most popular pieces of humorous folklore ever passed around the Faerie Realm. The story was that of Red Robina Hood, a young girl about his great-niece's age, who had the misfortune to be descended from werewolves on her mother's side. The gene was regressive and only showed up fully in Red Robina's grandmother, who was banished by the family to the forest cottage for her own safety and that of others. Red Robina was quite fond of the old girl and called on her often. But – and this was the part of the story that always sent faerie listeners into paroxysms of laughter – one night Red Robina quite forgot there was a full moon and arrived at the cottage to find her grandmother's bed occupied by a timber-wolf that promptly ate her.

What gave the story a special twist – and brought even more laughter from listeners – was that Red Robina's boyfriend, a woodsman twice her age called Pieris, hunted down the wolf and killed it . . . only to discover after the fact that he'd really killed the poor old grandmother. The incident started a feud between the families of Pieris and Red Robina that resulted in several more deaths until survivors on both sides were wiped out by plague. Ah, the hilarity of it all.

When the gardens were laid out, Hairstreak had arranged for the original cottage to be demolished and transported, stone by stone, to be rebuilt as their centerpiece. And now, he thought, his own dear, sweet great-niece was enjoying the precise facilities of a famous piece of faerie history. She must have heard the trundle of the barrow, for she was emerging from the doorway of the cottage now.

'Good morning, Mella!' Hairstreak called cheerfully. 'Come and give your uncle a kiss.'

Mella beamed and ran towards him.

Ten

The restaurant was owned, run and staffed by orange Trinians, which meant the food was good, the service fantastic, and the prices astronomical. Fortunately Chalkhill would be paying. Brimstone ordered steak with a side order of teeth, served on a bed of deep-fried potato batons, with grilled tomatoes and inkcap wafers. It was a lot more than he usually ate, but he hadn't had a thing since his morning rat and, besides, he felt like celebrating. He was free of the asylum, reconnected with his old source of income and, best of all, very much in control.

'Wine, sir?' asked their sommelier, addressing the words to Brimstone as the obvious senior of the dining duo.

'Two flagons,' Brimstone told him promptly. 'One red, one green.'

'May I recommend a Malvae for the red?' murmured the sommelier. 'A pretentious little vintage, quite new on the market, but with some interesting characteristics.'

A Trinian's recommendation would never be anything other than excellent. 'That will do very nicely,' Brimstone told him. 'And you can bring a half bottle of something cheap for my friend.' He smiled smugly at

Chalkhill, who scowled but failed to protest, yet another indication of how badly he needed Brimstone's services.

'Of course, sir.'

As the dwarf disappeared in the general direction of the kitchens, Brimstone said briskly, 'I've been out of circulation for a long time. You'd better bring me up to speed on what's been happening.'

Chalkhill shrugged. 'Blue's still Queen, you know that. Queen of Hael as well, although she's had to face two challenges. Last one was very nasty, damn nearly killed her, but she survived to rule another day. You know she married that human friend of her brother?' Brimstone nodded. Out of the corner of his eye he could see food coming, so the nod coincided with a stomach growl. Chalkhill went on, 'Iron Prominent. Now Consort Majesty King Henry, an empty title if ever there was one.' He glanced around as if worried the other diners might have overheard the treasonable utterance, but presumably decided they hadn't, for he continued easily enough, 'You had a run-in with the brother, didn't you?'

Brimstone blinked slowly, his eyes closing like the nictitating membrane of a serpent. 'Young Pyrgus? We both did, as I recall. He closed down our glue factory.'

'Nice little earner, that,' Chalkhill said thoughtfully. 'Pity you tried to sacrifice him to the Prince of Darkness.'

This time it was Brimstone's turn to shrug. 'We all make the occasional mistake.'

Chalkhill said, 'He's running an animal sanctuary somewhere down south.'

Brimstone sniffed. 'Waste of space, that boy. Can you

imagine wanting to devote your life to the welfare of smelly animals?'

'Maybe not a *complete* waste of space. He has a vineyard down there as well. That red you ordered is one of his.'

'I'll toast to his good health,' Brimstone remarked sarcastically. 'Any other news of the royals?'

Their table was suddenly surrounded by Trinians bearing groaning trays of food. Beyond the inner circle hovered the sommelier and his minions with their flagons of wine. Brimstone found himself staring at his steak, a massive cut of meat with its side order of teeth trembling beside it. He realised suddenly he was hungry enough to eat a camel and popped the teeth into his mouth. Gum contact triggered the spell and they began to gnash and chatter in anticipation. He speared the entire steak and allowed them to bite off a piece. They began to shred it very satisfactorily.

As the Trinians withdrew, Chalkhill said lightly, 'The younger brother, Comma – half-brother, I should say – is off on some heroic maritime mission. Madame Cardui is still in charge of the Secret Service. Apart from that, not much else is going on. Oh, and Fogarty's dead, but you probably know that.'

The great thing about being mad was that people tended to underestimate you. In the old days, Chalkhill was the one with the money and Brimstone the one with the brains. Chalkhill was still the one with the money, but now he thought himself far cleverer than his old partner. Far cleverer, far more dangerous, far more talented, far more insightful, wise, shrewd, prudent, sensible and astute, no doubt. Which was why he thought he could divert Brimstone's attention, tell him nothing of significance, avoid the one important subject. Brimstone poured himself half a glass of red, then added some of the green and watched the wine turn sludgy.

'Did Blue and Henry have any children?' he asked innocently.

Chalkhill contrived to look distracted. 'Children?' he echoed. 'Not sure faeries and humans can actually interbreed, can they?'

'Of course they can,' Brimstone told him. 'They produce faemans.' He smiled quizzically. 'Didn't Blue and Henry have a faeman child?'

Chalkhill frowned. 'Think I may have heard something of a faeman. Not sure whether it's a boy or girl. Don't pay much attention to these things.'

Brimstone managed to hold his face expressionless. Chalkhill was lying through his teeth. Even in the asylum, Brimstone had heard about the royal faeman, a girl named as Culmella Chrysotenchia, but more familiarly known as Mella. It was beyond belief that someone of Chalkhill's interests should not know everything there was to know about her. So why was he pretending not to? The obvious answer was that he wanted to channel Brimstone's attention away from the creature. And why would he want to do that?

All this clearly led back to the hankie now residing in Brimstone's nether pocket. When he'd sniffed it, at Chalkhill's insistence, he'd known at once it had never belonged to a faerie, Lighter or Nighter. But nor did it seem to belong to a Trinian, Halek wizard, endolg or any of the other races currently inhabiting the Faerie Realm. The possibility of a human had crossed Brimstone's mind, but the vibrations hadn't seemed to fit there either. But now they were talking *faeman* . . . He would have to check again to be sure, but he would have bet his new-found freedom that the handkerchief was the property of a faeman; and not just any faeman, but the very faeman Chalkhill was now desperately trying to avoid discussing.

It was an interesting development. Had the brat gone missing? Had Chalkhill been hired to find her? Most importantly, how could Brimstone turn this situation to his own advantage?

He took a short pull of his sludgy wine to wash down the shredded steak and turned his teeth on automatic as he allowed his mind to expand. Chalkhill thought he needed to sniff the hankie, or at least hold it in his hand, in order to contact its owner, but that was nonsense, of course. He closed his eyes, as if in ecstasy at the taste of his wine, listened in for a moment to the conversations in the kitchens, gave a brief nod to George, who was sitting at a table in the corner, then focused on the hankie in his pocket.

The mental image opened up like a doorway. He peered through cautiously and found himself looking into one of those ridiculous little kitchens so favoured in the Analogue World. There were two people inside, both female. One was a mature human, a little overweight and somewhat sly. The other was the owner of the handkerchief, a faeman girl for certain – the pointed ears and green eyes were a dead giveaway – and almost certainly the child of Blue and Henry: she had her mother's determined jaw and her father's gormless expression. So still in the Analogue World then – something Brimstone had known from the moment he first touched the hankie – although he was in no hurry to pass that information on to Chalkhill. He didn't know exactly where in the Analogue World. The focus was too tight at the moment, but he would probably get a clue when she moved outside. Once he had an accurate location, he could decide what to do about it. He might tell Chalkhill, or he might not. He might decide himself what to do with the girl. (Kidnapping could be profitable, or selling her into slavery.) It all depended what was best for Brimstone.

He opened his eyes again, vaguely wondering who had hired Chalkhill and for what.

Eleven

Henry blinked, rubbed his eyes and looked again. The girl – woman really: he'd have to stop calling her a girl since it only seemed to make her cross – sitting at the dressing table was Blue. She looked like Blue. She was dressed like Blue. She spoke like Blue. Her reflection in the mirror was Blue's reflection. But she couldn't be Blue, because Blue was standing beside him.

'What do you think?' asked the Blue beside him. Despite her worry about Mella she was smiling a little.

Henry looked at Blue a third time, then at the girl – woman – beside him. She was the one who'd accompanied him to their private quarters. Actually she was the one who'd demanded he stop what he'd been doing and accompany her to their private quarters, which sounded like the real Blue all right. But it would also be like the real Blue to try to trick him – she had a wicked sense of humour.

'Which of you . . . ?' he asked helplessly.

'I am,' said the Blue beside him.

'I am,' said the Blue at the dressing table.

Henry looked from one to the other. They were absolutely, positively identical and he felt as if he were drowning. The thought passed through his mind that Blue might be one of twins. But why had she never told him this before? And anyway, the Blue at the dressing table claimed to be Blue as did the Blue beside him. That wouldn't happen with identical twins. One of them would be called Lizzie or Maud or whatever. What he had here were two *versions* of Blue and he didn't know which of them he'd married.

The girl (woman!) beside him leaned across to whisper in his ear. 'You have a little heart-shaped birthmark on your bottom; she won't know about that. I like to kiss it when we're –'

Henry coughed. 'Quite,' he said quickly. He felt a flush rising from his neck. All the same, the resemblance was so uncanny, he thought he'd better make sure. 'Can you tell me where I have my birthmark?' he asked the Blue by the dressing table.

She gave him one of Blue's delightful smiles. 'On your ear?' she asked.

Henry shook his head in slow amazement. 'What is it – an illusion spell?'

'Doppleganger,' Blue told him, the real Blue by his side. 'I couldn't trust an illusion spell, not for this.'

'I thought dopplegangers were dangerous,' Henry said. Actually, what he really thought was that you died if you met yours.

'They're supposed to be bad luck, but that's just an old superstition. Isn't she great?'

She was great all right, Henry thought. She was Blue down to the very finest detail. The way she held her head, the way she moved her hand, that look in her eye when she was weighing up a situation . . .

'Where did you get her?' he asked. 'I thought dopplegangers just turned up, as portents of doom.'

'I arranged it with Madame Cardui,' Blue said. 'I was with her earlier to talk about Mella.'

Henry wanted to know how that meeting went, but

he could ask her about it in a minute. At the moment he was even more interested in the doppleganger. 'Where did Madame Cardui find her?'

'I didn't ask. But it's all right: she'll have taken all the necessary precautions. You know what she's like.'

Scary, that's what Madame Cardui was like. As was Blue when the mood took her. Dopplegangers were dangerous. It wasn't just an old superstition. And now this one was loose in the Purple Palace. The question was why.

'What's it all about, Blue?' he asked.

'Well, I can't go off looking for Mella and leave the Realm to look after itself, can I?'

'You're going off looking for Mella?' Henry echoed in his trademark turning-a-statement-into-a-question.

'You don't think I'd leave that to anyone else, do you?'

Now she came to mention it, he didn't. Even though they both knew Madame Cardui would leave no stone unturned in her search for their daughter, there was not the slightest chance Blue would leave something like that to anybody other than herself.

'So you're going to look for Mella and your doppleganger will . . . ?'

'Rule the Realm in my place,' Blue said triumphantly. 'Well, sort of. She'll keep people from thinking I've gone off and left the Palace unattended. Then, when I get back, I'll get rid of her and take over again and nobody will be any the wiser.'

That just raised so many questions he hardly knew where to start. Eventually he said, 'She's going – she'll be – I don't even know her name –'

'Blue,' Blue said. 'Her name is Blue. Same as mine.'

She gave him a kindly look. 'If you're getting confused, you can call her Orange.'

Henry looked at her, frowning. 'Why Orange?'

'Complementary colour.' Blue grinned at him.

'How?' Henry asked. 'How is she going to rule the Realm?'

'She's not really,' Blue said patiently. 'She'll just be a figurehead until I get back. She's perfectly fine for that job – she knows everything I do.'

'She doesn't know where I keep my birthmark,' Henry muttered.

'Not *intimate* things like that. She won't know about *birthmarks*. But all the important things, how to wave from an ouklo, how to shake hands with visiting dignitaries – she knows those sort of things.'

'How are you going to get rid of her?'

Blue looked puzzled. 'I don't want to get rid of her. I've only just managed to get hold of her.'

'When you've finished and you want to take over ruling the Realm again. How are you going to get rid of her then?'

Blue shrugged. 'I'll just tell her to go.'

Henry leaned towards her. 'And what happens if she doesn't *want* to go?' he whispered. 'What happens if she likes being Queen? What are you going to do then – kill her?'

'Don't be silly,' Blue told him sharply. All the same, he knew from her expression the question had shaken her.

Henry moved to press home his advantage. 'Suppose she decides to have you put in jail? The Palace guards will do what she tells them. They may be a bit confused, but they'll obey her, especially if she's sitting on the throne or wearing your crown. She could take the whole Realm away from you just like *that*!' He clicked his fingers.

Blue stared at him. After a moment, she said, 'We can set up safeguards. I'll talk to Madame Cardui.'

'There's another thing,' Henry told her.

'What?' Blue asked impatiently. She clearly disliked being brought down to earth about her little scheme.

'While you're off looking for Mella,' Henry said carefully, 'what am I supposed to do about my . . . ah . . . duties?'

'Your duties?'

'Keep your voice down!' Henry whispered. 'You know, my . . . *duties*.' He cleared his throat and swallowed. 'My . . . marital duties.'

Blue was looking at him in astonishment. 'Your marital duties?' The look dissolved into a grin and she giggled. 'Your *marital* duties?'

'Will you keep your voice down!' Henry hissed. 'If we're to pretend your doppleganger is you, if we're to do that and nobody is to suspect, then she and I would have to . . . you know . . .'

'No, I don't know,' Blue said loudly. 'What would you and she have to do?'

'Share the same quarters,' Henry told her. 'Share the same *bedroom*. For heaven's sake, Blue, you haven't thought this through at all!'

'Henry, there's no way you and she are going to share the same bed, even if she looks like me.'

'I didn't say bed, I said *bedroom*.'

'Yes, but you *meant* bed, didn't you?'

'Yes,' Henry said. 'Yes, I did. If this lunati—' He caught himself in time and hurriedly amended, '– if this idea of yours is going to work, I will have to behave towards your doppleganger exactly the same way I behave to you. *Exactly*. Otherwise people will notice, start asking questions, start wondering what's going on. So she and I would have to be . . . you know . . . affectionate with one another. Kiss each other occasionally, like we do. Hug and stuff. Sleep . . . sleep together. With one another. The way we do.'

Blue looked at him innocently. 'And you think of all that as your marital *duty?*'

'Well, not *duty*, exactly. That's just a turn of phrase. But it's the sort of thing that would be expected.' He looked at her soberly, then ended piously, 'And I don't *want* to sleep with anybody but you.'

'Relax, superstud,' Blue said cheerfully. 'All that's been taken care of.'

'Yes, but people will expect –' He stopped as a man walked out of the adjoining dressing room, wearing Henry's dressing gown.

'It won't be just me looking for Mella,' Blue told him. 'It will be the two of us. Together.'

The man smiled and gave a little wave. Henry stared at his doppleganger. 'Oh my God!' he said.

Twelve

Mella gave a sickly smile. 'Fairyland? I don't know what you mean.'

'I think you know exactly what I mean,' Aisling said. 'You're not from New Zealand, are you? I don't suppose you even know where New Zealand is.'

'Yes, I do!' said Mella hotly. 'New Zealand is an island nation in the South Pacific. It is a remote land. One of the last sizable territories suitable for habitation to be populated and settled, it lies more than 1,000 miles – that's 1,600 kilometres – southeast of Australia, its nearest neighbour. The country comprises two main islands – the North and South islands – and a number of small islands, some of them hundreds of miles from the main group. The capital city is Wellington and the largest urban area is Auckland, both located on the North Island. New Zealand administers the South Pacific island group of Tokelau and claims a section of the Antarctic continent. Niue and the Cook Islands are self-governing states in free association with New Zealand.' She'd memorised the speech word for word from the Encyclopaedia Britannica and could easily have gone on about the country's geographical features if she hadn't run out of breath. Not that it would have done her much good. She could tell from her aunt's expression that Aisling wasn't buying it.

'Your father isn't living in New Zealand either, is he?' Aisling asked.

Mella opened her mouth, closed it, opened it again and said, 'Ah –' She knew at once she'd hesitated too long, but by that point there was nothing she could do about it.

'I knew it!' Aisling exclaimed. 'I absolutely knew it, the lying little toad!' She looked around the room with pursed lips. 'He was always the same, always sneaking away doing things and not telling Mummy. So selfish.' She glared at Mella.

To cover her confusion, Mella took a long drink of her tea. Her mind was racing as she tried to figure how she was going to talk her way out of this one. She stared at Aunt Aisling, eyes wide. 'Ah . . . ah . . . I . . . ah . . .' she said. It was funny, but just the hint of a smile was beginning to play around Aisling's lips. A smile of triumph.

But then Mella suddenly realised it didn't matter. What did she care if Aunt Aisling knew she was from the Faerie Realm? (What did she call it? Fairyland?) What did she care if the whole world knew about her father? It wasn't as if anybody could do anything to him. Mella took another swig of tea and felt a really, really nice warm feeling in her stomach. Nice warm feeling. It wasn't as if Grandmother was going to *spank* him. Mella burped slightly and giggled. He was a grown man now, a big boy. No spanking for him any more. Besides, if Grandmother tried to spank him she'd have Mella's mother to contend with. And Mella's mother was a *Queen*.

Mella took another huge drink of tea, reached for the pot and poured herself some more. Tea was so *nice*. It made you feel relaxed and cheerful, both at the same time. It made you feel big and strong, which she was, of course, so she didn't have to worry about Aunt Aisling finding out anything. Not about her father, not about her.

'Well?' Aisling asked.

Mella shrugged. 'You're right,' she said. 'I'm not from New Zealand.'

'But you're my brother's daughter?'

'Oh yesh. That's what Mummy says when I've done something wrong: you're your father's daughter, she says. She says *father* 'cause that's what he is and he's not her brother, of course, he's her husband. But it's all the same man, isn't it? My father, your brother, Blue's husband.'

'Blue?'

'Mummy,' Mella said. She felt like giggling again, but didn't. This had become a very *serious* conversation.

'So you admit you're from Fairyland? You admit you're living there and so is Henry?'

Mella said soberly, 'We don't call it *Fairyland* – we call it the *Faerie Realm*.' She hesitated. 'Actually, we don't. We just call it *the Realm*. But it's the Faerie Realm. And my mummy runs it.'

Aisling looked at her sharply. 'Your mother *runs* the Faerie Realm?'

'Queen,' Mella said.

For a long moment Aisling just stared at her. Then she said, 'This gets better and better. Henry is married to the *Queen of the Fairies?*'

''S right.' Mella nodded. She wondered why she was having difficulty pronouncing her words properly and decided some more tea might help.

'What about Mr Fogarty?' Aisling asked suddenly. 'Is he with you or is he really in New Zealand?'

'Dead,' Mella said. Single words weren't so bad; it was whole sentences that gave her trouble. All the same, she thought she'd better make the effort to explain properly about Mr Fogarty. She took another deep, soothing, wonderful draught of tea. 'Got sick. Died. Now they have to talk to him through a Charaxes ark.'

Aisling stared at her. 'Fogarty's dead?'

'Yesh.'

'But Henry still talks to him? Like you're talking to me now?'

Mella shook her head and giggled. 'No, no, silly. That would be stupid. I told you, they use a Charaxes ark.'

'What's a Charaxes ark?'

''S a box that lets you talk to dead people. Henry – Daddy – got it from his friends the Luchti. They had one for ages and they made him a copy. Of course he was a blood brother of the Luchti. He got made one when he helped Lorquin kill his *draugr*.' She smiled. 'That was years ago. Lorquin's chief of the tribe now.'

Aisling looked momentarily confused, then shook her head and said, 'You're telling me Henry has a box, some sort of machine, that lets him talk to the dead?'

'Yesh. Talk to Mr Fogarty anyway.'

'And Mr Fogarty talks back?'

Mella nodded. 'Yesh.'

Aisling frowned suddenly. 'Have you been drinking, Mella?'

'Tea.'

'I meant alcohol.'

'Tea,' Mella repeated. She held Aisling's gaze.

After a long moment, Aisling said, 'Sit there and don't move. Don't go away. I've something I want to show you.' She stood up and hurried from the kitchen. 'Don't move,' she called over her shoulder.

Mella didn't feel at all like moving so she stayed exactly where she was and drank more tea. The warmth in her belly – she called it *belly* to herself now, which was a bit rude, but a lot more friendly than *stomach* – the warmth in her *belly*, good old *belly*, was spreading through the rest of her body and the world, this Analogue World, looked *wonderful*. Even this tiny little kitchen looked *wonderful*. And it was truly *wonderful* that she'd become such good friends with Aunt Aisling, who seemed so genuinely interested in the Faerie Realm and what was happening there.

Aisling came back, concealing something in her hand. She set it on the table in front of Mella. 'Do you know what that is?'

Mella blinked. She was having trouble focusing her eyes as well as talking, but even though it swam a little in her field of vision, she recognised the control at once. She made a huge effort. 'Yes,' she said with remarkable clarity.

'What is it?' Aisling asked. She was leaning forward now and actually seemed to be trembling a little with excitement.

'It's a *transporter*. Tha's a portable portal control,' Mella said. Even though she was concentrating very hard, she popped her *P*s. But that was because of the alliteration in *portable portal*. If there hadn't been any alliteration, she definitely wouldn't have popped anything. Definitely. 'Mr Fogarty invented them,' she added. 'When he was still alive, of course.'

'It opens up a gateway into the Faerie Realm, doesn't it?'

Mella nodded. 'Yesh.' It occurred to her to wonder how Aunt Aisling had managed to get her hands on a portable portal control. She didn't think her father would have given her one – he didn't like Aunt Aisling all that much according to his journal. Besides, he said in his journal that he'd kept the Faerie Realm a secret from his family.

'Do you know how to work it?'

'You just aim and press the button.'

Aisling pulled over a kitchen chair and sat beside her. 'That's right. Except it doesn't work any more. Can you tell why it doesn't work?'

Mella picked up the control and turned it over in her hands. Her fingers felt sausagey but she still managed not to drop it. It was an early model, quite possibly even one of Mr Fogarty's first prototypes, larger and more crudely made than the modern controls, but the basics were still the same. She slid her thumb along the side and discovered the safety switch was set to *on*. Aunt Aisling must have pushed it without noticing. There was no way the control would open a portal while the safety was in operation. She flicked it back and handed the control to Aisling. 'It should work now.'

Aisling handled the control as if it were a precious jewel. 'All I have to do is point and press the button?'

Mella nodded. 'Tha's right.' From somewhere far away she heard the sound of singing. Sweet singing. 'Maybe not indoors, though. Sometimes causes trouble with these old models.' She smiled benignly. Aunt Aisling wasn't really listening, but that didn't matter: it was such sweet singing.

Aisling's eyes had turned feverish with excitement. 'We're going on a trip, Mella, you and I,' she said loudly. 'I didn't get very far before, but now I have you as my guide things will be very different. Just press the button, do I? Just press the button?' She pressed the button.

A fiery portal opened in the kitchen, but Mella didn't see it. Mella had slid gently from her chair and was snoring softly on the floor.

Thirteen

'I think of Hodge every time we come down here,' Henry murmured a little dreamily. Hodge – Mr Fogarty's old tomcat – had always enjoyed hanging around the House Iris Portal Chamber and Henry still missed him.

'Mmm,' Blue said, her mind clearly on other things. She looked around. 'Where's Chief Portal Engineer Peacock?'

'Dunno,' Henry said. 'Listen, Blue, I think it's time you told me what you have in mind.'

Hodge had been an elderly cat when he first moved to the Realm, but something in the air suited him and he lived another twelve years before dying at the venerable age of twenty-eight. During a frisky moment in the interim, he surprised Madame Cardui's translucent pedigree queen, Lanceline, and the result was four kittens who looked exactly like Hodge and were now, as adults, beginning to show Lanceline's ability to talk. One of them appeared from behind the portal controls and polished Blue's ankle. 'Back in five minutes,' it said.

'Which one are you, darling?' asked Blue, who was almost as enamoured with Hodge's offspring as she was with Henry.

The kittens had been christened *Rodge, Splodge,*

Podge and *Emmeline*. 'Splodge,' said this one. 'Hello, Henry.'

'Consort Majesty King Henry to you,' said Henry, grinning.

'Cat may look at a king,' said Splodge philosophically. 'Five minutes. Good hunting.' He started to walk off, looking even more like Hodge from the rear than he did from the front.

'Don't go,' Blue called quickly. 'Who's back in five minutes?'

'Old Peacock,' Splodge told her over his shoulder. 'Gone to bandage his stump.' He disappeared behind the portal again with his tail twisting into a high question mark.

'Listen,' Henry said quickly, 'I'm glad we have a bit of time. I understand you didn't want to say much when there were people about, but why do you think Mella may be in the Analogue World?'

Blue looked at him in surprise. 'What makes you think I think that?'

'The way we're dressed for one thing.' They both had on Analogue clothing – jeans and shirt for Henry, jeans and T-shirt for Blue. 'The fact we're in the Portal Chamber, for another. I didn't really think you were planning a holiday.' A thought occurred to him and he added, 'No one else will either, if you're hoping to keep this a secret.'

'Oh yes they will,' Blue told him. 'Well, they won't, but you know what I mean. This will stay a secret all right, at least until we find Mella. C.P.E. Peacock hasn't really gone off to bandage his stump. I asked him to set up a *lethe* spell field round this chamber – I thought he'd have been back by now. But once we've gone, nobody will remember we've ever been here, including

Splodge and Mr Peacock himself. With our dopplegangers in place, it will seem like business as usual.'

'All right.' Henry nodded. He'd suspected something of the sort. 'But what makes you think Mella's in the Analogue World?' he asked again. 'Madame Cardui isn't looking there.'

'Madame Cardui is checking out the political implications as her first priority,' Blue said imperiously. 'As she certainly should, of course. It's just that I had reasons to believe Mella might have taken herself off to the human realm.'

'What reasons?'

'Reasons,' Blue repeated stubbornly.

'Which you didn't pass on to Madame Cardui?'

'No.'

'Even though she is in charge of the investigation into our daughter's disappearance?'

'Yes.'

'Why?' Henry asked.

For the first time Blue looked embarrassed. 'I wanted to be sure,' she muttered.

'No you didn't,' Henry said.

'No, I didn't,' Blue agreed. 'I'm sure enough. I found Mella's diary.'

'I didn't know she kept one.'

'Neither did I until she disappeared. It was very well hidden. Guardian spells and everything. Very grown-up.' She glanced across at him. 'Talking of which, I didn't know you kept a private journal.'

Henry blinked. 'How do you know I keep a private journal?'

'Mella mentioned it in her diary. Apparently she's read it.'

For a heartbeat he couldn't believe it. 'Mella's read my private journal?'

Blue nodded and touched her top lip briefly with the tip of her tongue. 'Oh, yes.'

'She can't have!' Henry gasped. 'There's private stuff in there. *Very* private. I mean personal. Like my underwear and that thing you found I liked last summer. That's very, very private.'

'Not any more,' Blue said.

'She shouldn't be reading my private journal,' Henry moaned. He still couldn't believe it. There were things in there he'd be embarrassed about Blue reading, let alone their own daughter.

'No, and I don't suppose I should have read hers,' Blue said. 'But I'm not going to get all guilty about it in the circumstances.' She gave an uncertain, but reassuring smile. 'I'm not as worried about her disappearance as I was. Madame Cardui is checking out the possibilities of kidnap, assassination and all that sort of thing, but I'm fairly sure this is just Mella being Mella. Mella being a normal teenager, I suppose. She's started to get curious about your background. It's what girls do about their father sooner or later. You can't blame her.'

'But I've *told* her everything she needs to know about my life,' Henry protested.

'Apparently you didn't tell her enough,' Blue said drily. 'Or maybe you told her too much. She's fascinated by your mother.'

'My mother?' Henry echoed. 'Why would *anybody* be interested in that old witch?'

'Because she's *human*,' Blue said quietly.

'I'm human,' Henry pointed out.

'Yes, but she's used to you, and besides you don't live in the Analogue World any more. Your mother is still making a life in a strange and wonderful world where they have trains and buses and porridge and don't even believe in magic. You have no idea how exotic that is for a teenager living in the Faerie Realm.'

There was a long moment's silence before Henry said, 'Don't be silly.'

To his irritation, Blue giggled. 'I'm not being silly. I think Mella is curious. I think Mella is curious about her human grandparents, who are strange creatures who live in a strange world she's never visited, and I think she's doubly curious about her grandmother, who happens to sleep with another woman. She's *fifteen*, Henry! We were all interested in sex when we were fifteen.'

'I wasn't,' Henry said automatically. He thought about it, decided it was a lie and glared at Blue as if that was somehow her fault.

Blue ignored him. 'And this isn't just sex, it's sex *in the family*. At her age, that's irresistible. I'm not saying she wants to do it. I'm just saying she wants to meet her fascinating old grannie.'

Henry clutched his head with both hands. 'Oh, God!' he said. 'You're planning for us to visit my mother!'

'Yes,' Blue said. 'Yes, I am. I think there's a very good chance we'll find Mella with her.'

'And what do we do? Just take her back?'

'Of course we take her back. What else would we do?'

'Suppose my mother won't let us?'

Blue stared at him in astonishment. 'She's our daughter. Your mother has no say in what we do.'

'I don't want to go,' Henry told her stubbornly.

'Why not?'

'There'll be a row. She doesn't approve of me wearing jeans.'

'Henry, you're a grown man now. Stop acting like a twelve-year-old.'

He *was* acting like a twelve-year-old: he knew that. The problem was he was frightened of his mother. Actually no, he was *terrified* of his mother, a manipulative guilt-tripper who'd made his early life a misery. When he was younger, he couldn't wait to get away from her. When he finally managed it, he hadn't been to visit her in years. As far as she was concerned, he was stuck in the wilds of New Zealand and might never come home. Not that she cared much anyway: she'd always led her own life. '*You* go to see her. You don't need me.'

'Of course I need you,' Blue said crossly. 'She doesn't know me. She's never met me, remember.'

Henry swallowed and looked around as if searching for an escape route. But it was no more than an empty reflex. He knew Blue was right. He knew he was behaving like a child. Above all he knew he had to go, knew he *would* go. And spot on time, as if in confirmation, Chief Portal Engineer Peacock limped through the door.

His peg-leg rattled as he snapped to attention before Blue. 'All set up, Ma'am.'

'Are we ready to go?'

'Soon as I set the coordinates and press the button, Ma'am. *Lethe* will cut in automatically.' He glanced across at Henry. 'Looking forward to going home, sir?'

'Not much,' Henry muttered. He nodded towards Peacock's leg. 'How's . . . ?'

'Fine, sir, fine. The new one's grown and they're attaching it next week. I'll be glad to get rid of old Peggy here.'

'Bet you will,' said Henry sympathetically. He licked his lips. 'Are you sending us directly to my old place?'

Peacock smiled self-effacingly. 'Still using the old-fashioned node-to-node technology here, I'm afraid, sir. No node anywhere near your parents' place, so we thought we'd send you via Mr Fogarty's old house. There's a node in the back yard, you remember.'

'We can take a public ouklo,' Blue said helpfully. She shook her head. 'Oh, you don't have them in the Analogue World. There must be something similar.'

'Taxi,' Henry muttered. Peacock had said *we*. Blue must have sorted the whole thing out. As usual. She probably had a pocketful of Analogue money to cover incidental expenses.

Peacock said, 'Well, Ma'am, sir, if you're ready . . . ?'

'We're ready,' said Blue, speaking for both of them. She moved towards the portal pillars.

Henry hesitated for a moment, then shuffled after her.

Fourteen

They emerged from behind the buddleia bush and Henry, who was ahead now, stopped so suddenly that Blue walked into him. 'What are you doing?' she asked crossly.

Nothing had changed. The tiny patch of lawn was still a mess, the house looked empty, the pane of glass in the back door was still cracked. Nothing had changed *in sixteen years!*

'It's still the same,' Henry told her.

'The same as what?' Blue frowned.

It was all a bit complicated. Henry had looked after the house for Mr Fogarty's daughter Angela, who lived in New Zealand, when Mr Fogarty emigrated to the Faerie Realm, pretending he'd died. Then Henry married Blue and emigrated to the Faerie Realm himself, pretending to his parents he'd gone to New Zealand to look after Mr Fogarty and pretending to Mr Fogarty's daughter he'd gone to university. He'd assumed Angela would find somebody else to look after the house or, more likely, sell it. But there was no sign of new owners, no sign of a caretaker, no sign that anything had changed. He wondered if there was still a spare key underneath the plant pot by the back door.

'The same as when I was looking after it,' Henry

murmured. He remembered gazing across that little patch of overgrown lawn at two intruders who turned out to be Pyrgus and Nymph and not recognising Pyrgus because the time disease had made him old. He remembered how Mr Fogarty had sent him coded messages and how close he'd come to not deciphering them. He remembered what a haven this old place had been when he wanted to get away from his mother and his rotten sister and the worry about his parents' divorce. 'Do you mind if we have a quick look inside?' he asked Blue. 'I know where there might be a key.'

'I think we should try to find one of your taxis,' Blue said. 'We need to know about Mella as soon as possible.' She caught sight of his face. 'Darling, what's wrong?'

Henry shook his head. 'Nothing.' But he couldn't stop the tears streaming down his cheeks.

There *was* a key under the plant pot and when they got inside, the kitchen was exactly the same. Henry even opened one of the drawers and found it still stuffed with Mr Fogarty's electrical bits and pieces – tangles of wire, old transistors and coils, needle-nosed pliers, circuit boards . . . Something in him wanted to look around upstairs, but he didn't think he could face it. Besides, Blue was right: their first priority was Mella, and while she was in no danger if she really had gone to visit his mother, it was as well to make sure and the sooner the better.

'We'd best go,' he said to Blue. 'There's a taxi stand about ten minutes' walk away.'

There was a bus stop even closer, but he didn't want to subject Blue to a bus ride: she'd only visited the Analogue World once before and the privacy of a taxi would be better. Besides, the taxi would be faster, even allowing for a ten-minute walk. On impulse he picked up the kitchen phone and found to his astonishment that it was still connected. 'I can call us a taxi,' he told her.

'Did Mr Fogarty live here all his life?' Blue asked while they were waiting.

'Just some of it, I think.' He didn't actually know when Mr Fogarty had bought the house – he'd been an old man when Henry met him. It had been a mistake to come inside: there were too many memories and the waiting was making Henry even more nervous about meeting his mother. 'Listen, let's wait outside, then we can see when the taxi arrives.'

'OK,' Blue said.

As they were locking the back door, Hodge emerged from the buddleia bush the way he used to and Henry's heart stopped. He felt the blood drain from his face, felt seized by the sensation of having stepped sixteen years back in time. What he had to do now was go in and open a tin of Hodge's cat food while the old tom curled around his ankles and howled at him to hurry up. He left the key in the lock – his fingers were suddenly too weak to turn it – and took a step forward.

'What are you doing here?' he asked.

'Followed you through the portal,' the cat told him and Henry felt a flooding of relief. Not Hodge, of course, but Splodge who looked so like him. The cat glanced around. 'I think, if you don't mind, I'll stay. Better hunting here than the Palace.'

'But there's nobody here to feed you,' Henry protested. 'And you're not used to Analogue World traffic. And –'

But Blue cut across him firmly. 'Splodge is a grown

cat now – he can take care of himself. He just wants to be in the same hunting grounds as his father.' She bent down to tickle Splodge behind the ears. As she straightened up again, she added, 'Just like Mella really.'

Mr Fogarty's old house was at the end of a cul-de-sac in the town. Henry's old home was on a country road a few miles outside it. The journey by taxi, allowing for traffic, would usually take about twenty minutes. As they climbed into the back, Blue said, 'I'm sorry, Henry.'

'What for?'

'Making you come with me. I could easily have fetched Mella on my own. I just didn't think how emotional a trip like this would be for you.'

Henry settled back in the seat and sighed. 'I wouldn't have let you go on your own. I know I said I didn't want to – and to tell you the truth, I'm still dreading meeting my mother – but I could never have left you to handle this, not really. Mella's my daughter too.' He gave a weak grin and shrugged. 'I should be the one apologising. Actually, I think we'll take it that I *am* the one apologising. I'm sorry. I'm sorry for giving you such a hard time.'

Blue said, 'Would it help if your mother didn't know you? If you were a complete stranger, who just happened to be with me?'

'Fat chance,' Henry said. 'I haven't changed *that* much in sixteen years.'

'Yes, but would it help?'

'Oh, it would help all right,' Henry said. 'Hypothetically. She was always perfectly civilised to other people. It was just me she used to get at. And Dad.'

Blue pulled a twist of paper from her pocket and unwrapped it to reveal a tiny white pill, like the

85

homeopathic remedies his father used to take for his migraines. 'Take this.'

Henry stared at the pill suspiciously. 'What is it?'

'It's a morphing tablet. I bought it for Mella – the teens are using them a lot these days. It changes the structure of your face. Temporarily. The kids take them for fun; like putting on a mask. Wouldn't fool anybody in the Faerie Realm, of course, but they're not used to magic in this world, so your mother won't know you. Unless she recognises your voice or your walk or something.'

'I can disguise my voice and do a funny walk,' Henry said promptly. 'Are you serious? Will it really change my face?'

'Yes, of course.'

'How long does it last?'

'Couple of hours. Three at the most.'

'How long does it take to work?'

'It's a gradual change, so it's quite slow. Maybe five minutes, maybe a minute or two longer for some people. But if you take it now, you should certainly be looking completely different by the time we get there.'

'Better looking, or ugly?'

'Oh, Henry! What does it matter?'

Henry swallowed the pill. He felt his face, then craned to try to see himself in the driver's mirror. 'What do I look like?'

'Yourself!' Blue hissed. 'I told you, the change is gradual. You won't notice anything at all for at least three minutes.'

Henry sat back again. 'Tell me when anything happens.'

The cab left town and moved sedately along a

tree-lined road. Henry was feeling his face again when the driver pushed back the glass hatch to ask, 'Round here somewhere, isn't it, Guv?'

Henry stopped feeling his face to check the road. 'Next on the right,' he said. He looked anxiously at Blue. 'Has it worked?'

'Beautifully,' Blue said. She smiled mischievously. 'Your own mother wouldn't recognise you.'

The cabbie made the turn, then slammed on his brakes. 'Jeez!' he gasped. 'Don't give us any warning, will you, mate?!'

The road ahead was closed, with no fewer than three police cars parked beside the barricade. A uniformed constable broke away from a group of his colleagues to stroll across.

'What's the problem, Guv?' the driver asked.

The constable bent down at the driver's window, checked out Blue and Henry, then told the driver, 'Can't get through, I'm afraid.'

'I can see that. What's the problem?'

The constable glanced back at Blue and Henry. 'Either of you two live here?'

Henry shook his head at once. 'No. Neither of us.' He thought Blue might be about to say something and squeezed her leg to shut her up.

The constable seemed to relax a little. 'House came down further up,' he told the cabbie. 'Debris all over the road. There'll be nothing getting through until they clear it.'

'Strewth,' the driver muttered. 'They're not building houses like they used to.'

'Didn't just fall,' the constable told him. 'There was an explosion. Boys from the fire brigade think it might have been a gas main, but I never saw a gas leak could do that sort of damage. The whole house is just a pile of rubble. Like a bomb hit it.'

'What about my fares?' the cabbie asked, indicating Blue and Henry with a backwards nod of his head. 'Can they get down on foot? They're visiting one of the houses on the road.'

The constable stuck his head through the window. 'Which one?' he asked Henry.

'*Chatleigh*,' Henry told him. He swallowed. 'It doesn't have a number.' He had a bad feeling about this, a very bad feeling indeed.

'Do you or the young lady have friends in *Chatleigh*, sir?'

'My mother lives there,' Henry told him. 'Why the questions, Officer?'

'Would you mind terribly stepping out of the cab, sir? The two of you.'

Henry grabbed Blue's hand and opened the taxi door. 'Come on,' he murmured. He knew for a certainty what the policeman was going to say, but he stopped himself from even thinking it.

The policeman looked at them soberly. 'I'm terribly sorry, sir. *Chatleigh* is the house that came down. They're searching the rubble for bodies at the moment.'

Fifteen

The security spells on the approaches to Lord Hairstreak's weather-beaten Keep were set to discourage
hawkers, messengers and casual callers by means of
lethal force, teleporting the resultant corpses to the
bottom of a disused, and now somewhat smelly, quarry.
But an exception was programmed in for the engineers of
Consolidated Magical Services who serviced Hairstreak's
Body in a Box, every six months as per contract, and
who required free access in the event of an emergency.

The man in the reception hall was clearly no engineer.
He wore a tailored suit in place of overalls and smelled
of cheap aftershave rather than oil. Hairstreak could
only assume the spell card had been confused by the
CMS logo on his blazer pocket and permitted him entry
in error.

The man stood up politely as Battus Polydamas
trundled Hairstreak into the room. 'Good morning,
My Lord. May I say what a pleasure – indeed *honour*
– it is to meet you.'

'What do you want?' Hairstreak growled. His toler-
ance of unexpected visitors, always low, had dropped
to zero since he lost his natural body. This man looked
like an accountant – he had flat, black, oiled-down hair
and a pencil-slim moustache – which probably meant

he'd come to try to raise the leasehold on Hairstreak's *Body*. Not that he had any chance. Hairstreak's lawyers had gone over the contract with a fine-tooth comb.

'My name is Sulphur, Lyside Sulphur,' the man introduced himself, 'and it's not so much what I want as what I can do for you, Your Lordship.' He smiled and maintained firm eye-contact.

Oh Gods, he was a salesman! How had he made it past the mastiffs? They should have sniffed him out a mile away, even if he'd fooled the security system. But then Hairstreak should have spotted him himself. The moustache was a dead giveaway.

'Have him fed to the alligators,' he instructed Batty. 'After you wheel me back to my study.'

'Yes, sir.' Battus began struggling to angle the barrow.

'We can give you back your body,' Mr Sulphur said.

'Belay that order,' Hairstreak said to Battus. He waited while his retainer manoeuvred him so he was facing the salesman again. 'What did you say?'

Sulphur started to smile, caught Hairstreak's expression and changed his mind. He swallowed audibly. 'Well, obviously not your old body – that's gone for good. Unfortunately. Or perhaps not. But we can give you *a* body.'

'We?'

'Consolidated Magical Services.' He pointed at the logo on his jacket.

'I know who you represent,' said Hairstreak quietly. 'I already have a CMS body.'

'I'm not talking about a *Body in a Box*, sir – I mean a *body*. One that can walk and lift things.' Sulphur was watching Hairstreak apprehensively, but clearly thought he'd grabbed an advantage because he pasted on the phony smile again and launched directly into his sales patter. 'What's more, sir, we have a special offer, one day only, for our existing customers. Trade in your present *Body in a Box* against our new, updated, stylish, fully automated *BodyFree* model and you will not only cover the down payment, but also qualify for an astounding twelve per cent discount on the overall purchase price, *plus* free head transfer and installation. What's more, sir, should you elect to buy the deluxe model – which I'm sure a man of your discernment and stature would certainly consider – you qualify for our new two-year-guarantee no-cost after-sales service and the gift of a free fountain pen that will write with green ink under water.'

'It can walk?' Hairstreak said.

Sulphur frowned. 'The pen?'

'The body, you blithering idiot!'

Sulphur nodded enthusiastically. 'Sir, this is one of the breakthroughs of the aeon. My company has taken the basic *Body in a Box* technology and revolutionised it. Our new entry-level model can not only support life just as effectively as the old-style cube, but walk under its own power, grip and lift objects with its mechanical arms and generally perform the motor functions of a normal human body.'

'I could walk?' Hairstreak said.

Sulphur was grinning broadly now. 'Walk, dress yourself, feed yourself . . . with practice, of course. Could I interest you in a demonstration?'

'Yes,' Hairstreak said shortly.

Lyside Sulphur opened the briefcase he'd left beside his chair and took out a small, brightly coloured box. He cracked the sealant with his thumb, set it on the floor and flipped the lid. A stream of silver vapour poured out to form itself into a headless humanoid robotic shape which then solidified. 'We have an artificial head,' Sulphur explained as he fished in the briefcase again. 'It runs on a chicken's brain, so it's very limited, but it'll give you an idea of the unit's capabilities.' He unfolded a silver sphere and screwed it expertly on to the body. 'Walk!' he commanded.

The silver body lumbered across the room in Hairstreak's direction, did a smart about-turn before it reached him and lumbered back again.

'Pick up the vase on the table!' Sulphur glanced reassuringly at Hairstreak. 'Don't worry, sir, we're insured for breakages.'

The creature – now it had a head of sorts, Hairstreak was beginning to think of it as a creature in its own right – clumped over to the table and picked up the vase with surprising ease.

'Now watch this,' Sulphur instructed excitedly. 'Toss the vase and catch it!'

Hairstreak wouldn't have bet tuppence on the fate of his vase, but the thing threw it several feet in the air and caught it expertly on the way down.

'Impressive or what?' Sulphur exclaimed.

'Impressive,' Hairstreak grunted grudgingly.

'Of course,' Sulphur said in that irritatingly informal way salesmen always seemed to adopt when they were circling for the kill, 'if you're concerned with looks, then the unit leaves a lot to be desired. It's a little better when you put clothes on it, but – and my boss would jail me if he knew I'd told you this – I don't like the design at all. The technology – wonderful. The design – well . . .' He shook his head sadly, then brightened suddenly. 'The deluxe model makes up for a great deal in that department.' He batted his eyelids in Hairstreak's direction and asked innocently, 'Would you like to see a demonstration of our deluxe model, Lord Hairstreak?'

'Yes,' Hairstreak told him. Within the confines of his present *Body in a Box*, the area of his stomach was feeling a tingle of excitement.

'I'm not taking up too much of your valuable time?' Sulphur asked.

Hairstreak wondered vaguely what the penalty was for strangling a salesman with your bare hands. Not that he had bare hands to strangle with, but if he bought the body that had tossed the vase, it could be one of his first actions as a newly mobile Faerie of the Night. For the moment, however, he bit back his irritation and simply answered, 'No, you're not.'

Smiling slightly to himself, Sulphur returned to his briefcase. This time the box he took out had none of the garish colours of the last one. Instead, it sported a sophisticated holographic design that incorporated – Hairstreak noticed at once – the Hairstreak family crest. It was a typical salesman's set-up. CMS had obviously created custom packaging for the body they hoped to sell him, perhaps even created a custom body. The basic model, robotic, clumsy, chicken-brained and ugly was still standing there to create a contrast with the deluxe super-duper model. What he was about to see would be very, very expensive indeed. But it might also be quite interesting.

It was certainly very different. Hairstreak saw that at once, the moment Sulphur flipped open the box. In place of the silver vapour (which was obviously based on the old genie technology) a pink and black origami sheet emerged. It began to unfold itself into an elaborate flower, from the centre of which sprang a life-sized hologram of a naked human figure that began to solidify visibly on contact with the air. Where the original metallic robot had been headless, this form was complete. As it stabilised, it turned slowly towards him and Hairstreak realised he was looking at a perfect representation of himself, head to toe. And not as he was now, but as he used to be when he enjoyed the fullness of his health.

He fought back the instinct to gasp, which would have given the oily little salesman an advantage in negotiations. The body was incredible, his replica in every way, yet with subtle exceptions. It was taller than he used to be and better muscled. The skin tone looked more healthy – smoother, with fewer blemishes and less body hair. There was an aura of strength and power about this creature that he liked very, very much.

'Of course the head is for display purposes only,' Sulphur said, disconcertingly passing his hand through it to demonstrate. 'But our designers have animated it to give you some small feel of how you would look should you decide to invest in our new *BodyFree* deluxe design.' He patted the solid shoulder and the head smiled at Hairstreak benignly. It was a beautiful smile, full of depth and wisdom.

Hairstreak knew he was going to buy this *BodyFree* deluxe whatever it cost. Knew he *had* to have it, and put Battus out to pasture for a long-overdue retirement. But he held tight rein on his emotions and said flatly, 'Let's see it move.'

'Certainly, Your Lordship. Perhaps if your factotum wheeled you back a bit, we could give it a little more room . . .'

Hairstreak gave an eye signal to Battus, who pulled the barrow back towards the door. 'That good enough?' Hairstreak asked.

'Admirable,' said Sulphur.

The demonstration was incredible. The figure burst into action like an athlete. It ran the entire length of the reception chamber with the grace of a gazelle, then cartwheeled back in the fashion of a gymnast. It leaped over tables and chairs, then hurled itself upwards to swing briefly from the chandelier before dropping lightly to the ground with its back arched, arms stretched and bum pushed out.

'I'll take it,' Hairstreak said.

'Our entry-level model or the deluxe?' asked Sulphur innocently.

'Don't be silly,' Hairstreak growled. 'Now talk to me about the head transfer.'

Sulphur was grinning broadly now. His commission on this single sale would probably earn him an obscene sum of money. 'That's another benefit of our deluxe model, sir. We find our customers are typically – and understandably – impatient to experience the benefits of their new bodies, so this model comes equipped as standard with the very latest magnetic slide technology which completely obviates the need for surgery. Essentially, what we do is to infuse your present *Body in a Box* with specially treated iron filings. These are absorbed by your natural head, thus rendering it magnetic. After that, a simple stasis spell allows us to remove your head from the box and transfer it to the shoulders of your new body – you experience the moment of blankness typical of the stasis spell. Once in place, the magnetic field of the body holds the head firmly in place – we've tested it against a pull of seven thousand tons; far in excess of anything your natural body could ever have withstood. The greatest benefit, of course, is that henceforth all your body–head connections are magnetic – far more efficient than the old flesh/blood/nerve connectors of a natural body.'

'What are the vulnerabilities?' Hairstreak asked.

'None. As I think I mentioned, the base technology is that of our *Body in a Box*, so the unit is solar powered and indestructible. Once you've been joined, you are essentially immortal and invulnerable.'

Hairstreak frowned. 'Essentially?'

'Your natural head remains vulnerable,' Sulphur explained. 'Although we can offer at extra cost a spray-on armour plating that will help somewhat with that problem. The body itself is immortal and invulnerable. It doesn't even require our after-sales service.'

Hairstreak licked his lips, his eyes bright. 'I assume all this involves a visit to the CMS clinic? How long does the transfer take?'

Sulphur picked up his briefcase again and began to shuffle papers. 'Actually, sir, this is the great benefit of magnetic slide technology. Once you have signed the contract, we can make the transfer, without any need of clinic facilities, here in your own home. Typically the whole thing takes less than half an hour.'

'Let's have the contract,' Hairstreak said.

Once the transfer was complete, Hairstreak celebrated the athletic abilities of his new body by slitting Sulphur's throat, disposing of the corpse, tearing up the contract and carefully destroying all evidence that the salesman had ever visited. No sense letting his enemies know he was fully mobile again. They'd find out eventually, of course, but in the interim, Sulphur's disappearance would give him a definite edge.

He had a slight problem with clothing – the new body *was* bigger than his old one – but he found some formal garments that hung well enough once he removed their padding. Then he walked – *walked!* – to the gardens in the central courtyard.

He found Mella seated on a bench talking to a rabbit: how much the sweet child enjoyed the small glories of the natural world! And how few things fazed her. She devoted no more than a passing glance to his new body before focusing on his face and smiling broadly. 'Why, Uncle Hairstreak, how kind of you visit. It's not your usual day, unless I'm very much mistaken.'

Hairstreak sat down beside her. 'Not mistaken at all. But I have something I wish to discuss with you.'

She shooed away the rabbit – which was just as well, Hairstreak thought, for even rabbits had ears – and turned to face him, knees primly together, a look of rapt attention on her face.

'You know, of course, that I have plans to make you Queen of our Realm in the very near future,' Hairstreak said.

'Indeed, Uncle, and I am very grateful,' Mella told him.

'Well,' said Hairstreak easily, 'it occurred to me that now I have regained my mobility, regained my body, so to speak . . .' He gestured at the new *BodyFree* and smiled slide-magnetically, '. . . it occurred to me that we might marry, so I could guide you henceforth as your husband and, eventually, as your King.'

'Why, Uncle,' Mella said. 'What an absolutely spiffing idea!'

Sixteen

Suddenly he'd lost her. One minute she was there, in that peculiar little Analogue kitchen, the next she was gone. As was the human with her and the kitchen itself. Brimstone extended his senses to their fullest limit. He could hear the hum of the city, listen to the eager sucking of a flea on Chalkhill's bottom, even catch the primitive, angry feelings of the prickleweed far below them, but the girl Chalkhill wanted him to track was gone without trace.

Instinctively, he reached for the handkerchief in his pocket, then stopped. The last thing he wanted was to give Chalkhill any hint that something was wrong. They hadn't agreed a deal yet and if Chalkhill found out he'd lost the girl, they never would. Best to keep him in the dark for the moment and try to pick up the girl's scent in private later. Assuming she hadn't died. That sort of *now you see it, now you don't* business used to happen when he stomped on cockroaches. One minute you were hearing their scritches and their scratches and their roachy little thoughts, the next . . . *stomp-squish* . . . nothing. Just the way it happened to the girl, except for the *stomp-squish,* of course. What a tragedy it would be, if she had died: the Queen's own daughter, finest flower of the Realm. All that potential ransom money gone. A tragedy. It was making him feel quite emotional, so that he had to suppress the urge to sniff.

But perhaps she wasn't dead. After all, there'd been nothing to suggest a threat. Perhaps she was just lying dreadfully injured somewhere. That would hardly affect her value at all; in fact in some ways it might enhance it. Actually, now he came to think of it, even her body might be worth a bob or two. People were so sentimental about corpses and where they should be buried, especially the Royal Family. It would be well worth trying to find out what had happened, even if she was dead.

They were back in the stretch ouklo, Brimstone, George and Chalkhill, on a course to Chalkhill's family estate on Wildmoor Broads. Chalkhill had drunk too much with the meal and was now nodding as if finding it difficult to stay awake. George was quiet too, having eaten two steaks and, apparently, a waiter, although in the rush at the restaurant, no one had seemed to notice. Perhaps he might risk using the handkerchief briefly, just to refocus himself.

With a quick glance towards the nodding Chalkhill – his eyes seemed to be closed at the moment – Brimstone slid the hankie from his pocket and sniffed it surreptitiously. At once he tuned in to a scene of utter desolation. A building lay in ruins, little more than a pile of dusty rubble. There were uniformed humans crawling over it, so this was presumably an Analogue World building, perhaps the same Analogue World building that had housed the Analogue World kitchen he'd seen earlier. Yes, that was likely; that would make sense. But if the building that housed the kitchen had fallen down and the faeman child was in the kitchen at the time, then young Mella was certainly dead – the uniformed humans were presumably searching for her corpse, probably in the hope of looting her jewellery. But that would be a good thing, because they wouldn't be interested in the body itself, which meant Brimstone might still have a chance of getting hold of it.

He stuffed the hankie in his pocket and sat back to have a little think. If he could figure out exactly where the house had collapsed, the trick would obviously be to persuade Chalkhill to fund a trip to the Analogue World. Just for Brimstone, of course – or Brimstone and George, to be exact: always safer with a bodyguard. The sooner they got shot of Chalkhill himself the better. But if Chalkhill had any inkling that Brimstone knew Mella was in the Analogue World, albeit not necessarily breathing, Chalkhill would want to come too. Which was back to square one. So . . .

Brimstone thought.

Brimstone thought.

Brimstone thought.

So . . . what he needed to do was persuade Chalkhill that he didn't know *exactly* where Mella was, but that he'd narrowed it down to two possibilities, one in the Analogue World, one in the Faerie Realm. No, belay that. Both in the Faerie Realm – the more he diverted Chalkhill's attention from the Analogue World the better. After that, it would be a small step to persuade him that they should then split up for the sake of speed and efficiency, with Chalkhill searching vainly in the Faerie Realm while Brimstone secretly visited the scene of the disaster in the Analogue World.

So where had the house collapsed?

Brimstone was familiar with parts of the Analogue World. He knew the more disreputable bits of New York quite well, for example. But the style of architecture around the collapsed building didn't look at all American. If anything . . .

The ouklo banked and swooped suddenly. Chalkhill opened his eyes. Brimstone stared through the window. They were over Chalkhill's family estate, a pretentious, spell-encrusted manor with manicured parkland far enough away from the city to be both comfortable and private, close enough to be worth a fortune. (How had an idiot like Chalkhill managed to keep hold of his money? Gods knew Brimstone had tried to take it away from him often enough.) A permanent fair-weather spell added to its value as well as its attraction.

They sat together by the swimming pool while Chalkhill's butler served them coffee cocktails. 'Any luck with the hankie?' Chalkhill asked on the first sip.

'Not easy,' Brimstone muttered. 'Even when you've been goosed by a cloud dancer.' He noticed George was dangling his enormous feet in the pool. George had always liked water.

Chalkhill followed the sip with a gulp. 'Well, if it's not going to work, it's not going to work. I'll have to find another way. Androgeous, perhaps you'd organise transport to the workhouse for Mr Brimstone.'

'No need to be like that, Jasper,' Brimstone said hurriedly. 'I only said it wouldn't be easy. I didn't say it wouldn't be possible.' A sly look crossed his features. 'Besides, we haven't talked terms yet.'

'Oh, so that's the problem,' Chalkhill said. 'Here's the deal. You find me the girl – you don't have to do anything to her, don't have to catch her, just find her. Five hundred up front – should give you a float after your little stay in the asylum, buy you a bar or two of soap; you could do with a bath – and five *thousand* if you find her.'

Five *thousand?* That was an enormous sum of money: enough to buy a town house and live without working for a decade. 'Ten,' Brimstone said instinctively.

'Seven and a half,' Chalkhill countered.

'Done,' Brimstone said. And Chalkhill certainly had been. Seven thousand five hundred, plus the five hundred up front: eight thousand altogether. That was more than they'd payed to ransom Scolitandes the Weedy. Chalkhill clearly wanted the girl very badly indeed. Which meant she was worth much more than eight thousand. An interesting situation.

But Chalkhill was talking. 'You'll have the five hundred before you leave here today, but you only get the rest after I get hold of the girl. It's yours once I have her in custody.'

'That's not fair!' Brimstone protested. 'Suppose I find her and you're too clumsy to catch her or so stupid you let her go? I've kept my part of the bargain. I should get paid.'

'That's the deal. Take it or leave it.'

'You'll have to cover my expenses,' Brimstone said.

'What expenses?' Chalkhill demanded. 'All you have to do is sit there, sniff and concentrate. I'm already paying for the cocktails.'

Brimstone treated him to a knowing smile. 'It's not as simple as that, Jasper. The cloud dancer made me sensitive and the sensitivity gives me a mental picture of the thing we're looking for. But I may not recognise the place. I mean, I could tell you she's standing under an oak tree looking at a sheep, but I wouldn't necessarily know where the tree was growing or who owned the animal.'

'Is she standing under an oak tree looking at a sheep?'

'No, that was just an example.'

'Do you have any idea where she might be yet?'

It was time, Brimstone thought, to dangle the bait. 'I do have a picture – not an oak tree or a sheep – but I'm not at all sure where it might be.' Which was a truthful lie. He wasn't quite sure where Mella was now, whether she was alive or dead, but he was convinced he knew where she'd just been. From his experience of the Analogue World, the scene he saw was never American, but it might be British. It had occurred to him that Mella's father – Consort Majesty King Henry – was a human, brought up in the Analogue World. What more natural for a girl of Mella's age than to want to visit her father's old home? Zero in on that and chances were you found the girl.

'Where do you think it might be?' Chalkhill demanded.

'Buthner,' Brimstone said promptly. He hesitated, then added, 'Or Haleklind.'

'Which one?'

'I don't know. But it shouldn't be too difficult to find out. The place I'm sensing is very distinctive: an escarpment with an enormous natural stone pillar that's been carved into the representation of a smiling dragon with emerald eyes. I'm surprised it's not known as a tourist attraction, but it's bound to be known in its own country.' He set his cocktail to one side and went on enthusiastically, 'I thought what I would do is take a trip to Buthner and make some enquiries. Then, if the place

I'm sensing isn't there, I can visit Haleklind and do the same.' He nodded soberly. 'That's why I'll need expenses.'

Chalkhill said, 'I don't have time to send you traipsing around two different countries.'

'Has to be done, I'm afraid,' Brimstone told him piously. 'What alternative do we have?' He waited.

Chalkhill swallowed the bait. 'You could describe what you're sensing and I can check one country while you check the other. That would halve the time.'

'So it would,' Brimstone said. He looked at Chalkhill with admiration, as if the thought had never occurred to him.

Seventeen

There were two fire engines at the scene as well as an ambulance and three more police cars. More than a dozen uniformed men were climbing over the rubble. Four of them had police dogs on leads. Henry walked across to where an ambulance driver was talking to a burly man who had plainclothes copper written all over him.

'Pardon me,' he said, 'but has anyone been injured?'

He addressed the question to the ambulance man, but the burly copper butted in at once. 'Excuse me, sir, but do you live along this bit of road?'

'No, I –'

'In that case, sir, you shouldn't be here. Can't have gawpers holding up the rescue operation.'

There was a time when Henry would have backed off apologetically: he'd been terrified of authority for most of his life. But that time was gone. He was King Consort of the Realm now and if he could hold his own with Blue, he could hold his own with anybody. He turned to look the big man directly in the eye.

'I was brought up in this house,' he said firmly. 'My mother still lives here. That hardly makes me a gawper.'

The man's tone and demeanour changed at once.

'I'm sorry, sir. Should have realised they wouldn't have let you through, if you didn't belong. I'm –'

Henry cut him off. 'You said "rescue operation". Does that mean there were people in the house?'

The ambulance man said, 'We don't know, truthfully. We're treating it as if there were – all we can do, really. We haven't found any survivors, but the good news is we haven't found any bodies either.'

'How long have you been searching?'

'Couple of hours.'

'That's a very short time,' Henry said.

'Don't know about that,' the ambulance man said. 'The sniffer dogs should have picked up something by now if there was anything to pick up.' He nodded towards the rubble. 'Just look at them: bored stiff, the four of them.'

The burly policeman was pulling a notebook from his pocket. 'Since you're here, sir, you might help us by confirming a few details. Neighbours say the householder was a Mrs Atherton. You wouldn't happen to know her first name?'

'Of course I know her first name,' Henry said crossly. 'She's my mother. It's Martha.'

'And I gather she lived here with another woman?'

Henry nodded.

'And that would be Aisling Atherton, would it?' the copper asked, consulting his notebook.

Henry glanced at him in surprise. So Aisling was still living at home, the lazy little cow. She must be nearly thirty now. Why couldn't she lead her own life? 'Aisling's my sister,' he said. 'Did the neighbours say she was living here?'

'Yes. Can you confirm it?'

'Not really. I've been away rather a long time.'

The policeman seemed to accept it. 'And your name, sir?'

'Henry. Henry Atherton.'

'But you haven't been living here for a while?'

Henry shook his head. 'No. Not for years.'

'So it would just have been Mrs Atherton and your sister? Or is there a Mr Atherton?'

'Divorced,' Henry told him.

'Recently?'

'No, years ago.'

'Any reason for him to blow up the house?'

Henry froze. 'What?'

The burly man closed his notebook with a snap. 'Mr Atherton, I'm Detective Inspector John Tyneside. I'm in charge of this investigation. Officially, we're checking out the possibility of a gas main explosion. Unofficially, the first thing we thought of when the reports started to come in was a terrorist attack. I –'

'A *terrorist* attack?' Henry echoed. 'Out here?'

D. I. Tyneside nodded. 'I know: we dropped that theory once we found that it was a domestic residence. But I'll tell you this, Mr Atherton. That house didn't come down because of a gas main. Just look at it. That was one hell of an explosion. It's a miracle the houses beside it are still standing. Some funny characteristics as well: didn't so much blow up outwards as inwards. We're talking high explosive here, Mr Atherton, and not your usual Semtex either: something new, something we haven't seen before. Your mother isn't mixed up in organised crime, is she?'

Wouldn't put it past her, Henry thought sourly. Aloud, he said, 'No, of course not.'

'Anybody want her dead? Sorry to ask. Your father wouldn't be an industrial chemist, by any chance?'

'Just a businessman,' Henry said. 'Management executive.' On second thought he added, 'Food processing. Nothing to do with explosives.'

'Doesn't hold a grudge against your mother, then? Because of the divorce?'

Henry shook his head. 'He's remarried and moved on.'

'How does she get on with your sister?'

'My mother? Like a house on fi—' He realised what he'd been about to say and amended it hurriedly. 'Very well indeed.' A thought struck him. 'Actually there's someone else living here – Anaïs Ward.'

Tyneside opened his notebook again. 'Neighbours didn't mention that one. Who is she – a lodger?'

'Lover,' Henry muttered. Despite himself he felt a flush rise in his face.

'Sorry?'

'She's my mother's lover,' he said firmly. 'I think she's still living here. As I said, I haven't been for a while.'

'We'll check it out,' Tyneside said, not at all perturbed. He looked directly at Henry. 'Now you, sir.'

'Me? What about me?'

'You say you haven't lived here for some years and now you're saying you haven't visited much either. Where have you been living?'

Fairyland, Henry thought. 'New Zealand,' Henry said.

Tyneside clicked a ballpoint. 'I'll need an address, sir.'

Oh God, Henry thought. But without hesitation he said, 'Twenty-two, Palm Grove Close, West Wellington Road, Auckland. New Zealand, of course.' It was completely bogus, but by the time they made the call to check it, he and Blue would be long gone.

'That's *palm* like the tree, not *Pam* like the woman's name?'

'That's right,' Henry nodded. He could see Blue approaching out of the corner of his eye and decided he needed to get away before she arrived to stick her oar in. It was hard enough keeping a story straight if you were the only one telling lies. Besides, he'd learned as much as he was going to from this policeman and the ambulance driver.

But Tyneside was looking at him curiously. 'Didn't get on all that well with your mother yourself, did you sir?'

Henry flushed again. 'What makes you think that?'

Tyneside shrugged. 'Moved out years ago, haven't visited much. Not exactly the loving son, are you?'

'I write,' Henry protested. Which he did, albeit rarely. The letters were composed in the Faerie Realm (not always by Henry himself) then transferred by apport to a university professor in Wellington, who happened to be a Spiritualist and believed himself under orders from the Other Side to forward them to Henry's mother.

'You don't happen to work in the explosives industry, do you sir?'

'No, I don't,' Henry said firmly. 'Now, if you'll excuse –'

'What do you work at, sir?'

I'm King of the Fairies, Henry thought. What could he say? If he hesitated, the District Inspector would know at once he was lying. But the fact was, he'd never had a real job, not a real Analogue World job. He hadn't even been to university: he'd married Blue straight out of high school and immediately taken up State duties in the Realm. And beside that, he hadn't even known what he wanted to do.

'I'm a teacher,' he heard his mouth say. His mother had always wanted him to be a teacher. That would please her. If she was still alive.

The thought brought him up short. He really did need to get away from this man. Essentially Henry hadn't learned much except that there was no confirmed bad news, while Tyneside had already winkled out enough false information to hang him twice over. He might easily suggest Henry take a little walk down to the station for further inquiries if Henry wasn't very, very careful, and Henry didn't have time to take little walks anywhere. His daughter was missing, and now his old home was blown up, his mother, sister and Anaïs were all missing, any one or all of them might be dead, God forbid, while Henry was faffing round getting nowhere as usual.

'Look,' he said, 'my wife is very upset about all this, as you might imagine, and I've left her alone too long. We'll be staying at the Dorchester if you've any news – or if you need me any further.' God knew why he'd picked the Dorchester, except it was a posh London hotel that made him sound impressive and respectable (*until Mr Tyneside calls and finds you're not on the list of guests*, a small voice whispered in his head). Then, before things could get any worse, he turned and walked away.

He headed Blue off by taking her arm. 'They haven't found bodies,' he said with quiet urgency, 'which is a good thing.' His natural pessimism seeped through a little and he added, 'Of course, they might find something yet, but there's sniffer dogs, and I think if they were going to –'

'Mella's not here,' Blue interrupted him. 'There's nobody here, nobody dead.'

'How do you know?'

'I used a follower.'

Henry looked at her in shock. 'You used a *what?*'

Followers were demons that followed people in the Faerie Realm, where they'd been illegal for centuries. Then he remembered they weren't illegal any more, one of the many reforms that came in after Blue became Queen of Hael. But legal or not, they were still considered terribly disreputable.

Blue must have caught something of the thought in his look, for she said fiercely, 'What do you expect me to do? She's our *daughter!*'

'No, no,' Henry said. 'You did the right thing.' He hesitated. 'Did it bring you any other information?'

'She *was* here,' Blue said, 'just as we suspected. She was here, but she's not now and there are no bodies in the rubble.'

'So where has she gone?'

'I don't know.'

'Didn't the follower tell you?'

'It lost her in the explosion – I've sent it hunting for her again, but we're not sure if she's here or back in the Faerie Realm. It's just possible she may have gone home.'

It sounded like wishful thinking, but it was cheering all the same. 'What makes you think that?' Henry asked hopefully.

'Look at what's happened,' Blue whispered. 'What does that remind you of?'

Henry blinked. 'A bomb blast?'

'Don't be silly. Bombs blow things outwards. Look at your mother's house now. I know there's rubble blocking the road, but look where most of it is.'

Henry looked. Most of it was where the house had stood, a huge pile of broken bricks and mortar.

'What does that remind you of?' Blue repeated.

'I don't know,' Henry said helplessly.

'You know the old portable portals Mr Fogarty used to make – the early ones, before he'd quite got the hang of it?'

Henry nodded. 'Yes.'

'You remember what happened when you used them inside a building?'

It came flooding back to Henry now. It hadn't always happened – in fact it hadn't often happened – but there'd been at least two cases he could think of when the portal had caused a building to collapse. Both times there'd been injuries, but at least the people had been rescued alive. When the portal closed, it created a super-vacuum that caused the building to implode. Blue was right. The remains of his mother's home looked more like it had imploded than exploded.

'Oh my God,' he breathed.

Blue said, 'That man you were talking to – he's waving at you. I think he may want to talk to you again.'

'Let's get out of here,' Henry said urgently. They were approaching the police barrier and at least he'd had the sense to tell the taxi to wait. As they hurried through, he had that weird feeling of somebody staring at the back of his neck, but when he glanced around, he could see nobody.

Eighteen

Chalkhill wrapped the shadow cloak a little tighter and peered out from behind the dustbin. What was Brimstone doing in Seething Lane of all places? The old boy had once had lodgings down here, but they were long gone. And they'd both owned a business here – the Chalkhill and Brimstone Miracle Glue Factory – but that was long gone as well, demolished by the interfering young busybody Pyrgus Malvae in the days when he was heir to the throne. Was Brimstone heading for the old factory site? It seemed unlikely. The demolished buildings had been replaced by a school, but the contractors neglected to defuse the cobblestone minefield attached to the original plant, so neither the school nor its pupils lasted very long. After that, the city authorities turned it into a carriage park for a while, but the high rate of vandalism meant it was seldom used. Prickleweed eventually invaded from the nearby Wildmoor Broads, so that the old site was a complete no-go area now.

One thing was certain: Brimstone hadn't come here to make the trip to Buthner as they'd agreed, any more than Chalkhill was looking for transport to Haleklind. Chalkhill knew the smell of bullshine when he heard it and he'd never bought Brimstone's story about the pillar carved into a dragon with emerald eyes. But that wasn't to say he didn't believe Brimstone knew where Mella was. The old fart knew all right: he just wasn't telling. Chalkhill could only presume he meant to grab the girl for himself, try to hold her for ransom or trade her as a slave. Complete madness, of course, but then – ha, ha – Brimstone *was* mad, wasn't he? If he hadn't been sent potty by the cloud dancer, he wouldn't have been able to locate Mella in the first place. All the same, his madness meant that if you followed Brimstone when he tried to carry out his loony scheme, you found Mella. And once Chalkhill found Mella, all he needed to do was quietly dispatch Brimstone, who was no further use and too old anyway, then deliver the girl to Hairstreak for slaughter. Mission accomplished double-quick time, fat payment received and on to the next job. Hey-ho the holly!

But what was Brimstone doing in Seething Lane? Was Mella hiding somewhere in this dungheap?

Brimstone stopped outside the barber's shop, glanced behind him suspiciously, failed to see Chalkhill in his shadow cloak, then scuttled across the street and up three stone steps into a dingy little shop opposite. Chalkhill waited for a moment, then crept closer. There was a faded sign hanging outside the shop:

TATTOO
PARLOUR
TATTOOS
PIERCING &
APPAREL

Chalkhill unfolded his shadow cloak and marched imperiously into the barber's shop. The chair, as he remembered, faced the window and gave him an uninterrupted view of the tattoo parlour. 'Short back and sides,' he snapped as he sat down.

'Not cutting hair any longer,' said the barber, a short, plump, balding man by the name of . . . Chalkhill searched his memory and found it . . . Nathalis. Filthy little sod, Faerie of the Night, of course – they all were round here – full of stupid jokes, but he'd been in the Lane for years.

'What do you mean you're not cutting hair any longer?' Chalkhill demanded. 'Your sign says *Open*.'

'I'm cutting it *shorter*!' Nathalis exploded into gales of laughter which faded only slowly under Chalkhill's glare. 'Ah, that's a good one. Gets them every time. But seriously, nice to see you again, Mr Chalkhill.'

Chalkhill glanced up at him in surprise. 'You know who I am?'

''Course I do, Mr Chalkhill. Place hasn't been the same since you closed down the factory, but we all remember you. Well, the old residenters, anyway. Lost a lot of trade when you pulled out, we did. And some of us miss the smell.' He picked up a pair of scissors. 'Just a trim, was it?'

Chalkhill settled himself in the chair. 'Yes, but take your time.'

'For sure, sir. Anything you say.' Nathalis ran his fingers through Chalkhill's hair and began to snip slowly, head to one side and tongue stuck out to aid his concentration.

'Who's running the tattoo parlour now?' Chalkhill asked casually after a while.

'Foreign bloke called Feniseca Tarquinius. Well, you could tell by the name, couldn't you? All your foreigners have stupid names. Imagine your mother lumbering you with something like *Feniseca*. Make you want to go and top yourself. But that's what it is. Most of us call him *Fens* for short, on account of his little sideline.'

'He fences stolen goods?' Chalkhill asked.

'Didn't hear it from me,' Nathalis said piously. 'But a nod's as good as a wink to a quiet bullfrog, so they say.'

Chalkhill frowned. Brimstone couldn't be trying to shift stolen goods: he was too recently left the asylum to have any. Maybe he was trying to buy some. But what? And why? 'Any other little sidelines?' he asked.

'This and that,' Nathalis told him unhelpfully. He clipped off another tiny lock. 'Still in the glue business then, Mr Chalkhill?'

'Not any longer,' Chalkhill said.

'Couldn't stick to it, eh? Ha-ha. What do you do now, if I may be so bold as to enquire, sir?'

'I'm an assassin,' Chalkhill said.

'You're an *assassin,* are you, sir? Kill people for a living?'

'That's about the size of it,' Chalkhill said.

'Business good, then?'

'Can't complain.'

Nathalis hesitated. 'Not on a job at the moment, are you, Mr Chalkhill?'

'One or two things in the pipeline,' Chalkhill said. He let the man sweat for a moment out of badness, then added, 'But not at this precise minute, no.'

'I'm relieved to hear it, sir.'

'You were telling me about Mr Tarquinius's little sidelines,' Chalkhill prompted him.

'Forgery,' Nathalis said quickly.

Chalkhill raised a surprised eyebrow. 'Money?'

'Documents. Travel documents, usually. Passports, destination slips, ID cards, that sort of thing. Good at it too, so I'm told. Goes with the artistic temperament, I suppose. Not a long walk from drawing a tattoo to drawing a new passport.'

'Costly?' Chalkhill asked casually.

'Not too bad if you're desperate. You could get the full set for under five hundred.'

Which was just the sum he'd given Brimstone up front. 'Interesting,' he murmured.

Nathalis set down the scissors and sprayed something smelly on Chalkhill's head. 'Thinning a little on top, I notice, sir. Would you like me to use some of our magical hair restorer? We find it gives excellent results, and no extra charge for you, sir, on account of you used to be in business on the Lane.'

Brimstone came out of the tattoo parlour clutching a brown paper bag and headed back up Seething Lane in the general direction of Cheapside.

'No thank you, Nathalis,' Chalkhill said politely. 'The baldness is part of my disguise.'

'Thought you said you weren't on a job at the moment, Mr Chalkhill?'

'I lied,' Chalkhill told him.

When Chalkhill left the barber's shop, he strolled across the street to the tattoo parlour. The walls were lined with illustrations of dragons, anchors, hearts, flowers, manticores, haniels, machine parts, swords and weapons, with a scattering of exotica like a London bus and a plate of Analogue fish and chips. A swarthy, broad-shouldered man, naked to the waist, was the only person in the shop. He was cleaning a set of needles with an oily rag.

'Ah, Fens!' Chalkhill greeted him easily. 'You don't mind my calling you Fens, do you? It's just that I think *Feniseca* is such a stupid name.'

Feniseca blinked, then began to climb to his feet. 'Now, just a minute, Smartass –'

Chalkhill caught him in a ninja nose-hold and stuck a stimulus in his ear. 'Listen carefully, turdface,' he whispered. 'A client of yours just left here a couple of minutes ago with a brown paper bag and he sure as Hael didn't look tattooed. Old boy, smells of rotted demons. I want to know what you sold him and I want to know it now.'

Feniseca was frozen with terror. 'Travel documents,' he said promptly. 'Full set.'

'Destination?'

'Analogue World.'

'Specifically?'

'London, England. Well, place near it: I don't remember the exact name. Have to look up my records. Listen, would you mind taking your finger off the button on that thing? They fry your brains if they go off accidentally.'

'Only if you have brains to fry,' Chalkhill said cheerfully, keeping his finger exactly where it was. 'You going to look up your records for me?'

'Absolutely, sir,' Feniseca told him.

Nineteen

It wasn't like the old days.

'It isn't like the old days,' Brimstone told George conversationally. In the oldest of the old days, when Brimstone was a boy, portals to the Analogue World were natural phenomena, generally caused by volcanic stresses, and only about five of them were known across the entire planet. Portals to Hael were a different matter: the magical techniques used for calling demons had been familiar – and used, despite their dangers – for centuries. It was only a matter of time before somebody thought of combining the natural phenomena with the magical techniques, and the result was the elaborate artificial Analogue World portals, so expensive to install and so costly to run that only the Great Houses of the Empire could afford them. These portals were directional . . . at least up to a point. You could only send somebody to a part of the Analogue World where a suitable node existed naturally or had been secretly established.

Then along came Alan Fogarty.

Brimstone had a sneaking regard for Alan Fogarty. He had a lot going for him when he first arrived in the Faerie Realm: he was old, he was bad-tempered, he was ruthless, he was paranoid, he was cunning. Now, of course, he had the additional advantage of being dead. But before that, he'd created the most revolutionary invention the Faerie Realm had seen in generations: the portable portal.

Some of his early prototypes had been a bit tricky. They couldn't be used indoors, for one thing, on account of an intermittent flaw that caused buildings to collapse. They were also node-based like the Great House portals. But they still represented a big improvement: the controllers were small enough to carry in your pocket, so you could open up a portal anywhere, even if you were limited in where it would send you. And they were cheap.

It was the cheapness that caused the spread of portable portals. Even while Mr Fogarty was still alive, everybody wanted one, and while House Iris never authorised their mass production, black market engineers ripped off the design and churned out copies by the thousand. But the real problems didn't start until after he died – a year or two after he died, to be exact. That was when a trainee engineer called Angelia Electrostrymon appeared on the scene.

Brimstone had a sneaking regard for Angelia as well, mainly because of her amazing name. Would she have invented her version of the portable portal if she'd been called Angelia Puddingbaker? He thought not. Any more than he would have become a demonologist if he hadn't been called Brimstone. Or Chalkhill would have turned into a great pale heap if he'd been called Goldenspheres. Names had a profound influence, Brimstone thought philosophically. But whatever about that, Angelia created a version of the Fogarty portal that made Fogarty's design look like it was nailed together from bits of wood. The great thing about it was that it didn't need reception nodes. You could persuade an Electroportal to take you anywhere in the Analogue World just by setting the relevant coordinates. The other great thing was that it was even cheaper to manufacture than the old Fogarty controllers. Angelia licensed her patent to Consolidated Magical Services and had been counting her money ever since.

The new style Electroportals might have sparked a travel revolution in the Faerie Realm if the authorities hadn't been quick to institute a clampdown. Couldn't have people trolling off to the Analogue World any time they felt like it. Would have given them ideas above their station, as too much freedom always did. So, however easy it was to get there, travel to the Analogue World became illegal – on penalty of having bits cut off you – unless you had the relevant documentation, which was both difficult and costly to procure in a procedure that typically took so long you missed the best days of your holiday anyway. At the same time, the Empire's State Public Relations Office, Propaganda Division, mounted a campaign designed to discourage spontaneous pleasure visits to the Analogue World, and the Royal Family set a good example by voluntarily using only their old-style node-based Family Iris portal with all its expense and well-known inconveniences.

'You can see why anybody sensible just buys false documents,' Brimstone told George, who sometimes listened in to his thoughts. He stored the last of his own forged documents in the various pockets of his travel suit. 'Now, I want you to stay close behind me and move through as soon as I do: there's only a small window of opportunity before the portal closes.'

George nodded.

Brimstone checked the coordinates. He'd taken them from an old Analogue World Ordnance Survey map and was by no means confident of their accuracy, but if he was off by a few yards, or even a few miles, he could still find his way to the exact location without too much difficulty: there was a sort of compass thing built into the Electroportal control that gave whispered instructions to the destination when needed.

'You ready?' he asked George.

George nodded again.

Brimstone squeezed the control and stepped through the portal.

Somebody's house had fallen down. He was standing behind a small ornamental hedge, but could see the ruin quite clearly on the other side of the road. George arrived behind him, pushing him a step forward, an action that automatically closed the portal. There were people about. He recognised police uniforms. His instinct was to hide, but he fought it down: he'd done nothing wrong. This time. So far. The coppers had nothing on him. In fact, he'd actually taken a step towards them when he saw the two retreating figures. Brimstone stared until the man glanced back, then stepped swiftly behind a bush.

The man was Consort Majesty King Henry Atherton. The woman was Queen Holly Blue.

twenty

Somebody's house had fallen down. Chalkhill suppressed a giggle, but sobered quickly. This was no time to rejoice in someone else's misfortune. He drew his shadow cloak around him and stepped into the shade of a nearby tree to evaluate the situation.

First off, there'd obviously been an accident, and a big one. His guess was that somebody in the ruined house had been running an illegal explosives factory. That sort of thing happened all the time in the Analogue World: since they couldn't do anything by magic, they were obsessed about doing it by explosives. It was obviously an *illegal* factory, since there were policemen crawling all over the rubble looking for clues.

Next, why had Brimstone come here? Brimstone definitely *had* come here, since Chalkhill could see the old fool skulking behind a bush across the road. The answer had to be that Brimstone knew Mella was running an illegal explosives factory in the Analogue World. The question was, had Mella perished in the blast? It seemed entirely likely. Teenagers were notoriously careless, and teenagers who went into the explosives business frequently blew themselves to bits. The second question was, could Chalkhill turn this to his advantage?

The simplest course of action would be to take credit for her death, report back and tell Lord Hairstreak he'd blown her up. A simple body part, such as he might find in the rubble, would be sufficient proof. Then Chalkhill could claim his fee without having had to earn it, which would be extremely gratifying. The only drawback he could see was that Hairstreak had insisted the girl be assassinated in Hairstreak's own castle. Was that stipulation negotiable? Hairstreak was not well known for his willingness to negotiate, but it was such a stupid thing to specify that he might. Especially if – reluctantly – Chalkhill dropped his fee a little.

But all this assumed Mella really was dead. And likely though that might be, it wasn't absolutely certain.

A policeman strode past just a few feet from where he was standing, but the shadow cloak did its work so that Chalkhill remained unseen. He allowed his gaze to drift back to Brimstone. With his expanded senses, Brimstone probably knew whether the girl was alive or dead. The trick would be persuading him to tell . . . and tell the truth. Brimstone was no longer looking at the rubble: he was staring at something a little way along the road. Chalkhill followed his gaze and discovered a couple of Analogue worlders hurrying towards the police cordon. The woman was too old to be Mella and he almost lost interest at once. But there was something familiar about her. Something familiar about the man too . . .

Chalkhill almost choked. The woman was Queen Blue! He looked again. Impossible, yet there she was. Furthermore, now he had his eye in, he could see the man with her was Henry Atherton, her human Consort. And maybe that wasn't impossible. They were Mella's parents, after all. Nothing more natural than for parents to go looking for their little girl, even if they were King Consort and Queen. He frowned thoughtfully. If Brimstone was here and Mella's parents were here, then it confirmed he was on the right track. Mella had to be here as well, somewhere close by, if she wasn't dead, of course. All he had to do was find her, snatch her, portal swiftly back to Hairstreak's Keep and slit her throat while His Lordship watched. Mission accomplished, payment received and on to the next job. Hey-ho the holly!

Another thought occurred to him, a dreadful, scary, hideously *exciting* thought. What sort of ransom could be raised for kidnapping Queen Blue? How much more would it be worth if you kidnapped King Consort Henry as well? Oh, what a thought that was! Riches beyond the dreams of avarice, but not beyond *his* dreams of avarice. On top of what he'd get from Lord Hairstreak for killing their daughter, it would make him the richest man in the entire Realm.

Chalkhill took three deep breaths to steady his nerves. One thing was certain: there would never be an opportunity like this again. Madame Cardui's security system was legendary. One Purple Emperor, Holly Blue's father, had been assassinated on her watch and she was determined that would never, ever, happen again. But even Cardui's long talons didn't reach into the Analogue World. Chalkhill suspected the headstrong Queen Blue had probably taken off impulsively without even notifying the old witch. Blue had a history of incognito jaunts. She might well be travelling with little security, possibly with no security at all. And while it would never do to underestimate King Consort Henry – he'd once killed a vampire with his bare hands – Chalkhill knew his own assassin's training made him more than a match for anybody.

Could he do it? Could he capture the entire Royal Family, Henry, Blue and Mella? Probably not alone – the logistics of an operation like that were almost certainly beyond one man. But he didn't have to do it alone. He had one potential ally already, albeit a tricky one. Between them, they could do the job . . .

Heart thumping, Chalkhill ran across the road and decloaked beside his old business partner.

'Yipes!' exclaimed Brimstone, jumping back a pace. Then he leaned forward to peer closely at Chalkhill. 'What are you doing here?'

There was no point in recriminations. Brimstone had lied to him, in all probability tried to cheat him, but it was no more than he'd have done to Brimstone had their positions been reversed. Now he needed Brimstone's help and he was certain he could keep the old man in line. After all, he'd managed it in the past. He drew another deep breath. 'Same thing as you – looking for Princess Mella. Did you know her parents are here? The two people in the entire Faerie Realm who are worth the most ransom.'

Brimstone may have been mad, but he wasn't stupid. He stared at Chalkhill with sudden interest flaring in his rheumy old eyes. 'You're not after them as well?' he asked.

Chalkhill gave a long, slow smile. 'I am now,' he said.

PART TWO

Twenty-One

'Pyrgus?'

Nymphalis found him in the vineyard, on his knees, talking softly to a vine. He was so focused on the plant that he obviously didn't hear her. 'Pyrgus!' she repeated more sharply.

Pyrgus Malvae turned his head slowly with the familiar, trance-like look he frequently got while he was tending to the grapes, then smiled his old, fond smile when he registered who it was. They'd been married seventeen years and the chemistry between them was as strong as ever. Except now wasn't exactly the time for a romantic interlude or even a short walk down memory lane.

'The manticore has escaped,' Nymph said.

'What?' he gasped. 'Are you sure?'

'Of course I'm sure. I've just been up to the sanctuary.'

'Nymph, she can't have! How?'

'Does it matter?'

Pyrgus suddenly tuned in to the reality of what she was telling him. 'Anybody at the sanctuary now?'

She shook her head. 'No.'

'Make sure it stays that way, Nymph. Nobody within a hundred yards – two if possible. We have to keep this quiet at all costs.'

'If we can.'

'I'm on my way,' Pyrgus said.

The sanctuary was a low-slung wood-frame building with special light panels in place of windows. Pyrgus, who'd lived in the Analogue World for a time, liked to think of it as Scandinavian in design, but any actual resemblance was slight. He'd built it as a home for rescued animals and since he was prone to rescuing any disadvantaged animal he came across, their needs were varied. At the moment the sanctuary housed the usual contingents of stray cats and dogs, a mountain llama, a rare desert haniel, two porkines, a herd of apts and a niff colony. The spell costs needed to provide suitable safe and separate environments for each were substantial, but fortunately Chateau Malvae wines were proving popular so that the vineyards funded the sanctuary, with enough left over to provide a modest living for Nymph and Pyrgus.

He could see the problem at once. An area of the south wall had been smashed outwards, leaving a gaping hole that even now still crackled with spell energies. Through the gap he could see the pillared environment that seemed to calm the manticore, but not, apparently, enough. Despite everything, Pyrgus felt a surge of admiration.

He moved cautiously towards the building. He might admire the manticore, but he respected her even more. While Pyrgus loved animals, he was far from sentimental about them. The wilder ones could kill you or leave you maimed for life; and there was no wilder, more unpredictable beast on the face of the planet than the manticore. More to the point, *his* manticore was one of the early prototypes, created before the Halek wizards realised the need to build in safeguards. The beast had proven so troublesome, so uncontrollable – even with magical restraints – that they'd been about to destroy it when Pyrgus intervened. Not that he got any thanks for the rescue – or theft, as the wizards insisted on calling it – but once he'd transported the poor thing across the Haleklind border they hadn't wanted to risk an international incident by following. Especially since he'd taken a problem off their hands.

And now, if his guess was correct, they were about to get it back.

He used his portakey to kill the securities – they'd proved useless anyway – and stepped warily through the gap. He was sure the creature had escaped – Nymph had told him it had escaped – but there was still a deeply ingrained part of his mind that warned him to be careful. The manticore was intelligent: he constantly reminded himself there were faerie genes in there along with lion and scorpion. She was quite capable of faking a breakout as bait for a trap. But as he peered around, there was no sign of the beast and few places where she might be hiding. To his right, half hidden by a pillar, was the creature's feeding table with a wooden bowl of half-chewed leaves. Pyrgus frowned, then went across and sniffed.

The smell confirmed his suspicions at once. The leaves were St John's wort, a mild euphoric for a human, a strong ecstatic for a faerie, but a berserker hit for a Haleklind creation like a manticore. No wonder she had found the strength to smash through the wall. Who fed her the wort? Not Nymph, a Forest Faerie skilled in herbal lore; not any of the sanctuary staff, who had strict instructions about the diets of their charges; not any of the vineyard workers, most of whom avoided the sanctuary like the plague; and certainly not Pyrgus himself.

He pushed the puzzle aside. The fact was he had a maddened manticore on the loose and a sinking feeling about exactly where she might he headed.

Pyrgus climbed back through the gap and almost bumped into Nymph.

'Definitely gone?' she asked, frowning.

He nodded. 'Yes. Some idiot fed her John's wort.'

'Bloody Hael!' She hesitated. 'You don't think . . . ?'

'I think she might. And can't say I blame her after what those bastards did.'

'What are you going to do?'

'Make sure, for a start.' He leaned over impulsively and gave her a kiss on the cheek. 'Do we have any glow-dust left?'

'I'm ahead of you,' Nymph said. She handed him a small packet. 'Go easy with it. There's more on order, but that's the last we have until the shipment comes.'

'Thanks,' Pyrgus murmured. He slit the packet with his thumbnail, squeezed and blew. The dust fanned out in a stream, ignoring both Pyrgus and Nymph, and began to glow almost immediately. Then it settled to leave a trail of luminous manticore padprints leading from the ruined wall towards the copse across the field. They set off to follow it together, quickly breaking into a panicky run.

'Where do you think she's heading?' Nymph asked. She seemed to be able to avoid obstacles by instinct, for she never took her eyes off the trail.

Pyrgus, who found himself struggling to keep up, said

breathlessly, 'Haleklind for sure.' He slowed slightly and Nymph slowed with him. 'She was created in Haleklind. You might say that was her birthplace.'

'Maybe she just thinks she's going home,' Nymph suggested. 'You know, to live in a forest or something.'

But Pyrgus shook his head firmly. 'No such luck. This is trouble, Nymph. Big trouble.'

The vineyard's southernmost fencing marked almost four miles of the border with Haleklind. From one point it was actually possible to see the towers and checkpoints of an official crossing post. Outside of such posts, the wizards maintained the integrity of their borders with magical protections – usually force fields – the most extensive and sophisticated in the known world. Indigenous wildlife could cross and recross without hindrance. Anything else was repulsed. The force fields extended deep beneath the earth and high above the skies of Haleklind. Without the necessary papers, nothing could enter the wizards' country.

Nymph and Pyrgus trotted through the copse, then stood side by side staring at the point where the manticore's luminous trail crossed the final limits of their estate. The high fencing was smashed as if it were matchwood, little problem for a creature that had burst through a solid wall. The trail continued deep into Haleklind, passing through the invisible force field as if it did not exist.

'The spell must have categorised her as wildlife,' Nymph murmured with a trace of awe in her voice.

But Pyrgus shook his head. 'She was *made* over there,' he said. 'All the component parts are Halek. As far as the spell is concerned, she's practically a *native*.'

They continued to stare gloomily for a moment. As

the glow of the trail began to fade, Nymph said, 'What are we going to do?'

'I'll have to go to Haleklind.'

'We'll both go,' Nymph said at once.

'There isn't time to arrange your documentation,' Pyrgus told her. 'As a Prince of the Realm, I have automatic entry.' It was one of the few perks of royal birth, maintained even after his abdication. 'Besides, one of us has to stay here to run the place.'

The marvellous thing about Nymph was she never argued about the inevitable. Still staring at the vanishing trail, she said, 'Do you think she can find the laboratory?'

'Given time,' Pyrgus said grimly. 'They're amazing creatures.'

'How much time?'

'Hard to say. I'm hoping I can head her off.'

Nymph licked her lips. 'If you can't, are you going to warn them?'

'I don't know,' Pyrgus told her honestly. 'There's part of me thinks they deserve anything they get.'

'But the manticore might be killed. Or hurt.'

'The manticore certainly will be killed. That's a given. But not before she takes a few of her old tormentors with her.'

'You can't let her die,' Nymph said. 'Not like that. You're going to have to head her off and bring her back.'

'If I can find her,' Pyrgus said.

twenty-two

'Look what you've done!' Aisling squealed furiously.

Mella opened her eyes and stood up. She felt groggy, but something seemed to have burned most of the drug effects out of her system. Aunt Aisling was waving the portal control under her nose; or what was left of the portal control. Half of it seemed to be missing. What remained was trailing wires with bits of electrical gear attached. The thing was broken beyond repair.

'Where are we?' Mella asked.

'How are we going to get back?' Aisling demanded.

Mella looked around. They were standing halfway up a narrow, twisting, wooden staircase in some gloomy place with wooden – or wood-panelled – walls. The stairs were so steep that they almost formed a sheer drop, yet there was no balustrade on either side. In its place was a thick length of knotted rope hanging down from a distant ceiling.

'Where are we?' Aisling asked Mella crossly, as if Mella hadn't just asked her the same thing. She looked at the control in her hand. 'This stupid thing blew up. Did you hear the explosion? Why did you tell me to press the button?'

'I don't know where we are,' Mella said. Her mind was still woolly from the tea, but not *that* woolly. They'd obviously passed through a portal: it was the only thing that made sense. So they were presumably back in the Faerie Realm. But *where* in the Faerie Realm she had no idea.

'You must know where we are,' Aisling insisted. 'You knew how to work the control!'

The woman was her aunt, but it was like dealing with a petulant child. 'Keep your voice down,' Mella told her urgently. Until she found out where they'd ended up, it would be as well not to draw attention to themselves. Not everywhere in the Faerie Realm was friendly.

'I will *not* keep my voice down!' Aisling snapped furiously; but at least she snapped it in a whisper. Mella suddenly realised her aunt was frightened.

'It's best you don't talk at all,' Mella said quietly, but very firmly. She looked around again. There was no one else on the staircase, no one at the bottom so far as she could see, and no sound of other voices. 'Now listen. Where the portal takes you depends on how the control was set. Did you do anything except press the button?'

Aisling shook her head. 'No.'

'Then it's taken us to wherever it was last set for.' She took a deep breath and asked something she'd wanted to ask much earlier. 'Where did you get the control?' She knew from her father's journal that Aunt Aisling had never been to the Faerie Realm, didn't even know about it, especially didn't know that Henry went there. And her aunt absolutely loathed Mr Fogarty, so it was very unlikely she'd got the portal control from him.

Aisling hesitated. Eventually she said, 'It's your father's.'

'Yes, but how did *you* get it? Did he give it to you?'

This time the hesitation was even longer. 'No, I found it in his room. He'd hidden it in a drawer under some of those magazines boys read for the pictures. I thought it might be for the television set. I mean, it *looks* like a TV remote. At least a bit.'

'So you took it?'

'Yes.'

'You stole it?' She was beginning to think some of the things her father said about his sister in the journal might be all too accurate. Mella was starting to build up a dislike of her aunt as well.

'No, of course I didn't steal it. I *borrowed* it.'

'But you never gave it back.' Mella made it as much a flat statement as a question.

'I didn't have a chance,' Aisling protested. 'He kept going off places.'

'Did you ever use it?'

'No,' Aisling said too quickly.

Mella stared at her. 'I thought you said you borrowed it for your television thing: what did you want it for if you weren't going to use it?' Aisling said nothing. Mella said, 'Are you sure you never used it?'

Aisling's mouth formed itself into the hint of a pout. 'Well, I might have. Once. Once or twice.'

'Indoors or outside?'

'Outside in the garden.'

'So you knew it wasn't a television control?'

Aisling suddenly sat down on the stairs. 'I knew he was up to something – him and that old pervert Fogarty. I knew they were doing things together. Mummy and Daddy never suspected, but I did. It was really creepy. He was always slipping out and staying away longer

137

than he should. Fogarty *made* things, you know. Electrical things. In his back kitchen. Henry never found out, but I followed him twice and I know he went to see Mr Fogarty and I watched through the window and he made some really strange stuff. I wouldn't be surprised if he made this.' She tossed the useless control on to the step beside her.

He certainly did, Mella thought, but said nothing. She continued to stare at Aisling in silence for a moment, then said, 'What happened?'

'When I used it? It opened up a sort of . . . thing. Just there, in the air in front of me. Like it did today.'

'What did you do?' Mella asked.

'Nothing the first time,' Aisling said. 'I mean, it looked like a fire and I didn't want to get burned.'

'And what about the next time?'

Aisling glanced away to one side. 'The second time I realised there was no heat, so I stuck my finger in carefully and the fire didn't burn me. Then I tried my whole arm and it still didn't burn me. I thought it might be some sort of doorway from something I heard Henry say to Mr Fogarty once. Well, I thought it might be anyway. So eventually I walked through.'

Mella blinked. 'Into the Realm?'

'A sort of desert place. It's the Faerie Realm, isn't it? What they used to call the Faerie Realm. I knew it! I absolutely knew it!'

'Parts of it are desert,' Mella said.

'One time I was inside a building with a long corridor with purple carpet and crystal chandeliers.'

The Purple Palace, Mella breathed. Aloud she said, 'So you went more than once?'

'Yes, but I didn't go very far – I was being careful.

And responsible. Usually I just stepped in and looked around and stepped back out again and then I closed the gateway or whatever it was. I never met anybody. Nobody ever saw me.'

'This is very important,' Mella said. 'Did you ever make adjustments to any of the dials on the control? Any buttons or switches or sliders or anything? Did you ever fiddle with anything except the on–off button?' She already knew the answer. Unless Aunt Aisling reset the control, it would have continued to take her to the same place. But it hadn't kept taking her to the same place, so she must have been fiddling with the settings, maybe not knowing she was doing it, but fiddling with them just the same. Fiddling *a lot*.

'I may have,' Aisling said defensively. 'I don't know. Perhaps I did, perhaps I didn't. And I only used it a few times. After a while it wouldn't work for me at all. I mean until today when you told me about the safety switch and that broke it.'

She could have reset it for *anywhere*, Mella thought. They could be anywhere in the Faerie Realm, in any country, friendly or unfriendly. Worse still, Aunt Aisling had broken the control, so they had no means of getting back.

'Come on,' Mella said and began to move cautiously down the winding staircase.

Aisling stood up quickly and followed. 'Where are we going?'

'To try to find out where we are.'

'Is that safe?'

Mella was getting fed up with her aunt. 'What else do you suggest we do?'

The staircase descended into a low-ceilinged room

with an open door. There was a murmur of voices from along the corridor outside. Aisling had been hanging back nervously, letting Mella take the lead. (Letting Mella take the risks!) Now she stopped dead. 'There's someone there!' she hissed.

'Yes,' Mella murmured. The voices were low-pitched, like a group of people engaged in a discussion. 'We'd better find out who they are.'

'What happens if they're hoodies or soccer hooligans or something?' Aisling asked. 'They might mug us.'

Mella threw her a contemptuous glance. 'And they might invite us for supper.' All the same, Aunt Aisling was right: it would be silly to barge into something without checking first. 'We'll just take a look. If we're careful, we should be able to scout things out without them seeing us.'

'You go,' Aisling said quickly. 'You're smaller.' When Mella stared at her, she added, 'You can hide more easily.'

'What are *you* going to do?' Mella demanded.

'I'll stay here.' Aisling looked around, clearly search-ing for a place of concealment.

Mella moved to the open doorway and looked out cautiously. What she'd taken for a corridor turned out to be a narrow balcony. She edged towards the railing and peeped over.

The balcony overlooked some sort of conference room, a little like the Discussion Chamber in the Purple Palace where her parents met up with visiting heads of state. It was equipped with three cabinets and a large oval table around which sat four men and three women, all dressed in identical red robes. Cowled hoods threw their features into shadow so that it was impossible to see their faces clearly. Double doors at one end of the chamber were conspicuously bolted and barred. A heady scent of incense magic wafted upwards. At least Mella assumed it was incense magic: she'd never seen it used before.

One of the men was talking in a precise, high-pitched voice. '. . . Just short of two thousand current stocks.' He looked around. 'You will recall the setback we experienced last year.' There was a murmur of angry agreement.

The woman at the head of the table had eyes that flashed red from under her hood. 'Our target figure is ten thousand, is it not?'

It was another of the men, a tall, upright figure, who answered. 'That was the minimum military estimate to ensure a successful campaign. Assuming suitable troop back-up, equipment and spell power.'

'There was some talk of less,' the woman said.

'There was,' the tall man agreed. 'Companion Marshal Houndstooth's plan called for only four thousand three hundred, but the troop back-up doubled, the necessary spell power tripled and so did the costs. That's why we abandoned it in April.'

'I am concerned about the timing,' the woman said flatly.

'Astrologically?' another of the women asked.

'Yes.'

The tall man said, 'That has been taken into consideration.'

'I don't see how it could be,' said the woman at the head of the table. 'If we still haven't managed to produce two thousand units and what we *have* managed to produce has taken more than a year, it will take *at least* five years to reach our goal total. I appreciate the loss of our prototype was something of a setback, but it cost us no more than a month or two as I understand it. Am I not correct in this?'

'You are correct, Companion,' the precise man said in his high-pitched voice. 'But you must appreciate that we are now no longer manufacturing, but breeding – a process that proceeds exponentially and is thus considerably faster.'

'Exponentially?' the woman echoed.

'To convert one item into one thousand items exponentially requires the time it takes for eleven separate operations, which is quite considerable. But to produce the next one thousand items requires only one further operation, as does the next two thousand and the next four.'

'The process accelerates?'

'Dramatically.'

'Are you claiming,' the woman said, 'that we may still reach our target in time for the eclipse?'

'We shall reach our target *before* the eclipse,' the man assured her.

'So our invasion of the Empire may proceed as planned?'

Mella's throat tightened abruptly. *Invasion of the Empire?* There was only one Empire in the Faerie Realm, the Empire ruled by her mother.

'Undoubtedly,' the man confirmed.

twenty-three

Henry had the taxi drop them off at Mr Fogarty's old house. It was as good a base as any for their operations in the Analogue World; and better than most. Clearly nobody was using it and, situated as it was at the end of a cul-de-sac, it was not overlooked and there were no casual passers-by – all reasons, no doubt, why Mr Fogarty had bought it in the first place. After his experience with D. I. Tyneside, what Henry wanted, quite desperately now, was somewhere quiet where he could think and talk to Blue in private without interruption.

As they closed the kitchen door behind them, Blue asked, 'Did he have some sort of living room? I find it a bit creepy in here.'

So, in fact, did Henry, although that was mainly old memories. 'Yes, he did. It's a bit cluttered – at least it used to be.'

It still was, mainly with piles of Mr Fogarty's abandoned books, but there was room on the couch for them to sit down side by side. Henry reached for Blue's hand. 'What do you think?'

'You know what I think: I told you at the site. I suppose Mella came to visit your mother.'

Henry pursed his lips. 'You think she used a portal indoors and that's what happened to the house?'

'Yes.'

'You think she's all right?' Henry took a deep breath and said it: 'Still alive?'

Blue looked sober, but certain. 'Yes.'

'Any ideas about where she may have gone now?'

'I've been thinking about that,' Blue told him. 'Obviously, the Realm. '

'Yes, but the Realm's a big place.' It was, in fact, a whole planet.

'I think we might be able to narrow it down a little,' Blue said. 'Where a portal opens up depends on how the controls are set. Well, you know I said she must have got hold of an old control?'

Henry nodded. 'Yes.'

'Didn't you wonder where she might have found one?'

'Well, yes, I did, but I thought . . .' He waved his hands vaguely in the air.

Blue waited a polite second for him to explain. When he didn't, she said, 'I thought she might have found one here.'

'*Here* here?' Henry asked. 'Here in this place? Mr Fogarty's house?'

'Unless you left one at your old home, there *is* nowhere else.'

'No,' Henry said thoughtfully, 'I didn't leave one at home.' He'd managed to lose one at home years ago, but that was a different matter. If he couldn't find it, Mella wasn't going to stumble on it either. What Blue said was making sense. Where else would Mella get hold of a portal control in the Analogue World except at Mr Fogarty's house? Their daughter must have come here first, before she went off to visit her grandmother. Which would make sense as well: he'd told her so much about Mr Fogarty the old boy must have felt like a hero to her. Besides, if she'd used any of the old node-to-node portals there was a node behind Mr Fogarty's buddleia bush.

'If it was a control that belonged to Mr Fogarty, it would probably be set to the Purple Palace,' Blue said. 'Or his old lodge in the grounds.'

Henry looked at her in admiration. She was absolutely right. Mr Fogarty only ever used portals to move from his home to the Palace and back again. A thought occurred to him. 'She might have reset it.'

'I don't think she did,' Blue said. 'I don't think she meant to use a portal at all. Why would she? She's only just arrived in the Analogue World. She wants to meet your mother, and probably your mother's girl-friend if I know our daughter. She wants to *explore* and see strange Analogue sights. She doesn't want to go home yet. Besides, Mella *knew* how dangerous it was to use those old controls indoors. I think she triggered the control by accident and managed to blow up your mother's home in the process. Fortunately there didn't seem to be anybody else in there at the time.'

'Oh my God,' Henry exclaimed. How was he going to explain this to his mother? Then it suddenly occurred to him that he didn't have to. He felt a delicious twinge of wicked guilt. He pulled his mind back to the impor-tant thing, which certainly wasn't his mother. 'You're quite sure Mella wasn't hurt when the house collapsed?'

'I'm quite sure she wasn't *there* when the house col-lapsed. The follower found no sign of bodies – I told you that. What it did find was Mella's energy trace. So Mella had been there, but obviously wasn't there when the house came down.'

'I'm not getting this,' Henry said. 'What do you think happened?'

'The house didn't collapse when the portal opened – it collapsed when it closed. That's the way it worked with the old controls. I think Mella must have opened it accidentally, then realised there was the danger of an explosion when it closed again. So she went through so she'd be on the right side if there *was* an explosion: she's quite clever, our Mella. At least she knows how to look after herself.'

'So she went back to the Realm, probably the Purple Palace?'

'That would be my guess,' Blue said.

'So we go home now, find her and ground her for the next ten years?' A thought occurred to him. 'Wait a minute: if she only went through to be safe, wouldn't she come right back again? Your follower devil said there was nobody in the wreckage, so she probably hasn't met my mother the way she planned, so –'

'There's somebody at the back of the house.' Blue looked up. 'I saw them passing the window.'

'It'll be kids,' Henry said dismissively. Kids sometimes came nosing round the place – he remembered from the old days when he'd come here to feed Hodge. 'What do you think? Wouldn't she come straight back? Anyway, she'd want to see if the place really had exploded – it didn't always happen with the old controls.'

'She might want to come straight back, but she mightn't be able to,' Blue said. 'Sometimes closing the portal actually *broke* those old controls. She wouldn't be able to come back until she got a new one. Or at least reached the House Iris portal. Except she won't be able to use it because I've told Chief Portal Engineer Peacock not to let her.'

'So,' said Henry, 'if the old control *didn't* break she's probably skulking somewhere near Mother's house, what's left of it. But if it did, she's probably back home in the Purple Palace trying to get hold of another control.' He frowned. 'And we're here, miles away from both.' He turned to look at Blue. 'Should we try portalling back to the Palace or –'

There was a loud, firm knock on the back door. The sound reverberated through the empty house. Henry felt Blue stiffen beside him. 'Who's that?' she asked.

'It'll be an insurance salesman,' Henry said. Insurance salesmen sometimes tried their luck door-to-door in this area. He remembered that too from his days feeding Hodge. 'I'll tell him to go away.' He stood up and headed for the door, then stopped. 'I'm not sure we should go back to the Palace. I mean, if that's where she went, she could well have come back again by now and even if she *is* there, she'd certainly be headed back here again by the time we found her.'

The knocking came again. 'Coming! Coming!' Henry shouted. To Blue he said, 'The other possibility if she *has* gone back is that Madame Cardui will catch her, but if that happens, Cynthia will let us know. So when you take everything into consideration, the sensible thing has to be for us to go back to my mother's house, what's left of it, and search for her there: you might even send your follower demon out again. And if she's not there, we wait, because it most likely means she's not there *yet* and will turn up eventually. What do you think?'

'I think you have the most extraordinary mind,' Blue said.

'Do you really?' Henry said, pleased.

'Perhaps you'd better deal with the salesman,' Blue said as the knocking repeated.

'Yes,' Henry said. 'Yes.' As he walked towards the kitchen, he called back over his shoulder, 'At least we know what we have to do now. At least we have a *plan of action.*' He entered the kitchen and saw the outline of the salesman silhouetted through the frosted glass of the back door. 'Coming!' he called again, cheerfully. He twisted the Yale lock. 'If it's insurance, I'm afraid –'

The door smashed in, hurling him backwards off balance. 'Get the Queen!' someone snapped. Then a figure hurtled towards him and, surprised though he was, Henry punched it in the face.

'Where is she?' someone asked querulously.

'Yipes!' gasped the man Henry had hit. He was dressed in black and masked, like somebody who'd gone to a fancy-dress party as a ninja. Henry kicked him between the legs and he jackknifed forward, then fell heavily to his knees.

'Come on, George.' An old man stepped through the open doorway. Even at a glance Henry recognised him as Silas Brimstone. But Brimstone was locked up in some lunatic asylum, eating flies. Henry aimed another kick, at the idiot ninja's head this time. The old man – Brimstone – raised a spell cone.

'Get down!' Blue's voice called. Henry glanced behind him to find her wielding a modified stimulus, the type that didn't need contact. It had an effective range of about twelve feet and he was directly in the line of fire. He dropped to the floor and rolled, but for some rea-son Blue was having difficulty firing.

'He sucker-punched me!' gasped the ninja and though his voice was overlaid with astonishment, Henry recognised it immediately. The voice belonged to Jasper Chalkhill.

Both Chalkhill and Henry climbed to their feet. Blue twisted her body violently and her stimulus, at long last, discharged a bolt of energy. It caught Chalkhill on the shoulder as he was reaching for Henry and spun him round, ripping off his mask. Brimstone cracked the spell cone and giggled as a filament net emerged like a plume of smoke. The thing enmeshed Blue at once, causing her to drop the stimulus, then reached for Henry. He jerked backwards, but it had his arm. His old allergy to magic cut in, so that he threw up on the floor. 'Oh, Henry!' he heard Blue say, whether in exasperation or sympathy he couldn't be sure. Then the filaments drew them closer together so that he was pressed against Blue, which was nice but didn't last long because he was having trouble breathing, then couldn't breathe at all, then he was sliding, sliding into darkness . . .

. . . darkness, silent darkness.

Twenty-four

The automated security system guided Pyrgus's flyer gently down to the reserved area of Creen International Airport, then, Prince Royal or no Prince Royal, disarmed his ship, confiscated several of his personal belongings, sprayed him to remove all microorganisms, conducted an internal examination to check for the presence of a wangaramus worm in his bottom, examined his identifications, photographed his tattoos and required him to answer a lengthy list of questions, the first of which was, *'Do you plan to engage in any action purposely designed or likely to lead to the overthrow of the lawfully constituted government of Haleklind?'* Pyrgus resisted the temptation to respond *'Sole purpose of visit'* and was eventually rewarded by a tone that told him the controls of his vehicle had been unlocked and he could now disembark without danger of being vapourised.

He changed unhurriedly into the standard blue-grey pilot's uniform, selected an enormous pair of darkened glasses that would mark him as a Faerie of the Night, pulled on a curly black wig, then ordered his elementals to provide a suitable ramp, opened the cabin door, and walked out to meet the inevitable reception committee.

The reception committee was an exercise in applied

hypocrisy. They must have known Crown Prince Pyr-gus Malvae had stolen their manticore – a hanging offence if he'd been caught – but with his flyer bedecked in royal insignia, they were forced by protocol to ignore the crime and treat him like the visiting dignitary he was. Not that it mattered, since they weren't about to meet with Crown Prince Pyrgus Malvae anyway, what-ever they expected.

The head of the delegation was the local mayor, to judge from his imposing chain of office. In his pressed new uniform, Pyrgus marched briskly across to him and saluted sharply. 'His Royal Highness is not to be disturbed,' he told the Mayor. 'He is currently sleeping.' He held the man's eye and added in a voice so low that only the Mayor could hear him. 'Sleeping it off, Your Honour.' He gave a slight nod and the hint of a wink.

The Mayor leaned over. 'Sleeping it off, pilot?' he repeated in a shocked whisper.

'The old problem.' Pyrgus nodded. He waited.

'Drink?' asked the Mayor. 'You're not trying to tell me His Highness –' He gulped, '– *imbibes?*'

'Like a fish,' Pyrgus said. 'Did no one warn you?'

The Mayor shook his head. 'No one.'

Pyrgus gave an ostentatious sigh. 'Diplomats. You wonder what we pay them for. You should have been told at the time they arranged this visit. You really had no idea?'

'None. Absolutely none.'

Pyrgus moved a little closer. 'Look, I feel sorry for you, I really do. Typical behaviour, does it all the time. Started –' He glanced around to make sure no one else could hear him, '– you know –' He made a glugging sound in his throat, '– shortly after we left the capital.

I'm supposed to stop him, but what can I do? He is a Prince of the Realm, after all, and he hides his supplies. By the time he reached Creen airspace, he was singing the national anthem and falling into his soup. Then he decided he was going to declare war on Haleklind. Fortunately he passed out just before we landed, so we're spared an international incident at least.'

'Yes, but what do we do?' the Mayor asked. He looked and sounded panic-stricken.

Pyrgus glanced around again, moved even closer to the Mayor and aimed his words into the waiting ear. 'In my experience he'll be out cold for the rest of the day and most of the night. I'd suggest you reconvene the reception committee late tomorrow afternoon to be on the safe side. He should be fit to make the visit then.'

'But what happens if he wakes up early? Won't he be insulted if there's no one here to greet him?'

'You have a point there,' said Pyrgus. 'Tell you what: I'll lock the flyer. He'll be quite safe inside. I'll do a little sightseeing, look up some old friends, and I'll be back in time for the official reception tomorrow afternoon. If he *does* wake up early – I don't think he will, but if he does – I'm the one with the key, no one else can let him out. It's entirely my responsibility, then, and since I haven't told you specifically where I'm going, there is no way you can trace me.' Pyrgus gave him the benefit of a broad smile. 'You're completely off the hook, Your Worship.'

The Mayor was frowning. 'But won't you get into trouble then? If he wakes early, I mean?'

Pyrgus shook his head vigorously. 'We pilots have a very strong guild,' he said. 'Besides, he won't want any accusations of prejudice against a Faerie of the Night – it's still a very sensitive issue in the Empire.' He shrugged. 'But he won't wake early, if my experience is anything to go by. He takes it by the gallon.'

'Right,' said the Mayor decisively, 'you lock up the flyer, I'll reconvene the committee for five tomorrow afternoon. That suit you OK?'

Pyrgus twiddled his Nighter spectacles. 'Admirably,' he said.

Although he was fairly sure he'd not be followed after the nonsense he'd spoon-fed the Mayor, Pyrgus left the airport by way of the visiting pilots' restrooms, where he hired a private cubicle. Once the securities were set, he stripped off his uniform, wig and glasses and stored them in an invisible locker. Then he unzipped the filament suitcase in the waistband of his undershorts and drew out the plainest of the suits stored there. Without the glasses and wig, he reverted back automatically to a Faerie of the Light, but the suit transformed him into a nondescript one. He looked, if anything, like a travelling salesman, one of the horde who flocked through Haleklind each year peddling parts for wands and reconditioned spells. He rummaged in the filament suitcase again and slid the Halek knife into the back of his belt where it was hidden by the jacket of the suit. He wasn't expecting trouble, but it was always best to come prepared. Hael, who was he trying to fool? He *was* expecting trouble. Trouble always seemed to find him on a mission like this. But that was an even better reason to come prepared.

Creen City was a curious mixture. The district immediately surrounding the airport was arguably the most spectacular on the planet. Here the wizards had built to impress, using some of the most ingenious spells ever created. The result was, to say the least, magnificent. There were buildings floating on clouds. There were galloping herds of fantastical beasts that appeared and disappeared at random. There were advertising hoardings that tugged your arm as you went past and hypnotised you into buying stuff you didn't want. Most noticeably of all, there were the gigantic ghost-like sculptures of the ruling Table of Seven that smiled down benignly from beyond the rooftops, dominating everything, instantly obvious, yet so insubstantial that they interfered with nothing. It was all very garish, very tasteless, very much what one might expect from wizards with more power than sense.

But beyond the airport district, beyond the tourist havens and the glittering illusion palaces, there was a different Creen. Pyrgus, who'd been visiting the country since before the revolution that brought the Seven into power, took one of the least-known walkways from the airport, a narrow, dingy, ill-lit track that held out the promise of threatening alleyways, simbala dens, dope deals, muggings and cut-purses. But the promise was deceptive, for, after a short rooftop walk, a humming distortion created a Möbius shape that bent the path back to the instant it began, allowing Pyrgus fresh entry; and now the walkway was an open avenue that led into the Old City.

The Old City dated back to the foundation of Creen, close to a thousand years ago, and Pyrgus loved it. The streets were narrow, but the timber-inlaid buildings that overhung them were enormous – structures that defied the laws of engineering with the help of spells so ancient no one now knew how they worked. At the precise geographical centre of the Old City lay its *suk,* a vast, open maze of market stalls, bathed in perpetual sunshine, that offered magical artifacts, ingredients, spare parts, potions, powders, clothing, weapons and machinery unlike anything found elsewhere in the Realm. Haleklind was the magical capital of the planet, known to its citizens by its traditional name, *Creen*. Creen City was Haleklind's capital, Creen Suk its beating heart. It was in the suk that Pyrgus once bought a prized possession, his first Halek knife. It was to the suk that he was going now.

Despite the teeming crowds, he found the secret walkway without difficulty, although mounting it unseen was so problematical that he wasted almost half an hour pretending to examine a selection of copper vessels designed to capture djinn. But then the crowd thinned suddenly and he made the transition. The walkway swept him outwards, then downwards into the subterranean labyrinth beneath the suk. When it emerged, he was standing outside a derelict factory plastered with *Unsafe Building* notices.

Pyrgus climbed on some disused spice drums to look through the dusty windows. He couldn't afford to risk the possibility of a security breach, but the interior was a deserted ruin with the only things of interest some scraps of rusting machinery, and the only signs of life the remains of a camp fire that had once warmed squatters. He tossed a pebble through a broken pane and listened as it echoed on the stone-flagged floor. A small stream of dust cascaded from cracks in the ceiling.

He climbed down, glanced around to make sure he was not being watched, then leaned on the broken pillar to one side of the boarded entrance. The spell coating recognised his DNA and sucked him inside.

The receptionist was a dark-eyed female demon, one of the very few he'd ever seen permitted to work outside of Hael. She glanced into the crystal ball set on her desk, then smiled at him. 'Crown Prince Pyrgus,' she acknowledged. 'What can the Society do for you today?'

'Is Corin still alive?' Pyrgus asked. There was considerable wastage in the Haleklind Society for the Preservation and Protection of Animals: the wizards hunted down its members without mercy.

'Yes,' the demon told him pleasantly. She looked at him expectantly. Literalism was a Hael characteristic. The demons never seemed able to *interpret* what you said, never got a jump ahead (without creeping into your mind, of course, which Blue had made illegal) so they reacted to every question a sentence at a time.

'Is he still your Executive Secretary?'

'Yes, Crown Prince Pyrgus.'

'Is it possible for me to see him?'

'Yes.'

After a moment, Pyrgus added, 'Now?'

'Yes, of course, sir,' said the demon enthusiastically. Her long, graceful hand reached towards a symbol inlaid in her desk.

'It's just *Pyrgus Malvae*,' Pyrgus told her. 'I don't use the title any more.'

'Of course, Pyrgus Malvae.' The smile was quite pleasant despite the sharpness of her teeth. The outstretched hand touched the symbol. 'May your Gods walk with you.'

The transition to Corin's office was instantaneous. Corin himself was rising from behind his desk, smiling broadly, hand outstretched. 'Pyrgus, dear boy, how good to see you! How is the lovely Nymphalis? Have you two had children yet? No, of course not: far too busy for that sort of thing. So little time and so many animals in need, eh? And I believe you're making wine now – some excellent vintages, from what I understand.'

Pyrgus took the hand and grinned at him. 'I'll send you a bottle or twelve. Meant to bring one with me, but I left home in a hurry. Bit of an emergency, I'm afraid.'

'Sorry to hear that,' Corin said, waving him into a seat. He was a small, balding, rotund middle-aged Haleklinder, who looked as far distant from hero material as you could possibly imagine. Yet he was probably the bravest man Pyrgus had ever known. 'Nothing serious, I hope?'

'My manticore's escaped,' Pyrgus told him bluntly.

Corin's eyes widened. 'The prototype? The one you liberated?'

Pyrgus nodded. 'I don't know what happened. She was perfectly happy for more than eighteen months, then suddenly she broke out and took off.'

'She'll have come on heat,' Corin said. 'She wasn't eating John's wort, by any chance?'

Pyrgus looked at him in surprise. 'She was, actually. I don't know who fed it to her.'

'Nobody, would be my guess. A full-grown manticore is perfectly capable of manifesting a few choice leaves of anything she fancies – the wizards built in magical capabilities. There's nothing they fancy more when coming into heat than John's wort.'

'I didn't know that: about manifesting,' Pyrgus said. 'She never did it before.'

'Probably didn't have to. They only manifest when they need something. It's a credit to you, Pyrgus. Shows she was happy with you. Shows you gave her everything she needed. Until she came on heat, of course. She'd be off like a rocket then, looking for a mate. And more John's wort.'

For the first time since Nymph told him the news of the break-out, Pyrgus felt something relax in his stomach. He'd come to his old friends in the Society hoping Corin might raise some manpower to help him track the manticore, but now it was beginning to look as if he might not have to. 'I thought she might head for the lab. The place where they constructed her.'

'What, try to get back at the wizards? Revenge for the pain they caused her?'

'Something like that,' Pyrgus said. 'Vengeance is a manticore characteristic.' He looked soberly at Corin. 'Actually, I wasn't so much worried about the wizards as the manticore. If she did attack the laboratory, they'd kill her. They'd have to and they wouldn't hesitate. I thought the only chance would be to head her off – that's why I came here. I was hoping you might loan me some men.'

Corin gave a faint smile. 'Let me show you something.' He pressed an inlay on his desk and a viewscreen emerged out of the floor behind him. As it rose, Pyrgus noticed it was one of the newer models with three-dimensional immersive capabilities: the Society must have robbed a few banks lately. Corin made a small adjustment to the inlay and the screen flared into life.

The immersive spells pulled Pyrgus in at once. He knew he was still seated in Corin's office, of course, but he still experienced the sensation of standing outside, on a small, grassy hillside with a breeze ruffling his hair as he stared down on the ruin of a distant building, now reduced to a heap of rubble, still smoking slightly.

'What is it?' he asked.

Corin's smile widened. 'The laboratory. We blew it up.'

Pyrgus snapped out of the illusion and gave him a startled, delighted look. 'I heard nothing about that!'

'The Seven kept it quiet: complete news black-out. It was their main research centre after all. Very bad for their image to admit they couldn't protect it against a ragbag of misguided elements, which is how they like to portray us.' He looked at Pyrgus benignly. 'The one thing you need have no worries about is your manticore attacking the laboratory. The laboratory doesn't exist any more.' He pushed his chair back so he could look at the picture on the screen. 'We used null-energy explosives so they can't build again for years: magic won't work there for the remainder of this century.'

'Casualties?'

'Oh, come on, Pyrgus, you know us better than that. The attack was at night, after the staff had gone home, and we moved all the animals out before we set the explosion. The only person hurt was one of our own operatives, and he cut his finger on one of their ghastly vivisection instruments.'

Pyrgus was frowning. 'I suppose she might still go there. I mean, she doesn't know you've blown it up.' He scratched the side of his nose. 'I wouldn't want her recaptured. Heaven knows what they might do to her, even without their precious lab.'

'She won't go there if she's on heat,' Corin said. 'Believe me, revenge will be the last thing on her mind. And actually even if she isn't on heat there's not much chance of her getting near the place. It's been a while since you visited Creen, hasn't it?'

'Nearly two years – why?'

'A lot's happened in two years,' Corin said. 'Let me show you something else.' His fingers beat a sharp tattoo on the surface of his desk and the picture changed.

For an instant, Pyrgus found himself hovering high above the ground. Below him was a sweep of plain and forest. Then suddenly he was dropping thousands of feet until he could see the details of the plain. It was teeming with game, a vast herd of . . . of . . . 'What are they?' But before Corin could answer, the scene went into close-up. 'Good Gods!' Pyrgus exclaimed. 'Those are manticores! Dozens of them!'

'Several hundred in that herd, actually,' Corin told him calmly. 'It's one of the biggest.'

'How?' Pyrgus asked. 'When I stole mine, there were only four in the entire country.'

'The wizards made two more prototypes, then switched from building to breeding. They're fertile creatures, are manticores. Get yourself a breeding pair and it doesn't take you long to knock up a herd. That lot are roaming the plains around where the laboratory used to be. If she's headed in that direction, she'll join them – it's in her nature. And if she isn't, she'll join another herd: they're dotted all over the country now, a score here, fifty there.'

Pyrgus felt a wave of relief so profound he felt like curling up and going to sleep. 'So I can stop worrying about her?'

'Yes.'

'I can just . . .' He made a helpless, delighted gesture with his hands, '. . . go home?'

'Yes.'

A hint of the earlier frown crept back. 'I want to make absolutely sure she's all right, make sure she joins a herd and goes back to the wild.'

'We'll do that for you,' Corin said. 'We monitor the herds as a matter of course. Shouldn't be too difficult to spot since she's an early prototype. Soon as we catch sight of her, we'll let you know.'

Pyrgus felt like hugging him. 'Thank you,' he said gratefully. 'That's taken a huge weight off my mind. Thank you, Corin.'

twenty-five

Mella felt a presence behind her and glanced around to discover her Aunt Aisling had found enough of her courage to creep on to the balcony. She was staring over Mella's shoulder down into the conference room below. 'What's going on?' she whispered. 'Who are these people? Can they help us?'

Mella pushed her back through the doorway and carefully closed the door behind them. Even with the door closed, she kept her voice low. 'Let's not make too much noise. I think we're in Haleklind,' she said.

Aisling looked at her blankly. 'Aren't we in Fairyland? The Faerie Realm, or whatever you call it?'

'Yes. Yes, we are,' Mella said impatiently. 'Haleklind is a *country* in the Faerie Realm.'

'I think,' said Aisling severely, 'it's about time we had a little conversation, you and I, about everything's that's been going on. I knew Henry was up to something – I've known it for years. Is he really living permanently in the Faerie Realm now?'

Mella nodded. 'Yes.'

'And he's really married to the Faerie Queen?'

Mella nodded again.

Aisling's face broke into a frosty smile. 'I can't believe Henry *married* a fairy! It's insane, even for him!' The smile disappeared and a thoughtful expression crossed her face. 'If he's married to the Queen, that makes him King, doesn't it?'

'Well, King Consort . . .' Mella didn't know where this was heading, but there was something about her aunt's tone she really disliked.

'But that still means he's a very important man, doesn't it? I mean he has *subjects* and servants and things like that? He *rules* people?'

'Well, he helps Mummy rule,' Mella said. 'He gives her advice and stuff and sometimes she takes it.'

'I expect he's rich now? Gold, gems, lives in a palace?'

This was *really* making Mella uncomfortable. 'Aunt Aisling, we're –'

'Rich!' snapped Aisling. 'Is he rich?'

'He gets an allowance from the State,' Mella said reluctantly. 'I expect it's quite large. And half of Mummy's family money automatically went to him when they got married, although I don't think he actually took it, and they do live in a palace, the Purple Palace. Because Mummy's Queen and Daddy's King Consort.'

A distant look crept into Aisling's eyes. 'My brother is King of the Faerie Realm!' she breathed. 'My brother is *King* of the Faerie Realm!' She refocused on Mella abruptly. 'I'm the King's sister, you're the King's daughter. Why are we creeping round like criminals? We shall order those people out there to stop their silly little meeting and provide us with transport to this Purple Palace of yours. I want to have a word with your father. He's behaved disgracefully. He's behaved disgracefully for *years*. I think it's time he tried to make amends, don't you? And not just to me, but to Mummy as well.

I don't *know* what she's going to think about all this when I tell her. But first, I want a word with Henry!' She half turned to reopen the door.

Mella caught her arm hurriedly. 'You can't just order those people to provide you with transport – this is Haleklind.'

Aisling looked at her blankly. 'What's that got to do with it?'

'Daddy's not King of Haleklind – it's an independent country. Actually Mummy's not really Queen of the Realm, not the whole Realm: that's just one of her titles. She's Queen Empress of the Faerie Empire. It's rather big, but there are still some countries outside it. Including Haleklind.'

'How do you know this is . . . where did you say? Haleklind? This building could be anywhere.'

Mella licked her lips. 'I'm *not* sure. But I think that might be a meeting of the Table of Seven, and the Table of Seven rules Haleklind.'

'Is Haleklind an enemy of the Empire?' Aisling asked quickly.

Mella stared at her. Haleklind didn't have an alliance with the Empire as far as she knew, but then again she didn't pay much attention to politics. She'd never heard anybody describe Haleklind as an enemy. The wizards kept themselves to themselves, except when it came to trade, and they were really, really paranoid about people entering their country for anything else (which would make things doubly difficult if this actually *was* Haleklind) but that was about it. Except for what she'd just heard. *Our invasion of the Empire may proceed as planned.* Haleklind *couldn't* be planning to invade the Empire, not her mother's Empire: it was too big, too strong. No single country could possibly hope to win a war against it; and Haleklind was surely too suspicious of everybody to have formed any alliances. Mella racked her brains trying to remember if there was any other empire in the Faerie Realm, wishing she'd paid more attention to her geography tutor, wishing she'd paid more attention to her politics tutor, wishing she'd paid more attention to . . .

Wait a minute! Hadn't her *history* tutor once mentioned a Chlorostrymon Empire? It fell hundreds and hundreds of years ago, but didn't the tutor say there was a remnant of that empire somewhere in the north? A little frozen alliance of Chlorostrymon states? Maybe that was what the Table of Seven was planning to invade, although for the life of her she couldn't imagine why: the only thing the Chlorostrymons had now was seal blubber. What Mella needed to do was get home at once and tell her parents what she'd heard: let them sort it out. Although in her heart of hearts she'd already sorted it herself. Nobody invaded to get seal blubber. But for now she had her aunt breathing down her neck.

'I'm not sure,' she said.

'Oh, you're being ridiculous!' Aisling snapped. She pulled the door open and nodded in the direction of the balcony. 'You think that's Haleklind's ruling council?'

'Yes.' The more she thought about it, the more sure she became. She wished Aunt Aisling would leave her alone to figure out the situation. Actually, she wished Aunt Aisling would just *go away!*

'Well,' said Aisling firmly, 'if Haleklind isn't an enemy, it must be a friend, or at least neutral; and that's the ruling council. If you knew anything about the way these things work, Mella, you'd realise that as the sister of the

King and daughter of the King we are entitled to be treated as visiting dignitaries, *will* be treated as visiting dignitaries. I shall go down now and explain we are here as the result of an unfortunate portal accident and request – request politely, even though I represent a powerful empire they would do well to respect – request that they arrange transport for us to our Purple Palace, where, I can tell you, I shall be speaking very frankly to *King Consort* Henry. Very frankly indeed.'

'Aunt Aisling, I –'

But it was too late. Aisling swept through the open door and, without any attempt at concealment, strode along the balcony towards the staircase leading to the council chamber below. Mella started to race after her, then stopped. If the Table hanged her aunt for breach of security or impertinence or stupidity, that was nobody's fault but Aisling's. It would do no good at all if she took Mella with her. Best to wait and watch and see what happened. Mella crept carefully to the edge of the balcony and looked over again.

The Goblin Guard appeared before Aisling was half-way down the stairs. In the old days, Goblin Guards used real goblins, silver-suited demons conjured from Hael and bound to service by the occasional sacrifice. But around the time Mella's mother was a teenager, the demon guards were replaced by cleverly crafted illusions with enough solidity to maim and murder with the same ferocity as an actual goblin. The illusion had originally been developed in Haleklind, but spread quickly when the wizards offered it for sale. Mella knew a Guard was coming, even before it actually appeared. She heard the distinctive insectile chittering underlaid with a *click-clack* sound like lobster claws.

'Don't move, Aunt Aisling!' Mella screamed as the goblins began to materialise. So much for waiting to see what happened. So much for maybe sneaking off while Aisling made a fool of herself. Seven heads turned towards her. She was absolutely caught. But what could she do? Aisling was her aunt and Goblin Guards *killed* people.

Aisling stopped. She could never have seen anything like a goblin in her life before, but to be fair, she took the Guard in her stride. From her vantage point half-way down the stairs, she called calmly to the seven round the table, 'I am the Lady Atherton, sister of His Consort Majesty King Henry of the Faerie Empire. Please ensure these creatures do not harm me.'

The *Lady* Atherton? You couldn't help admire her. But at least the demons were no longer moving and wouldn't move as long as she stayed still. Mella stayed still herself. If she moved while there was a Guard about, they might well attack her – and go straight through Aisling to get to her.

The woman at the end of the table pushed back her cowl to reveal sharp, almost cruel, features. She glared at Aisling. 'How did you gain entrance to our chamber?' she asked with more than a hint of quiet malice.

This had to be Haleklind, Mella thought. Only in Haleklind would that be the first question. Not *what do you want?* Not *what are you doing?* Not *who did you say you were?* But *how did you get in?* It occurred to her suddenly that Halek defences would be set to stop anyone portalling from the Faerie or the Hael Realms. It would never have occurred to the wizards to worry about the Analogue World, where nobody used portals, or magic of any sort, or even believed in wizards.

'I have no idea,' said Aisling, as if the question were of no importance. 'But if you will kindly instruct these things to step aside and allow me to come down so I don't have to *shout* all the time, I will tell you what I want you to do.'

One of the men round the table said, 'Consort Majesty King Henry of the Faerie Empire does not have a sister in this Realm.'

Mella focused on three of his words: *in this Realm.* Not *doesn't have a sister,* but *doesn't have a sister in this Realm.* This was Haleklind all right. The reach of the wizards' intelligence service was legendary, at least on a par with, if not actually ahead of, Madame Cardui's own. They knew her father had a sister back in the Analogue World, probably even knew her name. Mella just hoped Aisling wasn't going to lie to them. She'd already chanced it with her 'Lady Atherton' business.

'I have not come from this Realm,' Aisling said clearly. 'I have come from –' She stopped suddenly, obviously wondering what they might call the Analogue World, then went on, '– the Human Realm.'

There was an immediate buzz of conversation around the table and, even though she couldn't hear a word of it, Mella knew they were back to their old concerns, wondering how somebody from the Analogue World had broken through their defences to gain access to their chamber. The man who had spoken earlier cut through the buzz to ask, 'What is your forename?' He frowned, as if searching for the correct term, then added, 'Your *Christian* name?'

'I am the Lady Aisling,' Aunt Aisling told him, probably having figured *Lady Atherton* might not be the right form of address.

'*Lady* Aisling?' the man echoed. He raised an eyebrow. This was not going well, not going well at all. Mella wondered if she should simply cut and run, leave Aisling to it. But run where? The transporter was broken, so there was no open portal behind her. Running back the way she came might take her out of this building or might not. Since they'd entered on stairs, it might simply lead to an upper storey. And even if she did get out of the building, what good would that do her? She was somewhere in Haleklind. There were bound to be securities surrounding the building where the Table of Seven met. She would be captured the moment she ran into them. Captured or killed.

A cowled figure leaned across to whisper something in the ear of the woman at the head of the table. They both turned to look directly at Mella. 'Are you sure, Companion Aubertin?' asked the woman at the head of the table.

'I saw her once at a State occasion, Companion Ysabeau,' the man told her.

The woman Ysabeau called out, 'Are you Culmella Chrysotenchia?'

Mella swallowed. 'Yes, ma'am,' she called back.

'And this . . . lady, is your father's sister? From the Analogue World?'

'Yes, ma'am,' Mella repeated.

Ysabeau made a gesture and the Goblin Guard vanished. She stood up and walked towards the staircase. 'Lady Aisling, Princess Culmella, on behalf of the Table of Seven, may I welcome you to Haleklind.'

Twenty-Six

Companion Ysabeau showed them to a magnificently appointed suite of rooms and left them to freshen up. Aisling was ecstatic.

'See?' she said. 'See? Didn't I say we'd be treated like visiting dignitaries? Didn't I tell you?' She raced into her bedroom and, moments later, raced out again. 'My God, Culmella, come and see this!'

Mella dutifully followed her back in. Aunt Aisling had opened a massive wardrobe. 'Look!' she exclaimed. 'Look what she's given me!' There were dresses and frocks, evening wear and daywear, there were suits, there were jackets, there were tops, there were shirts, there were blouses, there were trousers, there were slacks, there was silk, there was satin, there was cloth-of-gold, there were hats, there were tunics, there were scarves, there were overcoats, there were furs and skins and fabrics with patterns and fabrics with prints and fabrics that had magically moving pictures. 'They fit!' Aisling exclaimed. 'They're all my size!'

Of course they fit, Mella thought crossly. *That's your basic clothing spell – where have you* been?

'Look!' In her enthusiasm Aisling jerked a drawer out of its fittings so that the contents cascaded in a glittering pile on to the floor. This one even brought Mella up short. The drawer was packed with accessories, mainly jewellery and gemstones. Mella recognised opals, sapphires, amethysts, rubies, emeralds, tourmalines, spinels, aquamarines, moonstones, agates, sunstones, turquoises, amber, topazes, aventurines, bloodstones, polished coral and garnets, jade, olivines, zircons and, most common of all, diamonds. Some were crafted into brooches, bracelets and pendants, some clearly meant as a gem dusting for clothing, but all, without exception, had been carefully hand-painted with spell coatings. As a result, they sparkled brightly, sang gently and emitted the most heavenly of scents. Some even moved sinuously or slowly revolved.

'I just want to . . .' Mella said, glancing at the door.

'But you simply have to see *this!*' Aisling sang, flinging open yet another wardrobe cabinet. Mella groaned inwardly. 'Shoes!' screamed Aisling delightedly.

The cabinet had been treated so that it expanded once the door was opened, converting into storage space equivalent to a small warehouse. Within it were racks upon racks, stacked like shelves, each one displaying thousands of pairs of shoes. Pinpoint spotlights flashed on and off at random to highlight one pair after another for inspection. Mella had seen the system before, but only in commercial premises and on a markedly smaller scale.

'You can walk in,' she said, hoping to get rid of Aisling. She needed to think. She mistrusted Companion Ysabeau – and all the other sinister hooded Companions – with every fibre of her being. She needed to get away from her over-excited aunt and take a little planning time to herself, away from the girlie concerns of clothes and shoes. She needed to warn her parents about the *invasion of the Empire.*

Aisling did walk in, a trance-like, blissed-out

expression on her face, and Mella took the opportunity to leave the bedroom. She was in the living area – vast, brightly lit, with ormolu furnishings and more spell coatings per square foot than she'd seen anywhere else in the entire Faerie Realm – when Aunt Aisling reappeared, noticeably taller than she'd been a few moments before.

'Look!' she cooed. 'Oh, Mella, *look!*'

Mella groaned inwardly. She had to stop this nonsense. They were in trouble – she *knew* they were in trouble – and they had to figure a way out. 'Aunt Aisling –'

But Aisling wasn't listening. She had put on a gold lamé, off-the-shoulder, ankle-length evening gown that somehow accentuated her height even more, and now twirled in the centre of the floor to show it off. 'See? Look at the shoes!'

Mella looked at the shoes. They were gold and jewelled high-heels and they floated – levitated – almost three inches above the surface of the floor, carrying Aisling aloft with them.

'Aren't they *divine?*' Aunt Aisling sang out. 'Aren't they just the most amazing things you've ever seen? And so *comfortable!* Honestly, Mella –'

But Mella had had enough. 'I'd like to show *you* something, Aunt Aisling,' she said firmly and walked to the door of their suite that led into the corridor outside. She waited.

'Well, there's no need to adopt that tone,' Aisling said sulkily. 'If you look in the wardrobe in *your* room I'm quite sure you'll find some very nice clothes that are perfectly suited to a girl of your age. Companion Ysabeau most certainly will not have left you out, so there's no need to be jealous. I tell you what, why don't we both go to your room together and I'll help you pick something appropriate. I think they're planning some sort of reception, probably a banquet in my – our – honour, so you'll need to be looking quite the proper little princess. I mean, you can hardly go in what you're wearing now, can you? Much too informal.'

Mella glared at her. 'Come . . . over . . . *here!*'

Aisling blinked. 'Honestly, Mella, I don't know what's got into you.' But she glided across just the same.

'Try the door,' Mella said quietly.

'What?'

'Try the door,' Mella repeated. She gestured towards the gilded handle.

Aisling frowned at her suspiciously. 'Why?' she asked. 'Why do you want me to go outside?'

'Try the bloody door!' Mella hissed furiously. She'd picked up the word from her father who'd once told her it had an impact on humans that was entirely missing in the Faerie Realm, where the adjective was strictly descriptive.

It had an impact on Aisling, all right. She recoiled visibly and her expression of suspicion changed instantly to one of shock. 'Mella!' she exclaimed. But all the same she floated forward, circled round Mella as if she might be exuding some miasmic plague, and reached for the handle.

The door was locked, as Mella knew it would be.

From the outside.

Twenty-Seven

They were lying side by side on a four-poster bed. Henry blinked. Somebody had made it up with black satin sheets. The brocade drapes were a deep, gut-clenching red. The curtains at the foot of the bed had been drawn back so he could see part of the room. A spell-driven mural on the wall featured a classical scene of nymphs fleeing listlessly from satyrs. The carpet on the floor was a bilious yellow. He sat up and his head throbbed suddenly, as if he'd drunk himself into a hangover the night before.

'What ghastly taste,' he muttered.

Blue gave that funny little moan she always did when she was waking up from sleep and opened her eyes. She looked at Henry, then the curtains, then the moving mural. After a moment, she sat up as well. They were both wearing the same clothes they'd chosen for their Analogue World visit.

'Looks like we're back in the Realm,' Henry said. The mural gave the clue. Unless somebody was using back projection.

'Yes,' Blue muttered. She swung her feet on to the floor and stood up. 'Have you any idea how long we've been unconscious?'

'None.' Henry shook his head; and wished he hadn't. 'Do you have a headache?'

'Yes.'

'Long enough for them to portal us back and bring us here, I suppose,' Henry said. 'That was Chalkhill and Brimstone.'

'Yes,' Blue said again.

'I thought he was insane.'

'Brimstone? He was. Probably still is.' She hesitated. 'It doesn't *feel* as if I've been unconscious for very long, but I suppose it's hard to tell.'

Henry gathered his courage and stood up as well. His head toppled a bit, but failed to fall from his shoulders. He squeezed his eyes shut, then opened them again and felt a little better. 'He used some sort of magic net thing on me.'

'Me too,' Blue said. 'Standard net spell. They play Hael with your nervous system. But it should wear off quickly now we're awake.'

They looked around the bedroom. The garish theme carried through to the furnishings, but the most noticeable feature was a mirrored dressing table that produced its own light when Henry touched the chair beside it. He caught a glimpse of himself in the mirror and thought, despite everything, he looked rather well.

'Positive distortion,' Blue muttered annoyingly. 'This is the bedroom of someone vain.'

'Chalkhill?' Henry said. Which would make sense since they'd been captured by Chalkhill and Brimstone – duh! But why would Chalkhill lock them in his bedroom? Why not in a dungeon somewhere? It was always hard for Henry to believe, but the truth was they were a King and Queen – well, King Consort, anyway. You didn't kidnap a King and Queen and lock them in your bedroom where anybody might walk in and find them and there was no proper security. That was like

175

something a child would make up as part of a fairy tale. But perhaps it wasn't a real bedroom. Perhaps it was a dungeon tarted up to look like a bedroom. But whether real or faked, there was just one priority. He looked around. 'The question is, how do we escape from it?'

'Window?' Blue suggested. They walked together to the window and looked out into a well-kept stretch of garden.

Henry ran the palm of his hand gently across the surface of the glass and felt the familiar tingling of his allergy to magic. 'It's spell coated,' he said. The thought occurred to him that the well-kept garden might be an illusion created by the coating. What was *really* out there might be an angry sea, a lava lake or a forest full of dinosaurs.

'Could still be breakable,' Blue said.

Henry doubted it. Chalkhill and Brimstone would hardly imprison them in a room with a breakable window. All the same, he knew better than to argue with Blue, who had a stubborn streak when ideas occurred to her. He looked around until his gaze fell on the dressing table chair. 'Stand back,' he said and picked it up.

Blue stood clear as Henry swung the chair against the windowpane. It struck the glass with a resounding *thwack* and bounced back violently. 'Jeez!' Henry gasped, dropping the chair and shaking the shock from his hands.

'Security glass,' Blue murmured. 'This isn't going to be as easy as we thought.'

Henry, who'd never thought it was going to be easy, put the chair back tidily beside the dressing table. 'I wonder if there used to be a fireplace . . .'

'In a bedroom?' Blue asked incredulously.

'If it's an old house,' Henry said. 'They used to have fireplaces in the bedrooms of old houses in my world: I thought it might be the same here.'

'Not since we discovered magic,' Blue said. 'I'm not sure we ever did. Anyway, there's no fireplace here.'

'No, I know there's not. But this is either a new house or an old house that's been renovated. If it's a new house there won't be a fireplace, but if it's an old house renovated, then one might be hidden.' If there was one hidden, they might be able to break through and climb up the chimney, assuming the chimney hadn't been blocked up. He began to tap the wall in the manner of a doctor sounding a patient's chest, hoping to detect a hollow.

Blue turned away in disgust and walked back to the window. 'There's something about that garden . . .' she said.

'I thought it mightn't be there at all,' Henry told her. So far, every bit of wall he tapped sounded solid as a rock, possibly because it was actually made of rock.

'What do you mean – not there?'

'Scenery spell, or whatever they call it,' Henry muttered. 'The tacky coating they use in piddling little town houses to make you think you're living on a country estate.' His mind went back to an earlier thought, but he decided not to mention the tarted dungeon theory, which would probably just upset Blue or, worse still, make her cross. He tapped another bit of wall. It sounded solid.

'I doubt it,' Blue told him. 'Scenery spells are cheap and nasty. If you look at them at an angle, there's nearly always a telltale sheen. There's nothing like that on this window.'

'Blue . . .' Henry said.

'Besides, there's something odd about the garden out there, something –'

'Blue . . .' Henry said again.

'– familiar. It's as if –'

'Blue,' Henry said, 'the door's open.'

She turned and her face took on a look of astonishment that quickly turned to admiration. 'How on earth did you do that?'

Henry was wondering about that himself. He'd been tapping the wall when he came to the door and something – force of habit probably – made him turn the handle and push. The door had opened easily. For a moment he considered claiming he'd cleverly picked the lock – he liked that look of admiration – but he knew she'd only ask how and the resulting hassle wouldn't be worth it. Instead he said, 'I didn't: it wasn't locked.'

Blue frowned. 'Are you sure?'

Henry gestured to the open door and raised both eyebrows.

'I suppose you are,' Blue said. She came across, took his hand and together they walked out of the room.

They were in the bedroom wing of a luxuriously – if garishly – appointed dwelling. No doors were locked nor were there any magical securities in place. There were no guards; indeed they seemed to be the only living creatures in the house.

As they entered a spacious living room, Blue said suddenly, 'You were right!'

'Was I?' Henry asked. 'About what?'

'Look at that white piano with the diamante legs,' Blue said. 'This is Chalkhill's house, definitely. I've been here before – that's why the gardens looked familiar. I came here once with Kitterick.'

Henry looked around. Why would Chalkhill kidnap them, then leave them with the run of his home? 'Why –?' he began.

'This was when he was being all camp and interior decoratory to hide the fact he was Lord Hairstreak's spy,' Blue said. 'He's left the place exactly the way he had it then. Come and look at the gardens – you won't believe them!'

She led him through French windows on to a tightly manicured lawn, then took a garden path flanking a flowerbed of foxgloves and bluebells that sang softly to them as they walked around the side of the mansion. The path meandered through a heart-shaped grove and past a croquet green with luminous pink hoops.

'Prepare yourself,' Blue murmured.

They turned the corner and Henry found himself looking at a swimming pool cut from a single piece of amethyst, then rimmed in gold and filled with sparkling water driven by machinery that maintained its fizz. The whole scene was bathed in warm, perpetual sunshine.

'My God!' he gasped.

'Quite something, isn't it?' Blue said.

Henry tore his eyes away from the pool. 'What I don't understand is why they kidnapped us and brought us here. I mean, you knew this was Chalkhill's place and other people must know it as well. It's the first place they'd look once he makes a ransom demand.'

'Assuming he's planning to make a ransom demand,' Blue said tightly.

'Well, what else would – oh. Oh dear. You think he might –?'

'I don't know,' Blue told him. 'It's probably ransom, but you're right about it being odd that he brought us here.'

'With no guards,' Henry mused. 'Although I suppose there has to be a security system, even if we haven't hit it yet. A force field surrounding the property or something.'

But Blue was shaking her head. 'He doesn't need one. This place is in the middle of Wildmoor Broads. We're surrounded by prickleweed. The only safe way in and out is by air.'

'And we don't have a flyer,' Henry said.

'And we don't have a flyer,' Blue confirmed.

They walked together through the gardens until they reached the boundary of the estate and stood staring over the wild expanse of the Broads. The prickleweed seethed and writhed like an angry ocean. A low, spell-coated fence stopped it encroaching on Chalkhill's property.

'Has anybody ever survived out there on foot?' Henry asked Blue.

'Somebody once made it for nearly a mile in an armoured car, although the vehicle dissolved soon afterwards. And there's a legend that two escaped prisoners got all the way across the Broads barefoot in the days of Scolitandes the Weedy, but nobody really believes it.'

'All the same,' Henry said, 'if we can't find a flyer, we'll have to try.'

Blue nodded soberly. 'I know. For Mella's sake.'

Twenty-Eight

'Simbala?' Corin suggested. 'There's a nice little parlour just around the corner.'

'I should be getting home,' Pyrgus told him unconvincingly.

'A small one for the road?'

Pyrgus grinned. 'Oh, go on, then! But only one, and only if I'm buying.'

'Wouldn't have it any other way,' Corin said.

They left the Society headquarters through a back door and emerged into an alley redolent with rubbish. 'Sorry about that,' Corin said. 'The smell keeps people from investigating this side of the building too closely – cheaper than spells. Just hold your nose and we'll be out of it in a minute.'

'How *is* the political situation?' Pyrgus asked. 'Are you still facing as much persecution?'

Corin shrugged fatalistically. 'More than ever. It's not that the wizards have anything against animals particularly – it's just that they treat them as *property*. It's the old scriptural attitude. Once you think you own the world, it's your Gods-given right to treat animals any way you want to, exploit them, whatever. They're not even supposed to experience pain, so you can cut them up in labs without feeling guilty.'

'Well,' Pyrgus said. 'It's not just Creen: we have the same attitudes at home. Maybe not as widespread, but . . .'

They emerged from the alley, walked down a narrow street.

'Actually, that's not really the problem any more,' Corin said. 'I mean we were making some headway in the old days. Not as much as we'd have liked, but some. We had a good propaganda machine. It carried the message and people were starting to listen. Who knows where it might have gone.' He took Pyrgus's elbow. 'We cross over here.'

They crossed the street to the opposite pavement and Corin stopped beside a narrow flight of stone-flagged steps winding downwards to some hidden basement. 'No, the real problem is the Table of Seven. Gods know, the old Wizards' Council was bad enough and I'd be the last one to tell you it wasn't corrupt to the core, but the Seven are ten times worse.'

They started down the steps with Corin in the lead. 'I thought they were against corruption?' Pyrgus remarked to the top of his head. 'I thought everybody welcomed the revolution?'

'Oh, we did. Even I did. Tell you the truth, Pyrgus, and I'm ashamed to admit it, but I actually helped the Table's cause. Small cog, admittedly, but still . . . They talked about animal rights in those days. The thing was, once they came to power, it went to their heads.'

'Often happens.' Pyrgus nodded.

They reached the bottom of the steps, which led on to a small cobbled courtyard. Corin headed across it to a narrow wooden doorway set behind an arch. 'They want to take control of everything and if you're not actively working for them, you're against them. You must have noticed how tight the restrictions are now when you're getting in and out the country.'

'Yes,' Pyrgus said without elaboration.

'It was only when the Haleklind Society for the Preservation and Protection of Animals refused to become an official government agency that the Table of Seven outlawed us. Did you know that?'

'No I didn't,' Pyrgus told him. He grinned. 'I thought you'd made them cross by blowing up their vivisection labs.'

Corin pushed the door and the heat and chatter met them like a wave. 'We only did that afterwards,' he said. He snorted cynically. 'When they decided to make everything illegal and anything that wasn't illegal was made compulsory. Slight exaggeration, but you know what I mean.'

They walked into the gloom of the simbala parlour. It was a very basic set-up. The walls were covered with maroon acoustic drapes while the range of bottles behind the bar was noticeably limited. But the chairs and couches were well laid-out and very comfortable.

'Is this place legal?' Pyrgus asked.

'Don't be silly,' Corin told him.

Pyrgus grinned. 'Grab somewhere to lie and I'll get us the music.'

He ordered half-hour shots from the barman, decided that was mean and changed the order to doubles. Carrying the humming glasses back on a small tray he handed one to Corin, who was already reclining on a couch. Pyrgus pulled an armchair to the head of the couch so they could chat and took his first sip of simbala. The music trickled down his throat like liquid gold. He leaned his head back and closed his eyes as the symphony gently filled his body.

Corin asked casually, 'Do you still have contacts in the Realm Government?'

It was an odd question, oddly phrased. Pyrgus opened his eyes a slit and said, 'Queen Blue is still my sister, if that's what you mean.'

'Yes, I know. But you don't have anything to do with day-to-day politics since you abdicated, do you? I mean, you're not in regular contact with her advisors, or anything like that?'

'She doesn't have many formal advisors – pretty much runs the show on her own: she's a born bossy-boots. Why do you ask?' The music, as it always did, wrapped around his words, giving them melody and tone. Out of the side of his eye he saw Corin drain half the contents of his glass in a single gulp. The volume inside his body must have been deafening.

'There have been rumours that the Table are on the edge of something major. I was wondering if Queen Blue's security service had heard anything about it.'

'What sort of something?'

'I don't know. Some sort of crackdown, maybe? I'm obviously concerned about my own organisation. But it may not even be internal. Just before you arrived, I had word that the Table were holding two outerlinders who claim to be representatives of the Empire.'

'At what level? Are they saying they're diplomats or a trade delegation, or what?'

'I don't know. But if the Seven are holding them, they obviously suspect something else.'

'Spies?' Pyrgus asked. The Table of Seven was para-noid, but that didn't always mean their suspicions were wrong: Madame Cardui was quite capable of sending agents into Haleklind, even though it was supposed to be a friendly neighbour. As was his little sister.

'I suppose so.'

Despite the music, Pyrgus frowned. 'Any names?'

The music must have been taking hold of Corin's bloodstream because he was smiling a little, like someone without a care in the world. But he caught himself quickly and the smile faded. 'Only one,' he said. 'Do you have a spy called Chirotentia?'

Pyrgus shook his head. 'No, but I don't know the names of all our spies. In fact I hardly know any of them. Even when they were preparing me to be Emperor, the identities of secret agents was on a need-to-know basis.'

'Camelia Chirotentia?' Corin persisted. 'Or Camelia Kissotentia? Something like that? Might even be Camilius. My source has a cleft palate.'

Pyrgus shook his head again. 'Rings no bells with me, but as I said –' He stopped, as a sudden thought struck him. It was silly. She was back in the Purple Palace and even if she wasn't, there was no way she was making a visit to Haleklind. And if she *was* making a visit to Haleklind, it would be a proper State visit properly arranged with all the formalities. The Haleklinders would never hold her. They wouldn't dare. It was against protocol. Unless, of course, she came into the country illegally, in which case she was an international incident. Which he'd have heard about, so it hadn't happened and was hardly worth thinking about; but all the same, Pyrgus couldn't stop thinking about it, or, more accurately, couldn't stop thinking about the things Blue used to get up to when she was still a teenager.

That sort of wildness was often hereditary. But what sort of wildness would take a kid to Haleklind illegally? And how would a kid *get into* Haleklind? Corin had just reminded him how tight the border restrictions had become. No, it couldn't have happened.

'No,' he said aloud.

'No what?' Corin asked.

'It wasn't Chrysotenchia, was it?' Pyrgus blurted.

From his place on the couch, Corin frowned. 'Could have been, I suppose . . .'

'Culmella Chrysotenchia?'

Corin sat up abruptly. 'The Crown Princess? Oh, I wouldn't think so.' He stared at Pyrgus. 'It's not possible, is it?'

'It's not likely . . .' Pyrgus said. Blue used to dress up as a boy and get into all sorts of trouble. 'But it's possible.' He grabbed Corin's arm. 'Come on!'

'Where are we going?'

Pyrgus headed for the door. The sudden adrenaline rush had flushed most of the music from his system. 'Back to your headquarters so you can ask your source if he meant to say 'Culmella Chrysotenchia'. If he nods his head, I think my niece may be in a heap of trouble.'

Twenty-Nine

Chalkhill seemed to know his way around Lord Hairstreak's Keep, Brimstone thought. He was certainly recognised by the securities, otherwise they'd both have been dead by now. But recognised didn't necessarily mean welcome, as they discovered when they reached His Lordship himself.

'What's he doing here?' Hairstreak demanded with obvious irritation.

Brimstone glared at him suspiciously. There was something wrong here. Chalkhill had told him His Lordship was a disembodied head now, but clearly Chalkhill had lied. Hairstreak was very much embodied, quite his old self in every way, fit and positively glowing with rude good health. He even looked as if he might have grown an inch or two, although that was probably just Brimstone's faulty memory. Which was obviously what Chalkhill was relying on. He was probably counting on Brimstone having forgotten what he'd said about a disembodied head. Obviously Lord Hairstreak and Chalkhill had hatched some dastardly plot together to murder Brimstone. It was just the sort of thing they'd do. Not that Brimstone was worried: he had George to protect him now. A bluebottle flew in through Hairstreak's window. Brimstone caught it expertly and dropped it into his pocket as a snack for later.

'He's helping me with my enquiries,' Chalkhill told Hairstreak shortly.

Hairstreak dismissed the information with a shrug. He stretched luxuriously, walked to the window and looked out through the spell-driven rain to the high cliffs and rugged rocks battered by a raging sea. 'I almost died once on those rocks,' he remarked inconsequentially. Then he turned back, eyes glittering. 'Where is the girl?'

'We don't have her,' Chalkhill said, then added quickly, 'yet.'

'Clock's ticking,' Hairstreak growled.

Chalkhill nodded. 'I know.'

'Then what in Hael are you doing here?' Hairstreak shouted suddenly. 'Wasting my time and your own! Why aren't you out there looking for her? You really really think I'm paying your outrageous fees so you can pop into my home every five minutes for a cup of tea?'

'No, sir,' Chalkhill said and Brimstone suddenly realised that for all his bluster, Chalkhill was still afraid of the little turd; or big turd, as he seemed to be now.

'Then what,' spat Hairstreak, 'are you doing here?'

'There have been developments,' said Chalkhill stiffly.

'Ooooooh – *developments!*' Lord Hairstreak exclaimed. He did a little dance and spread his arms through the air in a high, sweeping movement. Brimstone watched him with fascination. Perhaps, Brimstone thought, Chalkhill *hadn't* been lying about the disembodied head. Hairstreak was certainly behaving like someone who found a body a novelty. He'd hardly stood still for more than a moment since they walked through his door. But where had he got the new one? 'And, pray tell me,' Hairstreak said, spreading his hands like a pedlar and tapping his right foot, 'to what developments do you refer?'

Chalkhill gave a taught, triumphant smile. 'We have Queen Blue and King Consort Henry.'

There was absolute silence in the reception chamber and for once Lord Hairstreak stood stock still. He stared at Chalkhill as if he was unable to believe his ears. (His new ears, Brimstone wondered briefly, but then realised that if Hairstreak had been a disembodied head recently reembodied, then the ears would be his old ears. Probably.)

'You . . . have . . . *who?*' Lord Hairstreak asked.

Chalkhill, who was always a fool, never spotted subtle signals – or even not so subtle, come to that – allowed his smile to spread like a grinflower all over his face. 'Queen Blue and King Consort Henry,' he repeated. 'We have seized them both. We're holding them in my villa. As we speak.'

Hairstreak took a pace or two back into the room and picked up an ornamental marble egg from a side table. He weighed it gently in his palm, his eyes fixed on Chalkhill. 'You are holding the Queen and her Consort in your villa? Under lock and key?'

Still smiling like an idiot, Chalkhill shook his head. 'Oh, no, they have the run of the villa. Like honoured guests. They can't escape – it's in the middle of the Wildmoor Broads.' He obviously caught Hairstreak's expression, for he added, 'If they tried to leave the prickleweed would get them.'

'Prickleweed . . .' Hairstreak echoed.

'Yes, sir,' Chalkhill said enthusiastically. 'It's a

carnivorous plant that grows wild all across the Broads. The only way you can reach my villa –'

'– is by air,' Hairstreak finished for him. He was speaking very, very quietly. 'And while our Queen and her Consort are given the run of your villa "like honoured guests" – even though the prickleweed will flay them should they try to leave – you are doubtless demanding a ransom from the current Gatekeeper?' He frowned. 'Who is it now – I'm so very out of touch? Ah, yes, it's one of Madame Cardui's functions these days, isn't it? Accepting ransom notes. That and hunting down the man who sent them, since she's also Head of State Security. I do hope you didn't mention where you were holding them. That would make her job a lot less fun.'

Brimstone, who admired sarcasm, moved away from Chalkhill in case His Lordship decided to replace it with a physical attack, and took up a comfortable position beside the fireplace. Whatever developed – and something was certainly in the process of developing – was between Hairstreak and Chalkhill. Kidnapping the Queen and King had been Chalkhill's idea – nothing to do with Brimstone.

'Actually,' Chalkhill said (and you could practically hear the sound of spade on earth as he dug his grave deeper), 'I haven't sent a ransom note. To anybody.' That smile again. That glittering, spell-encrusted, sparkling smile Chalkhill was directing so vacantly towards Hairstreak. With his heightened sensitivities, Brimstone could almost feel the effect of it in his own body. Hairstreak was now poised like a coiled spring ready to mix metaphors in an uncontrolled explosion.

'You haven't?' Hairstreak asked, feigning surprise.

And Chalkhill *still* didn't spot the signs! 'Actually,' he said again, 'I thought *you* might like to have them.' *Don't offer them for sale*, Brimstone thought, *don't offer them for sale*. 'For a small consideration, of course,' Chalkhill concluded.

There was a sound like a pistol crack. It took Brimstone a moment to realise that Lord Hairstreak had gripped the marble egg so tightly that it shattered. A stream of powdered marble trickled through his fingers. 'How about,' Lord Hairstreak suggested, his eyes on Chalkhill, 'the small consideration is that I allow you to live another few weeks of your miserable life?'

Chalkhill blinked. 'I'm sorry?'

'Let them go, you cretin!' Hairstreak screamed. His face turned bright red and a vein began to pulse on his forehead. 'Get out of here at once and let them go!'

Chalkhill's jaw dropped. 'Don't you want them? You could ransom them for much more than I'd charge you.'

'Imbecile! Tort-feasor! Idiot! Goonberry! Crump-muckler! Your stupidity could ruin all my plans! Get back to your villa and release them. Release them at once!'

'But if you don't want them, I could ransom them myse—'

'No ransom!' Hairstreak shrieked. 'Let them go! Apologise! Grovel! Tell them you made a terrible mistake! Make up some story. Fly them out! Fly them home! Fly them anywhere they want to go!'

'But, Your Lordship, what will I –'

Hairstreak's small reserves of patience collapsed completely. Brimstone, who could see the trouble coming half a mile away, moved discreetly from the fireplace to take shelter behind a couch. He signalled George to keep clear and watched while Hairstreak hurled himself across the room to grip the lapels of Chalkhill's designer jacket. To Brimstone's surprise, he lifted Chalkhill bodily off the ground and slammed him against a wall, something which would have been quite beyond His (littler, shorter) Lordship in the old days.

Something weird happened. Afterwards, Brimstone decided Chalkhill must have overdone his ninja training and acted on reflex without thought of consequences. As Hairstreak held him, Chalkhill unleashed a rain of lethal blows, moving almost faster than the eye could follow, striking Hairstreak with fists, hands, elbows, knees and feet.

'Eeeeyah!' Chalkhill shouted.

Nothing happened.

'Fly them home,' Lord Hairstreak demanded. 'Then bring me Culmella.'

It was fascinating. Brimstone could tell Chalkhill was still acting on instinct as he produced a long, serrated knife and plunged it deep into Lord Hairstreak's heart.

Nothing happened.

Lord Hairstreak relaxed his grip so that Chalkhill slid slowly down the wall. 'Bring me Culmella.' Hairstreak gripped the knife and drew it slowly from his heart with a repulsive sucking sound. He smiled into Chalkhill's face. 'Otherwise I shall come after *you*.'

'That could have gone better,' Brimstone remarked in the ouklo.

Chalkhill glared at him, but said nothing.

'Now you've antagonised the Queen of the Realm and her King Consort and Lord Hairstreak. Powerful enemies.'

Chalkhill glared at him, but said nothing.

'And you don't know where to find Princess Mella,' Brimstone reminded him. 'So there's no way of getting back into Hairstreak's good books.'

Chalkhill glared at him, but said nothing. George was sitting on the seat beside him, his knees drawn up nearly to his chest because his legs were too long even for a stretch carriage. Not that Chalkhill noticed.

'And then,' said Brimstone cheerfully, 'there's the problem of getting away after you release Queen Blue. She knows who kidnapped her, of course – she must have seen you clearly before I cracked the spell cone; and besides she knows your house. No talking your way out of this one, is there? Once she gets back to the Purple Palace, she'll have every guard, soldier and policeman in the kingdom looking for you. Still, there's one consolation . . .'

'What's that?' Chalkhill asked, breaking his silence for the first time since they'd left Lord Hairstreak's Keep.

'Things can't get any worse!' Brimstone cackled.

But he was wrong. When they reached Chalkhill's villa, they discovered Queen Blue and King Consort Henry were no longer there.

thirty

'You're not hungry again?' Blue asked in astonishment. 'At a time like this?'

Henry looked at her blankly, then realised what she was going on about. 'No, no – this is a kitchen and in a kitchen there are knives. Chalkhill won't have left us any other weapons, but he might have overlooked something here.' Since there were no knives on obvious display, he began to pull out drawers.

Blue said, 'I hadn't thought of that.' She began to pull out drawers as well. In a few moments they were both equipped with lengthy knives and Henry was also carrying a chopper. 'Do you think this'll be enough to fight off the prickleweed?' Blue asked.

'I haven't finished yet,' Henry told her.

He led her back into the gardens and they walked to the edge of the estate. He gripped the low boundary fence with both hands and began to jerk it violently.

'What are you doing?' Blue asked him.

'I'm trying to break off a piece of this fence,' Henry said. 'Actually I'm trying to break off two pieces . . .' He renewed his attack, more violently this time.

Blue watched him. After a moment, she asked, 'Why would you want to do that?'

'Because the wood is spell impregnated to keep out

prickleweed – you can see the plants don't like to come near it at all. I thought we might be able to use it as shields.'

'Clever husband!' Blue grinned. She turned and began to walk back towards the house.

'Where are you going?'

'To see if I can find some rope or string,' Blue called over her shoulder. 'If we're going to use shields, we'll need something to carry them by. I thought I could make us a handle.'

She returned with a coil of rope in time to find Henry ripping out a piece of fencing and now in the process of breaking it in two so they could both have shields. Blue cut the rope to size with her kitchen knife and looped it in a cross over the piece of wood. Once knotted, it meant she could carry the makeshift shield on her arm. She stared at the gap in the fencing. 'Won't the prickle-weed get in?'

'Oh yes,' Henry said. 'But not before we're gone.' He looped his own piece of rope in imitation of Blue's and hefted his shield on his arm like a hero. 'With a bit of luck, it may have eaten the entire place by the time Mr Chalkhill gets home.' He took her hand and led her away from the gap in the fence to the entrance gates of the estate. Beyond them was a short, straight stretch of roadway, clearly spell protected since it was free of vegetation. But then the roadway ended and the prickle-weed began. The road itself was obviously not a real road at all, but just a landing strip for ouklos. 'I'm going to open the gate now – are you ready?'

Blue swallowed and drew her knife. 'Yes.'

Henry began to open the gate. 'As far as I know, the Broads aren't *all* prickleweed. It can't grow on rock, for example, and it avoids anywhere with Border Redcaps. Some of the thorn and shrub give it a run for its money as well, although we probably couldn't get through there anyway. But there are bits and pieces of roads, if we can find them.'

'Are there?' Blue looked at him in surprise.

'Just remnants,' Henry said. 'I came across it in one of the Realm histories. Apparently there was a proper network at one time, all magically protected. This was before they developed flying spells. Once that happened, people stopped using the network and it fell into disrepair. But there are still parts of it left and some of them even have their spell coating. I figured if we can get past the worst of the weed surrounding the estate, we might try to find the old roads and see how far they can take us. Might not be the most direct way, but . . .' He looked at Blue, letting the sentence trail.

'Hard to believe we're so close to the city,' Blue said. 'If only we had a flyer.'

'Well, we haven't. So we do it the hard way.' He grinned at her. 'Chin up, old girl – we've been through worse.'

It was meant as a sort of joke – not that Blue would know English people used to talk like that. She didn't grin back, but stared instead along the open road that stopped so abruptly in the seething mass of vegetation. 'Henry . . .' she said.

'Mmm?'

'Just in case . . .' She looked up at him soberly. 'You know . . .'

He knew all right. For all the knives and shields and brave talk of old road networks, their chances of crossing the Broads alive were slim. 'Mmm,' he said again.

'I want you to know I never regretted a single moment of our life together since we married,' Blue said quietly. 'I want you to know I love you.'

He took her hand and they walked together along the landing strip outside Chalkhill's estate. When they were a few yards from the weed, their hands parted as they arranged their knives and shields. The prickleweed leaned in their direction, as if it somehow sensed their approach. There was something else in the Realm history about the Broads, something about the weed he hadn't told her. It didn't strangle you, as many people thought. It secreted a toxic resin on to its thorns and used them to inject it underneath your skin. After a few moments, as the resin reached your bloodstream, you began to feel calm, then lethargic, then downright tired. A creeping paralysis would spread through your body, affecting every part except for your eyelids, your heart and your lungs. Thus, you remained wide awake, capable of seeing, hearing, feeling everything as the prickleweed crawled over your skin and flayed it, piece by piece, to reach the nutrients beneath. It was a brutally slow death, often taking days or even weeks, and, according to the history, perhaps the most agonising you could possibly experience. It occurred to him that if Blue was attacked while he still retained his freedom of action, he might use his knife on her to spare her the horror. He shuddered.

'I love you too, Blue,' he said quietly as they walked together towards the weed.

The prickleweed backed away from their shields.

'That looks hopeful,' Blue said in a tone of surprise.

'It does, doesn't it?' Henry was just as surprised. He stopped to consider the situation. 'Our problem is going to be our backs. Once we start to move through the weed, it can attack us from behind. But maybe we could try a trick the Romans used . . .'

'What are Romans?'

'Ancient civilisation in the Analogue World. If they were surrounded in a battle, the legionnaires used to fight back to back. That way, the shield didn't just protect your front, it protected the man behind you; and his shield protected you. If you and I went into the prickleweed back to back – sort of shuffled along and kept turning like a wheel and kept the shields up firmly and made sure our backs never lost contact and slashed out with our knives and were really, really careful – we might be able to work our way through.'

'Or else,' Blue said, 'we could break off some more fencing and tie shields to our backs as well.'

Henry looked at her with his mouth open, realised what he was doing and closed it again. 'Yes,' he agreed, 'we could definitely do that.'

They returned to the fence and Henry broke more pieces off quite easily. They roped them to their backs and bottoms. 'How do I look?' Henry asked, grinning.

'Very fetching,' Blue told him. 'Do you think it's going to work?'

'Actually I think it might. I'm surprised nobody's tried this before – I mean, not tying fencing to your backside, but a spell-coated suit you could wear on the Broads.'

'I suppose flying is easier,' Blue said. 'It's not as if anybody wants to stroll through the Broads on a nature ramble.'

'No, I suppose not. Shall we try it?'

They walked off the landing strip with some trepidation, but fronds of prickleweed snapped violently away from them as if stung. After they'd gone close to a hundred yards, Henry began to giggle. 'This is so easy,' he said. 'I think we're even heading in the right direction. Now all we need to do is find a road.' He turned to smile at Blue.

'I think I've scratched my hand on something,' Blue said, frowning.

Thirty-One

Once, when he was a boy, Pyrgus Malvae crashed a personal flyer into a tree that grew close to the main entrance of the Purple Palace. Now, he grazed the same tree by a whisker and, sirens screaming, ploughed up a stretch of turf on the lawn.

The Palace alarms were also sounding wildly as he dropped from his vehicle. He was vaguely aware that without the royal insignia – which he didn't always remember to display these days – the security systems would have blasted him from the sky. As it was, a stream of guards was pouring from the Palace and running in his direction. He sprinted towards them, fervently hoping their captain was someone who would know who he was. But his hopes were dashed as they came closer and he discovered their leader was a young woman he didn't recognise.

'I am Crown Prince Pyrgus,' he shouted loudly. 'Brother by blood of Queen Blue, brother by marriage of Consort Majesty King Henry. It is my charge that you take me at once to meet with them.'

The woman stopped a few feet from him and the guards, to his relief, stood down their weapons. She smiled at him benignly. 'Neither Blue nor Henry can see you at the moment, Pyrgus. Perhaps you might make do with me?'

Pyrgus frowned. The voice sounded familiar, but . . . 'Who are you?' he asked, a little sharply.

To his astonishment, the young woman stepped forward and embraced him, with a warm kiss on one cheek. 'Oh, you are such a *sweet* boy and always were. It's Cynthia Cardui, Pyrgus. I've had a head peel.'

'Good Gods, Madame Cardui! You look *amazing!*'

'Thank you, Pyrgus. It takes so much *effort* these days, I'm afraid, but it's always nice to know one is appreciated.'

'Why can't Blue and Henry see me?'

She slipped a hand through his arm. 'Now, my deeah, I think perhaps that's something we should discuss in private. Along with the purpose of your delightful surprise visit.'

Pyrgus allowed himself to be led not to the Palace, as it happened, but to a lodge in the grounds. He noticed their escort dropped away once they were within a hundred yards of the door. 'You're Gatekeeper now, aren't you?' he asked.

'Since poor Alan died. I don't often use the lodge – I still think of it as his somehow – but it does have such excellent security. One of the benefits of paranoia.'

'Do you speak to him much these days?'

'Not nearly so much as Henry does. I'm afraid I find it very difficult.'

They moved though the door and Pyrgus heard the familiar *click* of the securities sliding into place. 'Why can't Blue and Henry see me?' he asked at once.

'Because they're not actually here.'

'The flag is still flying.' He'd noticed it on his approach, despite his speed. The flag meant the sovereign was in residence. Henry might have taken himself off somewhere, but Blue must certainly be about.

'A small subterfuge, I'm afraid,' Madame Cardui told him. 'In the current emergency Queen Blue and I deemed it best that all seemed business as usual at the Palace. When they left, I substituted dopplegangers. Poor creatures are too silly to rule, of course, but they're quite capable of making small talk at State functions and waving from a balcony.'

'What emergency?' Pyrgus asked at once. Sometimes he almost regretted his life with the sanctuary and vineyard: it felt so cut off from the excitement of the capital.

Madame Cardui sighed. 'I'm afraid Miss Culmella has been misbehaving again. Would you like a drink? Or perhaps not, since you're flying. Unless you'd like to stay the night, of course. Although I don't know when your sister might be back. Mella has disappeared – run away. Blue and Henry are searching personally and I, of course, have my best agents at work. Without much result, I am embarrassed to tell you. I suspect it has been much the same for Blue and Henry, since I haven't heard from them.'

'I think I know where Mella is,' Pyrgus said.

Madame Cardui, who'd been fussing by the drinks cabinet, set the bottle down abruptly. 'What?'

'I think she may be in Haleklind,' Pyrgus said.

'I cannot imagine a less likely place,' Madame Cardui murmured, but her tone indicated she was taking him completely seriously. Her ability to adjust to the unlikely was what made her an excellent spymaster. She looked at Pyrgus soberly. 'Specifically where in Haleklind?'

'Specifically, being held prisoner by the ruling Table of Seven.'

This time, Madame Cardui failed to hide her shock. 'Are you sure?'

Pyrgus shook his head. 'No, I'm not sure. But I had it from someone I trust, who assures me his source is sound.'

'Does the Table of Seven know who she is?'

'I don't know. It's possible they may not, but you'd imagine she must have told them.'

'Unless she's playing one of her silly games. What is she doing in Haleklind? I assume she entered the country illegally?'

'I don't know that either.'

Madame Cardui felt for a chair and sat down. Despite the head peel, Pyrgus suddenly realised how old she really was; and how worried. There was tiredness in her eyes, but determination too. 'Help me here, Pyrgus: can you imagine any reason for your niece to go to Haleklind?'

'To tell you the truth, I don't know my niece all that well,' Pyrgus told her. 'I mean, I see her from time to time and I watched her turn into a young woman, but since I renounced the throne, I've kept away from the Palace as you know, so I'm not exactly in close touch. But I can tell you why *I* visited Haleklind at her age . . .'

'Why?' Madame Cardui asked.

'To buy a Halek knife. I don't suppose that would have much appeal to Mella, but most people visit Haleklind to buy magic – artifacts or crafted spells – that they can't get, or aren't allowed to get, at home.'

'So you think she may have been buying illegal magic?'

'It's a possibility.'

'Her parents think she may have gone to the Analogue World.'

'Is that where they're searching?'

'Yes.'

Pyrgus said, 'But you don't think they're right?'

Madame Cardui shook her head slowly. 'I wasn't convinced. Which was why I concentrated my own efforts elsewhere. Strangely enough, Haleklind was one of the places in the Realm that interested me.'

'But you said you couldn't imagine a less likely place for Mella.'

'I can't. But there's *something* going on in Haleklind. We've had our suspicions for several months now, although we haven't been able to discover any specifics. It's my experience that when one is presented with two unusual situations occurring simultaneously, it is always worth looking for a connection, however disparate they might be. Now you tell me Mella is being held in Haleklind. It does suggest they may indeed be connected.'

'What sort of activity is being reported from Haleklind?' Pyrgus asked her, frowning.

'Military,' Madame Cardui told him shortly.

Pyrgus felt a small chill. More than half a generation had passed since the faerie wars that had threatened to tear apart the Realm. Most people believed such a threat could never arise again, but Pyrgus knew better. Faerie nature never changed and there were always those, within and without the Empire, whose lust for power led them eventually down violent pathways. 'Troop movements?' he asked.

Madame Cardui sighed. 'No, that's the strange thing.'

'What then?'

'Increased signal activity, increased espionage activity – *greatly* increased espionage activity – stricter border controls. You must have noticed on your recent visit.'

'But no –' Pyrgus stopped short. 'How did you know I'd recently been to Haleklind? I didn't tell you.'

Madame Cardui gave a small smile.

'Oh, all right!' Pyrgus said. 'You're Head of State Security. You know every time a member of the Royal Family sneezes – even retired members.'

'Something like that.' Madame Cardui nodded. 'But when you read the intelligence reports on Haleklind over the past few weeks, they all point to a nation preparing for war. Not just the things I mentioned, but more frequent meetings of the Table of Seven, a vicious clampdown on subversive elements, a change of emphasis in the magical industry to weapons manufacturing . . . All signs of movement towards a war footing. But Haleklind has had a substantial standing army since the revolution and my spies show no unusual activity there at all. No troop relocation, no extra recruitment, no cancellation of leave. It's a vital part of the overall picture, and it doesn't fit.'

'Could be just the usual Haleklind paranoia,' Pyrgus suggested.

'You may be right. But I still don't like the signs of hostile intent, especially if they're holding Mella.' Madame Cardui stood up. 'Will you come with me to the viewroom? I need to alert Queen Blue.'

The viewroom was Mr Fogarty's invention: one of the strangest chambers in the entire Faerie Realm. It was a mix of Analogue World technology, Mr Fogarty's own developments in psychotronics and faerie communications magic. The overall effect was of a hi-tech bed of spreading fungus. The screens flared into life as Madame Cardui entered, but she gestured quickly so that all but one faded immediately.

'Did you catch any of that?' she asked Pyrgus.

'Catch any of what?' Pyrgus replied blankly.

'Well, I don't expect you'll use any information for subversive purposes, deeah. Come sit beside me and we'll make contact with your sister. I expect she'll be glad to hear from you despite her worries.'

Pyrgus slid into the chair beside Madame Cardui and watched as her slim fingers – slim, *young-looking* fingers: she must have had her hands peeled as well – stroked a series of bulbous, organic knobs. The screen remained bright, but blank. Madame Cardui thumbed the red *reset* button, waited for a second then tried again. The screen stayed blank.

'Something wrong?' Pyrgus asked quietly.

'I seem to have lost contact with your sister,' Madame Cardui said, frowning.

'Where were they when you last spoke?'

'Analogue World.' Madame Cardui's fingers were dancing in a complex pattern across the controls. Scenes kept forming and re-forming on the screen, but none stayed more than a fleeting second and none showed either Blue or Henry.

'Oh, yes, you told me . . . Nothing coming in from there?'

'They're not there any more. They can't be – there's no interdimensional stream with their cipher. I'm searching the Realm now, but I shouldn't have to. There should be a simple lock on Blue in this world: automatic discovery – it always works.'

'Are there any circumstances when it doesn't work?'

Madame Cardui turned to look at him. 'Only when the target is dead.'

They looked at one another. After a moment Pyrgus said, 'Maybe you should try locking on to Henry.'

Madame Cardui turned back to the controls without a word. Almost at once a picture began to form on the screen. It stabilised into the standard bird's eye view, then carried out a swooping zoom. Pyrgus leaned forward, his shoulder almost touching that of Madame Cardui. Together they stared at the scene.

'Oh, Gods!' Madame Cardui exclaimed in horror.

Thirty-Two

'Why did you lock us in?' Mella demanded. She had this thing of blushing when she was really upset, which was deeply annoying when you wanted to appear cool and grown-up and sophisticated. Which she definitely wanted to appear now, especially since Aunt Aisling had been treating her like an absolute *child,* making stupid comments that were meant to be reassuring, but were just *stupid* and not even anywhere near what was really going on. Probably.

Companion Ysabeau had changed out of her hooded robe into rather an attractive formal gown. She looked at Mella in mild surprise. 'Security,' she said. 'Aren't you locked in at the Palace?'

'I most certainly am not,' Mella told her sternly.

'I'm afraid it's routine here. Automatic, actually.'

'I'll bet you're not locked in when you go to your room,' Mella said sourly.

'But of course I am, dear.' Ysabeau gave her a beaming smile. 'All of us are in the Table of Seven. It's a standard precaution.'

Precaution against *what?* Against *who?* How could the Haleklinders live like this? Always under lock and key, always on their magical guard against intruders. It was like being in prison. Although perhaps it wasn't *all* the Haleklinders, perhaps it was just their rulers. Mella wasn't certain, but she thought the Table of Seven were fairly new to Haleklind. Hadn't they only come to power last year some time? Or maybe the year before? Perhaps that was it. Perhaps they hadn't got used to ruling yet. That was bound to make them nervous. It must be horrible to start running a country without any training. In the Realm, the Royal Family had held power for centuries. You were brought up to recognise your duty and your destiny. Which made *such* a difference.

Aunt Aisling was smirking in that totally unbearable fashion of hers. She'd been insisting there was a perfectly innocent explanation and now her whole expression said *I told you so*. As if you could actually trust the wizards. Everybody knew they were slippery. Mella made one more try.

'What happens if you want out? What happens if you have to go –' She was about to say, *to the bathroom*, but realised at the last moment there was a magnificent bathroom in their suite and changed it to a feeble, '– somewhere?'

'You simply knock on the door,' Ysabeau told her, as if it was the most obvious thing in the world. 'All security spells are tailored to the protected individual. You are completely in charge at all times.'

'Oh,' Mella said.

'You see?' Aisling chipped in brightly. 'Didn't I tell you there would be a perfectly reasonable explanation?' She turned to Ysabeau with a positively unbearable simper. 'I'm afraid my niece is a little young to understand the finer points of etiquette. So please allow me to express our thanks – on behalf of both of us – for your extraordinary hospitality. Our rooms are an absolute *delight* and the clothes and services you have provided . . . well, I simply can't imagine how I shall cope without them when we leave.'

Ysabeau made a depreciating gesture with her hand. 'The shoes and clothing are a small gift,' she said. 'You must take anything you please when you leave. We shall provide you with filament cases, of course. Now,' she added briskly, 'we have a small State reception and banquet arranged in your honour.' She glanced disapprovingly at Mella. 'Formal dress won't be absolutely necessary, Your Serene Highness, and my colleagues are waiting, so there's no time for you to change in any case. And you must be hungry at this time of day, so perhaps you would like to accompany me . . .' She took Aisling's arm, not Princess Mella's, Mella noticed, probably sensing a kinded spirit. Aisling continued to simper and chat and smarm and behave like a perfect *crawlcroop*, bought off with a few dresses and some shoes that would disappear the moment she got them home: everybody knew *that* trick. Mella hoped Aunt Aisling would be wearing them when they vanished, including the underwear. In public. It would serve her right.

The dining chamber was small and heavily lacquered. Mella found it more gloomy than intimate and all the shiny surfaces made her nauseous. But at least the rest of the Table of Seven had also changed out of their creepy red robes and were managing to look almost normal, or as normal as wizards ever looked. Ysabeau made the formal introductions and at least these were done the way they should be.

'Princess Culmella,' Ysabeau said, 'may I present Companion Oudine . . .' A small, bird-like woman with greying hair surveyed Mella with nasty, glittery eyes.

'. . . Companion Amela . . .' Amela was tall and slender and for some reason chose to dress like a man. She had one of those long, lugubrious faces that reminded Mella of a bloodhound. Her magical head-wear seemed to be short-circuiting, since it occasionally crackled and sparked, but this might just have been a current fashion in Haleklind.

'. . . Companion Marshal Houndstooth . . .' Mella knew he was military even before Ysabeau said his name, would have known he was military even if he hadn't been wearing uniform. She could tell by the short hair and the straight back and the heavy moustache (almost certainly dyed, if Mella was any judge). He'd probably been fit in his younger days, but now he was carrying a paunch that sailed in front of him like a battleship.

'. . . Companion Aubertin . . .' The tall, thin man, who might have been Amela's brother – who might *actually* have been Amela's brother: there was a decided family resemblance now Mella came to notice it – stared at Mella with dead-fish eyes. Mella decided she *really* didn't like Companion Aubertin.

'. . . Companion Naudin . . .' He reminded Mella of one of the gnomish accountants in the Purple Palace: small, fat, balding and very precise. Of all the Companions in the Table of Seven, he was the most oddly dressed. He wore a suit that was a fraction too small for him, but somehow contrived to look extraordinarily neat. The whole impression was of a small boy who'd been dressed by his mother and sent off to school.

'. . . and Companion Senestre.' At last, Mella thought, a wizard who actually looked like a wizard, with his deep-set eyes and goatee beard. She could easily imagine him in flowing robes throwing fireballs in the heat of battle. If he'd been twenty years younger, she might even have fancied him.

'How do you do?' Princess Culmella enquired politely as she shook hands with each Companion. 'How do you do?' they asked her in return. It was all very civilised and hypocritical, but Aunt Aisling seemed to be enjoying the experience when it came to her turn.

With the formalities over, Companion Ysabeau seated herself at the head of the table with Mella on her right and Aisling on her left. She waited until the remaining Companions took their seats, then rang a tiny silver bell. The chimes floated visibly upwards and circled the heads of the diners before rushing explosively from the chamber in all directions. At once, a pair of white gloves floated into the room carrying what proved to be an inexhaustible bottle of wine. Beginning with Mella, they floated round the table filling glasses, then moved back discreetly to hover in a corner. Mella, who wasn't allowed wine at home, took a quick sip and found she still didn't like it very much, although that wasn't going to stop her drinking now she had the chance. Aisling half emptied her glass, closed her eyes and murmured '*Divine!*' The white gloves floated over to refill her.

In the Purple Palace, dinners tended to follow a simple Analogue World pattern – starter, main course, pud, then perhaps tea or coffee substitutes – but that was just to make her father feel at home. Elsewhere in the Faerie Realm, meals were more elaborate: three starters, a small cup of ambrosia, salad leaves with fish, roast game, a boiled vegetable course, then a pause for digestion and a hearty song of thanks, finishing with bread and honey. In Haleklind, it transpired, the wizards followed a different pattern still. Two thimble-sized cups were placed before each diner by uniformed flunkies. In one, Mella discovered drops of silver liquid, in the other, golden, both clearly alchemical distillates. She watched from the corner of her eye to see what Companion Ysabeau would do and discovered the correct procedure was to drink the silver followed by the gold. The silver made her feel instantly replete, while the gold reversed the effect to make her feel ravenous. The few drops of liquid in each cup renewed themselves, she noticed, each time she drank them.

What followed was course after course, alternating sweet with savoury, in portions that were neither particularly generous nor particularly mean. By watching her hostess, Mella soon realised how the meal was to be eaten and the alchemical potions used. If a particular course was too small and left you wanting more, you sipped the silver and felt satisfied. If it proved too big, you sipped the gold and were at once hungry enough to finish it. Taking both potions at once changed your palate in such a way that food you disliked became instantly delicious. There were alchemical subtleties as well – silver followed by gold within three heartbeats made you thirsty, for example – but Mella had discovered only a few of them before Companion Ysabeau distracted her attention.

'Perhaps, Serene Highness,' Ysabeau said casually, 'you might like to tell us how we come to be honoured by this visit from yourself and your illustrious aunt?' She paused for a single heartbeat, then added, 'And how you managed to get here . . . ?'

Mella carefully set aside a forkful of seaweed. It was

an obvious question and one she'd been anticipating: indeed she was surprised it had taken so long. She'd thought hard about it in the interim and could see no reason why she should not tell the truth. Suitably embroidered, of course, to suit the diplomatic niceties. She gave Companion Ysabeau an inscrutable smile.

'It has long been our wish,' she said, deftly employing the royal 'we' that sounded so effective when her mother used it, 'to visit your delightful country and see for ourselves the fruits of your glorious revolution.'

'Indeed?' Ysabeau murmured, equally inscrutably.

'We had not had the opportunity,' Mella went on, 'of arranging an official visit, however.' She took an inadvertent sip of the golden potion and had to fight hard to stop herself savaging the seaweed again. 'So we are delighted to be here now,' she added hurriedly. It was a less satisfying explanation than the one she'd rehearsed, but it would just have to do. She speared the seaweed and forked it liberally into her mouth.

Companion Ysabeau said, 'And your means of entry into our country . . . ?'

Mella sensed she wouldn't get away with fuzzing the answer to this question: the Haleklinders were far too concerned about their security. At the same time, the seaweed was truly delicious. Then she remembered the silver potion, took a sip and the ravenous hunger disappeared at once. She pushed the seaweed to one side, swallowed the remainder of her mouthful and said, 'That was an accident. We portalled here by mistake.' She realised suddenly that the conversation between Ysabeau and herself was now the focus of attention of the entire table.

Ysabeau glanced quickly at her fellow Companions, then back at Mella. 'By mistake?' she asked.

Mella took a deep breath. 'We were using an old transporter that had been set all wrong, but we didn't know that and we didn't know the setting, of course, and my Aunt Aisling was a bit impatient –' She gave her aunt a brief, sideways look that made up for all the *told you so's* Aisling had been inflicting on her, '– and so instead of getting where we wanted to go –' Where *had* Aisling wanted to go? Anywhere in the Faerie Realm, Mella supposed. Anywhere she could get hold of her missing brother, who was now *King Consort*. '– We ended up here.' She treated Ysabeau to a beaming smile. 'We didn't even know where we were when we arrived. But it was so nice to find ourselves in Haleklind.'

Ysabeau's face remained impassive. 'You transported from the Purple Palace?'

Mella could feel the sudden tension in the room, but wasn't quite sure why it was there. Had she said something wrong? If she had, she didn't know what, or what to do about it. No matter how hard she thought, she *still* couldn't see any reason why she shouldn't tell the truth. She shook her head. 'Oh, no – from the Analogue World. My father is human, you know. I was visiting . . .' She hesitated, '. . . visiting my aunt in the Analogue World.' No reason to tell the *whole* truth. Besides, her plans to visit her grandmother were none of their business.

The atmosphere in the room lightened at once in a murmured general burst of conversation. Some of her dinner companions even allowed themselves tight smiles. 'Ah, the *Analogue* World!' Ysabeau exclaimed, as if the words explained everything. She turned to Companion Marshal Houndstooth and said sharply, 'Do we have protections against Analogue portals?'

'We do not,' said Houndstooth, not in the least

intimidated by her tone. 'Since there are no portals in the Analogue World.'

'Or at least so we believed,' put in Companion Naudin. His gaze flitted from Houndstooth to Ysabeau.

'And apparently we were mistaken,' Ysabeau said softly. She turned back to Mella. 'Are there any other transporters in the Analogue World?'

'I don't know. I don't think so,' Mella told her. 'This was a very old one of Daddy's that Aunt Aisling found.'

'And where is it now?'

'In my bedroom,' Mella said. 'But it's broken.' Out of the corner of her eye she saw Companion Aubertin slip quietly from the chamber.

Ysabeau turned to Houndstooth. 'Companion Marshal, we need to install securities against any further intrusion from the Analogue World. And we need to install them at once.'

'Yes, Companion Leader.' Houndstooth nodded.

'Level ten,' Ysabeau said.

'Of course.' Houndstooth nodded again.

'I want you to see to it personally.'

'Indeed, Companion Leader. They shall be in place within the hour.' He began to talk quietly into one of his medals.

Surprisingly, Ysabeau turned back to Mella with a beaming smile. 'I must thank you, Serene Highness, on behalf of the Table of Seven.'

Mella blinked. 'Must you?'

'But of course!' said Ysabeau expansively. 'Your visit – which we so much welcome – has alerted us to a potential flaw in our national security defences.' She leaned forward to tap Mella lightly on the arm. 'Obviously we would never consider you or your charming aunt a threat to our country, but the fact that you found your-selves here, in the very heart of our administration – albeit accidentally, we appreciate – certainly shows that an enemy might have arrived by the same route. An assassin, perhaps, or even, quite frankly, an entire invad-ing army. I know that might seem unlikely to one as young and innocent as yourself, but believe me . . .' She allowed the sentence to trail, then added, 'However, that particular loophole will soon be closed forever and –'

Houndstooth glanced up from his medal. 'Done, Companion Leader.'

'Ah, there, you see: closed already! And all thanks to you, Princess Mella.' Ysabeau's smile vanished abruptly. 'Now,' she said sternly. 'I want you to tell me what you overheard of our discussion in the Council Chamber.'

Mella froze. The question, coming when it did, took her completely by surprise. She had gone a long way to convincing herself the talk of attacking an empire couldn't possibly have meant *the* Empire and had almost managed to put it out of her mind. At least until she got back home where somebody else could worry about it. But now, suddenly, there was something in Ysabeau's tone that told her what she'd overheard was even more important to the Table of Seven than the security breach; and given how paranoid they were about security, that meant very important indeed. This, Mella thought, was no time to keep telling the truth. She needed to lie and lie convincingly, otherwise – her whole instinct told her – she was in a deep well of trouble. She opened her mouth, but before she could speak, Aunt Aisling said loudly, 'Well, I, of course, heard nothing.'

Ysabeau turned slowly towards her. 'Indeed?'

'I was back in the other room upstairs, quite out of earshot. Well, we could hear voices, but not what they were saying. I tried to tell the girl it might be a private meeting, but she's her father's daughter and *quite* headstrong, so ... I want to assure you, I personally heard nothing, nor did she tell me anything she may have heard. Not *anything*.'

Thank you, Aunt Aisling! Mella thought. To Ysabeau she said, 'Actually, I heard very little either. Something about pumpkins, wasn't it? I'm not sure. Honestly, we were so confused about where we were and how we might get back –'

'Pumpkins?' Ysabeau echoed. A twitch of her lips broke into a smile, then a laugh. 'Pumpkins!' she exclaimed again. Her companions joined in so that on the instant the room was filled with laughter.

'No, honestly –' Mella protested. Then, unmistakably, the smell of *lethe* was in her nostrils – heaven knows she'd used it often enough herself to recognise it – and Mella's chair toppled over with a crash as she tried to run from the chamber. But before she reached the door she forgot why she was running, forgot where she was, forgot who she was and certainly forgot everything she had seen or heard since she arrived in Haleklind.

thirty-three

'Don't die, my darling,' Henry whispered. 'My love, please don't die. Oh, Blue . . .' There were tears streaming down his cheeks. He cradled her head in his lap and stroked the long red hair. 'Don't leave me, Blue – I can't live without you.'

He was seated on a rocky apron that formed part of an outcrop rising up out of the Wildmoor Broads like the prow of some tall ship. Blue's body lay sprawled like one who had fallen from the clifftop. (Fallen and *died*, his mind kept insisting.) They were surrounded by a sea of prickleweed that seethed and writhed and reached in their direction, but did not – apparently could not – intrude on the rock.

There was blood by Henry's feet, quite a lot of it. The blood was Henry's own: a strip of flesh was missing from his forearm and there were lesions on his face, legs and hands. Blue exhibited scarcely a scratch, yet Blue was the one who was dead. 'You mustn't,' Henry said emphatically. 'Your subjects need you. I need you. You must not be dead.' Her eyes were open, but blank, staring upwards at a distant sky. There was no gentle rise and fall of her chest, no whisper of breath from her mouth. There was no heartbeat, no pulse.

Henry's mind kept replaying what happened. It was

at once so bizarre and so ordinary and, to start with, so triumphant. The fence-shields had worked. They had worked brilliantly. Chalkhill must have paid for some super-strong spell coating, because the weed could not touch them. It knew Blue and Henry were there. It reached towards them eagerly. But then it recoiled violently while it was still a foot or two away. That was distance magic, the costly kind. At the time, Henry thought it was their passport home.

He should have known better. The Broads had claimed hundreds of lives. If the trick to crossing them was that easy, somebody would have discovered it years ago.

But he hadn't known better and now Blue was dead. He couldn't believe it. He couldn't believe how sudden it had been, how simple it had been. When he saw how the plants were reacting, he'd turned to smile at Blue. He actually remembered saying, '*This is so easy. Now all we need to do is find a road.*' And then Blue said, '*I think I've scratched my hand on something.*'

He was stupid, stupid, *stupid!* He could hardly see the scratch on the back of her hand, it was so tiny. He almost told her not to make a fuss, but then, without warning, she fell. It was a dreadful, spine-chilling fall. Not a trip or a stumble, but a total collapse. Her eyes rolled backwards in her head so that she looked, for just the barest moment, like one of Madame Cardui's zombies, then her knees buckled and she sank in on herself like a squashed paper bag.

Her shield of fencing fell from her hand.

The weed was on her at once. Her back remained protected, but fronds whipped out viciously towards the front of her body and her face and there was not the slightest flicker of expression when they struck her. *She must have been dead already,* Henry thought. But at the time, Henry thought nothing, simply acted. He hurled himself forward with a roar, slashing blindly with his knife. Leaves and stalks flew and the weed, sensing attack, turned in his direction. He could feel the hundred tiny stings as it began to flay skin from his arms and legs. Something gouged his arm and blood began to flow, but he ignored it. Using his shield, he transposed himself between the writhing prickleweed and Blue, then grabbed her arm and heaved her up.

Something in him hoped she might be able to stand, perhaps even walk if he supported her, but she was deadweight. 'Arrrrgh!' Henry screamed and slashed out with his knife again. The creeping weed fell back a little, but then – he could scarcely believe it – circled slowly around them like an animal searching for a weak point to attack. Henry swung Blue's body across his shoulders in a fireman's lift, staggered a little, then planted both feet firmly. His shield protected her legs, the fencing tied to her back protected the rest of her body. He threw himself forward, desperate to get clear of the weed, desperate to find somewhere safe, even temporarily, where he could revive Blue.

After that, it was all a half-remembered nightmare, an ocean of prickleweed, a high forest of prickleweed, moving, scratching, slashing, driven on by desperation, half mad with grief and fear until, abruptly, he emerged by sheer luck on to the rocky apron.

He laid her down gently and stood for a moment, panting. He was aware of his own blood on his face, legs and body. Compared to himself, Blue looked completely uninjured. There was no blood, no swelling, no rash, no discoloration. If he closed her eyes, she would have looked almost peaceful. But he didn't want to close her eyes, because that would mean admitting she was really dead.

'Oh, Blue . . .' he moaned.

There was a sound behind him. Henry twisted, saw nothing, then quickly laid Blue's head gently on the ground and climbed to his feet. For a second he thought the prickleweed might be encroaching on the rock, but while it still surrounded him, it kept its distance. He could see nothing to explain the sound. His guess was a displaced pebble. But what had displaced it? In a less hostile environment he would have assumed a small animal – a rabbit or rat – but no animals survived on the Broads, not in the areas infested by the weed. Any that ventured into prickleweed territory were eaten.

He was about to return to Blue – to Blue's *body* his mind told him savagely: he had to face facts if he was to survive, and he had to survive for Mella's sake – when a movement on the cliff face attracted his attention. Something was crawling out of a dark opening about twenty feet above him. It emerged to cling to the cliff itself, then began slowly to edge its way downwards.

Henry watched, fascinated. The creature had the shape of a man, but was much, much smaller; scarcely larger than a cat, in fact. The thought that it was a monkey passed through his mind, but he dismissed it: he was in the Faerie Realm and there *were* no monkeys in the Faerie Realm. As it drew closer, he realised that the humanoid appearance was, in any case, quite superficial. The little 'man' had no features: no mouth, no nose, no eyes or ears, simply a bulbous ball of a head. The body was incomplete as well. Although there were rudimentary feet and hands, there were no toes or fingers. It was as if somebody had started to carve a human figure from a piece of wood, then left it unfinished. But the figure, a greyish black in colour, could move. And move swiftly. It had already reached the rocky apron and was heading towards him.

It never occurred to Henry he might be in any danger. The creature was too small to do him any harm. But when it headed towards Blue – towards Blue's body – he stepped forward quickly and placed himself directly in its path. The creature stopped. He was not at all clear on how it sensed his presence, but it did. It stood for a moment, head tilted back as if looking up at him with invisible eyes, then moved a cautious pace or two to its right, as if preparing to circle around him. When he moved to block it, the creature scampered left again, then stopped as Henry moved. It was like a child's game. It might even have looked cute if it were not so obviously determined to reach the body of his dead wife.

Henry decided to end the game and made a little dash towards it, hoping to frighten it away. The creature's head exploded.

A choking cloud of spores struck Henry's face, temporarily blinding him and sending him into a paroxysm of coughing. The spores were in his nose, in his mouth, in his eyes, in his ears. For a moment he could do no more than choke and retch, then his vision began to clear. The spores stung sharply where his skin was broken, but as he began to brush them off, he noticed that the gash on his arm was no longer bleeding. He blinked his eyes clear and caught sight of the little creature, headless now, climbing back up the cliff face towards its cave. As his gaze followed it, Henry noticed the sky had turned a luminous green. A nauseous, luminous green.

He felt, quite suddenly, like throwing up. Then the wave of sickness died down and the inside of his mouth turned icy cold.

Henry felt dizzy. The rock on which he stood was no longer firm, but undulated like the back of a great beast, throwing him off balance. For a moment it seemed it really *was* a great beast, but then he was on solid ground again.

The air began to sing. Henry's brother-in-law Pyrgus had once taken him to a simbala parlour and it was a little like that, except that then the music had flowed through the insides of his body while now it surrounded him in an expanding panorama that stretched out to distant horizons. He could see the music as well as hear it, smell it as well as see it. If he had reached out his hand, he might have touched it.

Blue moved.

Henry swung towards her, but she had not woken up, not returned from the dead. Her body was simply floating, drifting a little on the tonal currents of a sea of music. The music clung to her in a black lament.

There were giant birds. At first they were far away, gliding lazily in the distant sky, but soon they circled closer and he saw they were vultures come to feed on Blue. Henry waved his arms and shouted, but one of the birds kept coming, growing larger and larger until it hid the sun, then blacked out the entire sky above his head. He could smell the foetid stench of its breath, the sickly stench of death and decay, as it settled beside Blue, poor Blue.

Then it opened its stomach to lay a great, pale egg. As he stared, the egg emitted a tapping noise, cracked, then shattered. Out of it strode the Road Runner.

Thirty-four

It was nice to get out of the house. Lord Hairstreak stepped down from his gold-plated ouklo shortly after sunrise and stared up at Kremlin Karcist, the Creen citadel and Table of Seven administration centre for the whole of Haleklind. The place looked a lot less flamboyant than he remembered from the days before the revolution. No flags, no pennants, no decorative spells. In their place was a dun-brown military camouflage security coating and a series of stark notices warning about the use of lethal force. The gently winding serpentine of the entrance avenue had been replaced by a dead-straight road, aimed like an arrow at the entrance steps. Fearfully poor feng shui, but so much easier to defend since you could see an approaching enemy some half a mile away. Even the ornamental shrubs and flowerbeds had been rooted out to make way for a series of stark sentry posts. Interestingly, they were manned by heavily armed warrior guards: for all of Haleklind's world-famous reliance on magic, the Seven clearly did not altogether trust automatic spells. Paranoia was a wonderful thing, Lord Hairstreak thought: it made people so very easy to manipulate.

His own military entourage fell into place, four soldiers to secure the ouklo – would never do to have anybody discover what was hidden inside – the rest surrounding Hairstreak himself. He had little practical need of personal protection now he was equipped with a body that might as well have been armour-plated, but the psychological need for an impressive escort remained. It would never be enough that he had financed the Seven's coup, never be enough that he knew all their dirty little secrets. For total control, he needed to cut an impressive figure and that meant putting on a show. Not easy to do when you were confined to your Keep and wheeled round in a barrow. But now he had a whole new body, he could strut his stuff with the best of them; and Mella's capture was the perfect excuse. He smiled a little, took a deep breath and strode towards the steps.

Companion Ysabeau emerged to greet him, flanked by Marshal Houndstooth – a good sign since it suggested the military preparations were well underway. The Marshal saluted smartly, another good sign, but it was Ysabeau who skipped down the steps like a four-year-old, delivered a curtsy and an obsequious smile, then gushed, 'This is such an honour, Lord Hairstreak. I never thought I should have the pleasure of seeing you here in Haleklind, in person.' Her eyes swept over him as lightly as a feather duster. 'And looking so well.'

She couldn't hide her surprise, which pleased Hairstreak enormously. He'd been in two minds about this trip. On the one hand, Ysabeau could easily have transported Mella directly to his Keep and he'd had a long-term policy of maintaining a low profile. On the other hand, times were changing. He had his new body now and the manticore invasion was only days away. He no longer had to hide his connections with Haleklind: even if Cardui discovered the full extent of them, it would give her no clue to what was coming. And this trip had a wonderful cover story: he'd come to negotiate the return of Princess Culmella. What a comeback that would make to the political stage. What a preparation for the *real* comeback to follow.

'Thank you,' he said to Ysabeau, then added sharply, 'I should like to see the Princess immediately.' A part of him still wondered if they really did have Mella. It was beyond him to imagine how – or why – she had found herself in Haleklind. It was not at all beyond him to imagine the Table of Seven had made a mistake and captured some poor deluded child who perhaps *looked* like his great-niece.

'Of course,' Ysabeau nodded. 'We have her ready and waiting for you.' She hesitated. 'There's one thing . . .'

Hairstreak eyed her suspiciously. 'What?'

'We had to wipe her memory. As a precaution, you appreciate.'

'A precaution against what?'

'She overheard our invasion plan: at least she may have.'

Hairstreak frowned. 'How was that possible?' The manticore invasion plan was the most closely guarded secret in the whole of Haleklind. It was incredible that a teenage girl might stumble on it.

Ysabeau set her lips in a firm, hard line. 'That is something we are investigating at the moment. The girl was not alone. It will not be long before we have some answers.'

Hairstreak could well believe it. Haleklind interrogation spells were legendary. The Table of Seven would, quite rightly, be reluctant to apply them to a member of the royal house – they sometimes resulted in death and

often in brain damage – but if she was accompanied . . .
'Who was with her?'

'A woman claiming to be her aunt.'

Hairstreak frowned. He didn't think Mella had any aunts. 'Has her interrogation begun?'

'Not yet, but –'

'Take no action until I see her.' For all their skills, he trusted no interrogation methods but his own and preferred to apply them to someone who was neither brain damaged nor a corpse.

'As you wish, Lord Hairstreak, but –'

'That is as I wish,' he said, cutting her short again. He and Ysabeau had briefly been lovers before he financed her revolution, a tricky arrangement when one's body was a featureless cube. She had talked too much even then.

'Yes, of course,' she said, a little sulkily.

He decided to leave any further details for later. For now, his priority was to make sure they had the right girl. 'Very well,' he said tightly. 'Now, take me to the Princess.'

The interior of Kremlin Karcist was even more depressing than its new façade. The building had been a Grand Palace – a Winter Palace he believed – for the long line of Staretz Tsars who had once ruled Haleklind. The family specialised in high spirit contact and had a tradition of excellent artistic taste, so that the place had once been a veritable showcase of master paintings, stunning sculptures and magical installations that reached out to touch your very soul with their sheer and delicate beauty. All gone now. Rooted out to make way for featureless but functional corridors with automatic security checks every twenty yards. He sighed, inwardly. Perhaps it had been a mistake to back the Table of Seven's revolution, however successful it had been. But once the invasion was completed and he had direct control of both Haleklind *and* the Realm, he might remedy that. The Seven were useful enough at the moment, but they were essentially small fry, too unstable in their paranoia to hold power indefinitely. Once he became Supreme Ruler – once he *openly* became Supreme Ruler – he could execute the lot of them and replace them with interior designers. That would perk the palace up a bit, if nothing else.

A hidden security check emitted a delicate *peep* to indicate he was unarmed (as if he needed weapons now he had his super-body) and Ysabeau stopped before a doorway flanked by two dour guards. 'The Princess is inside,' she said. 'I take it you will wish to interrogate her?'

Interrogate. It was the way these people thought. All he really wanted to do was make sure it really was the Princess Mella in there, then get her out of the Kremlin so he could set the remainder of his plans in motion. But he only nodded. 'Yes.'

Ysabeau looked at him soberly. 'Alone, or would you prefer one or more guards to accompany you for your protection?'

Hairstreak almost laughed aloud. Even when he was only a head on a cube, he hardly needed much protection from a fifteen-year-old girl. He kept his face straight with an effort. 'Alone.'

Ysabeau looked stricken. 'Are you sure, Lord Hairstreak? I mean . . .' She tailed off under his withering stare. 'Of course, Lord Hairstreak.'

The girl in the room was Mella, all right. He knew it even as he closed the door behind him: he'd spent more than enough time in her company to be certain. She looked fit and healthy, despite whatever adventures she might have had with the Haleklinders, but there was a curious hint of blankness in her eyes. Ysabeau had had her confined in a small room, not exactly a cell, but certainly a sparsely furnished chamber with a single window too high up in one wall to provide an escape route. The guards outside the door completed the picture: no longer Princess Mella, but Prisoner Mella. Ah, well, no one had got her into this mess except herself.

She was seated on an uncomfortable little chair and did not bother to rise when he came in. 'Who are you?' she demanded in that sharp, feisty tone he admired so much.

There was no reason at all to lie to her. 'I am your uncle, Lord Hairstreak.'

'I don't remember you.'

Hairstreak leaned his back against the door and looked down at her. 'That's because you have had your memory removed using a *lethe* spell. Do you know who you are?'

The blankness in her eyes was replaced by a look of uncertainty. 'I'm not sure,' she mumbled.

'Don't worry about it. *Lethe* is only a problem if you don't know about it. Once I get you home, I can have the crystals removed quite easily. After that, you'll remember everything perfectly.' Actually, he wasn't altogether sure of that. Conventional *lethe* was easy enough to remove if one had the fee for an elemental physician, but the wizards might well have used one of their secret, military-grade spells that could prove far more tricky. Not that it mattered. *Lethe* was hardly going to interfere with his plans.

'We're going home?' she asked quickly. It was an interesting response. Most people would have demanded more details about their identity and the methods of restoring their memories.

'Yes.'

Now she stood up. 'When?' Memory or no memory, she was still the little princess. Almost a shame what had to happen to her.

'Soon,' Hairstreak promised. He stared at her soberly. 'There was someone with you when you arrived in Haleklind. Your aunt?'

'I don't remember.'

'There was,' Hairstreak insisted. 'I plan to talk to her now, after which I shall take you home.'

'And fix my memory?' Mella asked.

Hairstreak nodded. 'And fix your memory.' He reached behind to tap sharply on the door.

Ysabeau was still waiting outside. 'Is this woman with Princess Mella really her aunt?' he asked her.

'She *claims* to be the sister of King Consort Henry.'

The emphasis laid on *claims* might mean doubt, or could just indicate caution. Hairstreak frowned. 'I didn't know Henry had a sister. At least not in the Faerie Realm.'

'The Princess confirmed it. While she still had her memory.'

'Does this creature have a name? I assume she's human?'

'She is definitely human. The name she gave us was the Lady Aisling.' Ysabeau hesitated, then added, 'She seems . . . self-assured.'

'Do you mean self-centred?' He glanced directly at

Ysabeau and caught her checking out his new body. It was an interesting development. He was well aware that their brief affair when he was a cube had been entirely prompted on Ysabeau's part by her desire to curry favour and extract some of his money for her cause. Now, her look said there was actual desire. Well, perhaps, when he had a little more time . . . It would be intriguing to experience the differences.

Ysabeau glanced away quickly, flushing a little. 'Yes,' she said. 'I think I do mean self-centred.'

'I shall see her now,' Hairstreak said. Then, anticipating her next question, 'For interrogation.'

'Do you require spell cones?'

Hairstreak shook his head. 'I shall be using . . .' He blinked slowly, like a lizard, '. . . my own methods.'

Ysabeau licked her lips. 'May I watch?' she asked, a little breathlessly.

For the first time, Hairstreak favoured her with a smile. 'Why, of course, my dear,' he said.

The 'Lady Aisling', it transpired, had been no better treated than her niece (if indeed Mella *was* her niece.) Her door, like Mella's, was under guard. Hairstreak turned to Ysabeau. 'I shall need a little while alone with her. After that, I shall call for you to join me.' Fun and games with Ysabeau would have to take second place to his own interests. Whatever information he extracted from Mella's mysterious companion, he wanted to keep it to himself – at least for the moment. You never knew in advance what was useful and what wasn't, what needed to be kept secret and what didn't.

He pushed the door and strode into the room.

It was as if a thunderbolt had hit him.

thirty-five

'What's the matter with him?' Brimstone asked curiously. Even George was staring.

'*Meep, meep!*' Henry said. His legs were pumping furiously, but since he was lying on his side they weren't carrying him very far, although the motion did encourage him to move in a slow circle. There were strange pink lights in his eyes that spun in random spirals.

'Looks like a Border Redcap got him,' Chalkhill muttered. He was knelt beside the still body of Queen Holly Blue, his hands unusually gentle as he checked her pulse spots. He glanced back at Brimstone, caught his blank expression and added, 'They're a sentient fungus – you only ever find them in the Broads. Their spores induce hallucinations.'

'Have at you, Coyote!' Henry shouted suddenly.

'What do you think he's hallucinating?' Brimstone stepped back quickly as one of Henry's flailing feet came close to his leg.

'Something from his childhood,' Chalkhill ventured. 'It's often something like that. Something he saw or read in a book. He's a human so it's bound to be bizarre. Listen, Silas, I need your help.'

'He looks as if he's running,' Brimstone said. 'If he wasn't lying down, he'd be halfway to Yammeth Cretch by now.'

'*Whoosh!*' Henry said.

There was an answering rumble from somewhere high above them. Brimstone looked up. Although his eyes weren't what they used to be, even with his enhanced senses, he could make out distant shapes that might well have been personal flyers. He wondered vaguely if Chalkhill's souped-up ouklo could outrun them.

'Silas,' Chalkhill snapped, more sharply this time, 'get over here and help me put her in the recovery position.'

'Recovery from what – she's dead, isn't she?'

'*Meep, meep*, eeee-yah!' Henry murmured, waving both arms about in the manner of someone falling off a cliff. '*Thud!*' he said and lay still. Then he looked up wide-eyed, grimaced and jerked as if an anvil had fallen on his head. But his movements were growing less violent and there was a dopey expression on his face as if he was sliding into sleep.

Chalkhill nodded thoughtfully. 'Stung by the weed, I'm afraid. That's what prickleweed does for you.'

Brimstone wondered whether he should alert Chalkhill to the approaching flyers, but curiosity got the better of him. 'Doesn't that mean she's dead?' he asked. 'She looks dead to me.'

'She's dead, all right. But help me get her into the recovery position anyway. We need to be able to tell Hairstreak we did everything possible before admitting she snuffed it.'

'I think it might be better if you got her into the ouklo,' Brimstone said. 'We're about to have company.'

Chalkhill followed his gaze. 'You stupid old tort, why didn't you tell me?' He stood up as the first flyer circled for a landing. 'OK, don't panic. Nobody knows we kidnapped them and they're in no position to snitch about it. The story is we were flying to the city when we spotted them down below and landed to see if we could help.'

Brimstone smiled at him benignly. 'Oh, I'm not panicking, Jasper. It's not in my nature.' Besides, George could handle any trouble that might arise.

The flyer set down a short distance from their ouklo and an attractive young woman climbed out. 'Thank Gods you're here!' exclaimed Chalkhill loudly. 'We have no idea how these unfortunate people come to be in such dire straits, but they seem to have suffered some sort of an accident through no fault of ours and we landed in the hope that we might be of some assistance and now it appears they might be the very persons of Her Imperial Majesty our gracious Queen Blue and her honoured Consort Henry and – good grief, it's you!'

With his heightened perception, Brimstone had spotted Madame Cardui at once, even though the old bat had obviously undergone a head peel. He smothered a snigger. This was going to be interesting. Chalkhill was terrified of Cardui, and with good reason. He'd once betrayed her while he was working as a double agent. Now he'd kidnapped the Queen. So their enmity was both political *and* personal.

Cardui ignored Chalkhill and signalled to three further flyers circling overhead. Within moments, the entire rocky apron was swarming with Imperial troops, while Chalkhill continued to babble. 'Saw them from the air . . . our duty as citizens . . . no idea it was our majestic Queen and King . . . everything we could do to help . . . afraid the Queen . . . actions probably saved *his* life . . .'

'Don't suppose there might be a reward?' called Brimstone as the motionless body of the Queen and the far-from-motionless body of her raving – *meep, meep* – Consort were loaded on to Cardui's flyer. 'Few goldies for two loyal citizens who took time out to help the royals in distress?

Madame Cardui gave him a withering look. 'I must obviously get Their Majesties to a healer as quickly as possible,' she said quietly, 'but I shall investigate this incident thoroughly and should it come to light that either of you had anything, anything *whatsoever,* to do with their condition, I shall hunt you down and I shall catch you and I shall punish you. Personally. Severely. Do we understand one another?'

'Madame Cardui,' spluttered Chalkhill, 'I can assure you we had absolutely nothing, nothing *whatsoever,* to do with –'

But she was already climbing into the flyer. She ignored Chalkhill, signalled to her escort troops and all four craft took off in good order. Chalkhill glared at Brimstone. 'Another fine mess you've got me into,' he said.

Thirty-Six

Henry opened his eyes. There was someone bending over him and as the face swam into focus, he realised it was Pyrgus. 'Blue?' Henry whispered. There was a young woman standing behind Pyrgus, but she wasn't Blue.

'She's fine,' Pyrgus said. 'She's going to be fine.'

'Which is it?' Henry croaked. The inside of his mouth was cold, his tongue felt twice its normal size and his throat was parched.

Pyrgus repeated, 'She's going to be fine.'

Henry struggled to sit up. 'She was dead. Did someone do a resurrection?' He felt suddenly chill. Resurrection spells were a very recent development and not always successful. Sometimes they left the person brain damaged.

'She wasn't dead,' Pyrgus insisted.

'Tell me the truth, Pyrgus,' Henry said tiredly. 'I know she died out there on the Broads. The prickleweed got her.'

But Pyrgus grinned at him. 'Prickleweed toxin has an effect almost identical to a stasis spell. Everything stops, including your personal time field. If the weed doesn't eat you, you're usually fine once it wears off. She's still in bed recovering, but her death was strictly temporary. Had us worried for a while, though.'

The young woman – Henry suddenly realised it was

Madame Cardui with her head peeled – said, 'She's had treatment, deeah. The healers tell me she's now sleeping normally.'

'I want to see her,' Henry said.

'Yes, of course: as soon as she wakes up. But the healers haven't given us clearance on you yet.'

'I'm fine,' Henry told him stolidly. 'I'm in rude good health.' Then curiosity got the better of him and he added, 'What happened to me?'

'Border Redcap attack. The spores produce a state of temporary insanity.' Pyrgus grinned at him. 'I'm surprised anybody noticed.'

This was the old, jokey Pyrgus. For the first time, it struck Henry that everything actually *was* fine. 'Is Blue really all right?'

'She just needs rest; and so, apparently, do you. There may be some minor flashbacks, but they've flushed most of the spores out of your system. Although . . .' He hesitated, then went on, '. . . if you're feeling up to it, there's something we need to discuss with you.'

'I'm feeling up to it.' Henry started to climb out of bed, but Pyrgus placed a hand on his shoulder to restrain him.

'We should really be talking to Blue,' Pyrgus said, 'but the healers say it's best not to wake her yet, and there's a certain urgency about the situation . . .'

'Is it Mella?' Henry asked, suddenly remembering.

'Mella's part of it, deeah.' Madame Cardui pulled a chair to his bedside and sat down. 'But not the only part.'

'Is she still missing?'

'I'm afraid so, deeah, but at least now we know where she is.'

'Where?' Henry demanded. When she got back, she'd

be grounded for a month. Six months, if he had any-thing to do with it.

Pyrgus said, 'She's in Haleklind.'

Henry stared at him blankly. 'What's she doing in Haleklind?'

'Being held by the Table of Seven, apparently,' Pyrgus said.

'Being held by the Table of –?' Henry made another attempt to get out of bed and this time Pyrgus let him. Madame Cardui handed him a dressing gown. As he pulled it on, Henry said, 'The last thing Blue and I knew for sure was that she was in the Analogue World. She had a mad notion to visit my mother, then somehow managed to blow up her house. We thought she'd prob-ably come back to the Realm, but why Haleklind? And what do you mean, *being held by the Table of Seven*? She's their guest?'

'Or their prisoner,' Madame Cardui said quietly.

Henry looked from one to the other. 'Back up a little. What did she do in Haleklind that made them throw her into prison?' His daughter was nearly as wild as her mother, but this was *way* beyond anything he'd have expected.

'That's the whole point, Henry,' Madame Cardui said. 'So far as we can gather, she did nothing. The motivation appears to be political.'

'Political? How political? Why political? Haleklind's a friendly country. Bit paranoid, but we're not at war with them or anything.'

'Yet,' Pyrgus said.

Henry ignored him. 'OK, why do they *say* they're holding her? You must have had our ambassador ask them.'

'They're claiming no knowledge of her whatsoever, denying the whole thing.'

'So we think they have her and they say they haven't?'

'That's about the size of it.'

'We'll soon know the truth of it,' Madame Cardui chipped in. 'There's a sleeper in the ruling council. I'm expecting clarification from him soon.'

'There's something else,' said Pyrgus.

His tone seized Henry's attention. 'Go on.'

'We think Haleklind may be preparing for war.'

Henry frowned. 'Who with?'

'I'm afraid it's with us, deeah,' Madame Cardui told him.

Henry looked from one to the other with the expression of one who wonders if he's missed a joke. 'They can't go to war with us,' he said at last. 'They don't have the manpower.' Haleklind was an important country – and a wealthy one – because of its age-old speciality in magic. But while it had an extensive geographical spread, it was grossly under-populated. It had a well-trained standing army, but nothing to match the Empire forces. A thought suddenly occurred to him. 'They haven't developed a magical super-weapon, have they?' He was thinking of something like an H-bomb. The Faerie Realm was mercifully free from atomic weapons, but the wizards were quite capable of coming up with something just as nasty. Next to consumer magic, Haleklind's second largest source of national income was its weapons industry. So far the wizards had concentrated on improving traditional armaments – bows that fired themselves, heat-seeking spears, clubs that struck with giant strength – but sooner or later they were bound to start thinking of weapons of mass destruction.

'They have in a manner of speaking,' Pyrgus told him soberly. 'They're breeding manticores.'

'Manticores?' Henry echoed.

Pyrgus nodded. 'Yes.'

Henry said, 'They've been messing about with manticores for years now, haven't they? I keep reading news reports that they've built another one in their laboratories. Actually, I don't *keep* reading them: I suppose I've seen a couple in the past five years. That's the trouble, isn't it? Manticores are very scary creatures, but it takes you a couple of years to build one, so they're hardly a threat to national security.'

'I didn't say *build*, I said *breed*.'

'But that's impossible. Breeding manticores is impossible.'

'Apparently not,' Pyrgus said. 'They have herds of them now.'

'*Herds?*' Henry looked at Madame Cardui. 'Did we know about this?'

For the first time since he'd known her, Madame Cardui flushed a little. 'We did not.'

'Why not?'

'Partly because this has been a very recent development, but frankly also because Haleklind has never been a priority for our security services. Nor have manticores, come to that. The bottom line is we never considered them a serious threat.'

'So what's the Haleklind plan? Do we know?'

'Not in any detail yet. But we can speculate about the broad outline.'

'So speculate,' Henry told her.

But it was Pyrgus who butted in. 'Do you know much about manticores, Henry?'

'Big, scary, magical animals. Body of a lion, tail of a

scorpion, head of a man, three rows of teeth, like a shark. In my world they're considered mythical. Actually they're considered impossible. In my world unicorns are considered mythical, but you could imagine breeding one out of a horse. Nobody could imagine breeding a manticore.'

'The wizards imagined it,' said Pyrgus sourly. 'Actually, I like manticores. They're intelligent, but they don't think the way we do. The tail makes them poisonous: if they sting you, you're dead. The lion body and shark's teeth make them fearsome fighters – hand-to-hand combat with a manticore hardly bears thinking about. They can kill a horse with one blow, behead an armoured man much the same way. The one I had ate its way through a solid wall. The –'

'You had a manticore?' Henry interrupted.

'Used to,' Pyrgus said enthusiastically. 'I called her *Henry* after you. But she broke out and made her way back to Haleklind. Actually, that was how we discovered what the wizards were up to. I followed her to Halek—'

'You called a *manticore* after me?' Henry asked, appalled. 'A female manticore?'

'She had a human head,' Pyrgus said.

'Now, deeahs,' Madame Cardui put in, 'perhaps we should stick to the point at hand.'

'Yes, stick to the point at hand, Pyrgus,' Henry growled.

'The point is,' Pyrgus said, 'the Haleklind wizards have created manticores and now they're breeding them. My contacts in the Haleklind Society for the Preservation and Protection of Animals tell me they're modified manticores –'

'What's a modified manticore?' Henry demanded.

'Changed from what they are in the wild.'

Henry stared at him. 'There *aren't* any manticores in the wild. The wizards had to create them in the laboratory – you just told me.'

'All right,' Pyrgus said impatiently, 'modified when you compare them to the legends and myths about manticores in the wild, if you want to be pedantic. And I think there actually *are* some in the wild, if we could only find them. Nymph says –'

'We are in a crisis situation,' Madame Cardui interrupted firmly. 'Please let us stick to the point.'

Pyrgus glared at Henry. 'The point is the Haleklinders have manticores that are spell protected – terribly difficult to kill. They have manticores that fight like demons – better than demons; far better than demons. They have manticores that are spell-bound to obey orders and have no fear of anything. They have manticores who are just as smart as you and I are in a fight: smarter in some respects because they think differently to the way we do and that makes them creative. They have thousands of them and they're breeding more all the time. Can you imagine what sort of army that makes?'

Henry could imagine it all too easily. 'We need to wake up Blue,' he said.

'No need – I'm awake now,' said Blue's voice from the doorway.

Thirty-Seven

'Where are we?' Brimstone asked. He knew perfectly well where they were. They were lost, that's where they were. They were walking – creeping really – beneath a leafy canopy that filtered out the best part of the sunlight, leaving only a green gloom. The path they'd been following had long since become a track then petered out altogether, leaving grass and undergrowth beneath their feet. Around them, the forest stretched endlessly in all directions.

Chalkhill grunted.

Brimstone was not particularly worried: he trusted George to get him out of most tricky situations. But at the same time he was beginning to think it might be time he parted company with Chalkhill. The man had been useful in springing him from the lunatic asylum and for a while there he looked as if he might have some interesting plans – an assignment to kidnap the Princess had to be a nice little earner. But in true Chalkhill style, he'd already begun to cock things up. Not only had he annoyed Lord Hairstreak, but he'd managed to kill off the Queen, send the King Consort barmy and arouse some deep suspicions in the mind of the Head of State Security. Worse still, he'd implicated Brimstone in the mess. In the circumstances, it was difficult to see what Brimstone might get out of their old partnership. Perhaps best just to slit his throat and steal his purse, then make his way back to the capital, lie low for a bit and set up a little business with the money once the fuss died down.

The only thing that made him hesitate was that Chalkhill had used a concealment spell on the ouklo when they abandoned it and Brimstone had no idea how long it would take him to reach the capital on foot. He wondered vaguely if George could carry him.

Brimstone expanded his consciousness to see if that would help. There was an incredible amount of life in the forest – his old enemies the cockroaches were there, lurking and waiting, as were termite colonies and insects of every description, each and every one carrying its own unique threat. (If he hadn't had George for protection, they'd certainly have eaten him by now.) There were wolves and badgers and sliths and haniels, not to mention militant diseases and those dead things that ate dried leaves and faerie meat. The place was crawling with them.

'Where are we?' he repeated.

'Where are we?' Chalkhill mimicked crossly. 'Where are we? Where are we? We're in an assassin's tunnel so we can get through the magical defences.'

What magical defences? Whose magical defences? Brimstone thought. Aloud he said, 'What's an assassin's tunnel?'

'An assassin's tunnel,' Chalkhill said with heavy patience, 'is a knot in spacetime established by the Assassin's Guild that allows its members secret access to every country in the Realm. Everybody knows that.'

Everybody doesn't, Brimstone thought vaguely. This

must be a new development since they'd locked him away in the Double Luck. So many technical advances: it was positively bewildering. To keep the conversation going before Chalkhill lapsed back into gruntspeak he asked, 'So we're walking through a knot in spacetime?'

'Yes.'

'Put there by the Assassin's Guild?'

'Yes.'

'It doesn't feel any different.'

'How would you know what walking through a knot in spacetime felt like, you old fool?' Chalkhill muttered, quite audibly as it happened, given Brimstone's expanded senses.

'Where are we going?' Brimstone asked.

'Haleklind,' Chalkhill told him shortly. 'The tunnel means we skirt their magical defences.'

Brimstone opened his mouth to ask another question, then closed it again. Haleklind was probably the best place they could go. Haleklind was a country independent of the Realm and while theoretically the two were on friendly enough terms, there was no extradition treaty between the two, unless that was something else had changed. So even if Madame Cardui discovered Chalkhill had been ultimately responsible for the death of Queen Blue and King Consort Henry's madness, there was nothing she could do about it legally. She'd probably have him quietly bumped off, of course, but she'd never bother with Brimstone himself, who'd only played a small part in the whole affair. Well, smallish. Or not the major part, anyway; and besides he could always plead insanity. It would still be prudent to lie low for a time, but far more prudent to lie low in Haleklind rather than the capital.

The thing to do, Brimstone thought, was to follow this mysterious 'assassin's tunnel', which, in practice, meant following Chalkhill. Once they reached *Haleklind*, he could slit his throat and steal his purse. Actually, Haleklind would be an even better place to set up a little business. They didn't have any stupid regulations about black magic and with his previous experience as a demonologist, he could certainly manufacture some very interesting spells. The whole magical industry was very sophisticated in Haleklind. He wouldn't even have to open up a shop: he could wholesale the cones direct to a distributor and saturate the nation within months. Might even make him rich.

'Keep close,' he said to George.

'Pardon?' Chalkhill asked.

'Just clearing my throat,' said Brimstone.

Whatever he knew or didn't know about it, walking through a knot in spacetime didn't feel much different to walking through a normal forest. There were the same trees, the same undergrowth, the same bushes, the same plants, the same flowers, berries, nuts and fruits along with the occasional sight or sound of some animal. But after a while Brimstone did start to sense the strangeness. Although there was no noticeable path, they somehow managed to keep moving. Trees and bushes blocked their way, yet they somehow managed to avoid them. His expanded senses told him that the whole place teemed with life, yet somehow nothing managed to attack them. There was an oddness about the sounds as well. Birdsong echoed creepily. The rustle of a passing beast hung in the air long after the movement had gone.

Then suddenly it stopped. There was a path beneath their feet again and the sighing on the wind sounded just like the sighing of the wind should sound. They walked another hundred yards before emerging from the trees on to an open plain.

'Is this Haleklind?' Brimstone asked. He sniffed the air for any scent of magic, but there was only the distant tang of manure.

'Yes.'

'I thought we'd be in a city. Creen or somewhere.'

Chalkhill sighed. 'You can't have an assassin's tunnel opening into an urban complex – far too noticeable. Creen is about a day's march away if we can't steal some transport. But we're inside the magical border checks and I have forged papers for the two of us that will see us through the rest.' He shouldered his backpack. 'Come on.'

Brimstone hesitated. 'What are those?' he asked.

Chalkhill followed his gaze. 'What are what?'

With his expanded senses, Brimstone could see a herd of creatures grazing close to the horizon. They might have been cattle, except he knew they weren't. The trouble was, he couldn't make out exactly what they *were*. His perception kept sliding off them, slipping sideways as if he were trying to grasp a heavily greased pig. That meant only one thing: the creatures were magical. But he'd never heard of a magical creature that went about in herds; and certainly not in herds this size – it was vast. Brimstone pointed. 'Over there,' he said. 'Near the little copse.'

'Oxen,' Chalkhill told him promptly. 'Farmer must have turned them out to graze.'

Brimstone was frowning. 'Those aren't oxen.' The distance made it difficult to judge, but he thought they might be bigger than oxen. Maybe even a *lot* bigger. What he was sure of, absolutely sure of, was that the herd had spotted them. The animals had begun to move in their direction.

'Cows, then,' Chalkhill said. 'Doesn't matter. They won't bother us if we don't bother them. Now come on – we haven't got all day.' He turned and began to walk off briskly westwards.

Brimstone hesitated. Chalkhill couldn't hear it yet, but there was a rumble like muffled thunder building up from the direction of the herd. It was the most ominous sound Brimstone had ever heard. The beasts were about to bother them, whatever Chalkhill believed. The rumble was the sound of a rolling stampede.

Chalkhill stopped and turned. 'Are you coming?' he shouted impatiently.

They had no chance on the open plain. The creatures were already moving fast. Even if they were only cattle, they'd flatten anything that got in their path. But the sound they made was not the sound of hooves, unless the hooves were padded. Brimstone was certain now they weren't cattle: they were some sort of magical monster. They were huge and the herd seemed to stretch for miles. Their only chance, his and Chalkhill's, was to get back to the forest, maybe even get back into the assassin's tunnel. But when he glanced behind him, they seemed to have wandered further from the forest than he'd realised.

'What's that noise?' Chalkhill asked abruptly. 'You don't think it's going to rain?'

Brimstone closed down his expanded senses, but even without them he could see the herd now, hear the approaching rumble Chalkhill had mistaken for thunder. They were coming at an incredible speed. 'Look!' He pointed again.

'Oh my Gods!' Chalkhill gasped.

The herd was filling the whole horizon, bearing down on them with the inexorable inevitability of an army of ants. And like ants, there was something insectile about them. Every second brought them closer and now Brimstone could make out the waving stings that served for tails. The smell of the creatures preceded them, carried by a sweeping wind. It was a hot, magical smell. A sudden, deathly terror gripped Brimstone's abdomen.

'Manticores!' he gasped. It was impossible, yet he was watching them approach with his own eyes. He could see their faces now, their glowing eyes. They only had one chance. 'We have to get back to the forest!'

Chalkhill was already running, abandoning his old partner to his fate. He was a younger, fitter man than Brimstone, but even so, his chances of escape seemed nil. The herd was almost upon them now. Brimstone allowed himself the smallest of chill smiles. He might have rescued Chalkhill if Chalkhill had played fair, but Chalkhill had chosen to make it every man for himself. Which was A-OK with Brimstone.

'George,' he called imperiously. 'Carry me to the forest at once. Just me. Not Chalkhill.'

To his surprise, nothing happened. The manticores bearing down on them were gigantic. He looked around desperately for George. But George, the great, hulking, invisible idiot, was gambolling delightedly to meet the manticores, a big cheese-eating grin pasted wide across his face. And now, Brimstone realised, it was all too late. Whatever about George, the herd was upon him.

Thirty-Eight

Lord Hairstreak had heard of the phenomenon, all right. It had been whispered about in the playground while he was still a child as one of the most amazing things that could happen to a boy. According to the stories, it always came out of the blue when you least expected it. It changed your life because it changed *you*. It turned you into a simpering, whimpering, well-washed, over-dressed, mouth-dribbling, verse-scribbling, soppy, floppy, stupidly happy, fun-loving factotum in the service of . . .

Well, it could be anybody, of course, but the play-ground consensus was it was most likely to be a *girlie* with whom you would become so instantly enamoured that you would be prepared to *kiss her bum!* There were gasps at this revelation, sniggers too, and expressions of doubt or disgust from the more squeamish. Young Hairstreak was not among them, for even at the age of six he was aware depravity knew little bounds. All the same, he could never imagine bottom kissing would ever appeal to *him*.

The phenomenon was called *the thunderbolt* because of its likeness to a weapon once used by the Old Gods to punish – actually to obliterate – recalcitrant faeries. The original thunderbolt, according to the children's tales, was always unexpected, always amazing and always absolute in its effects.

The thunderbolt once again became a topic of serious conversation when the young Hairstreak reached adolescence. By now the emphasis had moved on to the interesting myth that the thunderbolt never struck just once. If it happened to you, it invariably and automatically struck the focus of your affection as well. With hormones racing through the bloodstream, this was an important, even vital, point. Aroused young men no longer thought what they might be called on to do for the girl of their dreams, but rather what the girl of their dreams *might do for them* . . . and bottom kissing was the least of it.

When called to university, Hairstreak discovered the self-styled Thunderbolt Club, a student organisation devoted to researching the phenomenon. He joined out of curiosity and was only mildly disappointed to discover the society had a strictly academic emphasis and was generally concerned with the thunderbolt as a belief system. At its meetings, speakers presented learned papers tracing the roots of the belief to prehistoric times. One particularly clever young man suggested that the term 'thunderbolt', with its undercurrent of violence, might actually derive from the prehistoric practice of clubbing faerie women into submission. When a terminally bored Hairstreak polled his fellow members about whether they believed the thunderbolt phenomenon, as described in the myths, might actually exist, the No camp achieved a solid ninety-six per cent. He was far from disappointed. Even as a boy he had decided the thunderbolt fell into the same category as the Reindeer King of Crippenmass or the Tooth Human.

And now, to his astonishment and consternation, the thunderbolt had struck him.

Despite wearing what was clearly faerie clothing, the woman in the room was human – he could see that at a glance: she had unfashionably short hair, for one thing, without a hint of reddish highlight, and her eyes lacked any characteristic of either Faeries of the Night or Faeries of the Light. He could see too that she was genuinely Henry's sister. The family resemblance was definite, if understated, and fortunately she lacked the weaker characteristics of his great-niece's King Consort. There was determination in her jaw, steel in her gaze, a subtle cruelty about her lips. He could imagine her rending her partner after mating, as humans did. Or was that spiders? In any case, the thought excited him.

Hairstreak swallowed and licked lips that had suddenly gone dry. He took a step forward, then stopped. She was staring at him in amazed adoration. *The thunderbolt never strikes once!* Oh, joy! Oh, bliss! Oh, frabjous day! With every ticking second she looked more beautiful, more glorious, more *delicious* than the last. She looked cunning and ruthless and brutal and strong – all the qualities he had always searched for in a woman, yet never seemed to find. For once the Gods were definitely with him. Had this incredible meeting occurred as little as a month ago, life would have been an unmitigated disaster. How could she have coped with his wheelbarrow and his cube? How could *he* have coped?

A thought struck him. Was the passion he felt an aspect of the thunderbolt or a feature of his remarkable new body? Certainly his whole body seemed electrified now, far beyond even the elation he'd felt following the initial transplant. Did it matter which was the chicken and which the egg? On reflection, he didn't think so.

The woman took a step towards him. She was the most beautiful creature he had ever seen, surpassing even the silk mistresses who were renowned throughout the Realm as examples of feminine perfection. Her eyes had locked on his and there was a single, delightful bead of sweat above her brow. The expression on her face was one of hunger. Her voice was throaty as she gasped, 'Who . . . who are you?'

For some reason his own voice locked – or was it actually his brain? He found it suddenly impossible to answer the simple question. *I am Lord Hairstreak . . .* impressive, of course, but far too formal. What was needed was warmth, intimacy, hints of future wonders and delights. *I am Black . . .* but she might not recognise it as a given name, might think it a colour, might grow confused. *I am Blackie . . .* the Duke of Burgundy had called him that, in the days when they were bosom friends, but it was more a military comrade thing. Divorced from the military context, it made him sound like a terrier. Besides, a first-name salutation gave no hint of his status and he knew, instinctively, she was a woman to whom status was important. *I am Lord Black?* Just as bad, in its own way, as *I am Lord Hairstreak.* Could he say *I am Lord Black Hairstreak,* inviting intimacy while trumpeting his own importance? Or was that too pretentious? His mind began to spin out of control. How about a pseudonym? *I am Bron Fane . . .* that sounded suitably romantic, but it wasn't a faerie name, so she might think he was concealing something. *I am Papilio Cresphontes . . .* a genuine faerie name to be sure, but unfamiliar and a little working class. Besides, how could he possibly explain it was not his own name when the time came to reveal he was, in fact, Lord Hairstreak?

Suddenly he was back in his kindergarten playground listening to his friend Rubidus joyfully explaining that the thunderbolt left you simpering, whimpering, soppy and floppy with brains so soft they oozed out of your ears. It was happening! It was happening to him now! His mouth was opening and closing like a grounded fish; and emitting just as little noise. Yet the woman, this beautiful, adorable, perfectly delightful woman was looking at him as if he was a god.

Lord Hairstreak found his voice at last. 'I am your future, Lady Aisling,' he told her firmly.

Thirty-Nine

They did what they often did in times of crisis: went into private conference in the high-security conservatory Blue's father had built behind the Throne Room. Henry went at once to pull out the Charaxes ark from underneath one of the benches.

'He's not going to like this,' Blue murmured.

'It's an emergency,' Henry told her firmly. 'He'll just have to lump it.'

The Charaxes ark was closely modelled on the Ark of Euphrosyne, an ancient artifact Henry had discovered years ago in the care of the Luchti, a desert tribe in far-off Buthner. But it was nowhere near identical. The Luchti Ark had to be triggered by a full ceremonial and even then only operated under certain limited planetary positions. Although the core technology was identical, Henry's Charaxes ark was more like an old-fashioned two-way radio: you extended an aerial, cranked a handle and asked the built-in microphone if anybody was there. The call sign, though traditional, was a little off-key. It was never just *anybody* who was there: the box was attuned to a single consciousness, who either answered or didn't as he saw fit. Which in recent times was less and less often. Henry prayed he would allow the contact now.

The box emitted the familiar high-pitched whine as he turned the handle, vibrated a little, then beeped twice to indicate readiness. Henry took a deep breath. 'Is anybody there?' he asked.

'I thought I told you not to call me at the office.' Mr Fogarty's growl came through at once, distorted somewhat by the tinny speaker, but instantly recognisable.

Not for the first time, Henry had trouble believing Mr Fogarty was dead. He'd sacrificed his life for the sake of the Realm some seventeen years ago now, but the Ark of Euphrosyne and later the Charaxes ark had allowed Henry to keep in touch, albeit reluctantly on Mr Fogarty's part. The business about the office was a silly joke between them, but the sentiment behind it was serious enough.

'I need your advice,' Henry said, cutting through any further preliminaries.

'She's not pregnant again?'

Henry flushed a little. 'No she's not; and she's here with me.' He meant *So mind your manners,* but alive or dead he was still a bit afraid of Mr Fogarty, so he didn't say it.

'Hello, Blue,' Fogarty called. He seemed cheerful enough, which was unusual. Since his death, he'd made it quite clear he did not like to be disturbed and was often downright rude when Henry managed to make contact. It was something Henry never really understood. He'd have imagined that when you died, you would be only too happy to chat with somebody still living.

'Hello, Gatekeeper,' Blue said warmly. Even now she still used the title Mr Fogarty had held while he was still alive. 'Are you well?'

'Don't be silly,' Fogarty responded. There was a audible sniff across the speaker, then he said, 'I suppose there's a crisis on?' Somehow he always sounded more sympathetic to Blue than he did to Henry.

'We're facing an invasion,' Henry said.

'Haleklind?'

It brought Henry up short. 'How did you know?'

'Those clowns were spoiling for a fight long before I moved on. It was only a matter of time.' A pause. 'How much time has it been, incidentally?'

'Since you died? Sixteen, seventeen years – something like that.' Precision didn't matter. Henry knew Mr Fogarty wouldn't retain the information. He'd asked the question before; at least once during every contact. The answer meant little to him. Apparently time ran differently on the other side.

'How's Cynthia? She's not with you?'

Mr Fogarty asked about her every contact as well. Henry pushed down his impatience. Mr Fogarty had been a difficult man while he was alive and death had not improved him. 'She's busy,' he said bluntly. 'But well. Very well. She asked after you.' He'd made up the last bit, but he knew it would please Mr Fogarty and possibly stop him diverting any more. 'About Haleklind . . . ?'

'Uppity clowns, wizards,' Fogarty said. 'Comes of having too much power. They were bound to give you trouble eventually. What is it? Some sort of magical weapon?'

'In a manner of speaking,' Henry said. 'They're breeding manticores.'

To give him his due, Mr Fogarty got it at once. 'A manticore army?'

'Yes.'

'I didn't think that was possible.'

'Neither did we,' Blue put in. She hesitated, then added, 'There's something else – they have Mella.'

There was a pause so long that Henry wondered if the connection had gone down. Although she hadn't been born until after his death, Mr Fogarty had a soft spot for Mella. It dated from the day when Mella, aged six, had stolen the Charaxes ark and called him.

'Ransom?'

'Not yet. No demands. No contact of any sort.'

'But your intelligence is they have her and are preparing for war with a manticore army?'

'That's about the size of it,' Henry said.

'Timing?'

'Not sure. Days, maybe? A week if we're lucky. Soon, anyway.'

'What's our state of preparation?'

Henry liked that *our* – it meant Mr Fogarty still thought of himself as on their side. It was by no means a foregone conclusion. During some of his more recent contacts, the old boy seemed to be withdrawing not just from the affairs of the Realm, but from the living world in general. Henry glanced at Blue, who said, 'The standing army is one third the size it was when you were with us, Gatekeeper. Enough for local emergencies, but we were not expecting all-out war.'

'How long to bring it up to full strength?'

'Ten days. But even at full strength we can't hope to beat a manticore army.'

'What about demons?' Fogarty asked. 'I know you don't want to use them, but . . .'

. . . But Blue was still Queen of Hael, a position she had held, despite several challenges, since she'd slit the throat of Beleth, Prince of Darkness. Henry felt himself shudder slightly. He'd married one tough lady.

Blue said, 'I'll use them, Gatekeeper, if it means saving the Realm. They will take longer to mobilise, perhaps as much as fifteen, perhaps twenty, days. I –'

'Give the order to mobilise,' Mr Fogarty interrupted.

'I already have,' Blue said calmly. 'But my generals advise me that even with demonic back-up, we could not hope to defeat a manticore army of more than a few thousand.'

'How many can the Haleklinders field?'

'More than that, possibly *much* more than that.'

Henry said, 'We were wondering, Mr Fogarty, if you could help.'

Fogarty's voice gave a tinny sigh. 'We've been through this before, Henry. Even if I could raise an army here, you know how dangerous that would be.'

The trouble was Henry didn't. They *had* been down this road before, ever since the time Mr Fogarty had let slip his discovery that Emperor Scolitandes the Weedy once raised a battalion of the dead to help in a skirmish against the Ancient Theclinae. He'd lost, as it happened, but that was the result of bad leadership – the dead had fought brilliantly, so much so that the Theclinae never really recovered and went into decline as a culture to disappear from faerie history within a century or so. Admittedly a skirmish fell short of a war and a battalion was a far cry from an army, but if Mr Fogarty *was* prepared to bring across even a few thousand troops, it was bound to stop the Haleklinders in their tracks. Not even manticores could prevail against death.

Henry said, 'I realise there's a risk involved, but not half as great a risk as facing the manticores without help. If we don't do something –' He nearly said, *If you don't do something,* but stopped himself just in time, '– the Haleklind Table of Seven will rule the entire Realm before the year is out.'

'I want to talk to you about something, Henry,' Fogarty said; and there was a note in his voice that made Henry instantly uneasy. His unease increased as Mr Fogarty hesitated. Mr Fogarty *never* hesitated about anything. He was the most decisive, straightforward man Henry had ever known.

'What?' Henry asked, when he could stand it no longer. He glanced at Blue, who was frowning.

Eventually Mr Fogarty said, 'I'm leaving.'

Henry found himself staring at the Charaxes ark. 'Leaving?' he echoed. He wanted to ask where. He wanted to ask why. But he was afraid to ask either.

In a tone that was almost conversational, Mr Fogarty asked, 'You ever wondered, Henry, why your grandfather didn't come back to give you help and advice after he died.'

'I never knew my grandfather,' Henry said. 'Neither of them. They were both dead years before I was born.'

'Bad example,' Mr Fogarty muttered. 'All right. Have you ever wondered why kind, loving parents who die never come back to help the children they leave behind? Or hardly ever? Don't even pop in for a word of reassurance? *I'm all right, even if I'm dead . . . I still think about you . . . You'll find a few quid in the biscuit tin . . .* that sort of thing?'

'Because the dead can't come back?' Henry ventured.

'Are you stupid or what, Henry?' Mr Fogarty asked crossly. 'You're talking to me now. You're asking me to raise a bloody army. You've read the ghost stories. Of course the dead can come back. It's not even all that difficult. Look how many séances go on back home. There's a spiritualist church in every city – mightn't be very big, but they're there.'

A little stung by the *stupid* remark, Henry said, 'Then they *do* come back – communicate anyway – through mediums.' He was increasingly confused about what Mr Fogarty was getting at.

'That's the children getting in touch with *them!* The dead aren't making the first move,' Mr Fogarty told him impatiently. 'How many people die in our worlds every day? Millions and millions. And how many pop back for a quick word with the loved one they left behind? A handful. A tiny handful. And you never wondered why that was?'

'Actually –' Henry began.

But Mr Fogarty cut him short. 'I'll tell you why it is. Life's a lot different when you're dead. You see things differently. I don't just mean you change your opinions about things – although you definitely do that all right – I mean your *perception* of the world is different. You can *see time*, for heaven's sake. That was my biggest surprise: took some getting used to, I can tell you.'

That meant he could see the future, Henry thought with a sudden surge of excitement. He could tell what was going to happen, how they might get Mella back, exactly when the Haleklinders were going to invade. He opened his mouth to ask a string of questions, but Mr Fogarty cut him short again.

'And before you start wittering at me with all sorts of stupid questions, that doesn't mean I can tell you the future,' Mr Fogarty said. 'When you're dead, you see time like a huge field. People go wandering all over it.

You can see where they've been, but they decide where they're going, so everybody's future changes all the time depending on where you decide to go. I can tell you what might happen, not what definitely will, but I could do that before I died. You could do it for yourself if you ever bothered to think.' He coughed, as if clearing the throat he no longer possessed. 'Anyway, I don't want to get sidetracked. The point is things change when you die. *You* change. Things that used to be important just aren't important any more. Don't get me wrong: people are important – you still love them or hate them – but what happens to them isn't as important as they think it is because you see where they've been and where they could be going and how they could double back and so forth.'

Henry glanced at Blue again. This wasn't making very much sense to him. 'Mr Fogarty,' he said, 'this isn't making very much sense to me. I –'

'You die twice,' Fogarty told him.

Henry blinked. 'You what?'

'There's a second death,' Mr Fogarty said. 'You die once – your body dies – but it doesn't actually kill you. You get to fart around as a ghost, sometimes in your old familiar physical world – great fun that, nobody can see you – sometimes in the dream worlds. Hard to say how long it lasts: time's weird when you don't have a physical body – that's why I keep asking you how long it's been. From your point of view it could be hours or years, from mine it's almost like time doesn't pass at all. Except it does; and mine's nearly up.'

Henry held himself completely still. Despite the threat to Mella, despite the impending war, he was suddenly focused on a different, chilling fear.

'The thing is,' Mr Fogarty went on, 'the ghost body you're in doesn't last forever. It dies as well, exactly like your physical body. The second death. Mine's coming close.'

'What happens to you after . . . ?' Henry asked. 'What happens to your . . .' He wanted to say *soul*, but it sounded prissy and Mr Fogarty had never been a religious man, '. . . consciousness?' he finished softly.

'Don't know,' Mr Fogarty told him shortly. 'But in the circumstances, I wouldn't hold my breath waiting for me to raise you another army.' Henry thought there was genuine regret in his voice as he added, 'Or help you about Mella, come to that.'

forty

Mella sat on her chair, staring thoughtfully at the floor. She should have felt happy. The man who said he was her uncle would take her home soon and restore her memory. Soon she would know who she was and how she'd got here. Soon she would be able to get on with her life; and it sounded like an interesting life if she had a Lord for an uncle. What more could she ask for? Yet she felt uneasy and, when she tried to talk herself out of it, she continued to feel uneasy. Uncle or not, there was something about Lord Hairstreak that repelled her.

She heard the sound of the securities before the door itself opened and Hairstreak came in. There was a woman behind him. Both were smiling. 'Time to get going,' Lord Hairstreak said cheerfully. He held out his hand to her.

'Who's she?' Mella demanded suspiciously. The woman was pleasant enough looking and very well dressed, but she had much the same effect on Mella as Lord Hairstreak, although that might just have been because she was with him and they were obviously friends.

Hairstreak looked around to smile benignly at the woman. 'This is your aunt Aisling,' he said.

Mella stared at the woman. She was very slightly

overweight, with a self-satisfied expression behind her smile. Uncle Hairstreak and Aunt Aisling. 'She's your wife?' Mella asked. Aunt Aisling looked too young to be Lord Hairstreak's wife – *far* too young.

Lord Hairstreak's smile broadened. The woman's smile metamorphosed into a simper. 'Not . . . yet!' Lord Hairstreak said. Aunt Aisling giggled like a schoolgirl.

Mella found herself wondering if either of these people was telling the truth. How could she be sure Lord Hairstreak was her uncle? How could she be sure this Aisling woman was her aunt? How could she even be sure that Hairstreak was a Lord, or that his name was actually Hairstreak? He could be anybody, anything. He might be a brigand or an axe-murderer or some horrid pervert who liked young girls. The woman might be his accomplice. What better way to set a victim at ease? First you have her memory wiped, then you introduce yourself cosily as her uncle and auntie. Lull her suspicions. Except Mella's suspicions were definitely not lulled. She had no proof this creepy pair were who they said they were, no proof at all.

Mella ignored the outstretched hand. After a moment, Hairstreak (if his name really was 'Hairstreak') shrugged and said, 'Aisling, dearest, perhaps you would take her out to the ouklo. You know what to do when you get there. I shall have Ysabeau make sure there is no one to see you except our own guards.'

The self-satisfied expression was momentarily replaced by a frown. 'Ouklo?'

'My carriage,' Lord Hairstreak explained. 'It's what we call a flying carriage in the Realm. You can't miss it – it's gold plated.'

'Ooooh,' Aisling said. 'Gold plated!'

Mella's mind was working at top speed. Why did Aisling have to have the term explained? Even with her memory wiped, Mella knew what an ouklo was. And why say *It's what we call it in the Realm* as if Aisling wouldn't know what things were called in the Realm? Did she come from somewhere else? She was clearly no shape-shifter, so it couldn't be Hael. The only other possibility was the Analogue World. But what was a woman from the Analogue World doing with a so-called Lord of the Realm? And that answer of Hairstreak's – *Not yet* – suggested that if they weren't married now, they soon would be. (The woman had looked *so* pleased by that prospect.) Why would a noble of the Realm choose to marry someone from the human realm? It just didn't happen. Or hardly ever. There was something wrong with this couple, something very wrong.

'Aunt' Aisling (who couldn't possibly be Mella's aunt) put on a (phoniest of phony) smile and walked across to take Mella firmly by the arm. 'Come along, dear,' she said. 'The sooner we get you home, the quicker we can fix your memory and then you won't feel so confused and miserable.' She was surprisingly strong. Mella found herself virtually frogmarched from the chamber, noticed Aisling gently stroking Lord Hairstreak's back *en passant*, wondered if she should struggle, but decided not yet. What was the point of staying locked up in a little room? If she went with Aisling, there was always the possibility she might escape. Actually (the thought suddenly occurred to her) if she went along with their little charade, if she pretended to buy into their story, she might lull them into a feeling of false security, which would surely make escape a little easier.

She hadn't actually been struggling, but now she

ceased to resist altogether and covered her suspicions with a sudden smile. 'Thank you, Aunt Aisling,' she said cheerfully. 'That would be wonderful.' She even managed a second smile flashed in the direction of his pervy Lordship and felt Aisling's grip on her arm relax at once. The woman was an idiot. So long as Hairstreak did not come with them, escaping from her should be a doddle.

To her delight, Hairstreak didn't. Aisling led her from the chamber and along a corridor. The guard on her door did not accompany them, nor did any others. The sun was still climbing over the horizon as they reached the outside and Mella found she was leaving an enormous building set in its own grounds. Aisling took her arm again. 'Just a moment . . .' They stood at the top of a short flight of stone steps and watched as armed soldiers left their guard posts one by one to form what Mella at first took to be an escort detachment. But to her surprise, they simply marched off and disappeared without once glancing in their direction. As they disappeared, Aisling said, 'Come on . . .'

The ouklo was obvious. Its gold plating gleamed copper in the early-morning sun. Mella licked her lips. Perhaps the Hairstreak person really was a Lord: he was certainly extremely rich, whoever he was. But being a Lord didn't mean he was her uncle and being her uncle didn't mean he was telling the truth. Her mistrust was deepening. There was something about Hairstreak she simply didn't like. And the dislike extended to Aisling. Besides, if they weren't married . . . *yet* . . . how could she be her aunt if Hairstreak was her uncle? Mella frowned. Actually she could, quite easily. She could be her mother's sister or her father's sister with no married ties to Hairstreak at all. And Hairstreak could be her mother's brother or her father's brother or a stepbrother or even a friend of the family – family friends were sometimes given the honorary title of 'uncle'. And it *still* didn't matter because there was something positively *creepy* about Uncle Hairstreak and Aunt Aisling.

'Come on,' Aisling said again, impatiently this time.

Mella went with her. Aisling, she could see, was almost blinded by the ouklo; and not just in the literal sense. She had the look of a child shown the greatest toy in the entire world, the most precious plaything. Gold obviously unhinged her; at least the amount of gold that was plated on the carriage. Which meant, Mella thought, she was vulnerable because she was distracted.

Mella glanced around. A straight road led away from the entrance steps. To her right were open fields. To her left, beyond the sentry posts, were lawns, some ornamental shrubs and, beyond them, a treeline. Neither the road nor the open fields would give her any cover if she ran, but the terrain to her left looked more promising. She wondered why the guard posts had been vacated. Clearly there was more going on here than she knew, but this was no time to worry about it: just give thanks to her guardian gods that she would not have soldiers chasing her . . . at least not until Aisling sounded the alarm and got them back. But by then she might have a decent head start.

She walked to the bottom of the steps. The ouklo was less than a hundred yards away. She glanced left again, surreptitiously. She could see distant trees now, tall shapes against the lightening sky. They might be no more than a copse, or a single stand, but if they were the edge of a wood, or, better yet, a forest, they would give her good shelter. Once there, she had an excellent chance of hiding herself from any pursuit; once there she had an excellent chance of escape.

What then? a small voice whispered in her mind. *You have no memory.* She pushed it away. She would worry about the *what then?* later. For now she had to concentrate on getting away from creepy Uncle Hairstreak and Aunt Aisling.

She made the decision. She would run left. She would run through the space between the first two sentry posts, run fast until she reached the ornamental bushes, then use them as cover until she reached the trees. Even if Aisling came after her at once, Mella was younger and lighter and fancied her chances of being faster. But she didn't think Aisling would come after her. Somehow she seemed a little too . . . soft, a little too concerned about dirtying her fine clothes. Mella reckoned if Aisling did anything, it would be to call for help; and by the time help arrived, Mella could be long gone.

As they passed the gap between the first two sentry posts, Aisling took her arm again; and there was nothing soft about her grip.

'It's all right,' Aisling said reassuringly, her voice positively dripping with insincerity. 'There's someone in the ouklo I have to take back. You can wait while I do so, then we will take you home and make you well again.'

There were four guards by the ouklo! Their black uniforms bore the same insignia Lord Hairstreak wore on his tunic. She hadn't noticed them before: they were standing behind the ouklo and shielded by its bulk. How could she escape now? They would be after her at once – fit, strong young men who were probably equipped with net and other capture spells. And how could she break away from the tight grip Aisling had on her arm? With surprise on her side, she might jerk herself free, but if she failed first time it would result in a struggle. Once Aisling called the guards – and Aisling would certainly call the guards – her chances of escape vanished.

It was too late for her to run through the gap as she'd planned, probably too late for anything much now. The black-uniformed guards were moving forward to meet Aisling. Oddly, they seemed almost threatening, but they stepped back at once when Aisling opened her right hand to show them an authorisation token. The scent of magic wafted into Mella's nostrils and she saw, beyond doubt, that Aisling was authorised by Lord Hairstreak, the genuine, the one-and-only, Hairstreak. (Whoever Lord Hairstreak might be; but the guards accepted him all right.) After that, it was definitely too late for any-thing. Mella was being bustled towards the ouklo, Aisling's grip still firmly on her arm, the guards now ranged around her so there was no possibility of escape. The door of the carriage opened.

'Mella!' called Aunt Aisling: it was a strangely familiar name.

Mella dived inside, shot across the carriage and out the other door. She had the faintest impression of some-one crouched inside the coach, but no time for anything except slamming the door behind her, racing across the lawn, diving behind shrubs and then, at last, headed like an elated gazelle towards the treeline.

She had almost reached the forest by the time stupid old Aunt Aisling thought to raise the alarm.

forty-One

There was the sharp snap of a breaking branch some way behind her. Mella felt her heart sink. She'd been so certain of her luck when she reached the treeline. It was not a single stand, not a copse, not even a small wood, but exactly what she had hoped for: the edge of (almost certainly) a forest – a forest that would provide her with a thousand places to hide from her pursuit. There *was* pursuit, of course. She'd heard the guards blundering through the shrub beds, but by the time they reached the trees she was deep inside the forest, surrounded by exotic plants, and had no difficulty at all in losing them. All had been silence for a while, except for the expected background sounds, but now there was something following her; and somehow she didn't think it was a guard.

It was gloomy in the forest. A leafy canopy filtered the sun into a pale, green light, but once her eyes adjusted, she could see well enough. She stopped to listen, staring behind her. There was no sign of pursuit, no further sound of any sort. Gradually she began to relax. Eventually she started off again.

She didn't know where she was going. But now she'd made her escape, her mind was racing. She needed desperately to retrieve her memories, find out who she was, where she was, what she was doing here. Only then could she work out what to do. In her mind, she began with first principles, starting with what she knew and what she could know.

She knew she was wearing decent clothes. They were clean and well cut and probably expensive, which would tally with the idea that she was the niece of a Lord. She knew what she looked like – there was a little mirror in her pocket. But despite the clothing and the mirror, she had no money, not a single golden coin. (Why did she think of gold rather than silver or copper? She filed the fact away for future explanation.) Perhaps she was a pauper who'd stolen the clothing, but somehow she didn't think so: it fitted her too well. She thought it might be tailored, in which case it could be even more expensive than it looked. So someone had taken her money, along with any clues to her identity.

But there were some things they couldn't take away. The skin of her hands was pale, soft and smooth. There was no dirt beneath the fingernails. These were not the hands of a labourer. These were not the hands of a merchant or an artisan or a gardener. These were pampered hands. *The niece of a Lord.* She found herself staring at her feet. She had dainty feet – *faerie feet,* her father used to call them – encased in fashionable green leather shoes. She tried to remember where she'd bought those shoes, then suddenly focused on the thought that had passed almost unnoticed through her head. That thought brought a sudden surge of excitement. Her father once told her she had faerie feet! She remembered her father!

Except she didn't. The excitement ebbed. She could not remember his face or who he was, or anything about him, only that one remark; and she couldn't even remember when he had made it. Perhaps yesterday, perhaps long ago. She felt sad she could not remember his face, but at least she had a father, whoever he was. A father who remarked on the size of her feet. Did she have a mother? No picture emerged in answer to the question, no comment about her feet; or anything else. Did she have a home? Nothing. She thought instinctively of gold, she wore expensive clothes and shoes, her hands showed little sign of work . . . she was a rich girl (but one without money) who had faerie feet and pretty shoes and well-cut clothes and no other memory about herself.

Mella entered a clearing, but felt immediately exposed and headed out of it at once, taking a narrow pathway that carried her back into the shelter of the trees. She found herself jogging beside a stream that widened to a narrow river, then the river ceased to follow her path and disappeared. After a moment she heard a steady roaring sound that blocked out any other noise. It grew louder and louder until she emerged on the shore of a lake fed by a magnificent waterfall.

The lake shore was even worse than the clearing in the forest – far too exposed for safety. Mella turned back immediately and almost walked into the girl.

The girl was standing on the path only yards away, any sound of her approach masked by the noise of the waterfall. She was about Mella's age and build. She stood quite still, her face in shadow, but obviously staring directly at Mella herself. Two words sprang at once to Mella's mind: *Feral Faerie*. Or *Forest Faerie* if she was concerned about being polite. This had to be a Forest Faerie. Were Forest Faeries dangerous? Her memory was vague on that point, but this one didn't seem to be armed and at least she wasn't one of Hairstreak's guards.

Mella made a snap judgment and decided (for the

moment) not to run. She too froze into immobility, thought about it for an instant, then called hesitantly, 'Who are you?'

The girl stepped forward so that her face was in full sunlight. 'Hello, Mella,' she said softly, using the name Aisling had called out as she dived through the carriage. 'Don't be frightened.'

But Mella *was* frightened. Mella was suddenly very frightened indeed. She turned and ran. She broke from the trees and ran along the lake shore with the roar of the waterfall pounding her ears. But the girl ran with her, no more than a pace or two behind and there was no shaking her. Eventually, breathlessly, Mella stopped and turned. 'Get *away* from me!' she screamed. Out from the trees, in the full light of the sun, there was no mistaking it. The girl who followed Mella was Mella. Mella was being chased by herself, had been caught by herself. 'Why do you call me Mella?' she asked wildly.

'Because that's your name – don't you remember?' Mella said. She smiled. 'It's mine too.'

'I've had my memory wiped with *lethe*. I don't know who I am.'

'You're Faeman Princess Culmella of the Faerie Realm,' Mella told her. 'Mella for short. Your mother is Queen Holly Blue. Your father is Consort Majesty King Henry. Now do you remember?'

Mella shook her head. 'No,' she said miserably.

'Take my word for it,' Mella told her.

'Who are you – my doppelganger?' Mella asked. She knew that doppelgangers could be created or called, but if your doppelganger turned up spontaneously, it meant you were going to die.

Mella shook her head. 'I'm your sister,' she said.

'I'm your twin. Uncle Hairstreak made me. I'm your clone.'

Uncle Hairstreak? The man she instinctively mistrusted. 'What's a clone?' she asked.

'I think it's a spell from the Analogue World.'

'They don't use magic in the Analogue World.'

Mella shrugged. 'Maybe it's a science then. Uncle Hairstreak used it to make me from a lock of your hair. He definitely used magic to make me grow. I'm you, Mella. All the cells of my body are your cells. I'm Mella too.'

'You're Mella II?'

'He calls me Mella.' Mella II reached out and took her hand. This time Mella did not try to run away. 'He plans for me to take your place, so obviously he calls me Mella. Our Uncle Hairstreak is a wicked man.'

Take my place? Aloud, Mella asked, 'Is he really our uncle?'

'He's really your great-uncle by marriage, once removed. His sister was married to your mother's father before he married your mother's mother. I suppose you could say he's my father, since he made me, but he's always encouraged me to call him *uncle*. Besides, if he's my father, I think that would make you my mother.'

'Your *mother?!*'

Mella II shrugged. 'It was your hair.'

'I don't want to be your mother.'

'Neither do I. I'd rather you were my sister.'

Mella said, 'I don't understand this; not any of it.' Part of the problem was her missing memory, but she suspected she would still have problems understanding even if she remembered everything. But at least her fear had nearly gone now.

'You don't have to understand. You just have to trust me. But I'll try to help you understand.'

They had begun to walk slowly, hand-in-hand along the side of the lake. Now her initial panic was dying down, Mella discovered she trusted Mella II. It was an instinctive thing, like her mistrust of Uncle Hairstreak and Aunt Aisling.

'Is Aisling really my aunt?'

Mella II nodded. 'You do have an aunt called Aisling. She's your father's sister.'

'I don't like her.'

'Neither does he, apparently.'

'Do you know my father?'

Mella II shook her head. 'I've not met him yet. I've not met anybody of importance yet, except Uncle Hairstreak and some servants and now you. But I know a great deal about everybody because Uncle Hairstreak thinks I'm stupid.'

'Why? Why should he think you're stupid?'

'Because I *was* stupid when he made me. I didn't grow up the way you did. He cloned me – cloned you, I mean – then used a growth spell. So I had no childhood. I jumped from birth to teens. I looked like you, but I was just a shell. He used an educational enchantment programme to give me the formal information I needed – about our mother and father and the Palace and so on – but that didn't amount to life experience. It was difficult because he had to keep me secret, so he couldn't turn me loose in the world. But he let me roam through his estate and deal with servants and so forth – people he really trusted – so I would be at ease. He never thought I'd read his private papers and find out what he was planning.'

'I'd have done that,' Mella said.

'Yes, I know you would. You're me. And I'm you. Sort of. That's the other thing he never thought of. I was always nice to him and he always thought I was just a silly clone who'd do what she was told when he needed her to. He never thought I'd identify with you once I knew about you. He never thought I'd be horrified at what he planned to do to you. But I was, because it was like he was going to do it to me.'

Frowning, Mella asked, 'What *did* he plan to do?'

Frowning, Mella II said, 'This is all so complicated. Listen, I said you had to trust me. *Do* you trust me?'

Without the slightest hesitation, Mella nodded. 'Yes, I do. I don't know why, but I do.'

'I know why. It's because you're sort of me and I'm sort of you. It's almost like being the same person in two bodies. If you can't trust yourself, who can you trust?'

'Yes, who?' Mella agreed. She found herself agreeing with a lot of things Mella II said. If she only understood what was going on, she might enjoy being the same person in two bodies.

Mella II said, 'I've always spent a lot of time wandering in Lord Hairstreak's grounds and reading books in his library. There are berries that counteract the effect of *lethe*. More or less. I read about them in a book on herbs. There were some growing on a tree in his garden so I was curious.'

'I don't suppose you brought any with you?'

Mella II shook her head. 'No, but I saw some growing in the forest. We could go back . . .'

There was something she wasn't telling. Mella knew it at once. 'What aren't you telling me?'

Mella II looked pained. 'Actually, the book doesn't

recommend the berries as a *lethe* cure – the usual thing is to inject elementals into your bloodstream and let them dig the crystals out of your brain with little spades. People *used* to use these berries, but nobody does any more.'

'Why not?'

'The dosage is a bit tricky. If you take too few berries, it doesn't work. But if you take too many, they poison you.'

'You get sick?'

'You get dead.'

After a moment, Mella said, 'These berries – do you think you can find them again?'

They walked together back into the forest and it was really, really nice having a sister. Mella thought of Mella as her sister: *clone* seemed cold and impersonal, and *twin*, for all they *were* twins and absolutely identical, was somehow wrong as well. Having Mella beside her was like finding a long-lost sister, finding someone who would always be on your side. It was . . . comforting. Even the forest seemed less threatening.

'There,' said Mella II. She pointed.

They were growing on a bush rather than a tree, bright yellow, with a speckle of red. 'Are those them?' Mella asked.

'Yes.'

'That's a bush, not a tree.'

'I know. I must have forgotten.'

'But you remember the right dosage.'

'I think so.'

'What is it?'

'Five berries,' Mella II said. She hesitated. 'Or was it four?'

'I'm not taking them if you don't remember.'

'I do. Honestly, I remember. I think it was five. Unless that was the overdose that poisons you and you die in agony . . . No, it's not the overdose. Five is definitely the right dose. For an average bodyweight.'

'What's an average bodyweight?' Mella asked desperately.

'I don't know.' Mella II plucked five berries off the bush. 'I tell you what – I'll take these to test them. If they work for me they'll work for you.'

'How can you test them?' Mella asked. 'You've still got your memory. Either they won't work at all or they'll kill you: that's no test. Besides, there aren't many more berries on the bush. We can't afford to waste them.'

'So you're prepared to risk it?'

'What risk?' Mella demanded. 'You said you remembered.'

'Yes, I do. It's five berries. I'm nearly sure.' She handed five across and Mella swallowed them.

'Nothing's happening,' Mella said after a moment.

'It takes a bit,' Mella II told her. 'You have to digest the berries for the active ingredient to get into your bloodstream. That's what makes them so dangerous. Once there's an overdose in your bloodstream, there's no way of stopping it. You can puke up the berries but they'll still kill you.'

'How long does it take?'

'What, for you to digest them? Five minutes? Ten? I don't know. It didn't tell you in the book. Do you want to sit down? You look a bit . . . funny.'

After five minutes, Mella suddenly glanced at Mella II with an expression of trepidation. She licked dry lips, convulsed, then gasped. 'Something's happening,' she said.

forty-two

'I'm not sure I like this,' Blue said.

'We've run out of alternatives,' Henry told her firmly. He was helping Pyrgus into his invisibility suit, an extraordinarily difficult business since neither of them could see where the arms were. In a moment, Pyrgus would be helping Henry into his, which would be even more difficult since both Pyrgus and Henry's suits would be invisible.

They were standing, all three of them, in the Situation Room, a modified cavern deep in the bedrock beneath the Purple Palace. Banks of crystal spy globes surrounded the huge Operations Table where segments of the Realm landscape were available – in three dimensions – once someone voiced the proper sonic trigger. Just now, the visible segment was a stretch of the Haleklind border. Vast herds of manticores were massing on the Haleklind plains. A faerie army faced them on the other side. So far, no one had made a move to cross the vital boundary, but young women moved briskly between the globes and the table, constantly rearranging the display, so that the position might change at any moment.

Although the Situation Room was a bustle of activity, with uniformed operatives scurrying in all directions, there was a rectangle of empty space to the right of the table avoided even by the most hurried. This was, Henry knew, the space occupied by his SWAT team, hideously efficient, finely honed, muscular commandos who'd had no difficulty at all climbing into their suits and now stood (presumably to attention) waiting for their leaders to get a move on.

'The manticores aren't in any particular formation,' Blue said, staring at the table.

'No, but they're *there*,' Pyrgus said with much more obvious impatience than Henry would ever have dared. 'They're *ready*. And if we wait for the wizards to make a move, it will be too late.'

'What worries me,' Blue said, 'is that this operation might spark off the very war we're trying to avoid. We haven't come anywhere near exhausting the diplomatic alternatives yet.'

What worried Henry was Blue's guilt. She'd carried it since the Civil War, shortly after she became Queen, blamed herself for the deaths of thousands of brave soldiers. Because of the guilt, she had a horror of war that was almost pathological. It clouded her judgment in ways a Queen could not afford and sometimes made her swing to extremes. He opened his mouth to speak, but Pyrgus beat him to it. 'If we wait, we may lose our best chance of rescuing Mella. Maybe our only chance.'

Henry weighed in on his side. 'We know where she is and we know she's still safe. We know we can reach her and we have the element of surprise. All of that could change.'

'Yes, I know,' Blue said. She didn't sound convinced. She turned to General Vanelke, the only surviving member of the trio who had run the Empire's military operations at the time of the Civil War. 'What do we know about Kremlin Karcist?'

Vanelke tore his eyes away from the viewglobes. 'Its defences, Ma'am?'

'Yes.'

'It's the former Tsarist palace, so it has all the securities you'd expect against direct attack. Old magic, not particularly sophisticated, but very reliable. They can be breached, of course, if we bring enough firepower to bear, but we're not planning a frontal attack at this stage, so they're not entirely relevant.'

'But the Table of Seven have added their own systems?'

'Of course they have,' Vanelke said.

'Including anti-infiltration spells?'

'So Madame Cardui assures me.'

'In your opinion, General Vanelke, what percentage success might we expect if an infiltration operation was attempted by professionals – your men, specially trained?'

'Attempted and *led* by professionals, Ma'am?' Vanelke asked, striking to the nub of the matter with irritating precision.

'Yes.'

'It won't *be* led by professionals,' Henry put in quickly. 'The whole poi—'

'Approximately eighty per cent,' Vanelke said.

'And led by amateurs?'

'Come on Blue, we're not exactly amat—'

'Less than forty per cent.' Vanelke managed to make it sound like Armageddon.

Blue turned. 'You see, Henry? I can't think why you

didn't ask the General before you and Pyrgus hatched this . . . this . . .' She shook her head helplessly.

Because it was none of his damn business, Henry thought crossly. Aloud he said, 'General Vanelke doesn't have enough information to answer your question accurately. Your figure was based on standard infiltration techniques, was it not, General?'

'Yes, sir, it was.'

Henry looked severely at Blue. 'Our plan isn't based on standard infiltration techniques. We're going to get into Kremlin Karcist the same way Mella did.' He didn't spell it out for the sake of security. There were a lot of people wandering past in the Situation Room.

'The same wa—?' Blue, who was sharp as a tack, got it almost at once. 'Oh, I see.' After a moment, she added, 'Suppose the Table of Seven have closed that loophole?'

Pyrgus had disappeared. At once Henry felt hands on his leg and noticed that his foot had vanished. 'If they've closed it we'll have to find another way. But with luck they won't have discovered yet how she got there. Either way, it argues for us moving fast.'

To give Blue credit, she never argued for the sake of it. What he said made sense and she knew it. All the same, she looked directly at Henry. 'I'm missing a daughter,' she said. 'I don't want to lose a husband and a brother as well.'

'You won't,' Henry assured her. 'And you can stop worrying about an international incident that will trigger war. These suits are the latest technology. We'll be quite undetectable. Once we're in and find Mella, we'll have her out of danger in minutes.' He glanced at Vanelke. 'And that's guaranteed one hundred per cent.'

Most of Henry's body had disappeared now, but

Blue leaned across and kissed the floating head. 'Just be careful,' she whispered.

'I will,' Henry promised. He turned away, wondering where Pyrgus was, and discovered they'd been joined by Madame Cardui.

'You can take the suit off,' she said gravely.

He'd known her long enough to realise at once something was badly wrong. 'What's happened?' he asked.

Pyrgus's head reappeared, floating in the air a few feet from Henry's. 'What's wrong?' he echoed.

'Mella is no longer in Kremlin Karcist,' Madame Cardui told them. The effects of her recent head peel were beginning to wear off and she now looked increasingly like a mature woman. Somehow it suited her better than the girlish appearance created by the peel.

'Are you sure?' Blue asked at once.

'I've just had word from my agent in the Kremlin. They were holding her captive, but now she's disappeared.'

Blue's face turned to stone. 'This isn't some sort of cover-up? They haven't . . . harmed her and are pretending . . . ?'

Madame Cardui shook her head. 'Mella wasn't killed,' she said emphatically. 'She seems to have escaped. They didn't harm her, Majesty. At least . . .'

'At least . . . ?'

'Apparently they erased her personal memories. I don't know why. Possibly she saw something she shouldn't.' Madame Cardui shrugged. 'If it was a standard *lethe* treatment, it will be easily enough reversed once we have her back. If not . . .' She shrugged, '. . . we'll just have to cross that hurdle when we come to it.'

'Do we know where she is now?' Pyrgus put in.

Madame Cardui sighed. 'No, deeah, we do not. But all my agents in Haleklind are now on highest alert. We'll know it once she surfaces again.'

Blue said, 'But in the meantime our daughter is wandering somewhere in enemy territory with her memory erased . . .'

'I'm afraid that is exactly the situation we face,' Madame Cardui said grimly.

forty-three

'I'd never met Lord Hairstreak,' Mella said. 'Not before today.' She looked at her sister, who looked back at her like a reflection in a mirror. The dammed-up memories were flooding in now, leaving her excited to the point of breathlessness. 'My parents both said he was a very bad man. After the war, they thought he was dead to begin with: for a long time too – over a year, I think. Then, when they found out the only bit of him left was his head, they took pity and decided to forgive and forget and leave him alone.'

'Big mistake,' murmured Mella II.

'We never visited him. At least I didn't. I suppose Blue and Henry thought I'd be squeamish about talking to a head with all its veins and sinews and yucky bits dripping into a cube. They think I'm still a child. You wouldn't *believe* how over-protective they can be.'

'You call your parents by their first names?' Mella II exclaimed in obvious surprise.

'Not usually,' Mella told her. 'Do you?' She realised abruptly what she'd said and added hastily, 'Would you? Might you? Will . . . ?' She tailed off.

'I suppose your parents are my parents, sort of,' Mella II said a little sadly. 'If I had real parents, if I knew my real parents, I'd call them Mother and Father.

Or Mummy and Daddy. I'd never call them by their first names, not even sometimes.'

'So we're not really so much alike,' Mella said.

'Yes, we are!' Mella II told her fiercely. 'We're absolutely identical. It's just that we were brought up differently. I miss having parents. I miss having a childhood.'

To change the subject, Mella said, 'You'd better tell me what Lord Hairstreak was up to. With you, I mean. Do you know?'

'Of course I do.' Mella II still sounded a little heated. 'He talked to me about everything. He thought I was his obedient little creation, ready to do absolutely everything she was told. It never occurred to him that being you, all my sympathies would be on your side.'

After a moment, Mella prompted, 'Go on.'

'It's funny. I keep thinking you should know all this. But of course you don't.' Mella II reached out and took Mella's hand. 'Lord Hairstreak made me so he could have you killed.'

'What?!' Mella stared at her.

'He came up with the plan before he got his new body; while he was still just a head on a cube. He knew the Realm would never accept him as King – he was just too creepy. The original idea was that he would kidnap you and have you killed in his Keep, then substitute me for you and send me back *as* you to take my place in the Purple Palace. I was supposed to do everything he told me, of course.'

Mella stared at her. 'But what about Mummy and Daddy?' she asked.

'Oh, they were going to be killed too.'

'Assassinated? Like me?'

'Not exactly. Actually, not at all. He had too much

time on his hands while he was just a head on a cube.' She hesitated. 'Not that he had any hands then, but you know what I mean.'

'Oh, go on!' Mella told her impatiently.

Mella II grinned at her. 'He came up with the idea of having Haleklind attack the Realm. The old wizards would never have done it, of course – they were peculiar, but they weren't interested in international politics and they certainly had no territorial ambitions – so he financed a coup and had them overthrown and set up the Table of Seven. They were supposed to be the new Revolutionary Ruling Council, but actually they took their orders from Lord Hairstreak when it came to the things that mattered.'

'Wait a minute,' Mella said. 'Whoever was in charge, Haleklind would never have stood a chance of invading the Realm. Not successfully anyway. They only have a smallish army: even I know that. The whole country is just one big magic industry. All they've ever thought of for centuries is selling their spells.'

'Quite right,' said Mella II. 'But Lord Hairstreak's idea was for them to develop a *magical* army. He wanted them to breed manticores.'

'*Manticores?*'

'They're great mythic beasts, half lion, half scorpion, half –'

'Yes, I know what manticores are. But you can't *breed* magical beasts. You have to make them one at a time. Everybody knows that.'

'And apparently everybody is wrong,' Mella II told her emphatically. 'The plains of Haleklind are swarming with manticores now and that's Lord Hairstreak's secret army.'

After a long moment Mella said, 'So the Haleklinders attack the Realm with manticores and kill Mummy and Daddy . . .'

'. . . then Lord Hairstreak steps in and negotiates a truce, hero of the hour, applause, applause, and you become Queen, only you're dead so it's really me, and Lord Hairstreak runs the Realm through me because, of course, I'm his sweet little creation so I'll do what I'm told and then, when I'm old enough, he marries me and –'

Mella almost choked. 'He does *what?*'

'Marries me,' Mella II repeated. 'He can do that quite legally because I'm supposed to be you, remember, and he's not a blood relative, so he marries you and becomes King. He's wanted that for years and years.'

'I think I need to sit down for a minute,' Mella said. She propped her back against a thick tree trunk and sank down to the mossy forest floor. 'What a pervy *pervert!*'

Mella II sat down beside her. 'He hired an assassin to get you, but you ran away and that spoiled his plans.'

Mella held her head. Between the flood of memories and the fresh information, she felt as if it might explode at any minute. 'But then I played into his hands by ending up in Haleklind.'

'Yes, you did,' Mella II confirmed. 'The original idea was for us to be swapped at his Keep, but when the Table told him they had you in their Kremlin, that was even better. He packed me into his ouklo at once. I was supposed to wait until he'd confirmed it really was you, then he was going to kill you and make the switch. Or make the switch and kill you, I forget which. I was trying to figure out a way to save you when you made the escape yourself – I should have known you'd manage perfectly well: you're very resourceful, just like me.'

'Why is Aunt Aisling helping him?' Mella frowned. Nothing Aunt Aisling did was making much sense.

Mella II glanced at her in surprise. 'I didn't know she was. What can she do in the Analogue World?'

'She's not in the Analogue World: she came here with me and now she's helping him for some reason.'

'I didn't know that,' Mella II repeated.

Mella pushed the mystery from her mind – there were obviously far more important things to think about. She pushed herself abruptly to her feet. 'We have to get back to the Palace and warn everybody what's going on.'

'I was going to say that,' Mella II told her. 'The only thing –'

'What? What's the only thing?'

'The only thing is how we're going to do it. We're lost in a forest somewhere in Haleklind, probably being chased, and even if we find our way out we won't know how to get to the Realm, and even if we find out how to get to the Realm I know there are all sorts of guards and security spells at the border because Hairstreak once told me. So how do we do it?'

'Perhaps I can help you with that,' said a weird, growly voice behind them.

forty-four

'How did this happen?' Lord Hairstreak demanded. Normally he would have strangled the messenger: one had to have some compensation for bad news. But it was Aisling who brought him word of Mella's escape, so he strangled his emotions instead and put up with the frustration. And to be fair, now he thought about it, the news wasn't all that bad. Because Mella, it seemed, had foolishly run into the forest, which was infested with the fiercest manticores as part of Kremlin Karcist security, so her chances of survival were slim. It would be only be a matter of time before one of the beasts found her and carried her off to feed its young. And even if she somehow avoided the forest manticores, there was no way of avoiding the herd on the plains beyond. The perfect way of getting rid of her. The manticores would leave no bone unchewed, no trace of her at all. Such an unfortunate accident. He couldn't imagine why he hadn't thought of it before. With Mella out of the way, the substitution of her clone became child's play.

Except that he was looking into an empty ouklo. There was no sign of the Mella clone.

'I don't know,' Aisling said.

If he was brutally honest with himself, she sounded

as if she didn't really care. But he could hardly expect her to grasp the devious intricacies of his plan, or its overriding importance, come to that. After all, they'd only just met and he'd scarcely had time to tell her more than the bare bones of what he was doing. 'What exactly happened?'

Aisling's face had taken on a bored, petulant expression. She examined her fingernails and spoke without looking at him. 'The girl got into the carriage then ran out the other door.' She looked up at him. 'It wasn't my fault.'

'No, of course not,' Hairstreak muttered. Actually, she was right. He should never have given her responsibility for Mella at this early stage of their relationship. Not that it would probably have been much different if he'd escorted the girl himself. Who'd have thought that Mella with her memory wiped would run away? Why on earth should she? Her actions were quite unpredictable and he would not have predicted them. But that was water under the bridge. He had to be careful now. Ysabeau and the other Table members could appear at any moment. None of them knew all the details of his plan and he wished to keep it that way. In particular, he preferred to keep the existence of the clone secret. 'Was there anyone else in the carriage at the time?'

'I don't know,' Aisling said.

Hairstreak considered his position. Mella might have run away – although for the life of him he couldn't think why – but the Mella clone never would: she'd always been a model of obedience. She'd probably just got bored waiting and wandered off. Which meant she was in the grounds somewhere, possibly even in the house. But he needed to find her before anyone else did.

It was important she didn't go on public display before he was sure the original Mella was dead. He looked around him.

'Where are my guards?' he demanded.

'I sent them off after the girl when she escaped,' Aisling said. 'They followed her into the forest.' She hesitated. 'So did the other girl.'

'What other girl?'

'I saw another girl creep out of the bushes and follow them in. I don't know where she came from.'

It was the Mella clone. It had to be – there simply wasn't any other girl about. Now the two Mellas were in the forest. This was turning into a nightmare. What if he lost the clone? What if she was savaged by a manticore? He'd trained her perfectly for the job she had to do, but that training had taken time. He couldn't possibly start over with another one.

'Lord Hairstreak –'

Hairstreak groaned. This was all he needed. Ysabeau was headed down the path towards them with other members of the Table of Seven straggling behind her.

'Is everything all right, Lord Hairstreak?'

Hairstreak came to a decision. 'Companion Ysabeau,' he said firmly, 'how do you control the forest manticores?'

Ysabeau looked at him blankly. 'Control?' she frowned. 'Manticores?'

'The forest manticores,' Hairstreak snapped impatiently. 'They're part of your security system. There must be some way you control them to allow free passage through the forest when you need it.'

'Oh, I see,' Ysabeau exclaimed. 'Yes. Yes, of course. You mean, as when our technicians need entry to the forest to check the system overall. We use a manticore repellent.'

'Is that a spell?'

Ysabeau shook her head. 'It's a whistle. You hang it round your neck and when you press the button it emits a sound the manticores don't like.'

'So they keep away?'

'Single manticores, yes.'

'What about a herd?'

Ysabeau shook her head again, more violently this time. 'You mustn't use them near a herd. When they're clumped together manticores can't get away from the sound quickly enough, so they usually panic and trample each other. But it works well enough in the forest.'

'I'll need two whistles,' Lord Hairstreak told her. 'Can you arrange that?'

'Yes, of course, Lord Hairstreak.' Ysabeau glanced around her in bewilderment. 'But . . . why?'

'The Lady Aisling and I are going for a little walk,' Hairstreak told her. 'In the forest.'

forty-five

The creature, on four legs, stood higher than Mella's shoulder while she was standing on two. It was far and away the most terrifying thing she'd ever seen. Its body was that of a giant lion, tawny and heavily muscled with great clawed feet. It might even have *been* a giant lion, but for two things. The first was that its rear end was nothing like the hindquarters of a lion. Instead, it tapered and curled upwards into a vicious scorpion sting the size of an ogre's spear. The second – and Mella *really* couldn't get her mind around this one – was that in place of a lion's mane and jaw was the broad, reddish-brown head of a man. Or perhaps not *quite* a man, for the nose was flat, the teeth immense and the tongue lolled from the mouth like the tongue of a dog.

'Oh my Gods!' whispered Mella II.

Mella took a small step backwards. Instinctively, she kept herself between the creature and her newfound sister. Not that she could be any real protection. A single leap and the thing would be upon them. A single slash of one paw and they'd be dead.

'What is it?' gasped Mella II.

'It's what you've just been talking about,' Mella told her quietly. 'That's a manticore. Haven't you ever seen one before?'

Mella II was staring at the thing with eyes like saucers. She shook her head. 'No. Have you?'

'No, but I've seen pictures.' She hesitated, then added, 'I never thought they were so big.'

'Do you think we should run?' Mella II asked her.

Mella had been wondering the same thing herself. The truth was, she didn't know a lot about manticores, despite seeing pictures and reading a bit about them. Some wild animals chased you if you ran, and killed you when they caught up. Some ate you if you stood still. The trick seemed to be figuring out which was which, and nothing she'd read ever seemed to give a hint how. Besides, she wasn't sure she should think of a manticore as a wild animal. Didn't magical creatures fall into a different category? She wasn't sure, but she did know they were unpredictable. But the bottom line was that *this* magical creature wasn't growling like a lion, wasn't pawing the ground like a bull, didn't have its ears flattened like a cat or its lips curled back in a snarl like a wolf. In short, it was making no threating gestures. It wasn't moving at all, in fact: not stalking them, or chasing them or creeping up on them or anything.

She wondered who'd spoken. Maybe they weren't facing a wild manticore. Maybe this manticore had a keeper. After all, if Lord Hairstreak planned to use them as an army, there must be some way of training them.

'Best not to startle it,' she told Mella II.

She looked around for the animal's keeper. 'Hello . . .' she called, but quietly so as not to startle the beast. 'Can you come out and show yourself?'

'Who are you talking to?' asked Mella II. Despite her previous question she didn't look ready to run.

The manticore rolled its tongue back into its fear-some mouth. 'My guess is she thinks she's talking to my keeper,' it said, a little thickly.

Mella felt as if a claw had clutched her heart. 'Manti-cores can *talk?*' There was nothing about that in the literature.

The manticore shook his head so that leaves rustled in his mane. 'Just this one. I have a special dispensation and a bit of extra magic from our leader.'

Who was their leader and how could he get a manti-core to talk? But before Mella could ask, Mella II said, 'We don't mean you any harm.'

The manticore stretched: he was actually bigger than both the girls put together. He raised one paw and extended claws that looked like sabres. He grinned slightly, showing fangs that would have done justice to a shark. 'I was a bit worried about that,' he said.

A manticore with a sense of humour! The creature could swallow their whole heads with a single gulp, but somehow Mella started to feel at ease. 'Did you say you could help us?' she ventured.

'If you'd like to come with me . . .' the manticore told her. 'My name is –' It was even thicker than his usual speech, but sounded something like *Aboventoun*, '– by the way.'

Mella glanced at Mella II. 'Excuse me,' she said to the manticore. The two girls clumped together for a hurried conference.

'He wants us to go with him.'

'Yes, I heard.'

'What do you think?'

Mella II stretched around Mella to look at the manti-core. 'He's terribly big.'

'Yes, isn't he? I don't suppose you know what they eat?'

'You mean, like, people?'

'We're vegetarian,' the manticore said helpfully.

'This is a private conversation,' Mella told him firmly. 'Please don't listen in.'

But Mella II said to him directly, 'You're vegetarian with *those* teeth?'

'They're for fighting, not eating,' said the manticore. 'My ancestors didn't evolve: they were *created*.'

Mella II placed her mouth close to Mella's ear and whispered, 'What if he's one of Hairstreak's manticores?'

Mella had been trying not to think about Lord Hairstreak, who was presumably tracking them by now. She looked at Aboventoun, who looked back at her blandly. 'Why do you want us to go with you?' she asked bravely.

'Well, not to eat you, that's for sure. Our leader wants to meet you.'

The girls looked at one another, then back at the manticore. 'How did your leader know we were here?' they asked in unison.

'Our leader knows *everything*.'

Mella had the uncomfortable feeling that leaders who knew *everything* were usually megalomaniacs. This manticore seemed friendly, but he still looked deadly dangerous. Did she really want to meet another one?

Suddenly, without the slightest warning, she realised that she did. She trusted the manticore and she knew exactly why. The creature was a mixture. Haleklind wizards had taken bits of lion, bits or scorpion, bits of man and bits of heaven knew what else (those teeth!) to make its first ancestor. For the wizards, the result was a war machine. For the creature itself, the result simply had to be confusion. It was an extraordinary mixture, a prey to strange thoughts, and perplexing emotions. Mella knew this because she was a mixture herself, human and faerie. She and the manticore were two of a kind.

She turned to Mella II. 'I vote we go with him,' she said.

'So do I,' said Mella II without the slightest hesitation.

They were deeper in the forest than they thought and reaching the manticore's companions – he called them his *herd* – took longer than Mella had anticipated. By the time they emerged from the trees, her feet were sore and she was exhausted and breathless from trying to keep pace with a creature who tried to move at her pace, but whose long legs covered an enormous amount of ground even at an amble. She stood stock still, wondering if she had made the right decision. Mella II stepped out of the forest to join her. Together they stared out across the open plain.

'Oh my Gods!' Mella whispered.

It was a spectacle drawn directly from a madman's dream. The entire plain was black with manticores – hundreds, perhaps even thousands, stretching as far as the eye could see. They were grazing as the girls emerged, but now, like a vast wave on a giant ocean, heads came up and turned to look towards them. The eyes of the beasts glowed in the sunlight.

'Which one's the leader?' Mella II murmured.

'I'll take you to him,' said their guide. 'Just follow

me.' Aboventoun strode forward and the edge of the herd parted to allow him through.

'I'm not going in there,' Mella said decisively. Following a single manticore was scary enough, but walking into a herd of thousands took courage of a whole different kind.

'We have to,' Mella II told her.

'Why? Why do we have to?' Aboventoun might be able to talk (by special dispensation) but these were wild beasts, dangerous and unpredictable.

'Because we don't know what else to do,' Mella II said firmly (as firmly as Mella herself might have said if she had anything to be firm about). 'We have to get to the Palace and we don't know how and Aboventoun is the only creature who's volunteered to help us.' She glanced at the waiting Aboventoun. 'Sorry to call you a "creature",' she added.

'That's all right,' said Aboventoun. 'It's exactly what I am. Now, are you coming before our leader gets impatient?'

Mella hesitated a second longer, then moved forward with her sister. Mella II was right: they simply didn't know what else to do.

The herd opened a pathway to allow them through. Aboventoun ambled along it without looking back. The smell of the great beasts enveloped them. It was by no means unpleasant and after a few paces became actively comforting, as if they too had become part of a protective herd. A few of the creatures stretched out their heads to sniff them as they walked past. None showed any sign of aggression.

With the manticores all around them, they could see nothing but Aboventoun's great swinging scorpion tail.

Mella was beginning to wonder how long it was going to take to meet the leader when, without warning, the manticores scattered, leaving a large circular open space in the middle of which stood . . .

Aboventoun lowered his head, then slowly, carefully, bent his forelegs. Mella wondered what on earth he was trying to do, then realised he was kneeling. She stared, open-mouthed, at the thing he was kneeling *to*.

If she'd thought about it at all, Mella must have assumed that the leader of the manticores would be a manticore himself. Or possibly herself. But she should perhaps have thought to ask herself how one dumb beast, however dominant, could persuade another of its kind to talk. What she was looking at was big and strong and fierce all right, but it was no manticore. It was huge and fanged and humanoid and feathered, with fiery saucer eyes and strangler's hands. It rose to tower above her as it towered above Aboventoun and every other nearby creature. She could see it, she could smell it – it had a heavy spice scent – yet in some peculiar way it did not seem to be really there at all.

It sniffed her scent through twitching nostrils, then smiled a smile of recognition. 'I knew your mother once,' it told her in a voice that reverberated through her head.

Mella opened her mouth then closed it again. It seemed impossible for her to speak. If the manticores were frightening, this thing was positively terrifying. *I knew your mother once?* Mella tried again to speak and failed.

'I am Yidam,' said the creature. 'But thou may call me George.'

forty-six

There was no way Mella was going to call this creature George. The way it shimmered on the edge of existence made her wonder if it somehow *permitted* her to see it, permitted the manticores to see it. They seemed respectful, but at ease, although this thing, this *Yidam*, was even bigger than they were and radiated an aura of power that was almost overwhelming. She knew what she was looking at, even though she had never seen anything like it before or heard the name. *I knew your mother once.* If that was true, it was something her mother had never spoken about.

Mella felt Mella II move to her side. 'What is it?' Mella II whispered.

'It's one of the Old Gods,' Mella whispered back without taking her eyes off the creature: it was impossible to take her eyes off the creature. 'They sometimes intervene in faerie affairs.' That was something she *did* know about from her mother. Blue had often told the story of how Henry rescued her from the dragon, and while Mella always thought it had to be grossly exaggerated – both her parents assumed she was positively *naive* – there was one detail that had lodged firmly in her mind. Another of the Old Gods – his name was Loki – had intervened big time in the whole affair.

But it wasn't the intervention that impressed Mella. After all, there were loads of ancient legends about the Gods appearing when they were least expected. No, what impressed Mella was the reason Blue gave for the intervention. She could still hear the words sounding in her mind:

'A priest once told me the Old Gods believe that mortal lives are lived to act out certain stories. Sometimes they intervene to make sure the stories turn out the way they should – they way they were fated to.' Then the coy little smile. *'So I suppose your father and I were fated to get married and have you.'*

The sentimentality of the *fated to get married and have you* bit usually made Mella want to puke, but while she would have died rather than admit it, there was something fascinating about the idea of acting out your own story, your own *heroic* story, with the help of the Gods. Was she too wrapped up in a story, the way her mother had been once? Other words of Blue's slid into her mind:

'Never get the idea the dangers aren't real. The stories aren't made up: they're the patterns of the ways we lead our lives. Some of them end in tragedy. Your father could have been eaten by the dragon – we both could. He was brave and he was strong and it didn't happen … but it could have. There are no guarantees.'

Mella wondered if she had the courage and the strength to live the sort of story her parents had once faced. Perhaps she wouldn't have to, but surely the very fact that the Yidam was standing before her showed she had some important, heroic, story to live? The question was, what? Actually, the question was, could she survive it? As her mother said, there were no guarantees.

At her side, as if reading her mind, Mella II murmured, 'We can get through this together.'

Mella felt a flooding of courage. 'Lord Yidam,' she said, 'how did you know my mother?' Was it permitted to question a god? Too late – she'd just done it.

If the Yidam disapproved, he gave no sign. 'She called me to ask a question about war and peace.'

'She never told me that,' Mella murmured. Her mother had never ever mentioned the Yidam at all. Not once. Which was seriously weird. Surely if you met an Old God, you'd boast about it for years?

'Nor should she. It was part of her burden of shame.' The Yidam leaned forward and held Mella's eye. 'There are echoes in thy story.'

Mella licked her lips. 'What do you mean, Lord Yidam?' She was aware the Old Gods were dangerous, far more dangerous than any manticore, yet somehow she felt no fear of this one. Respect and caution certainly, but no real fear. Having Mella II at her side made a difference. It was as if all her courage had been doubled.

'Is there not the threat of war?' the Yidam asked.

'Yes,' Mella II said promptly. She turned to Mella and whispered, 'What I was telling you – the Haleklinders and the manticores and Lord Hairstreak and everything.'

'Yes, yes, I know!' Mella hissed back impatiently.

'And art thou not the only ones who can stop it?' asked the Yidam.

Mella blinked.

They held a conference, all three of them, squatting cross-legged on the earth, surrounded by the manticore herd. The Yidam's head remained higher than a manticore's back and the Old God still towered over the two Mellas, yet their little circle seemed somehow . . . friendly. What they discussed, by contrast, was terrifying.

'Why me?'

'It is thy story.'

'How can one person stop a war?'

'Thou are not one person: thou art two.'

'How can two people stop a war?' A note of desperation had crept into Mella's voice, but the Yidam was relentless.

'Thy story is thy fate.' The Yidam stared at her silently.

After a while, Mella ventured, 'Will you help us?'

'The Old Gods cannot interfere in the affairs of faerie,' the Yidam told her piously.

Mella lost it. 'Of course you can!' she shrieked. 'You're interfering all the time! You're interfering *now!*' She was shouting at an Old God and she didn't care. Loki had interfered. The Yidam knew her mother. The Yidam was the leader of the manticores. Of course the Old Gods interfered! The Old Gods were practically *control freaks!*

The Yidam grinned at her benignly.

After a while, Mella calmed down enough to ask, 'What am I supposed to do?' She had a vivid mental picture of herself as a tiny, tiny figure at the head of rebel soldiers they'd drummed up from somewhere. It was ludicrous, but the picture would not go away. Maybe she could wear high heels.

'That is not for me to say,' the Yidam told her irritatingly.

'He means we have to figure out for ourselves what to do,' said Mella II brightly.

'That is what I mean,' the Yidam echoed.

Mella looked from one to the other, half in fury, half in panic. 'We can't figure out something like that!' she shouted so loudly that a nearby manticore shied away. 'That's politics and military decisions and the fate of nations and the future of our empire and I'm not even sixteen yet! We can't do stuff like that! We can't! We can't!'

'Yes, we can,' said Mella II.

'Go back to first principles,' suggested the Yidam.

Mella decided she hated the Yidam, even if he had known her mother. He was smug and he was bossy and he was totally unhelpful. She wasn't all that keen on Mella II at the moment either: she was far too gung-ho for their own good. She took a deep breath and asked sourly, '*What* first principles?'

The Yidam didn't answer, but her irritating sister did. 'He means we should think carefully about what's happening here; and what's about to happen. He means we should think about Lord Hairstreak's dastardly plot to take over the Realm and how he's proceeded with it so far. We know . . .' She sat up straight and began to count briskly on her fingers, '. . . *dastardly plot step one* that Hairstreak made me to replace you . . . then, *dastardly plot step two*, he arranged a coup to overthrow the legitimate government of Haleklind . . . then, *dastardly plot step three,* he encouraged the new revolutionary Haleklind Table of Seven to breed manticores as weapons . . . and finally, *dastardly plot step four,* he plans to unleash the manticores on the Realm, probably any minute now.'

'Yes, I know all –' Mella began.

But Mella II would not be interrupted. 'Now the great thing is we've *already* foiled dastardly plot step one. He can't replace you with me, because we've both escaped his dastardly clutches –'

'I wish you'd stop saying 'dastardly',' Mella muttered. 'It sounds silly.'

'All right,' said Mella II mildly. 'We've escaped his dastardly clutches – I won't say it again after that – and we're working together so he can't replace you with me and even if he did, I wouldn't do what he told me, so it would be pointless. That means all we have to do now is undo the other steps of his das— of his plot and we've won. We need to warn our parents about what's going on and especially about Lord Hairstreak's involvement. That's probably the most important thing. We simply have to get a message to the Purple Palace.' She hesitated. 'I don't suppose you could do that, could you, Lord Yidam?'

'No,' the Yidam said shortly. But he was watching her with interest.

'No, I thought not,' Mella II muttered, frowning. 'Actually they might not believe a message unless we delivered it personally.' She looked back at Mella. 'But that wouldn't be enough, of course. Ideally we also need to stop the Table of Seven launching an attack. Once we've done that, *everything* falls into place. War averted, parents saved, Lord Hairstreak locked away in some deep dungeon, perfect ending to your story. *Our* story, as it must be now.'

'Why don't we just change the entire world while we're at it?!' Mella snapped. '*How?* You tell me *how!* We're surrounded by manticores somewhere in Haleklind with no transport, no money, no weapons and a big fat toothy supernatural entity who tells us what to do but won't raise a finger to help us.' She glared at the Yidam. 'Well, come on – tell me how!'

The Old God gazed at her almost fondly. 'Nobody knows thy story except thyself,' he said. 'But thou hadst better think of something quickly. Lord Hairstreak is already in the forest.'

Mella felt herself go cold. 'How do you know?'

'I know everything,' the Yidam told her. 'Except thy story, of course.'

'Is he close?'

'Not yet. But he is on thy trail and following his own story. Thou dost not have much time.'

Mella stared at him wide-eyed. 'He can't get us while we're surrounded by your manticores, can he?'

'Perhaps, perhaps not,' the Yidam said softly. 'But thou canst not hide forever . . .'

Mella wondered if there was some penalty for strangling an Old God. The Yidam was the most infuriating creature she had ever met. She wasn't *planning* to hide forever. She wasn't planning to hide at all. All she wanted was a little *support* from –

'I have an idea,' said Mella II abruptly. She grabbed Mella's arm. 'Let's go somewhere private for a minute.'

'Stay thou clear of the trees,' the Yidam told them. 'Aboventoun was my messenger, but I do not control the forest manticores.'

Forty-Seven

'Can you suggest an alternative?' Blue asked coldly.

Henry hated it when she was in this mood, although he had to admit it went with the territory. Above everything else, above being his wife, his lover, his very best friend in two worlds, Blue was Queen. Her prime responsibility was the welfare of the Realm (along with the welfare of Hael, but he didn't like to think of that too often) and just now the Realm was threatened as it had never been before.

'Not as such,' he said carefully. 'But that doesn't mean we shouldn't examine the proposal carefully. It's an extreme course of action.'

'It's an extreme situation.'

'I don't like it,' Pyrgus said. 'They're innocent animals.'

'They're military weapons,' Blue said shortly.

The proposal had been voiced by Madame Cardui, promptly backed by General Vanelke, who, Henry suspected, was still irritated about the abortive plan to save Mella without involving his soldiers.

'Look,' Henry said, 'I think we should concentrate on Mella. We still –'

Mella's disappearance was driving Blue crazy, not that Henry would have expected anything else: mother love always beat father love hands down. It would be killing her that there was nothing they could do for Mella until they had new information on her where-abouts. But Blue's way of handling it was to go on the attack.

'You know we have no way of finding Mella yet,' she snapped. 'So perhaps you could stop wasting every-body's time and –'

Henry avoided conflict whenever he could, but that didn't mean he was afraid to push when it was neces-sary; and it was definitely necessary now. He held Blue's gaze and said firmly, 'It's no waste of time where our daughter's safety is concerned. Can't you reactivate your follower?' He caught the startled glances in the Situa-tion Room. Followers might no longer be illegal, but they were considered extremely bad form among Faer-ies of the Light. The thought that the Queen of Faerie might actually use one was as unthinkable as the idea that the Queen of England might appear on Horse Guards Parade dressed in frilly knickers. He knew Blue wouldn't thank him for mentioning the follower in public, but he was getting desperate.

Blue glared at him. 'All right,' she said angrily. 'Since you insist on shouting from the rooftops, my follower was never deactivated. It finally found her as she entered Haleklind.' She hesitated, but only barely. 'At which point it fell foul of Haleklind's advanced magical secu-rities. The follower is dead, Henry. I sent its body back to Hael for cremation an hour ago.'

'Oh,' Henry said, chastened. But he couldn't afford to stay chastened for long. 'All right, scrub the fol-lower. So we don't know where she is and we don't have a quick way to find out, but we can be reasonably sure she's still in Haleklind. How sensible is it for us to start a war against Haleklind while she's still there?'

'We're not starting a war,' Vanelke grumbled. 'They are.'

'We're not starting a war,' Blue echoed. 'We're making a pre-emptive strike. The whole idea is to *stop* a war.'

'We're *discussing* Madame Cardui's *suggestion* of a pre-emptive strike,' Henry corrected her.

'And I don't like it,' Pyrgus put in fiercely. 'Not that sort of a pre-emptive strike.' He snorted bitterly. 'It's obscene.'

'It involves the least loss of faerie life,' Madame Cardui said mildly.

'And the slaughter of thousands of innocent animals!' Pyrgus had gone red in the face now, as he often did when talking about animal welfare. In another couple of minutes he would lose his temper, as he often did when talking about animal welfare. That made him likely to shout at his sister, shake Madame Cardui and quite possibly bop Vanelke on the nose.

'There are political implications to a neutron spell,' Henry said to turn the discussion in a different direction.

There was silence for a moment. They all knew about the political implications of a neutron spell. It had been outlawed in warfare by international treaty for more than a century. The spell was officially listed both as black magic and a weapon of mass destruction. You could lay it on an entire population if you had a big enough power source. It killed living creatures, but left property intact for looting. Henry shivered. Pyrgus was right about one thing: neutron spells were obscene.

He looked pointedly from one face to another. The first – and prime – provision of the treaty was that neutron spells should never be used against fellow faeries or allied races in warfare. The second was that neutron spells should no longer be manufactured. The third was that all existing stockpiles of neutron spells should be destroyed. Since the signing, in Blue's great-grandfather's day, the first provision had held, more or less. (There had been some small-scale use of neutron technology in the Battle of Inkcap, but the claim was that it had been accidental and less than a score of people died.) The second and third provisions had been resolutely ignored. Most countries maintained secret laboratories where neutron spells and other banned magics were created. Most countries maintained clandestine stocks of the weaponry. What stopped their use, frankly, was fear. Nobody wanted to be the first to cast a neutron spell in case the enemy had sufficient power reserves to strike back in kind. Until now, that was.

Madame Cardui, who'd made the suggestion in the first place, said, 'My calculations are that there may be fewer implications than one would imagine.'

'How do you make that out?' Pyrgus demanded, his voice still angry.

'Firstly,' Madame Cardui said coolly, 'all our intelligence on the matter suggests there are very few countries with the power resources to do us much damage. They have the spells, of course, but not enough power reserves to drive them to anything like their ultimate potential.'

'Haleklind has the resources,' Henry interrupted. Haleklind's reserves of magical power were massive, exceeded only by the combined reserves of the entire Empire.

'Haleklind does,' Madame Cardui nodded. 'But the question is whether Haleklind would wish to be seen to be the first to break the prime provision of the treaty.'

'Yes, but they wouldn't be the first, would they?' Pyrgus snorted. 'We would.'

This time Madame Cardui shook her head. 'No, we would not,' she said firmly. 'The treaty specifically bans the use of neutron spells against faeries or allied races. It says nothing about manticores or other animals.'

'Well, it should do!'

'That may be so, Pyrgus,' Madame Cardui told him, 'but at the moment it does not. If we specifically target the manticore herds –' She gestured towards the view-globes, '– the effects will be isolated from all the main population centres and there should be no collateral damage whatsoever. Once we make the strike, we will announce that the Haleklinders had developed breeding manticores as weapons for military purposes and that our aim in removing these weapons is purely to preserve peace. Legally, the Haleklinders have no grounds to strike back at us and if they were tempted to strike anyway, even they do not have sufficient power reserves to wipe us out completely. We, on the other hand, have sufficient reserves to remove every living being in Haleklind.'

It was the fact she said it so calmly that chilled Henry so much. 'That's what I mean,' he told her soberly. 'Every living thing in Haleklind includes our daughter at the moment.'

It had a chastening effect on Blue. He knew that, even though she tried to hide it. She started to say something, but Pyrgus cut across her. 'Listen,' he said, 'do we have to act at once? This very minute? Can we wait a day or two before wiping out the manticores?'

Blue glanced towards Madame Cardui and General Vanelke, who were standing together – like newfound allies, Henry thought – near the edge of the Operations Table. Vanelke glanced in turn at the viewglobes. 'They're not positioned for an immediate attack,' he said. 'But they're positioned to *be* positioned.'

'How long?' Blue asked.

'The ones closest to our border . . . half a day . . . twenty-four hours at the most.' Then he added unexpectedly, 'But if you take the whole strategic situation into account, it would be longer – somewhere between forty-eight and seventy-two hours, I would estimate. They're not stupid. They know what they're facing and they'd want to make sure of every detail. That takes time.'

'Cynthia?' Blue asked.

Madame Cardui shrugged. 'I have no specific information that an attack is imminent. What worries me is the very existence of the manticores. As the General says, we could have a border incursion in half a day.'

Blue turned back to her brother. 'All right, Pyrgus, what did you have in mind?'

'Two things,' Pyrgus told her. 'I'm more familiar with Haleklind than anybody here. I suggest I go back there. Prime objective to find Mella and get her to safety. I have contacts who could be helpful. Secondary objective, to find out if there's any way to defuse the situation. Call it a diplomatic mission. At very least I might be able to buy time. With Mella still in Halkelind somewhere, time may be the most important thing.' He stopped and stared at her expectantly.

Henry opened his mouth to support Pyrgus, then

closed it again. Blue could get stubborn if she thought they were ganging up on her. He waited. After a long moment, Blue said, 'Yes. Yes, Pyrgus, that's a good idea. Can you go at once?'

Pyrgus nodded. 'Yes.'

'Alone or with back-up?'

'Alone,' Pyrgus said.

'I'll come with you,' Henry told him hurriedly.

But they both turned towards him.

'Not a good idea,' Pyrgus said.

'I don't trust the Table of Seven,' Blue said soberly. 'It's bad enough to risk a Crown Prince. I'm not prepared to risk my King Consort.'

'It would also be bad politics,' Madame Cardui put in. 'We would be acting at too high a level.'

'Pyrgus,' Blue said.

'Yes?'

'I can give you two days – at most.'

'I understand.'

Blue said, 'That's assuming there's no change in the present situation.'

'I understand,' Pyrgus said again.

But Blue clearly wanted to make absolutely sure he really did understand. 'If there is any evidence – any hint or suggestion – of an attack by the Haleklinders, or Madame Cardui brings me any intelligence that such an attack is imminent, I shall order the immediate use of neutron spells specifically targeted to wipe out the manticores. All the manticores . . .' She turned to Henry with a bleak smile. 'At least we can be sure Mella will be safe. Whatever she's up to, there's no way she will be anywhere near a manticore herd.'

Forty-Eight

Hairstreak was in the forest for almost an hour before he heard the screams. They were some distance off, but carried an interesting degree of urgency. It was difficult to be certain, but he thought it might be a female scream. Specifically a girl's.

'What's that?' Aisling asked.

Aisling had been slowing things down. With his new body, Hairstreak could walk indefinitely without tiring, but Aisling was a bundle of complaints after the first few hundred yards. Her feet hurt. Her legs hurt. She scratched her hand on a thorn bush. She was out of breath. The forest was smelly. Couldn't they rest a little while?

'Somebody in trouble,' Hairstreak said tritely. 'You stay here: I'll go and find out.'

He expected she might protest, but she only said, 'Please be careful, darling.'

It was odd to be called *darling,* but he rather liked it. 'Use your whistle if anything comes near you.'

'Of course,' Aisling said. She stood on tiptoe to give him a brief kiss. He liked that as well.

The scream came again.

Hairstreak flicked his new body into turbo mode and ran. Mostly he kept to the paths, but from time to time found it convenient to push his way directly through shrub and bushes. Although his mind was occupied, he was aware of the scrapes and scratches that resulted; and also the pain. Consolidated Magical Services had enabled the body to feel pain in the normal course of events, since pain was a necessary – and familiar – signal of malfunction. But the pain was less intrusive than it would be in a natural body and if it grew troublesome, he could always switch it off using a small stud built into his left nipple. On the whole, he was too distracted to care. The screams – they were definitely girlish screams – had to mean Mella was in trouble: after all, the forest was not exactly teeming with young women. She'd been caught by a manticore, perhaps, or fallen down and broken her stupid leg. But the question was, which Mella? With luck, it would be the real one. In which case he could finish her off and resume his search for the clone. But if it was the clone . . .

He kicked his speed up another notch.

The screams were continuous now, and closer. There was an overlay of other noises, an animal growl and a snapping sound like the breaking of bones. Someone was under attack, but so long as she was screaming, she was not dead. Hairstreak put on another burst of speed. He ran along a narrow pathway, then left it for a more direct route. He broke through a screen of bushes and found himself in a broad clearing. He was no longer alone.

The manticore seemed seized by a frenzy. It was crouched over the girl, stabbing at her viciously with its scorpion tail, tearing at her flesh with its hideous fangs. The girl's clothing was ripped and her body streaming blood. If she had fought the beast when it first attacked, she was not fighting it now. Her body was as limp as a rag doll. Her eyes were closed, her throat bloody and exposed. The girl was Princess Mella, to judge from the remnants of her torn clothing. She was not the one screaming.

For Hairstreak, it felt as if he had been struck by a slo-mo spell. The pace of time dropped to a crawl. The great scorpion sting thudded like a background drum-beat, stabbing the ground in some hideous reflex now the girl was dead. He turned slowly towards the source of the screams and uttered a profound, slow prayer of thanks to the powers of Night: the girl screaming was the Mella clone, standing paralysed several yards from the manticore, her back against a tree. She looked terrified, but physically unharmed.

The manticore dropped the body of the girl and swung its head around to stare at him with glowing, insane eyes. It opened a mouth packed with blood-stained teeth and roared, a sound so vast the trees on either side of him reverberated and rustled their leaves. Then, still with the appalling slowness that character-ised the whole encounter, it launched itself forward and began to run towards him. Rippling muscles propelled padded feet in stately haste.

The manticore was huge. This was the first one Hairstreak had seen close up, outside of the laboratory. They were about the size of a medium-sized dog when they were finally released into the wild, but it seemed as if they only started growing at that point. This one was larger than an ox, large as an elephant in height and appreciably longer when it uncurled the scorpion tail. Despite its size, Hairstreak pondered for a moment on the possibility of fighting it. At another time he would never have entertained the thought, but there was something in his new relationship with the Lady Aisling that spurred him towards heroic deeds. And it was a practical thought. His new body was virtually indestructible – or so the salesman claimed.

But there remained a weak point: his natural head was as vulnerable as it ever was. One crunch of those massive teeth and he was dead. He remembered a time when he would have welcomed that outcome, but that time was long gone. He was on the brink of the coup of his entire career, poised to rule the Realm and countries beyond, poised to become the greatest Emperor history had ever known. This gory scene showed beyond all doubt his luck had changed. Princess Mella was dead. Her terrified replacement stood unharmed only yards away. He would have to calm the clone down, of course, persuade her to forget the horror of the last few minutes. But she had always been amenable and he expected no trouble. So perhaps best to waste no time in dangerous heroics. Especially when Aisling was not even here to see them.

Slow time reverted and he was faced with a beast hurtling towards him at breakneck speed. For something so large, it managed to move with the swiftness of a striking snake. The long forelegs ate distance at an alarming rate. It was already more than halfway across the clearing. In seconds he felt a wave of heat from its foetid breath. Strangely, the predominant smell was that of ageing fruit. The creature roared. Hairstreak pressed the control on the whistle around his neck.

The tone was too high-pitched for faerie ears, but the manticore reacted at once. It stopped dead, only yards away from him and stood for a moment, swinging its great head from side to side. Then, in a curiously cat-like gesture, it raised one foreleg to brush against its ear, as if trying to remove a flea. A puzzled expression crept into its eyes and it backed off a few steps. Then, suddenly, it swung away, and bounded across the clearing. Hairstreak had assumed it would simply run, but it took time to swoop and grab the limp corpse of the dead Mella. It turned towards him, her body hanging from its mouth. (The face looked surprisingly serene in death.) Then the manticore blundered away into the depths of the forest.

'Uncle Hairstreak!' shrieked the Mella clone. 'I was so frightened, but I knew you'd come to find me!'

He had been wondering if he might have trouble with his Mella clone since he entered the clearing and realised the two girls must have met. It was difficult to predict the effect of an encounter with one's clone. It might even have shaken his Mella's carefully induced determination to become Queen. But her words reassured him. She was still the same old Mella he had nurtured so carefully over the past few years. Hairstreak walked across and put one arm around her shoulders. She was trembling, but she looked up into his face with trusting eyes.

'Come on,' he said, 'I need to get you home.'

'To your Keep?' asked Mella.

With a sudden surge of satisfaction, Hairstreak shook his head. 'To the Purple Palace,' he told her. 'I think it's time you took your rightful place.'

Forty-Nine

Blue would kill him, Pyrgus thought, if ever she found out. And in truth he might deserve it. However informal the arrangements, the fact remained he was on a diplomatic mission. It was also a fact that he had ignored protocol, skirted sanctioned arrangements, evaded Madame Cardui's official spy (delicately designated Personal Assistant to the Crown Prince), given his entourage the slip and disappeared to carry out a mission of his own. It was practically treason, but what could he do when the lives of thousands of innocent animals were at stake?

'You never sent that wine you promised,' Corin said, grinning, as they shook hands.

Pyrgus smiled bleakly. 'I've been tied up. Bit of an emergency on, actually.'

Corin waved him to a seat and pulled up a second chair beside it. The gesture was typical; and not simply because he and Pyrgus were old friends. Corin was a man who disliked formality and never felt the need to sit behind a large desk in order to impress people. 'There had to be trouble, otherwise you wouldn't be back so soon. Is this about your niece?'

'Not exactly,' Pyrgus said. 'She *was* in Haleklind – still is, we think – but that's not the problem.'

'I'm afraid there's no news of your manticore,' Corin said. 'But I'm sure she's safe. She'll certainly have joined one of the major herds by now. They've spread all over the country.'

'Actually . . .' Pyrgus said uneasily. This was the point of no return. He was about to discuss Realm policy and military plans with a citizen of what might be classified an enemy nation. But he would have trusted Corin with his life. 'Actually, it's the manticores I want to talk to you about . . .'

'I thought it might be. I assume you've heard the rumours?'

'What rumours?' Pyrgus asked quickly.

'There's been talk that the Table plan to use the manticores for military purposes. Turn them into war-horses or something.'

It occurred to Pyrgus suddenly that with all the talk of manticores as weapons, he'd never thought to wonder exactly how they would be used. 'Do you imagine that's true?' he asked.

Corin shook his head. 'Absolute nonsense. A soldier would have to do the splits to mount a full-grown manticore. And if he managed that, he'd never control it. These are wild beasts, Pyrgus. Magnificent animals, but you know how difficult they are. Difficult and unpredictable. One minute they're grazing quietly, the next they're ripping you to shreds if you aren't careful.'

'So you think there's nothing in the rumours?'

'I didn't say that. I just said they couldn't be used as mounts. They might still be used as weapons.'

'How?'

Corin spread his hands in a helpless gesture and smiled broadly. 'You think the Table of Seven let me know their plans?' The smile faded and he added soberly, 'But I can guess. At least I can tell you what I'd do if I wanted to use manticores as weapons.'

'What?'

Corin took a deep breath and released it as a sigh. 'I'd herd them into position, feed them St John's wort, then stampede them into your army.'

Pyrgus stared at him. 'My Gods!' he exclaimed as the implications sank in. He found himself picturing the scene. St John's wort sent manticores berserk. One great beast could kill a score of soldiers before it was slaughtered in its turn. A herd of them would decimate an entire army within minutes. The bloodshed would be unimaginable.

Corin shrugged. 'May never happen, Pyrgus – it's only rumours. May not be what the Table is planning at all. Haleklind is always full of gossip.'

Pyrgus said, 'Did you know there's a colossal herd massed on the Empire's border?'

'Of manticores? No, I didn't.' He looked seriously at Pyrgus, waiting.

Pyrgus closed his eyes briefly, reopened them and said, 'We have intelligence that the Table of Seven plan to attack the Realm using manticores as their secret weapon. I don't know exactly how they propose to use them, but after what you've just said . . .' He let his words trail off.

Corin, who knew Pyrgus very well, was staring at him intently. 'That's not all, is it?'

Pyrgus shook his head. 'The Realm may retaliate with a neutron spell.' He could not quite bring himself to tell the whole truth, which was that Blue had no intention of waiting to retaliate. At the first definite sign of threat, she would order a pre-emptive strike.

There was silence between them. 'Oh,' Corin said at length. He looked away, as if unwilling to meet Pyrgus's eye. 'Neutron spells are illegal under international law.'

'Nevertheless . . .' Pyrgus said.

'A neutron spell would kill the entire Haleklind army and wipe out the manticores.'

Pyrgus realised he would have to tell him. 'Actually, it could be just the manticores. My sister may not wait for the Haleklind army to get involved.'

'*Just* the manticores?'

'I know, I know,' Pyrgus agreed. He reached out and gripped Corin's arm. 'We have to do something.'

'How can I help you? How can the Haleklind Society for the Preservation and Protection of Animals help you?' Corin glanced briefly towards the door. 'Hael, we're a subversive organisation now: there must be something we can blow up.'

'I've had an idea,' Pyrgus said. 'How many men can you muster?'

'Muster for what? Are we talking soldiers here for fighting? Or saboteurs? What?'

Pyrgus knuckled his eyes tiredly. 'Corin, I don't suppose you know how manticores might be safely herded? Large numbers of them. Without too much risk of stampede.'

'Actually I do,' Corin said. 'You use torches made from rosemary.'

Pyrgus looked up. 'The plant?'

Corin nodded. 'Manticores don't like fire, but they're not nearly as afraid of it as other animals. You might shift them using torches, but they could just as easily turn on you. They don't seem to mind taking a small burn if it allows them to disarm you – knock the torch

325

away, I mean. But burning rosemary has a peculiar effect on them. They won't come near it for one thing, so you're safe from attack; and at the same time it seems to sedate them, so you can usually persuade them to move where you want them to without too much difficulty. Is this what you need men for?'

'What worries my sister is the herd on the border. I thought if we could move it away . . .' He sighed and made a helpless gesture. 'It would buy us time, at least. But the operation would have to be quick and clean. If the manticores move *towards* the border . . .'

'Queen Blue will use the neutron spell?'

'She might. Dammit, she *will*! I know Blue.' He looked at Corin. 'Can you find enough men for the job? They'll have to be sensible and quick off the mark and able to follow orders precisely and have enough initiative to deal with emergencies – if a manticore left the herd, for example.'

'It's a huge herd,' Corin said, shaking his head. 'We'd need an awful lot of good men.'

'So you can't do it?'

'I didn't say I couldn't do it,' Corin told him. 'If you supervise the making of the torches, I'll round up the men.'

fifty

'Something's happening,' Henry said quietly. There was no change on the Operations Table yet, but it looked like definite movement on the viewglobes. He leaned forward for a better, closer look.

There was a lot of noise in the Situation Room – people talking, people moving, people shouting orders – but Blue seemed to be attuned to him because she was at his side at once. 'What's the matter, Henry?'

What was the matter was that the manticores were moving. He was almost sure of it. And if he was right, it was war and his wife would vent the fury of a neutron spell on Haleklind. 'I'm not sure,' Henry said. 'Maybe nothing.'

Blue stared past him at the globe. 'You think they're moving, don't you?'

'Blue,' Henry said, 'about the neutron thing –'

'Don't make this any more difficult for me, Henry. I must preserve the Realm.'

'Yes, but not that way. Not by killing thousands . . . probably tens of thousands . . .'

Blue said tiredly, 'Tell me another way. You were here when we discussed it. Tell me a better way.' When Henry didn't answer, she turned her back on the globes. 'There's no sign of troop movements,' she said firmly.

'They won't use the manticores without conventional back-up. It would make no sense.' She stopped to stare around the bustle in the Situation Room, then added almost dreamily, 'I'm sure Madame Cardui will alert us to troop movements.' Henry thought she looked exhausted, which she probably was. They'd both missed sleep lately.

He turned back to the globes. The technology was not a million miles away from what he was used to in his own world. The feed came from cameras strategically placed at points along the border. What the cameras saw could be changed, at least to some degree, by remote control. Since the equipment used magical energy, the enemy could cut no cables, could block no television signals; and the cameras themselves were so well protected they were virtually indestructible. But there were three serious flaws. The first was that the picture quality was poor. The second was that the pictures themselves were small, with no means of enlargement. (Mr Fogarty had once explained why: something to do with a geometric progression of energy needs.) The third, and most troublesome of all, was that the picture could not be refreshed in real time. Instead it reacted to the position of the moon. The result was that in certain phases, the pictures on the viewglobes ran as smoothly as a movie, while in others the update was jerkier than an old dial-up internet connection. Unfortunately they were in a jerky internet moon phase at the moment.

Blue was probably right. If there were no troops to back them up, it would make little sense to send the manticores stampeding across the border. Except that he thought he'd spotted movement close to the herd. Not troop movement, to be sure – so far there were only a few figures – but maybe the preliminary to troop movement: forward scouts searching out the best positions for an approaching army. Or maybe nothing at all, a small party of Haliklind tourist hikers who'd wandered off the beaten track. Henry shut his eyes. He really would have to stop thinking the worst in every situation. If this went on, he'd start imagining Lord Hairstreak had made a miraculous comeback and was plotting to take over the planet.

'Excuse me, Consort Majesty, Lord Hairstreak wishes to see you and Her Majesty the Queen.'

Henry stared down at the messenger, a fresh-faced young woman in uniform, wondering if he'd misheard or was just hallucinating. He noticed Madame Cardui was standing beside the girl and switched his attention to her at once. 'I thought Lord Hairstreak was dead – or as good as. Isn't he on life support?'

Madame Cardui nodded. 'He was kept alive with a *Body in a Box*. Nightmare existence: just a head on an onyx cube. But it seems CMS have sold him something better now – I sent a memo to Queen Blue about it. He has full-functioning mobility. Quite his old self, in fact. His old *dangerous* self.'

There were a lot of things Henry suddenly wanted to know. 'You don't think he's mixed up in the Haleklind invasion plan, do you?'

Madame Cardui said soberly, 'I doubt it, given his long incapacity. At the same time, I've just had intelligence that Lord Hairstreak came calling on the Companion Leader immediately before Mella vanished – an interesting coincidence . . . if you believe in coincidence.'

Blue, who had been locked in close conference with General Vanelke, was suddenly beside them. 'What's an interesting coincidence?'

'Hairstreak's here,' Henry said. 'He's managed to acquire a mobile body.' He looked at the messenger.

'Majesty, Lord Hairstreak is seeking an audience with Your Majesties.'

'*Hairstreak?*' Blue frowned. 'Where is he?'

'Above in the Palace, Majesties, waiting in the ante-room to the Throne Room.' The girl had an excited look in her eye. She hesitated, then suddenly blurted, 'Majesties, the Princess Mella is with him.'

Despite the need for decorum, Henry was almost running when he reached the ante-room, but had to stop to allow Blue to enter ahead of him. As he stepped inside a pace behind her, it registered at once how tall Hairstreak had become. Madame Cardui was right: he had regained a fully functioning body, and a bigger, stronger one than the body he used to have. If it was made by CMS it had to be artificial, but it looked the real thing. The face on the old familiar head was contorted into an expression of attempted benevolence that made Henry instantly suspicious.

Then, standing to the right of Hairstreak and a little behind, he saw Mella. She was wearing different clothes to the last time he'd seen her and looked a little the worse for wear, but overall, to his intense relief, she seemed fit and healthy.

Blue must have spotted her as well, but was constrained by protocol to say, 'Lord Hairstreak, how good to see you functioning again.'

Henry, who accepted no such constraints, ran to

Mella. As he reached her, he heard Hairstreak said, 'I have brought your daughter home from Haleklind.'

'Indeed you have,' Blue told him, still every inch the Queen. 'And we are grateful. How may we express it? Will you accept a reward?'

'Mella!' Henry exclaimed and threw his arms around her. He'd have her grounded for a month for running away and worrying them like that, grounded for six months for using *lethe* on them. He'd ban all her favourite foods, forbid her use of magic, deny her all servants, refuse her new shoes, have her travel privileges withdrawn and give her a severe talking to. But all that was for the future. All he wanted now was to kiss her and hold her and make sure she was all right.

Mella hugged him back. She smelled a little different – probably hadn't bathed in a while, although it was not the smell of stale sweat – and her eyes seemed unusually sober, worried almost, although that would easily be explained if she had got herself into trouble, since she ran away. Or perhaps she was just anticipating punishment, as well she might.

'There is no need for a reward,' Lord Hairstreak said. His voice had improved since he found a new body, taking on more resonance and giving him a certain charisma. 'Mella is my favourite great-niece.'

Mella is your only *great-niece,* Henry thought inconsequentially.

'Daddy, I need to talk to you,' Mella whispered in his ear. 'Take me out of here somewhere private.'

'Then you must stay for a meal,' Blue said; and you would never have thought she loathed Lord Hairstreak ... or that the Realm was poised on the brink of war. 'We have to hear the story of how you found her –' Blue glanced at Mella for the first time, '– and what she was doing in Haleklind.'

Henry felt a surge of admiration for his wife. She too must have been beside herself to hug Mella, kiss Mella, find out if Mella was all right, but she was coolly, calculatingly putting her Realm duty first. If Hairstreak agreed to stay for a meal – and protocol insisted one should never decline an invitation from the Queen – Henry could imagine her subtly quizzing him about the Haleklind situation (and the reason for his recent visit) under the pretext of asking him about Mella. There was only one problem with her plan. Now Hairstreak was equipped with a brand new artificial body, had he begun to eat again? Henry was fairly sure that when the little crud was just a head on a cube, he'd lived on sunlight.

'Daddy!' Mella hissed urgently.

Henry turned his attention back to his daughter. 'We can't leave yet,' he whispered. 'It would be impolite to Lord Hairstreak. And your mother will want to talk to you in a minute.' The exchange was attracting the attention of Lord Hairstreak, who glanced towards them. To his surprise, Henry noticed that his daughter caught Hairstreak's eye and a most curious look passed between them. Then Lord Hairstreak turned away and the moment was gone.

Mella stood on tiptoe and leaned forward until her mouth touched his ear. 'If you don't get me out of here at once, Daddy, I intend to pee, very publicly, on your foot.'

Fifty-One

Pyrgus had done something like this before when he was a boy, and he still loved it. Corin's men weren't at all what he'd expected. He'd assumed the best his old friend could do would be members of the Society, and probably not even activists. Instead he produced soldiers – tough, hard men with marine training. They didn't carry weapons (at least not visible weapons), which was a small disappointment, but they wielded their torches like projectile rifles. Corin introduced Pyrgus as their new leader and they all came to attention, saluted smartly and stamped so violently that the nails in their heavy-duty boots emitted sparks. Then they trotted into marching formation, shuffled into final positions and fell in behind him. It was a fantastic feeling, spoiled only by the fact he had to ask Corin where they were going.

The march – it was a proper march with rude counting songs and everything – proved fairly easy, which was just as well since Pyrgus quickly discovered he was disgracefully unfit; at least by comparison with his men. He felt a distinct sense of relief when Corin whispered that they were approaching the manticore plain that abutted the border. But when they topped a rise and looked across the plain itself, it was immediately obvious something was wrong.

'Where are the manticores?' Pyrgus asked. There was not a single beast in sight, let alone a herd.

Corin looked as surprised as he was. 'I don't know.'

'Are you sure this is the right place?'

'Yes,' Corin said. 'Of course.' He pointed. 'That's the border over there. If you look carefully you can see the shimmer of the securities.'

'But there aren't any manticores.'

'Yes, I can see that,' Corin said. 'They must have . . . gone.'

'This is turning into a really stupid conversation,' Pyrgus said grumpily. 'Of course they're gone, otherwise they'd still be here. The question is where? They were massing on the border, Corin, I can promise you that. You know what I told you.' He looked at Corin and nodded knowingly. He had to be careful what he said because of the men who were now pressing up behind them, but once Corin thought about it, it had to be obvious that a manticore herd, bred as weapons and poised for an invasion, didn't simply wander off somewhere. If there had been any sign of major movement, any sign at all, the Table of Seven would have ordered them driven back to their former position at once. Even Pyrgus's own plan to move them back from the border was only a way of buying time.

Corin lowered his voice. 'Perhaps the invasion has started.'

Pyrgus stared at him in sudden shock. It said a lot for his naiveté that the thought had never occurred to him. But now Corin had expressed it, Pyrgus realised, with a sweeping chill, it was the most obvious explanation. 'Do you really think so?'

'I don't know,' Corin said. From his face he was as

shocked and worried as Pyrgus himself. 'But I think we should find out.'

'How do we do that?'

'We go down there and look at the tracks.'

'Manticores aren't easy to track.' Pyrgus frowned. He'd had a hard enough time following the one that escaped from him and she wasn't on open ground where there were no broken bushes to give a clue.

'Not single manticores, no,' Corin agreed. 'Those pads don't leave much of a mark. But a herd's different, especially a big one; and especially if it's moving quickly. They extend their claws and that chews up the ground. If we go down there, we'll soon know where they went – which direction, anyway.'

There was something else worrying Pyrgus. 'I don't suppose you'd know if the Table of Seven have view-globe cameras set up on the plain?'

'Bound to,' Corin said. 'Their military would want to keep an eye on the herd. And the border, of course. Are you worried about being seen?'

'A bit.' Actually he was less worried about being seen by the Haleklind military than he was about being seen by Blue, who thought he was on a diplomatic mission to Kremlin Karcist. When he had planned on moving the herd, he knew the manticores themselves would shield him, and in any case he was unlikely to be spotted among a mass of milling beasts and men. But if he went down on to an empty plain, he would stand out like a sore thumb. Blue would know at once what he was up to, of course. They'd been so close since child-hood that she could practically read his mind. At which point she'd go ballistic.

Corin, who was quick on the uptake, said, 'Is this

that you don't want the men seen, or you don't want to be recognised personally?'

'Recognised personally – it's a complication I really don't need. It doesn't matter who sees a party of men wandering about, not now: not in an empty field. But I'd rather –' He broke off to ask, 'What are you doing?'

Corin was holding a spell cone under his nose. 'Easily fixed,' he said.

Pyrgus drew back suspiciously. 'Where did you get that?'

Corin grinned. 'I may not like the Government, but I'm still a Haleklinder – we carry spells for every occasion. This one's a NewFace®. The kids use them a lot at dances – they make you look handsome.'

'I'm handsome already,' Pyrgus grinned back.

'Matter of opinion,' Corin told him. 'But in any case they change your whole appearance: your own mother won't recognise you. The best thing about it though is that when you get fed up with looking different, all you have to do is rub your face vigorously and the effect dissipates.'

'Crack the cone!' said Pyrgus briskly.

Corin proved right about the tracks. Once they went down to the plain, it was obvious a manticore herd had grazed there; and recently. It was a little less obvious where they'd gone – parts of the plain were so churned up they looked as if they'd been ploughed – but fortunately one of Corin's men had experience as a tracker.

'They moved into the forest,' he said.

'That's not possible,' Corin said at once. 'Plains manticores dislike the forest and vice versa.'

The man shrugged. 'Only telling you what the tracks show.'

Pyrgus felt a cautious flooding of relief. If the manticores went into the forest, it meant there'd been no invasion yet. But like Corin he was still unsure about this information. He turned to Corin and asked, frowning, 'Where would they go in the forest? Where does the forest lead to?' He didn't seem to be making himself clear, so he added, 'I mean, if you go right the way through the forest, where do you come out?' His grasp of Haleklind geography was abysmal, but the thought occurred that there might be better living conditions for the manticores on the other side. The beasts were nomadic to some extent and could simply have taken off in search of better pastures. Plains manticores might not like to live in a forest, but they might be prepared to pass through one. Against that, if the Table of Seven was planning on using them as a weapon, had moved them to the border and had cameras tracking them, it seemed very unlikely they'd simply have been allowed to wander off. Or if they *had* wandered, wouldn't their military minders be appearing soon to bring them back?

Corin looked at him thoughtfully for a moment. 'The forest has a long stretch northwards and it eventually extends right into the Realm if you go south, but if you move directly across you reach the grounds of Kremlin Karcist eventually.'

'That's where I'm supposed to be,' Pyrgus muttered thoughtfully. His mind was running at full speed. Wherever they might be, the manticores were no longer massing by the border, so the mission he'd set himself was accomplished, even though he'd had nothing to do with it. Which meant he could now get on with his *official* mission. If he reached the Table of Seven quickly, he could start his search for Mella at the place where she was last seen and at the same time find out if there was any diplomatic leeway in the current threatening situation. He was actually more optimistic than he had been when he started out. He kept thinking about the missing herd, finding it difficult to imagine anyone other than the Haleklind military might have moved them. And if the military *had* moved them, that marked a change in the situation, just possibly a change for the better. He came to a decision and turned to Corin.

'Old friend, I want to thank you for your help.'

'Can't say we did much,' Corin shrugged.

'You were here for me – that's what counts. And however it happened, the manticores are out of danger for the moment. So now I need to make official contact with the Table of Seven.'

Corin glanced at him quickly. 'You're not thinking of hiking through the forest, are you?'

'Shouldn't I be?'

'Not on your own, you shouldn't. First of all, knowing you, you'd probably get lost. Secondly, the forest manticores are by far the most dangerous breed of the whole species. Dangerous and unpredictable.'

'Yes, but if you leave them alone, they'll leave –' Pyrgus began to protest.

Corin cut across him. 'Get real, Pyrgus. I know you're an animal-lover, but they can still kill you. We'll come with you.'

Pyrgus looked at Corin, looked at the men ranged in military ranks behind him. 'Will you? Would you? Will you really?'

Corin glanced across his shoulder. 'What do you say, men?'

And the men raised their torches in salute and shouted, *'Yes!'*

The march through the forest was uneventful – so much so that Corin began to worry. 'With a party this size we should have hit at least one security spell by now,' he told Pyrgus eventually. 'This forest edges the grounds of Kremlin Karcist. There's no way they'd let it go unprotected – open invitation.'

'Maybe they rely on the forest manticores to keep people out,' Pyrgus suggested.

'Have *you* seen any manticores?'

'Actually no,' Pyrgus said. 'But I thought it was just the sounds of a big party that was keeping them away.'

'Then a fat lot of protection they'd be, would they?' Corin said. 'But I happen to know there *were* magical protections in this area. At least there used to be. Some of them set to stop large groups as well. One or two people you can leave to the manticores, but a group the size of ours should set off alarm bells all over the place. I've been using a detector since we moved into the trees and there's not a sign of anything. It's as if . . .' He hesitated. 'If I didn't know the Companions better, I'd say it's as if somebody switched them off.'

'Let's just thank the Gods there aren't any,' Pyrgus said philosophically. 'Makes life easier for us. Once we reach the Kremlin we'll be fine: I'm known to Table members and I shall vouch for the rest of you. I'll tell them we came through the forest to keep my mission secret: they'll appreciate something like that.'

'OK,' Corin said, without much conviction, and Pyrgus noticed he continued to keep a cautious watch at every step they took. But Pyrgus knew something was wrong the moment they stepped from the forest into the Kremlin grounds.

The manicured lawns and carefully tended borders were a mess. Shrubs, bushes, even ornamental trees had been uprooted and the grass was shredded so badly he could see the brown soil beneath. Beyond, the sentry posts were all but flattened, and there was no sign of any guards. He stared across at the building itself and saw at once that the window to the right of the main entrance was broken. The entrance itself was unguarded and the double doors wide open – unheard of in the annals of revolutionary Haleklind.

Pyrgus and Corin turned to look at one another. 'Something's happened,' Pyrgus said unnecessarily. They stared together back at the building, then, driven by some instinct, began to run towards it. Corin's men hesitated, then ran with them. As they approached the main entrance, a small figure emerged.

Pyrgus stopped dead. 'Mella!' he exclaimed.

Mella looked at him. 'Who are you?' she asked.

fifty-two

It was one of those conversations that was destined to be replayed in Henry's mind until the day he died: bewildering, astounding, memorable . . . although it began mundanely enough:

Henry said, 'How dare you threaten to pee on my foot. That's absolutely disgraceful behaviour for a young lady. And I will not stand for it.' *Especially not on the foot you've just peed on*, his mind told him irreverently. He tried to sound stern, but was having trouble keeping a straight face.

Mella said, 'Lord Hairstreak's behind it.'

'Lord Hairstreak's behind *what?*'

They were together in the Throne Room now, with the door to the ante-room firmly closed and spell securities protecting their privacy. Their sudden departure had earned him a glare from Blue and he couldn't blame her: walking out like that wasn't merely rude, but massively undiplomatic. Still, it was done now and Mella was looking up at him with that world's-about-to-end expression teenaged girls adopt when they're trying to convey something they think is important. She wasn't much older than her mother had been on the day he first saw her. He tried very hard not to look at Mella fondly.

'Lord Hairstreak is behind the Haleklinders' invasion plan. You have to throw him into a deep, dark, smelly dungeon.'

'Lord Hairstreak is behind the Haleklinders' invasion plan?' Henry echoed. The urge to smile at her had suddenly evaporated. How did Mella know about the Haleklinders' invasion plan?

'Daddy,' Mella said severely, 'Mother's told you not to repeat things back to people in the form of a question. You have no idea how irritating it can be.'

'You have no idea how irritating it can be to have a brat for a daughter,' Henry told her. 'How did you know about the invasion plan and what makes you think Lord Hairstreak has anything to do with it?'

'My sister told me,' Mella said.

'Stop playing games, Mella. You don't have a sister.'

That was when she told him everything.

Blue was in a foul mood when she joined them in the Throne Room. 'Have you any idea how big a breach of protocol –' she began.

Henry opened his mouth to interrupt her, but Mella beat him to it. 'Mother,' she said, 'you have to lock up Uncle Hairstreak.'

'I don't want another word out of you,' Blue said sharply. She shook her head grimly, lips tightly pursed. 'You've caused *so* much trouble for your father and me –' She stopped suddenly and stared at her daughter. 'I have to *what?*'

'He tried to make the Haleklinders invade us and then he was going to kill you and Daddy and put the other Mella on the throne and –'

Blue picked up on it as quickly as Henry had. 'How

do you know about the Haleklinders' invasion?' she asked at once.

The trouble was, Henry thought, his wife and daughter were exactly alike: stubborn, opinionated, bossy, impatient. As a result, they fought all the time, even when Mella wasn't behaving like a brat. He adopted his most calming voice, although he knew from experience it usually irritated them both, and said firmly, 'Leave this to me, Mella. And you, Blue, please be quiet and listen.' He almost added, *for a change,* but stopped himself in time.

Blue glared at him. From the corner of his eye he could see their daughter glaring at him as well. Henry ignored them both. He'd decided there was only one way to handle the new developments – heck, even to make sense of them – and that was to take one step at a time. The most urgent step, it seemed to him, was to tell Blue what Mella had just told him. The next most urgent was to decide what to do about it. Assuming Blue believed it. Henry wasn't sure he believed it himself. He took a deep breath.

'This is a bit complicated,' he began, 'but Mella's just told me –'

The Throne Room doors burst open to a howl of protest from the magical securities, but Pyrgus was still a Crown Prince, so they could do nothing to stop him. He slammed the doors shut with his foot and hurried excitedly towards them. 'You'll never believe what's happened in Halek—' he began, then caught sight of Mella. 'How did you get here ahead of me? That's impossible!'

Mella smiled at him benignly. 'Hello, Uncle Pyrgus.'

'Has she told you?' Pyrgus asked. He looked from

Blue to Henry, suddenly smiling broadly. 'Has she told you what she did to the Table of Seven?'

'That wasn't me, Uncle Pyrgus,' Mella said. 'That was the other Mella.'

'You're behaving like a *child!*' Blue snapped. 'What have you done to the Table of –?'

'Look,' Henry said, 'if the rest of you can be quiet for a moment, I think I should explain that Mella claims there are two –' He stopped dead as the Throne Room doors opened again. He stared. It was one thing to have Mella tell him that utterly fantastic story about Lord Hairstreak and his clone. It was quite another to come face to face with the living proof of it.

'Hello,' said the young figure in the doorway. 'I'm Mella II.'

Fifty-Three

It was so *cool!* First off, there was lots and lots of seriously good food, including her fave, candied mushrooms. Then there was sitting at the top table with the other Mella beside her. (She was wearing her official princess crown and they'd sweetly made a replica for Mella II, which just showed their parents could be quite decent really when they put their minds to it.) Then there was the fact that everybody, but everybody wanted to hear their story, even though it was the talk of the city and they'd heard it all before. Then, best of all, there was Victorinus – Papilio Victorinus – the Duke's grandson, who was so fit he was positively *radical*. She could hardly wait to see him with his shirt off in the celebration games. But he wasn't in the games yet: he was sitting beside her, staring into her eyes, and asking her to tell him (again!) how she'd saved the entire Realm. She could imagine that Victorinus might have caused just the teeniest, tiny bit of trouble between her new sister and herself if he hadn't been a twin. His brother, Papilio Pharnaces, was distracting Mella II even as they spoke.

'It confuses me, *bella*,' Victorinus told her breathlessly, 'this story I have heard, that you were eaten by the beast.' He spread his hands helplessly and smiled.

'Yet, here you are, so beautiful my poor heart aches.' His eyes were huge and brown, his lashes long. He was *two years* older than she was – how fabulous was that?

Mella gave a brittle little laugh. 'I wasn't eaten, silly,' she told him happily. 'It was all a set-up to fool Lord Hairstreak.' Her mother had warned her not to mention Lord Hairstreak's name, but she couldn't see how to tell the story without it; and besides, everybody *knew* about Lord Hairstreak's involvement, even though he kept denying it. 'Mella II and I changed clothes to make him think she was me and I was she and the Yidam – you know what a Yidam is, don't you, Victorinus –?'

Victorinus reached out langorously to take a grape. 'Big scary Old God,' he said.

'– the Yidam could make the manticores do anything and he had this special one called Aboventoun who had loads of fake blood and *pretended* to attack me and kill me and carry me off, only it wasn't really me, it was Mella II and I was watching and screaming and dressed like Mella II so Hairstreak would take me back to the Palace *thinking* I was Mella II. You see, he thought Mella II would do everything he told her and take my place at the Palace, but instead he brought me right back to where I wanted to be so we could be sure my parents would believe it when I told them everything. Wasn't that cool?'

'I wish I could have watched you and your sister changing clothes,' Victorinus told her softly.

Along the table a little way, Mella II was talking to Victorinus's brother Pharnaces. Or rather listening, warmed by the steady gaze of liquid eyes. 'So beautiful and yet so brave,' he was saying. 'Such a *devastating* combination.'

Mella II giggled nervously. 'Oh, I wouldn't say I was all that brave,' she said coyly.

'But, *bella,* you *were,* you *were!*' Pharnaces exclaimed. 'Single-handedly you overthrew the dreadful regime of Haleklind and removed the greatest threat to our beloved Realm the world has ever known.'

Mella II was having trouble breathing, due to unfamiliar body sensations. Her heartbeat was raised, her skin was tingling, her mouth kept smiling of its own accord. It was like being dreadfully, wonderfully ill with a fever. For some reason, Pharnaces seemed to send her into a delirium of delight. She licked dry lips and admired the curl in his hair.

'Hardly single-handed,' she protested. 'I was helped by more than a thousand manticores.'

'Ah, beauty and the beasts!' Pharnaces breathed in the husky way he had that sent shivers down her spine. 'Thrill me again, *bella,* with the story of what happened!'

'Oh, it was nothing really,' Mella II sighed. 'But I'll tell you anyway,' she added quickly. 'When Aboventoun carried me off, he brought me back to the herd and the Yidam – you know what a Yidam is, don't you, Pharnaces –?'

Pharnaces reached out to take a grape. 'Big scary Old God,' he said.

'– the Yidam could make the manticores do absolutely anything and he suggested that if I took the whole herd with me to Kremlin Karcist, it might help me persuade the Table of Seven not to use them as a weapon, but when the Companions saw them – you know what a Companion is, don't you, Pharnaces –?'

Pharnaces placed the grape between his perfect white teeth and bit into it very slowly. He did not take his eyes off hers, not for a single, shivery instant. 'Big scary old Haleklinder,' he said softly.

Mella II swallowed. '– When the Companions saw them, they ran away because manticores are really sweet, but they're really, really scary at the same time, especially when there's a whole lot of them, and then Uncle Pyrgus arrived, and of course I'd never met him before so I didn't know who he was, but he had this Haleklind friend called Corin with him who wanted to overthrow the rotten old Table of Seven and free the manticores and make Haleklind much nicer and he took over the Government and called off the whole war. Corin did.' She'd spilled it out all of a rush, which wasn't remotely cool, but Pharnaces was still looking at her adoringly, so that was all right.

Queen Blue was climbing to her feet. Conversations round the tables ceased immediately as heads turned in her direction. 'My friends . . .' Blue said. She was speaking quietly, but had the knack of projecting her voice so that it carried clearly throughout the banquet hall. '. . . We are gathered here this evening to celebrate the arrival of a new addition to the Royal Family . . .' There was a sudden burst of excited applause and a few strident whistles. Blue waited for the din to die down, then went on. '. . . A new addition to the Royal Family who has arrived from a most –' She hesitated, pretending to search for the appropriate word, '– *unexpected* source.'

'And nothing to do with King Henry!' shouted a racous young earl who'd clearly had too much to drink.

Blue smiled as she waited for the laughter to die down. 'A gift from my uncle – who unfortunately cannot be with us tonight – my uncle and former leader of the Faeries of the Night, now thankfully fully recovered from his tragic . . . accident, my uncle Lord Hairstreak . . .' She waited for applause and it came, although notably subdued from those Faeries of the Light who were present. 'My uncle Lord Hairstreak who has generously presented us with a perfect, fully grown, cloned sister for our beloved daughter Mella.' She gestured, turning smiling towards Mella II. 'My Lords, Ladies and Gentlemen, I would ask you to please be upstanding and raise your glasses in a toast to . . . Mella II!'

As Blue sat down again, Henry murmured, 'You overdid the *uncle* bit.'

Blue was still smiling and acknowledging the congratulations of their guests. Out of the corner of her mouth she said, 'I wanted to emphasise family unity. The last thing we need now is another Lighter–Nighter split.'

'I think we should have jailed the old tort-feasor,' Henry growled. 'Locked him up and thrown away the key.'

Blue turned towards him. 'Where's the proof? We have no documentary evidence of his involvement with Haleklind, no evidence at all except hearsay. We may claim he wanted to replace our daughter with a clone. He says he was merely grooming Mella II as a gift. It would be political madness to move against him without a cast-iron case. Remember he used to be the leader of the Faeries of the Night and could well be again, now he's got a new body. There's nothing we can do except play along.' She reached for her goblet and took a small sip. 'There's one positive thing about what's happened: Hairstreak's now out in the open, where we can keep an eye on him.'

'Two,' Henry said.

Blue frowned, puzzled. 'Two?'

'Two positive things . . .' He glanced down the table.

Blue followed the direction of his gaze.

'We now have twins,' said Henry, grinning.

Epilogue

'Do you think she'll go back?' Henry asked, gnawing away at something that had been troubling him.

'Mella?' Blue asked.

'Yes.'

'To the Analogue World?'

'Yes.'

'To see your mother?'

'Yes.'

'I expect she will,' Blue said mildly. They'd had this conversation before and Blue was sick of it. She cast around for something that would shut Henry up. 'Maybe you should take her.'

'What?!' Henry exploded.

'Better than having her run away.' Blue dropped her head as if studying some State papers so he couldn't see the smile.

It had the desired effect. Henry stopped obsessing. Or at least stopped obsessing aloud.

After a while, Blue said, 'That's nice. I think.'

'What's nice?' Henry asked her.

They were together in the His 'n' Hers study on the top floor of the Purple Palace. Sunlight streamed through the high windows, giving what was essentially an office space a bright, cheerful, holiday look.

'We've been invited to a wedding,' Blue told him.

'That's nice,' Henry said. His nose was buried in a book and he didn't make the effort to look interested.

Blue looked up. 'Don't you want to know who's getting married?'

'Who's getting married, Blue?' Henry asked her.

Blue threw a small white card on to her desk. The purple ribbon marked it as one of the new, spell-driven invitations that had become so popular in Court circles lately. A built-in illusion spell introduced the bride and groom to anyone who handled the card.

'Lord Hairstreak,' she said dully.

'Lord Hairstreak? And he's sent us an invitation to the ceremony?'

'I suppose it's an olive branch,' Blue said.

Henry set his book down. 'Who's he getting married to?'

'Somebody called the Lady Aisling. She's not at Court. Actually, I don't recall I've ever heard of her.'

Frowning, Henry said, 'Aisling: that's not a faerie name.'

'Analogue World, isn't it?' Blue asked.

'Let me see the invitation,' Henry said.

Glossary

Key:

FF: Forest Faerie
FOL: Faerie of the Light
FON: Faerie of the Night
HMN: Human

Analogue World (a.k.a. the Earth Realm). Names used in the Faerie Realm to denote the mundane world of school and spots and difficult parents.

Antiopa, Nymphalis (Nymph). (FF) Daughter of Queen Cleopatra, Princess of the Forest Faerie and wife of Crown Prince Pyrgus Malvae.

Apatura Iris. (FOL) Father of Prince Pyrgus, Prince Comma and Princess Blue. Purple Emperor for more than twenty years.

Apport. The magical precipitation of a small object from one place to another. Apports usually arrive during Spiritualist séances for reasons nobody really understands.

Apt. Tiny (Faerie Realm) horse about the size of an Analogue World mouse.

Atherton, Aisling. (HMN) Henry Atherton's younger sister, now grown up and still a pain in the ass.

Atherton, Henry. (HMN) King Consort of Queen Holly Blue and father of Princess Mella.

Atherton, Martha. (HMN) Headmistress of a girls' school

in the south of England. Divorced former wife of Tim Atherton and mother of Henry and Aisling.

Atherton, Tim. (HMN) Successful business executive. Former husband of Martha Atherton, father of Henry and Aisling.

Blue, Holly. (FOL) Younger sister of Crown Prince Pyrgus Malvae, daughter of Apatura Iris, Queen Empress of the Faerie Realm and Ruler of Hael.

Bob. Silver coin in use in the Faerie Realm.

Border Redcap. Sentient, lunatic, psychedelic-spore-throwing humanoid fungi who live in cliff communities in Wildmoor Broads.

Brimstone, Silas. (FON) Elderly demonologist and former glue factory owner who went insane following an attack by a cloud dancer.

Bus. Faerie term for a kiss, human term for a large, noisy, diesel-driven motor vehicle or (Old Eng.) a kiss. The use of the term by Shakespeare suggests, but does not prove, the Bard was in touch with the Faerie Realm.

Buthner. A poor, primitive and largely desert country in the Faerie Realm whose leaders have proven broadly supportive of Queen Blue's empire.

Cardui, Madame Cynthia (a.k.a the Painted Lady). (FOL) Elderly Head of Queen Blue's Imperial Intelligence Service and former lover of the late Alan Fogarty.

Celadon. Famous Forest Faerie garden designer.

Chalkhill, Jasper. (FON) Former business partner of Silas Brimstone, former head of Lord Hairstreak's intelligence service and now a professional assassin (freelance).

Cheapside. An area of the FOL capital.

CMS. See *Consolidated Magical Services*.

Cobblestone minefield. The security area surrounding the old Chalkhill and Brimstone Miracle Glue Factory. See the historical reference work *Faerie Wars* for details; also see www.faeriewarsgame.com.

Coffee. A bitter drink that leaves humans wired and gives faeries a psychedelic experience.

Comma, Prince. (FOL/FON) Half-brother of Prince Pyrgus and Princess Blue. (Same father, different mothers.)

Consolidated Magical Services (CMS). Major manufacturer of high-grade magical equipment in the Faerie Realm.

Control. See *Transporter*.

Copper. British slang for policeman or a small denomination coin; also the name of a metal or a cauldron used for boiling clothes. All in all, one of the more confusing human expressions.

Corin. A Haleklind revolutionary opposed to the ruling Table of Seven, particularly where their policies on animal welfare are concerned. Executive Secretary of the illegal Haleklind Society for the Preservation and Protection of Animals.

Crawlcroop. Derogatory faerie expression denoting a person who sucks up to those in authority.

Creen. What Haleklind natives tend to call Haleklind; also the official name of Haleklind's capital city.

Crumpmuckler. A professional picker of goonberries, an occupation reserved in ancient times for faeries of low intelligence.

Culmella Chrysotenchia (Mella). Only daughter of Queen Blue and Consort Majesty King Henry.

Danceflower. A tulip-shaped bloom about the size of a full-grown man that undulates sexily to attract pollinating insects.

Dead things that eat dried leaves and faerie meat. Brimstone was thinking of ghoulampires. (q.v.)

Demon. Form frequently taken by the shape-shifting alien species inhabiting the Hael Realm when in contact with faeries or humans.

Djinn. A desert elemental.

Doppleganger. In its basic form a freeze-dried replica, much used by spies and adventurers, that could temporarily replace a person in a location while the real person escapes. Recent improvements in spell technology have allowed dopplegangers to walk, talk and function in a way that closely mimics their originals, albeit in a limited way.

Endolg. An intelligent animal that looks much like a woolly rug. Endolgs have a unique ability to sense truth which makes them popular companions in the Faerie Realm.

Faeman. A faerie/human hybrid.

Faerie of the Light. (Lighter) One of the two main faerie types, culturally averse to the use of demons in any circumstances and usually members of the Church of Light.

Faerie of the Night. (Nighter) One of the two main faerie types, physically distinguished from Faeries of the Light by light-sensitive cat-like eyes. Make use of demonic servants.

Faerie Realm. A parallel aspect of reality inhabited by various alien species, including Faeries of the Light and Faeries of the Night.

Faerie Standard. The *lingua franca* of the Faerie Realm.

Fanfern. A fan-shaped fern that opens and closes seductively to reveal anything concealed behind it.

Feral Faerie. A wild, nomadic, faerie people who live and hunt in the depths of the great primeval forest that covers much of the Faerie Realm. The Feral Faerie are not known to hold allegiance to either the Faeries of the Light or the Faeries of the Night.

Filament suitcase. An ingenious use of interdimensional portal technology to create an area of non-geographical space that can be used to store bulky personal items in a thread-like filament typically sewn into a traveller's undergarment.

Flyer, personal. A Realm aircraft roughly equivalent to a flying sports car.

Fogarty, Alan. (HMN) Paranoid ex-physicist and bank robber with an extraordinary talent for engineering gadgets. Fogarty gave his life to save the Realm during a lethal temporal plague and now communicates with members of the Royal Family from the Other Side.

Fogarty, Angela (a.k.a. Mrs Barenbohm). (HMN) Alan Fogarty's daughter.

Follower. Demonic spy.

Force, the. What British policemen call themselves

collectively. What American policemen call a mysterious energy in *Star Wars*.

Forest Faerie. The way you refer to a Feral Faerie if you don't want to give offence.

Gatekeeper. Ancient title used to describe the chief advisor of a Noble House.

Ghoulampire. A dead thing that 'lives' in forests, subsisting on dried leaves and the occasional faerie. For reasons not altogether clear, ghoulampires prefer the taste of Faeries of the Night to Faeries of the Light.

Glowdust. A fine powder that reacts with magical energies by glowing brightly. Often used to detect traces of magical creatures, or show the recent use of magic in a specific area.

Goonberry. An extraordinarily stupid berry, fruit of the magenta goonberry bush, which forms such an important focus for the traditional faerie rites that welcome Spring.

Great House. Noble family.

Great Myphisto, The. Madame Cardui's late husband.

Grinflower. A semi-intelligent plant noted for the manner in which its petals curl upwards when it is told a joke. (Some botanists claim the effect only occurs if it is a *good* joke.)

Hael. Faerie name for Hell.

Hairstreak, Lord Black. (FON) Noble head (literally) of House Hairstreak and former leader of the Faeries of the Night.

Halek knife (or blade). A rock crystal weapon which releases magical energies to kill anything it pierces. Halek knives are prone to shattering occasionally, in which event the energies will kill the person using them.

Halek wizard. Non-human, non-faerie. Reputedly the most skilful of the magical practitioners in the Faerie Realm. Halek wizards typically specialise in weapons spells technology.

Haleklind. An independent nation in the Faerie Realm, run by wizards and noted for its production of the deadly Halek blades.

Haniel. A winged lion with a forest habitat native to certain areas of the Faerie Realm.

Highgrove. An area of the FOL capital.

Hodge. Mr Fogarty's old tomcat, now long dead, alas.

House Iris. The Royal House of the Faerie Empire.

Illusion Palace. Haleklind's equivalent of a movie theatre, but different from Analogue World cinemas in that patrons take part in an immersive adventure indistinguishable from physical reality.

Imperial Island. The island where the Purple Palace is located.

Iron Prominent. Henry's first honorary title in the Faerie Realm. The title *Consort Majesty* now takes precedence.

Kitterick. An Orange Trinian in the service of Madame Cardui.

Kremlin Karcist. Literally, 'Magical Citadel'. The centre of power in Haleklind.

Lanceline. Madame Cardui's translucent cat.

Lethe. A spell that wipes out general or selected memories from the person to whom it is applied. To the best of my recollection . . .

Loman Bridge. The main bridge spanning the river that flows through the FOL capital.

Luchti. A desert tribe in Buthner of which Henry Atherton is a blood brother.

Lucina Hamearis, Duke of Burgundy. (FON) War hero and former ally of Lord Hairstreak, once owner of Hairstreak's present home.

Malvae, Crown Prince Pyrgus. (FOL) Former Purple Emperor for about five minutes, now owner of an animal sanctuary and vineyard in the south of the Faerie Realm.

Manticore. An interesting experiment carried out by the wizards of Haleklind that enabled them to create a new and highly lethal species combining human, leonine and scorpion characteristics.

Mella. See *Culmella Chrysotenchia.*

Niff. (Hael wildlife.) A heavily armoured, steel-fanged animal slightly smaller than a fox.

Olbonium. A symphony of scents presented as a popular public entertainment in the Faerie Realm.

Ouklo. Levitating, spell-driven carriage.

Outerlinder. What Haleklind natives call foreigners.

Peacock. Chief Portal Engineer of House Iris.

Porkine. A sea-faring Faerie Realm mammal, believed by some to be the distant ancestor of Analogue World dolphins.

Portakey. A remote control used to switch magical securities on and off.

Portal. Inter-dimensional energy gateway, either naturally occurring, modified or engineered.

Prickleweed. A semi-intelligent carnivorous plant.

Purple Emperor or Empress. Ruler of the Faerie Empire.

Quercusia. (FON) Comma's mother.

Scolitandes the Weedy. An early Purple Emperor not best known for his courage in battle.

Seething Lane. Former site of the Chalkhill and Brimstone Miracle Glue Factory.

Shadow cloak. A magical garment that enables the wearer to pass unnoticed, especially when standing out of direct sunlight.

Simbala. An addictive form of liquid music sold legally in licenced outlets and illegally elsewhere.

Spell cone. Pocket-sized cones, no more than an inch or so in height, imbued with magical energies directed towards a specific result. The old-style cone had to be lit. The more modern version is self-igniting and is 'cracked' with a fingernail. Both types discharge like fireworks.

Spy globe. See *viewglobe*.

Staretz. A holy wizard.

Staretz Tsar. A member of the long line of magical kings who once ruled Haleklind.

Stimlus. Small, lethal energy weapon sometimes used in the Faerie Realm for personal protection, sometimes just to kill people.

Suk. Haleklind term for open market. Curiously, the Arabic term *suq* or *suk* also denotes a market or commercial quarter of an Arab or Berber city, suggesting some ancient connection between Halek and Arab cultures.

Table of Seven. Haleklind's ruling council.

Tea. A popular Analogue World drink that makes faeries drunk.

Theclinae, the. An ancient faerie people who flourished before the split between Faeries of the Light and Faeries of the Night. Their written language remains undeciphered, so what is known of their history is drawn entirely from Empire archives.

Thunderbolt, the. What faerie mythology calls love at first sight.

Tort-feasor. One who feases torts.

Transporter (a.k.a control). Mr Fogarty's hand-held version of a portal, based on the thing they use in *Star Trek*.

Trinian. Non-human, non-faerie dwarven race living in the Faerie Realm. Orange Trinians are a breed that dedicates itself to service, Violet Trinians tend to be warriors while Green Trinians specialise in biological nanotechnology and consequently can create living machines.

Trubong. A spring-shaped plant native to the southern regions of the Faerie Realm that bounces from one area to another seeking soil nutrients.

Viewglobe (a.k.a spy globe). A magical sphere of quartz crystal that can be set to generate an updating three-dimensional image of specific territory.

Walkway. (Specifically in Haleklind.) An ingenious device invented by Halek wizards that allows users to follow a pathway that curves in such a way as to bring them back to their entry point at, or before, the time they set out. While the Haleklind authorities encourage the belief that walkways are spell driven, the devices are actually based on the principle of a closed timelike line – an area of physics currently under investigation in parts of the Analogue World, notably America.

Ward, Anaïs. (HMN) Henry's mother's lover.

Whitewell. A district of the FOL capital.

Wildmoor Broads. A flat area of thorny shrubland north of the faerie capital much favoured by the wealthy of the Realm for their estates, since the difficulties of travelling through the area goes a long way towards ensuring their privacy. The only really viable means of transport is by levitating carriage. Ground transport is attacked by prickleweed, a semi-sentient plant that will typically swarm over any vehicle and bring it to a halt in minutes. Crossing the area on foot is impossible – the prickleweed paralyses pedestrians, then rips them apart for their nutrients.

Yammeth Cretch. Heartland of the Faeries of the Night.